2/25

STRONG RAIN FALLING

STRONG
RAIN FALLING

A CAITLIN STRONG NOVEL

Jon Land

A TOM DOHERTY ASSOCIATES BOOK
NEW YORK

This is a work of fiction. All of the characters, organizations, and events portrayed in this novel are either products of the author's imagination or are used fictitiously.

STRONG RAIN FALLING

Copyright © 2013 by Jon Land

A Forge Book
Published by Tom Doherty Associates, LLC
175 Fifth Avenue
New York, NY 10010

www.tor-forge.com

Forge® is a registered trademark of Tom Doherty Associates, LLC.

ISBN 978-0-7653-3150-2 (hardcover)
ISBN 978-1-4299-9279-4 (e-book)

Tor books may be purchased for educational, business, or promotional use. For information on bulk purchases, please contact Macmillan Corporate and Premium Sales Department at 1-800-221-7945, extension 5442, or write specialmarkets@macmillan.com.

First Edition: August 2013

Printed in the United States of America

0 9 8 7 6 5 4 3 2 1

For the brothers of Delta Phi Fraternity of Brown University,
past, present, and future.
As the song says, "Long life to Delta Phi!"

ACKNOWLEDGMENTS

Must be that time of year again, and I promise you a great ride this time. Before we start, though, I need to give some much-deserved shout-outs.

Stop me if you've heard this before, but let's start at the top with my publisher, Tom Doherty, and Forge's associate publisher, Linda Quinton, dear friends who publish books "the way they should be published," to quote my late agent, the legendary Toni Mendez. Paul Stevens, Karen Lovell, Patty Garcia, and especially Natalia Aponte are there for me at every turn. Natalia's a brilliant editor and friend who never ceases to amaze me with her sensitivity and genius. Editing may be a lost art, but not here, and I think you'll enjoy all of my books, including this one, much more as a result.

Some new names to thank this time out, starting with Mireya Starkenberg, a loyal reader who now suffers through my butchering the Spanish language in order to correct it. My friend Mike Blakely, a terrific writer and musician, taught me Texas firsthand and helped me think like a native of that great state. And Larry Thompson, a terrific writer in his own right, has joined the team as well to make sure I do justice to his home state.

SPOILER ALERT! I'd be very remiss if I didn't mention a pair of terrific books that were crucial to my research on this one. They are noted below next to the * but you may want to ignore them until you finish so as not to give anything away. A major thank-you also to Professor John Savage of Brown University, a true expert on the book's subject who offered his two cents that were worth a million to me.

Check back at www.jonlandbooks.com for updates or to drop me a line. I'd be remiss if I didn't thank all of you who've already written or e-mailed me about how much you enjoyed the first four tales in the Caitlin Strong series. There may be big news to report soon on the Hollywood front (knock wood!), so rest assured that your opinions are being echoed and I never would've gotten even that far if not for your support. Rest assured you will be even more pleased with this latest adventure. To find out if I'm as good a prophet as I am a storyteller, just turn the page and begin.

P.S. For those interested in more information about the history of the Texas Rangers, I recommend *The Texas Rangers* and *Time of the Rangers*, a pair of superb books by Mike Cox, also published by Forge.

*Clarke, Richard A., and Robert K. Knake. *Cyber War*. New York: Ecco, 2010.
*Mark Bowden. *Worm: The First Digital World War*. New York: Atlantic Monthly Press, 2011.

The world to me is like a lasting storm.

—WILLIAM SHAKESPEARE,
Pericles

PROLOGUE

Then mount and away! Give the fleet steed the rein—
The Ranger's at home on the prairies again;
Spur! Spur in the chase—dash on to the fight
Cry Vengeance for Texas! And God speed the right!

James T. Lytle, "The Ranger's Song"

Smokeville, Texas; 1919

The boy walked out of the desert, the late-afternoon sun in his face, his skin burned red, parched lips marred by jagged cracks. His tattered clothes carried the thick, smoky scent of mesquite mixed with the acrid stench of burned wood, as if his journey had taken him through a brush fire burning to the southwest.

But it was the flecks of blood staining his face, shirt, and sweat-soaked hair, tangled with wisps of tumbleweed, that caught John Rob Salise's eye more than anything.

"You all right, son?" Salise, a town selectman and constable, asked with hands laid on the boy's shoulders to hold him in place. "What's your name?"

The boy continued to gaze straight ahead without regarding him, his shock-glazed eyes barely blinking. His breaths came in rapid heaves, his exhaustion showing in knees that had begun to buckle with the burden of his weight, and Salise thought the boy might keel over if he lifted his hands from his shoulders. Salise noted the boy's boots were badly scuffed and sun-bleached, making him wonder how long exactly the boy had been walking, how far he'd come.

And whose blood had showered him as if it were the product of a spring downpour.

Salise handed the boy a small canteen he always wore clipped to his belt during his rounds. The kid snapped it up, peeled back the cap, and guzzled the water so fast twin streams ran down both sides of his mouth, the drops drying almost as soon as they touched the ground.

"Where'd you come from, son?" Salise asked, figuring him for ten or eleven, although his wan appearance made it difficult to tell.

The boy drained the rest of the water, still ignoring him.

Salise snatched the canteen from his grasp. "I'm trying to help you out here."

When the boy remained unresponsive, hands dangling limply once more by his sides, Salise turned his own gaze down Smokeville's single commercial thoroughfare. The street featured a strange combination of horses hitched to posts and motorcars parked awkwardly against a raised wooden walkway near a saloon, where legend had it Wild Bill Hickok had shot a man intending to do the same to him.

"Well, then it's a good thing for you we got a Texas Ranger in town. What do you say we go find him?"

Ranger William Ray Strong sat across the table from his son, Earl, the boy having followed him into the Texas Rangers just short of his nineteenth birthday. A bottle of whiskey rose between them, two full shot glasses accounting for what was missing from it so far.

William Ray raised his glass in the semblance of a toast, eyeing the *cinco pesos* badge pinned to his son's chest. "Here's to you, Earl, on following me and your granddad into the Ranger service. 'No man in the wrong can stand up against a fellow that's in the right and keeps on a-comin'.'"

And upon finishing the quote from the great Ranger captain Bill McDonald, William Ray downed his whiskey in a single gulp, leaving Earl to sip at his glass, wrinkling his nose the whole time.

"I'll tell you, boy, it's a good thing you shoot a hell of a lot better than you drink, though I suspect such things have a way of catching up with each other over time."

That's when a man William Ray recognized as a town constable entered the bar with a boy in tow. He'd met the man a couple times but couldn't for the life of him remember his name.

"Constable Salise," his son, Earl, greeted, rising to his feet and brushing the holstered Colt further back on his hip, "what have we here?"

Salise noticed the badge originally worn by Earl's grandfather who'd been killed in the Civil War not long after William Ray was born. The new Ranger looked like a younger version of his famed father, albeit thinner with sinewy bands of muscle instead of bulk and without the sun-dug furrows lining his face.

"I come in here expecting to find one Ranger," Salise said, "and here there are two."

"Believe you know my father, sir."

"'Course I do. The great William Ray Strong, late of the Frontier Battalion."

"Just for the final days, sir," William Ray said, his eyes falling on the boy. "And if this is your son, I'd recommend a bath as opposed to a shooting lesson or an autograph."

"He's not my son, Ranger. I found him wandering in the street. Looked like he came plain out of the desert."

"Is that a fact?" William Ray said, coming out of his chair to draw closer to the boy. "You got a name, son?"

The boy didn't say a word, not even tilting his gaze to acknowledge the Rangers' presence.

Salise laid a dust-covered hand atop the boy's shoulder. "I can't get a word out of him crossways."

Earl gave the boy a better look, dabbing his kerchief in his mostly full glass of whiskey before patting it against some of the blood matted on the boy's shirt. "Day old at most," he reported to his father.

"How you figure that?"

"Whiskey got it off quick. Any more than a day, it would have taken some wiping or swabbing."

"Is that a fact? 'Course, I didn't need to know that to see that the soles of his boots got close to a full day's worth of red sand stuck in their grids. Any more than a day, and it would've turned a brownish shade by now. Any less, it'd be more orange."

"Is that a fact?" Earl echoed, drawing a smile from his father.

William Ray returned his attention to Constable Salise. "We can't get a name out of the boy, let's see if we can get a rise. Earl, what towns be a fair day's walk here through the desert?"

Earl Strong aimed his answer at the boy. "There's Franklin Notch, Bald Pass, Willow Creek—"

Earl stopped when the boy's eyes narrowed in fear at the mention of Willow Creek. He shuddered just once and then lapsed back into whatever trance had overtaken him.

Earl crouched his gaunt six-foot frame down so he was eye to eye with the boy. "That where you're from, son, Willow Creek?" he posed as gently and reassuringly as he could manage.

The boy rubbed his nose with a pair of fingers that were black at the tips, leaving a smudge that looked like soot.

"You got nothing to fear. You're safe now."

"No," the boy rasped, eyes swinging for the doors as if expecting someone to burst through in the next moment. "They'll be . . ."

"Yeah?"

"They'll be . . ."

"What, boy, what?" William Ray asked, his own gaze and Earl's cheating toward the saloon doors now too.

". . . coming."

"Who?" Earl Strong asked this time.

The boy didn't look at him, didn't seem to be looking at anything when he drew a tattered piece of thick paper, folded in quarters, from his pants pocket. He started to extend it forward, but stopped halfway to Earl, who plucked it from his grasp. Earl laid the piece of paper atop the bar table and smoothed it out.

"What the hell?" William Ray said, squinting at the sight of its contents.

It was a drawing rendered in the same black ink that stained the boy's fingers, a drawing of man-sized skeleton figures wearing pistol belts and bandoliers. Some of the skeletons in the drawing wore sombreros over their exposed skulls and some didn't.

Now it was William Ray who knelt down in front of the boy, holding the drawing close for him to see.

"What's this exactly, son?"

No response.

"You see something that looked like this back home in Willow Creek?"

The boy muttered something.

"What was that, son?"

"Night," the boy rasped.

"How's that?"

"They come at night."

William Ray looked up toward Earl. "How far a ride you figure it is to Willow Creek?"

"Six hours if we push things, eight if we don't."

William Ray held his son's stare as he stood back up. "Then we better get a move on if we wanna get there 'fore nightfall, Ranger Earl."

WILLOW CREEK, TEXAS; THE PRESENT

"You have no reason to be scared, muchachos *and* muchachas."

But the woman's assurances did nothing to soothe the fears of the five children huddled before her, tear-streaked grime from the dusty air coating their faces.

"Do you know why you're here today?" Ana Callas Guajardo asked them.

The children shrugged, shook their heads. They'd been taken from their schools back in Mexico without explanation and driven to what had once been a town over the Texas border, where the woman was waiting, introducing herself simply as "Ana." She was in her early forties, boasting the tight lines and features of a younger woman at ease in the white silk blouse and snug-fitting jeans aged off the rack. The boots she wore looked comfortably worn, new soles belying their true age. Her raven black hair was streaked with gray and bound up in an elegant chignon.

"Because this is where it all began . . . and now, where it will begin again. Do you know what Steve Jobs once said? 'Have the courage to follow your heart.' It was one of his primary lessons of business, one I follow religiously. That is why I had you brought here. This way, *muchachos* and *muchachas*."

The children trailed her down what was little more than an outline of what had been the central thoroughfare of a town long dead. Three boys and two girls ranging in age from nine to thirteen from four different schools. Their dark hair and full, deep-set eyes of an identical shade made them look like siblings, cousins at the very least, when in fact none save for one brother and sister were even related. Their young faces glistened under the sun, their school uniforms marred by wrinkles from the trip there and the dust sprayed through the dry desert air. The ground roasted beneath their feet in the merciless afternoon sun, fluttery heat waves rising where the town's residents had once traipsed.

"Your lives all share a legacy that calls Willow Creek home," Guajardo continued, her tone flat and firm. "Ever since hell rose to take the town in its grasp. Willow Creek died that day at the hands of creatures known as *esos Demonios*. Now you will learn of that day, and your place in it."

Moving through the center of what had been a town, the children could see debris in the form of rotted, dried-out wood collected in areas where buildings once stood. The ground was darker in these spots, looking sallow and dead, unable to reclaim the life the structures had once stolen from it. Besides the stray patches of debris, the only evidence of civilization ever having been there was a set of train tracks lost to moss and blown gravel. Those tracks remained unfinished, unconnected; no train had ever touched them, making them seem even more ghostly, as if the brambles and brush were actually trying to draw the rails and ties into the earth to bury them forever. And yet over this scene of decay rose the sweet scents of juniper and piñon wafting in from a desert watched over by sentinel-like mesas that gleamed beneath the white puffy clouds floating across the sky. The sun cast those mesas a soothing shade of red that would darken further as evening bled the heat from the air.

Guajardo stopped in view of the raised lip of the railroad tracks and faced the children, some of whom were sniffling, wiping away the tears that had begun to fall anew. Her upper lip flirted briefly with the semblance of a snarl, the muscles in her jaw tightening visibly and a vein that had risen on the left side of her neck starting to pulse. "What you need to know today, *muchachos* and *muchachas*, is that *esos Demonios* are real, that monsters are real. And the monsters that killed this town all those years ago have returned to embark on a new beginning, so that old scores can be settled at long last."

She turned to face north, beyond Willow Creek, beyond Texas.

"*Esos Demonios* will be unleashed again, this time on a country that has to be called to account for its crimes. *Esos Demonios* will show the *Estados Unidos* what true pain is like, so much that she will never recover. Not in my lifetime or yours. She will drop to her knees and beg for mercy from the wrath *esos Demonios* will visit upon her."

"There's no such thing as monsters," the oldest boy said to her, standing defiant as if assuming the mantle of leadership for the others.

"What if I could prove that you're wrong?" Ana Guajardo asked him.

"*Señora?*"

"It's like I told you, *esos Demonios* are real and I can prove it," she said to all five of them now. "Come, let me show you."

Some still sobbing, the children resisted at first, but then, with a collective shrug, followed in step behind her. Guajardo led them toward a grove of Mexican blue oaks on the south side of town, shaded by a large stone mesa to the west. The trees were wild and overgrown, their thick-leafed branches scratching against one another in the breeze. They'd risen higher in the patches where the sun remained over the mesa deeper into the afternoon, looking like gnarled fingers reaching for the sky.

Guajardo stopped half in the sun and half in the shade, her back to the children.

"What are we supposed to be seeing, *señora?*" the oldest boy prodded.

Guajardo turned and held all the children in her stare, making sure they could see her eyes. "Proof that monsters really do exist, because one of *esos Demonios* stands with us now, *muchachos* and *muchachas*," she said, something shiny appearing in her hand. "Right before you."

A cloud slid before the sun, darkening Guajardo's silhouette as she started forward, to the oldest boy, who'd stepped out in front of the others first.

The screams that followed stole the breath of even Ana Guajardo's hardened gunmen standing vigil at the other end of the former town. High-pitched wails that merged into one another to become a single screeching banshee-like cry, echoing off the rock walls of the canyon before following Willow Creek into oblivion.

PART ONE

Men in groups with long beards and moustaches, dressed in every variety of garment, with one exception, the slouched hat, the unmistakable uniform of a Texas Ranger, and a belt of pistols around their waist, were occupied drying their blankets, cleaning and fixing their guns, and some employed cooking at different fires, while others were grooming their horses. A rougher looking set we never saw.

Scouting Expeditions of McCulloch's Texas Rangers,
as quoted in Mike Cox, *The Texas Rangers*

I

Caitlin Strong was waiting downstairs in a grassy park bisected by concrete walkways when Dylan Torres emerged from the building. The boy fit in surprisingly well with the Brown University students he slid between in approaching her, his long black hair bouncing just past his shoulders and attracting the attention of more than one passing coed.

"How'd it go?" Caitlin asked, rising from the bench that felt like a sauna in the sun.

Dylan shrugged and blew some stray hair from his face with his breath. "Size could be an issue."

"For playing football at this level, I expect so."

"Coach Estes didn't rule it out. He just said there were no more first-year slots left in the program."

"First year?"

"Freshman, Caitlin."

"How'd you leave it?" she asked, feeling dwarfed by the athletic buildings that housed playing courts, training facilities, a swimming pool, a full gym, and the offices of the school's coaches. The buildings enclosed the parklike setting on three sides, leaving the street side to be rimmed by an eight-foot wall of carefully layered stone. Playing fields took up the rear of the complex beyond the buildings and, while waiting for Dylan, Caitlin heard the clang of aluminum bats hitting baseballs and thunks of what sounded like soccer balls being kicked about. Funny how living in a place the size of Texas made her antsy within an area where so much was squeezed so close.

"Well, short of me growing another four inches and putting on maybe twenty pounds of muscle, it's gonna be an uphill battle," Dylan said, looking down. "That is, if I even get into this place. That's an uphill battle too."

She reached out and touched his shoulder. "This coming from a kid who's bested serial killers, kidnappers, and last year a human monster who bled venom instead of blood."

Dylan started to shrug, but smiled instead. "Helps that you and my dad were there to gun them all down."

"Well, I don't believe we'll be shooting Coach Estes, and my point was if anybody can handle an uphill battle or two, it's you."

Dylan lapsed into silence, leaving Caitlin to think of the restaurant they'd eaten at the night before, where the waitress had complimented her on having such a good-looking son. She'd felt her insides turn to mush when the boy smiled and went right on studying the menu, not bothering to correct the woman. He was three quarters through a fifth year at San Antonio's St. Anthony Catholic High School, in range of finishing the year with straight A's. Though the school didn't formally offer a post-graduate program, Caitlin's captain, D. W. Tepper, had convinced them to make an exception on behalf of the Texas Rangers by slightly altering their Senior Connection program to fit the needs of a boy whose grades hadn't anywhere near matched his potential yet.

Not that it was an easy fit. The school's pristine campus in historic Monte Vista just north of downtown San Antonio was populated by boys and girls in staid, prescribed uniforms that made Dylan cringe. Blazers instead of shapeless shirts worn out at the waist, khakis instead of jeans gone from sagging to, more recently, what they called skinny, and hard leather dress shoes instead of the boots Caitlin had bought him for his birthday a few years back. But the undermanned football team had recruited him early on, Dylan donning a uniform for the first time since his brief stint in the Pop Warner Football League as a young boy, when his mother was still alive and the father he'd yet to meet was in prison. This past fall at St. Anthony's he'd taken to the sport again like a natural, playing running back and sifting through the tiniest holes in the defensive line to amass vast chunks of yardage. Dylan ended up being named Second Team All TAPPS District 2-5A, attracting the attention of several small colleges, though none on the level of Brown University, a perennial contender for the Ivy League crown.

Caitlin found those Friday nights, sitting with Cort Wesley Masters and his younger son, Luke, in stands ripe with the first soft bite of fall, strangely comforting. Given that she'd never had much use for such things in her own teenage years, the experience left her feeling as if she'd been transported back in time, with a chance to relive her own youth through a boy who was as close to a son as she'd ever have. Left her recalling her own high school days smelling of gun oil instead of perfume. She'd been awkward then, gawky after growing tall fast. Still a few years short of forty, Caitlin had never added to that five-foot-seven-inch frame, although the present found her filled out and firm from regular workouts and jogging. She wore her wavy black hair more fashionably styled, but kept it the very same length she always had, perhaps in a misguided attempt to slow time, if not stop it altogether.

Gazing at Dylan now, she recalled the headmaster of his school, a cousin of Caitlin's own high school principal, coming up to her after the victorious opening home game.

"The school owes you a great bit of gratitude, Ranger."

"Well, sir, I'll bet Dylan'll do even better next week."

The headmaster gestured toward the newly installed lights. "I meant gratitude to the Rangers arranging for the variance that allowed us to go forward with the installation. That's the only reason we're able to be here tonight."

She'd nodded, smiling to herself at how Captain Tepper had managed to arrange Dylan's admission. "Our pleasure, sir."

Now, months later, on the campus of an Ivy League school in Providence, Rhode Island, Dylan looked down at the grass and then up again, something furtive lurking in his suddenly narrowed eyes. The sun sneaking through a nearby tree dappled his face and further hid what he was about to share.

"I got invited to a frat party."

"Say that again."

"I got invited to a party at this frat called D-Phi."

"D *what*?"

"Short for Delta Phi. Like the Greek letters."

"I know they're Greek letters, son, just like I know what goes on at these kind of parties given that I've been called to break them up on more than one occasion."

"You're the one who made me start thinking about college."

"Doesn't mean I got you thinking about doing shots and playing beer pong."

"Beirut."

Caitlin looked at him as if he were speaking a foreign language.

"They call it Beirut here, not beer pong," Dylan continued. "And it's important I get a notion of what campus life is like. You told me that too."

"I did?"

"Uh-huh."

"I let you go to this party, you promise you won't drink?"

Dylan rolled his head from side to side. "I promise I won't drink *much*."

"What's that mean?"

"That I'll be just fine when you come pick me up in the morning to get to the airport."

"Pick you up," Caitlin repeated, her gaze narrowing.

"I'm staying with this kid from Texas who plays on the team. Coach set it up."

"Coach Estes?"

"Yup. Why?"

Caitlin slapped an arm around the boy's shoulders and steered him toward the street. "Because I may rethink my decision about shooting him."

"I told him you were a Texas Ranger," Dylan said, as they ap-

proached a pair of workmen stringing a tape measure outside the athletic complex's hockey rink.

"What'd he think about that?" Caitlin said, finding her gaze drawn
to the two men she noticed had no tools and were wearing scuffed
shoes instead of work boots.

"He said he liked gals with guns."

They continued along the walkway that curved around the parklike
grounds, banking left at a small lot where Caitlin had parked her rental.
She worked the remote to unlock the doors and watched Dylan ease
around to the passenger side, while she turned back toward the hockey
rink and the two workmen she couldn't shake from her mind.

But they were gone.

2

PROVIDENCE, RHODE ISLAND

"What's this WaterFire thing?" Dylan asked, spooning up the last of
his ice cream while Caitlin sipped her nightly post-dinner coffee.

"Like a tradition here. Comes highly recommended."

"You don't want me going to that frat party."

"The thought had crossed my mind, but I'm guessing the WaterFire'll
be done 'fore your party even gets started."

Dylan held the spoon in his hand and then licked at it.

"How's the ice cream?"

"It's gelato."

"What's the difference?"

"None, I guess."

They had chosen to eat at a restaurant called Paragon, again on the
recommendation of Coach Estes. It was a fashionably loud, lit, and reasonably priced bistro-like restaurant on the student-dominated Thayer
Street, across from the university's bookstore. Dylan ordered a pizza
while Caitlin ruminated over the menu choices before eventually opting

for what she always did: a steak. You can take the gal out of Texas, she thought to herself, but you can't take Texas out of the gal.

"I hear this WaterFire is something special," Caitlin said when she saw him checking his watch.

"Yeah? Who told you that?"

"Coach Estes. What do you say we head downtown and check it out?"

They walked through the comfortable cool of the early evening darkness, a welcome respite from the sweltering spring heat wave that had struck Texas just before they'd left. Caitlin wanted to talk, but Dylan wouldn't look up from his iPhone, banging out text after text.

They strolled up a slight hill and then down a steeper one, joining the thick flow of people heading for the sounds of the nighttime festival known as WaterFire. The air was crisp and laced with the pungent aroma of wood smoke drifting up from Providence's downtown area, where the masses of milling people were headed. The scent grew stronger while the harmonic strains of music sharpened the closer they drew to an area bridged by walkways crisscrossing a river that ran the entire length of the modest office buildings and residential towers that dominated the city's skyline. A performance area had been roped off at the foot of the hill, currently occupied by a group of white-faced mimes. An array of pushcarts offering various grilled meats as well as snacks and sweets were lined up nearby, most with hefty lines before them.

The tightest clusters of festival patrons moved in both directions down a walkway at the river's edge. Caitlin realized the strange and haunting strains of music had their origins down here as well, and moved to join the flow. The black water shimmered like glass, an eerie glow emanating from its surface. Boaters and canoeists paddled leisurely by. A water taxi packed with seated patrons sipping wine slid past, followed by what looked like a gondola straight from Venice.

But it was the source of the orange glow reflecting off the water's surface that claimed Caitlin's attention. She could now identify the pungent scent of wood smoke as that of pine and cedar, hearing the familiar crackle of flames as she and Dylan reached a promenade that ran directly alongside the river.

"Caitlin?" Dylan prodded, touching her shoulder.

She jerked to her right, stiffening, the boy's hand like a hot iron against her shirt.

"Uh-oh," the boy said. "You got that look."

"Just don't like crowds," Caitlin managed, casting her gaze about. "That's all."

A lie, because she felt something wasn't right, out of rhythm somehow. Her stomach had already tightened and now she could feel the bands of muscle in her neck and shoulders knotting up as well.

"Yeah?" Dylan followed before she forced a smile. "And, like, I'm supposed to believe that?"

Before them, a line of bonfires that seemed to rise out of the water curved along the expanse of the Providence Riverwalk. The source of these bonfires, Caitlin saw now, were nearly a hundred steel braziers of flaming wood moored to the water's surface and stoked by black-shirted workers in a square, pontoon-like boat, including one who performed an elaborate fire dance in between tending the flames.

The twisting line of braziers seemed to stretch forever into the night. Caitlin and Dylan continued to follow their bright glow, keeping the knee-high retaining wall on their right. More kiosks selling hot dogs, grilled meats to be stuffed in pockets, kabobs, beverages, and souvenirs had been set up on streets and sidewalks above the Riverwalk. The sights and sounds left her homesick for Texas, the sweet smell of wood smoke reminding her of the scent of barbecue and grilled food wafting over the famed San Antonio River Walk.

Caitlin was imagining that smell when she felt *something*, not much and not even identifiable at first, yet enough to make her neck hairs stand up. A ripple in the crowd, she realized an instant later, followed almost immediately by more of a buckling indicative of someone forcing their way through it. Instinct twisted Caitlin in the direction of the ripple's origin and the flames' glow caught a face that was familiar to her.

Because it belonged to one of the workmen she'd glimpsed outside the hockey rink back at Brown University. And the second workman stood directly alongside him, their hands pulling their jackets back enough to reveal the dark glint of the pistols wedged into their belts.

3

PROVIDENCE, RHODE ISLAND

Caitlin saw the men's eyes harden, semiautomatic pistols yanked free and coming around.

She shoved Dylan behind her, feeling the muscles that weight-room workouts had layered into his shoulders and arms, as she drew her own SIG Sauer P226.

The last thing she saw before she opened fire were flashes of steel in both workmen's hands, rising fast in the glow off the nearby flames. Her spin toward them had obviously surprised the workmen, but her gunshots shocked them even more.

She fired through a tunnel in the night air, imagining she could feel the heat of the bullets blazing a path forward. She kept pulling the SIG's trigger, standing rigid amid the panicked jostling and sudden surge her gunfire had unleashed.

She realized she was still holding fast to Dylan in her off hand, dimly aware of the muzzle flashes and the thuds of her nine-millimeter shells clacking against the concrete beneath her. The impacts forced the workmen backward, where they crumpled to become land mines in the path of the throngs sent fleeing by the gunshots.

Caitlin pushed her way toward the downed gunmen, able to catch sight of their lost pistols being kicked about by feet thrashing over the concrete. No thought given in that moment to the fact that this wasn't Texas and she'd just gunned down two men in a state the size of a postage stamp, where the authorities might not be nearly as sympathetic to her methods as D. W. Tepper.

She released the hand holding tight to Dylan and stooped to retrieve the stray pistols, realizing she had no plastic evidence gloves, when the sudden roar of an engine grabbed her attention anew. Instinctively, she lurched back upright, facing the sound's origins on the river with Dylan planted behind her again.

A motorboat sped toward the scene, cracking a gondola from its path and then slamming a small skiff tending the braziers out of its way. Impact sprayed fresh fuel and kindling across the water's surface, the motorboat jostled just enough to keep a gunman poised in the rear from opening fire with his assault rifle when he'd intended to. Caitlin resteadied her SIG and parted the crowd as she aimed, a clear path between her and the gunman now.

He got his weapon leveled.

Caitlin fired hers. Three times, the pistol's roar echoing over the panicked cries and Baroque music. She hit the gunman twice, stealing his balance and pitching him into the outboard motor. Plenty of bullets left to use on the boat's driver, whose right hand had dropped from the wheel.

Caitlin fired at him until she heard the click of the hammer striking an empty chamber as the SIG's slide locked in place, the motorboat now veering straight for one of the braziers. The violent crash caused a flame burst that showered fiery embers into the air to rain down on the fuel and kindling pooled on the surface.

POOOOOOFFFFFFF!

The exploding speedboat sent a hot wind blowing up against Caitlin as flames erupted on the water, faces twisted in fear along the Riverwalk framed by the glow. Caitlin managed to steady herself with a shallow breath and grabbed a second magazine from her jacket.

"Caitlin!"

Dylan's cry reached her before she'd jacked it home and she swung toward the boy in the same moment he rushed past her, straight for a big man she hadn't noticed wielding a big knife.

"Dyl—"

Caitlin wasn't sure if she started to scream his name or only thought to, as the boy hit the man low with a classic football tackle that drove him up and over the retaining wall. He splashed into the water below with Dylan ready to spill over after him involuntarily, until Caitlin grabbed the boy's baggy Brown University sweatshirt and drew him backward before he lost the rest of his balance.

Fresh magazine in place, she moved back to the wall in search of the man lost amid the fiery sheen caught in the river's reflection. She rotated her eyes and pistol, but the river and the night gave up nothing.

Caitlin stepped back, even again with Dylan, the boy's face shiny with perspiration and looking like a Halloween mask in the river's angry orange glow.

"Water fire, all right," she said, falling well short of a smile when fresh footsteps pounded her way.

She shoved Dylan behind her, pistol coming back around.

"Drop the gun!" ordered a blue-uniformed Providence police officer now in her line of vision. "I said, *drop the gun!*"

Caitlin let the SIG fall to her feet and raised her hands in the air, making sure Dylan did the same.

4

Fiesta, Texas

"SkyScreamer?" Cort Wesley Masters posed to his younger son, Luke.

"Come on, Dad," the boy prodded, "take a chance. You never do anything exciting."

Cort Wesley wasn't sure where Luke was going with that, until the boy grinned over his own comic reference to the last few years that had seen Cort Wesley and Caitlin Strong taking on just about every bad guy Texas had to offer. He let the boy lead him about the day-glow brightness of Six Flags in Fiesta, just outside San Antonio, located in an old limestone quarry where the two-hundred-acre park was surrounded by majestic ten-story cliffs. From the parking lot, Luke made straight for the SkyScreamer, the sight of which left Cort Wesley's stomach fluttering. The latest park attraction turned out to be a towering twenty-story swing ride that spun at speeds in excess of forty miles per hour.

"You're scared," Luke said, as they took their place in line under the crystal clear night sky.

"No, I'm not."

"Yes, you are. You're gritting your teeth. You never grit your teeth."

Cort Wesley stopped gritting his teeth as the line began to move. "I thought we were gonna do the Go-Karts."

"Later," Luke told him. "After we do the Boomerang."

"Boomerang?"

"A super-coaster. My favorite part is when it goes backward."

"Backward," Cort Wesley repeated.

"You look pale, Dad. We can skip the Rattler if you want."

"I appreciate that, son," Cort Wesley said, moving up yet further in line and hoping the SkyScreamer would break down before their turn came.

After missing the first nine years of the boy's life, Cort Wesley reveled in moments like this. With Luke having just celebrated his fourteenth birthday, who knew how many more of them there'd actually be? But the truth was he missed Caitlin Strong and his older son, Dylan, more than he'd thought, finding the mere days almost as tough to bear as the months he spent a couple years back in Mexico's infamous Cereso Prison. He'd finally made it home after nearly a year away to find his sons almost like strangers again to him, like they were living the early part of their lives in dog years. Luke was filling out, wearing his hair longer, disappearing for long stretches into his room with only a cell phone for company—in short, becoming a teenager. Cort Wesley had spent so much time worrying over Dylan these past few years that he hadn't even considered the possibility of his younger son following right in the older one's footsteps. Just when it seemed Dylan had finally got his head turned straight, if his recent dedication to his studies and finding the right college was any indication.

A Masters boy visiting colleges, an Ivy League one no less!

It was hard for Cort Wesley to imagine that, and he wondered what his lifelong criminal father, Boone, who never finished high school, would've made of it. Boone had gone to the same high school as Caitlin's father, Jim, where they played football together before losing touch until a legendary bar fight years later sent both of them to the emergency room. Cort Wesley found himself wondering what his late dad would have thought of him shacking up with the Texas Ranger daughter of Jim Strong too.

But that's the way it was, whether Boone Masters or anyone else liked it or not. And, truth be told, it was nice to have a few days alone with his younger son, especially since Luke was morphing quickly into the more extrovert and daredevil ways of his older brother. Except for the fact that he'd started to look a bit more like Cort Wesley, while Dylan continued to boast the strong, dark features and tumbling, tangled hair of their mother. Maura Torres had been the last woman Cort Wesley had grown really close to before Caitlin Strong, close enough for him to give her two sons he'd not met until her murder. Looking at Dylan always reminded him of her, while looking at Luke reminded him too much of himself. The boy's hair was starting to thicken into waves and his eyes were the same steely brown as Cort Wesley's, in contrast to Dylan's hauntingly black ones. Luke had the same long neck, high cheekbones, and even held his head slightly to the side when listening to others or pretending to. And like Cort Wesley, sometimes his smile carried a menace with it that belied the gesture—sometimes, though more often lately.

Cort Wesley had never been to Six Flags Fiesta before, and he found himself feeling guilty over the notion that too often his boys got dragged into the violent parts of his life, and yet he'd never just up and taken them to this nearby amusement park on a whim. He and Caitlin had talked about it a few times, but one of the four of them was always too busy with something else.

Now, soon to be seated next to Luke in a swing with his feet dangling two hundred feet above the ground, Cort Wesley was beginning to wonder if he could have found a less stomach-churning way to have some quality time. Strange coming from a man who had jumped out of airplanes in the dead of night for Special Ops missions back in his army days, and had inspired fear in pretty much every Mexican drug runner who worked the streets of San Antonio while he was playing enforcer for the Branca crime family. That stage of his life had happened before he'd met his sons or Caitlin. Cort Wesley didn't even recognize that man anymore; the one who looked back at him in the mirror now was an entirely different being, albeit with the same powerful frame and deep-set eyes.

As of late his reflection had come to take on the look of his own father, especially the gray patches that were starting to advance backward from his temples. In Cort Wesley's memory, the graying hair was the only thing that ever really changed in his father, Boone Masters being the same man in his late twenties as he was in his early fifties when cancer claimed him fast. Man had managed to survive all manner of the law and rival criminals seeing vulnerability in Boone's independence, only to lose his life to a bum pancreas ruined by too much alcohol.

Cort Wesley thought of his dad these days only when he was with his sons, wondering if the worry he felt over Dylan and Luke might have been matched by that which his father had experienced over him. Boone Masters never showed much emotion, but then again neither did Cort Wesley, both of them real good at turning their faces into masks that could be swapped out given the situation.

"Dad, move up. It's almost our turn," Luke was saying, and Cort Wesley realized they were almost to the front of the line.

Above them, the SkyScreamer's lighted arms whirled into a single glowing ribbon that seemed to brighten the entire night. So focused was Cort Wesley on the ride that he barely noticed the Latino man, wearing sunglasses in the dark, almost directly across from him on the opposite side of the ride's base, raise a cell phone to his lips.

"*Le tengo*," he said. "I've got him."

5

"A Texas Ranger," the detective said again, shaking his head. He'd introduced himself as Finneran, but Caitlin had stayed with "Detective" so far.

He'd offered her a chair at the table in the interview room equipped with a one-cup coffeemaker that dispensed barely half that after Finneran had pressed the start button, but she refused it. The room was overly bright and Caitlin paced along the length of the counter while the detective fiddled with the Keurig machine before trying another K-Cup.

"I'd like to speak to the young man," she said, forcing herself to sound polite. "That's going to be the last time I ask you nicely."

Finneran shot her a look, appearing ready to respond when the machine spit out yet another half cup that he added to the first. "As soon as his interview with another detective is complete. They know anything about patience in Texas?"

"We're not talking about 'they,' we're talking about me and the young man I'm responsible for, and right now you're treating us like suspects."

"We call that routine procedure up in this neck of the woods," said Finneran.

"Well, Detective, I call it a load of crap."

"Maybe you should watch your mouth, Ranger."

"I was; that's why I said 'crap,'" Caitlin told him.

Finneran smirked, seeming to enjoy the superiority he thought he held over her. "When was the last time there was a gunfight on your River Walk, Ranger?"

"A gang incident six months ago. Several bystanders still healing after being caught in the cross fire. I wish you'd have been there to help us sort things out, Mr. Finneran."

"That's *Detective*."

"Not from where I'm standing right now." Caitlin watched him sip the coffee without adding cream or sugar. "You call my captain back in San Antonio?" she asked Finneran, trying to picture D. W. Tepper's reaction when he learned she'd gunned down four men while taking Dylan on a college visitation trip.

"My own captain did. Your captain said he wasn't surprised and that we could keep you as long as we wanted."

"And you seem to be doing just that, sir."

The Providence Police Department was headquartered in a modern, gray-steel and glass building spiraling six stories into the air maybe a mile from the site of WaterFire. From this fourth-floor interrogation room, Caitlin could actually see the glow of flames still burning and soft wisps of smoke dissipating as they wafted into the air.

"But now I'd like to speak to the young man," Caitlin continued. "If you can just tell me what room he's in . . ."

Whatever Finneran was about to say dissolved into a glare. He was a beefy man with red spiderweb veins growing out of his ruddy cheeks and a stomach that tested the bounds of his button-down shirt. "What were you doing carrying a gun outside your jurisdiction?"

"Texas Rangers don't have a jurisdiction."

"State lines don't count?"

"Our rules and regs require us to be armed at all times anywhere anytime."

"This is Rhode Island, Ms. Strong." Finneran was breathing noisily through his mouth, seeming to squeeze words in between breaths. "Your rules and regs don't mean a goddamn thing here."

"Where's Dylan Torres?"

"Being interviewed in another room."

"Outside of my presence."

"His ID says he's eighteen. That means we can speak to him alone."

"To interview or interrogate? Maybe you're forgetting he just survived a pretty tough scrape and could use some support instead of being treated like one of the gunmen who came after us."

Finneran sipped some more of his coffee, ignoring her.

"Is he a suspect?"

No response.

"Am *I* a suspect?"

"You killed four men tonight and fired off at least a magazine's worth of rounds into a crowd. Would a Rhode Islander be a suspect in Texas if they'd done the same thing on your streets?"

"That would depend on whether the men he or she killed were trying to do the same to them. We tend to give awards to such people, instead of treating them like criminals." Caitlin moved away from the counter, facing Finneran halfway between it and the table. The empty holster felt strange on her hip. "Your crime scene techs find the victims' guns?"

"They found two pistols, yes, but we've yet to determine who they belonged to."

"So it's normal at this WaterFire thing for speedboats toting men with assault rifles to be part of the show?"

"You're not exactly in a position here to be a smart-ass, Ranger."

"They got anything like Rangers in Rhode Island, Detective?"

"Closest thing we have is the state police."

"Then maybe we should call them," Caitlin said, holding his stare. "What about the man who dropped into the river? You find him?"

"Not a good time to dredge the bottom," Finneran sneered, checking his watch impatiently.

"The man Dylan pushed into the water wasn't shot. He probably swam away. You should be looking for him."

"Really?" the detective said, crossing his arms. "And what else should I be doing?"

"Telling me everything you've learned about the two men whose bodies you recovered."

"They weren't carrying IDs."

"What about fingerprints?"

"We're running them now."

"They were Latinos, Mexicans probably."

"We figured that much out all by ourselves."

"I've made a lot of enemies south of the border in my time."

"From what your captain said, it seems like you've made enemies in lots more places than that, Ranger."

Caitlin looked Finneran straight in the eye. "And I seem to keep making new ones."

Finneran drained the rest of his coffee and laid his cup down on the countertop. "Rhode Island doesn't have much need for gunfighters up here, given that we don't share your border problems."

"That's right. Last time I checked you weren't in an all-out shooting war with Massachusetts or Connecticut."

Finneran's eyes widened, his nostrils flaring as he opened his mouth to speak, when Caitlin ran right over his words.

"You ever been in a gunfight, Detective?" she asked, leaning forward.

"You think being in the number you have is what law enforcement's supposed to be about?"

"Ever fired on a suspect?" Caitlin resumed, instead of responding. "How about even drawn your gun? Let's try that one."

"This is Rhode Island, Ranger," he said finally. "We tend to look down on violence here, not embrace it."

"Maybe you'd feel different if you'd come up against the kind Texas Rangers deal with on a regular basis."

Finneran continued to hold her stare. In the small room's overly bright light, the veins on his cheeks looked like Magic Marker drawings a child might have left while he was napping.

"We did an additional check on you, Ranger. I can't even add up all the men you've killed. You're supposed to be some kind of goddamn legend."

"Not at all. I'm just doing my job, like you're supposed to be doing yours."

"You say you came up here to visit Brown University with this eighteen-year-old boy you're not related to. You say these men were watching you earlier in the day and likely trailed you to WaterFire."

"Somebody's pulling their strings. You let me out of here, and I'll find out who."

"Back in Texas?"

"The general vicinity, anyway."

Finneran gave her a long look, as if seeing Caitlin for the first time. "Know the last time anybody up here killed four people in self-defense?"

"I'm afraid I don't, sir."

"Never, Ranger, never. Looks like you've made history in a second state."

"You find anything else on the dead men's persons?"

"Pertaining to you, no. But you may want to take a look at this," he said, taking a picture enclosed in evidence-seal plastic from his jacket pocket.

He laid it on the countertop, and Caitlin moved up between Finneran and the Keurig machine to regard it.

"Oh, shit" was all she could say.

6

San Antonio

Guillermo Paz sat in the back of the classroom, trying to make himself as insignificant as possible. It wasn't easy, given the stares the other students, all younger and of college age, kept casting back his way as if to make sure he was real and not some kind of apparition. They didn't know his name, his background, even the fact that he'd once been wanted in the city for murder until someone in Washington made it all go away. What they knew was that a seven-foot man with long black hair twisted into ringlets falling well past his shoulders, and arm muscles the size of softballs, had joined their philosophy class.

This unit was being devoted to Arthur Schopenhauer, whose writings had grabbed Paz's attention as of late. This was his first night visiting the class, and he resolved to cling to the rear, fit in as best he could by being silent, and hopefully find the solace that had been missing lately in his regular visits to church confessionals.

Those visits had begun years before in his home country of Venezuela, to which Paz could never return, begun when his own conscience got the better of him over the increasingly murderous deeds he'd been entrusted to perform. His estrangement from the Chavez regime was followed almost immediately by a job in Texas that brought him face-to-face with the Texas Ranger who'd both changed his life and sent him searching for the purpose behind it. Paz considered himself, that very life, a work in progress. And now that priests seemed no longer able to help guide him through that evolution, he had turned to San Antonio College on San Pedro Avenue because of the school's generous collection of night classes. Guillermo Paz, former colonel in Venezuela's infamous secret police, figured nights were best for all concerned.

"Schopenhauer," the professor, whose name Paz had already forgotten, was saying, "claimed that the world is fundamentally what humans recognize in themselves as their will. His analysis of will led him to the conclusion that emotional, physical, and sexual desires can never be fully satisfied. The corollary of this is an ultimately painful human condition. Consequently, he considered that a lifestyle of negating desires was the only way to attain liberation."

Paz shook his head, unable to keep himself quiet. He raised his hand. The professor tried his best to ignore him until Paz waved his hand in the air, feeling the tiny desk he was squeezed into creak from the strain.

"Yes?" the man said finally, still reluctant to look in Paz's direction very long.

"I was wondering if you'd like to rethink your last statement, Professor."

"Excuse me?"

"This shit about controlling desires being the only way to find freedom," Paz said. "That's not really what Schopenhauer had in mind, is it?"

Now everyone in the classroom was looking at him, or at least trying to. Even the professor, previously reluctant to even acknowledge Paz's presence, took a tentative step toward him, as if to defend his territory.

"I don't recall seeing you in this class before," he said.

"I'm just visiting, getting a feel for things, trying to figure out if it's worth my time."

"Would you like directions to the registrar's office? I'd recommend coming back tomorrow during business hours."

"I'm open twenty-four hours a day and you won't see me here again." He ran his eyes around the students whose eyes were uniformly riveted upon him. "In fact, you're lucky if you ever see any of them here again. Let me enlighten you, *Profesor*. For Schopenhauer life was all about will, the ability to exert yours over someone else's. Yes, he believed the primary motivation of human beings lies in their most basic desires, but he was only saying this in reference to how little we'd evolved from the animal kingdom. He said what he said just to make that point, but it doesn't really cover his core philosophy. You should know that, shouldn't you?"

"What's your name, sir?" the professor asked instead of responding.

"Oh, I'm not enrolled in this class. I'm kind of just auditing, looking for someone who can shine a light on something I haven't seen before."

"I think you should leave."

Paz rose, his classroom desk shifting from the strain and nearly toppling when he stepped away from it to reveal his true size. "I figure I better enlighten your students first, *Profesor*." Addressing them now, seeking out eyes reluctant to meet his or looking the other way entirely. "The word on Schopenhauer was that he was a defeatist, a believer in the fact that human desire itself was futile and, by extension, life was pointless since desire was everything. He might have said both those things at some point, but there was never a connection between them."

"I'm going to call security," the teacher said.

"The thing I take from Schopenhauer," Paz continued, ignoring him, "is that man's will at its basest level poses a challenge that is in our capacity to overcome, to become the master of. He believed life was about cause and effect, becoming the champion of cause in order to control effect."

"Security's on their way," said the professor, holding his cell phone for Paz to see.

But Paz continued to ignore him, aware that more eyes were regarding him now, the reluctance dissipating as the younger students began to see in him some form of rebellious kindred spirit. "I've been reading Schopenhauer a lot lately because his philosophy kind of follows my own life path. Five years ago I killed because I was told to, obeyed my orders and felt nothing over the pain they left behind. I wasn't doing it for me, so taking all those lives left me feeling empty inside. Then I met my Texas Ranger and she showed me how the missing ingredient was belief. I realized, and all of you should too, that Schopenhauer was really saying that pain exists in the absence of passion. When you believe in something, your desires will reflect that which defines your morality. It's the distinction between purpose and action, or action undertaken as a result of moral purpose, being what makes us human and gives us hope."

He stopped, realizing *all* eyes in the room were rooted on him now.

"Isn't that right, *Profesor*?" he asked the man still holding his cell phone as if he'd forgotten it was there.

The professor could only swallow, consumed by the shadow Paz cast over him.

"Your teacher isn't graced with the grandest of thinking," Paz told the class. "Maybe that explains why his quote about Schopenhauer's view of the world came straight out of Wikipedia. Isn't that right, *Profesor*?"

This time the professor didn't even swallow.

"Ever since I met my Texas Ranger, I realized that man is the master of his own will, that he can make himself into whatever he wants. Too many think Schopenhauer was saying man is a prisoner of his will when the point he was really making concerned the rewards of overcoming it. But you won't find that in Wikipedia."

A few of the students actually smiled smugly, their body language taking them closer to Paz's viewpoint, if not Paz himself.

"Any questions?" he asked, when he heard his phone buzz with an incoming text message.

He eased the phone from his pocket and checked it fast, stiffening and seeming to grow taller and broader right before the students, who recoiled inwardly again.

"Sorry, gotta go," he said, turning for the door.

Paz was halfway out it before anyone had even noticed he'd moved, the class more startled than scared.

"Looks like my Texas Ranger needs me again," he added, poking his head back inside the classroom, continuing with his gaze fastened on the professor. "And all of you need another teacher."

7

PROVIDENCE, RHODE ISLAND

Caitlin laid her cell phone down on the counter, willing it to ring with Guillermo Paz's voice on the other end. After Cort Wesley's phone went straight to voice mail, she'd considered calling D. W. Tepper, but he lived ninety miles from San Antonio. Company F headquarters wouldn't have another Ranger readily available and, since she'd come to figure that the San Antonio police had permanently blocked her number from their phone lines, there was no sense calling them either.

"You want to tell me what that was all about?" Finneran said, having hovered over her while she sent Paz a text message that read simply CALL ME.

Caitlin noted for the first time that the detective's hair was a strawberry blond color tinged with gray at the temples. The room's harsh fluorescent lighting exaggerated the strawberry tones, making it look painted on, more the work of an artist than a barber.

"You saw everything you needed to."

"Not if it's connected to the shooting up here tonight, I haven't."

"Those gunmen aren't exactly in a position to get anywhere fast, Detective. Four of them, most ever killed in a gunfight up in these parts, remember?"

Finneran's gaze tilted toward the picture sealed in an evidence pouch. "That picture is evidence. It still belongs to us."

Caitlin slid the picture back toward him, a picture not of her.

But of Dylan.

One of the killers carrying it to make sure their target was properly identified. Caitlin could visualize them checking the picture back outside Brown University's athletic complex, making sure they had the right kid. Because Dylan must've been who they'd been gunning for at WaterFire tonight, not her.

An eighteen-year-old kid who happened to be the son of a man who had as many enemies as she did.

And if Dylan was a target, it stood to reason that Luke might be too. But neither he nor Cort Wesley were answering her calls or texts, meaning they must be somewhere with them turned off, leaving her to place all her hope in her enigmatic protector, Colonel Guillermo Paz.

"I'm talking to you here," Finneran was saying, when Caitlin's phone rang at last, UNKNOWN lit up in the Caller ID.

"Hello, Ranger," said Guillermo Paz.

Caitlin pictured Paz's huge shape on the other end of the line as she laid everything out for him.

"I don't know where Cort Wesley is, Colonel," she finished. "I think his cell phone's turned off."

"I can still trace its location, Ranger," Paz said, leaving it there.

Caitlin pretty much figured he was still in the nebulous employ of a mutual acquaintance of theirs in Washington, accounting for his new-found skills.

"Make it fast, please," she told him, ending the call and turning back to Finneran. "You need to take me to Dylan, Detective. You need to do that now, because he's still in danger."

"This is a police station, Ranger. I think we're capable of keeping him safe."

Caitlin moved right up into his space, tilting her head back just enough to look him in the eye. "You have any idea what we're dealing with here?"

"No, I don't."

"Well, neither do I, and until I do that boy isn't safe *anywhere*."

"Anything else?" Finneran asked her.

"Yes, sir. I need my gun back."

8

SAN ANTONIO

Luke was eating a funnel cake slathered in whipped cream and drizzled with chocolate, Cort Wesley's stomach still too queasy to even think about food.

"You feel any better, Dad?" the boy asked, biting off another wedge that left swipes of chocolate where his mustache had just begun to sprout.

Cort Wesley shifted on the picnic bench in an area of tables set on a blacktop promenade between food stands wedged in amid the rides and attractions. He positioned himself to avoid eyeing people munching on anything, a sight that for the time being continued to make his own stomach flutter.

"Sure," he told his son anyway. "Plenty."

"How about we try the Rattler roller coaster?" Luke suggested. "It only goes sixty-five miles per hour."

Cort Wesley caught the amused glint in the boy's eyes and just nodded. The SkyScreamer had spun him around in a hundred-foot arc at only forty miles per hour, the San Antonio skyline passing by faster and faster until it became a blur at the same time his stomach began to rumble in protest. It hadn't settled down yet, but Cort Wesley refused to let himself spill up the contents that had turned bitter and were now bile-laced. If he disappeared into the men's room, he wouldn't be able to face his younger son for a week.

"Why don't we try the shooting gallery over there?" Cort Wesley suggested instead.

"'Cause I suck at shooting and you know it."

"Caitlin's lessons haven't helped?"

"Not much. Pistol keeps jerking in my hand and my thumb keeps getting torn to shreds."

"That'll pass."

Luke blew the hair out of his face with his breath, just like Dylan. "Who taught you how to shoot, your dad?"

"Well, he gave me a gun and told me to go learn for myself, if you call that teaching."

"Would I have liked him?"

"My dad? When he was sober, yeah. He was a good enough man without any drink in him. But he had a peculiar idea of parenting."

"Like what?"

Cort Wesley took a moment to reflect on the fact that he'd seldom spoken to Luke, or Dylan for that matter, about their infamous, and in some circles notorious, grandfather Boone Masters. "Like the fact," he answered finally, "that for my dad being a role model meant having me help him lift stolen goods into the back of his truck and then riding atop it to hold everything steady. You know what he gave me for Christmas one year?"

"No."

"A television I'd dropped at the place where he stored all the stuff. He told me breaking it cost him the money he was going to use on my gift, so I got the busted TV instead."

"That's not nice," Luke said.

"Line at the shooting gallery's next to nothing."

Luke frowned, his lips puckering. He wedged the last of the funnel cake into his mouth and rose from the bench. "I don't want you telling me all the stuff I'm doing wrong. Just let me mess up on my own."

"Son, this is the night you win yourself a Kewpie doll."

"What's that?"

"Never mind," Cort Wesley said, as fireworks erupted in the sky over another section of the park.

He felt his stomach muscles seize up, flashback memories of his time in the Gulf War hitting him hard and fast. Just like they always did when something bad was about to happen.

But not tonight. No odd feeling or misplaced memory was going to spoil tonight.

"Something wrong, Dad?" Luke asked, sensing him stiffen.

"No, son," Cort Wesley said, believing it even less, "not at all."

9

SAN ANTONIO

Cort Wesley liked mowing down the figures moving and rotating against the shooting gallery's rear wall, each recorded hit drawing a *ping* and a boost to his LED score readout on the overhead board. These carny-like attractions didn't seem to fit in with the rest of the park, the space they'd been squeezed into looking carved out of the grounds only on a temporary, maybe trial, basis. For tonight, though, the feel of pulling the trigger followed by the satisfying sound as another moving target bit the dust refreshed him to the point of even settling his stomach.

"*Sir,*" a voice said from somewhere behind him, as Cort Wesley watched Luke step up to take his turn, "*you can't be wearing that in here.*"

"You're holding it wrong, son."

"That's what Caitlin always says."

"Well, maybe you should start listening."

"Dad," Luke spat at him, elongating the word and shooting him a glare that brought the rumbling back to Cort Wesley's stomach.

"Sorry."

"*Sir, I'm going to have to ask you to stop.*"

Cort Wesley heard the man's voice again in the back of his mind, the front devoted to watching his son begin pecking away at the bad guys, the gallery rifle clacking off pellets a bit bigger than what he remembered as a boy. Missing more than he hit, the soft click of a shot followed every second or third time by the clang of a strike. Luke's concentration was intense, so much so that he looked like he was trying to squeeze the paint off the rifle and Cort Wesley had to gnash his teeth to avoid telling him to ease up on his grip. Luke's current score was a fraction of what he'd managed, making him think he should have missed more on purpose.

"Sir, the park has a strict no guns policy!"

For Cort Wesley, the night changed then and there. The cool, comfortable breeze turned hot against his skin, and suddenly the smooth darkness became nothing more than a ribbon of black set against the bright lights piercing it. The scents of popcorn, cotton candy, barbecue, and grilling food all got sucked into the vacuum of Cort Wesley's defenses snapping on. He spun just as a lanky Latino shoved an unarmed security guard aside and drew his pistol in the same motion.

Cort Wesley yanked the gallery rifle from Luke's grasp and steadied it on the gunman, opening up with full awareness of the load's minimal capabilities. Because he targeted the man's sunglasses, all wrong to be wearing at night, which made Cort Wesley remember the same man standing across from him at the SkyScreamer talking on his cell phone.

The pellets cracked the glass of both lenses and sent flecks flying toward his eyes. The man used his free hand to tear the glasses off and swipe at his now red and watery eyes, even as he opened up wildly with his nine-millimeter pistol.

Cort Wesley shoved Luke up and over the game's heavy wood, waist-high front wall and then pulled himself over with his legs swept to the sides. The gunman's initial shots found nothing as a result, his next bullets flying even more askew with his aim further upset by the unexpected turn of events.

"Dad . . ."

"Stay down!"

"Dad!"

"Down!" Cort Wesley ordered again, yanking a pair of freshly loaded gallery rifles down from the counter.

Ridiculous to think their rounds could accomplish much at all, but Cort Wesley figured this was the best time to try, with the gunman's original intentions thrown all out of whack. He timed his lurch upward to coincide with a time lag he took to mean the gunman was jacking a fresh magazine home, and found the man in his sights just as he was bringing his pistol back up from fifty feet away.

Cort Wesley peppered him with a barrage of pellets from both rifles, his shots all aimed at the man's face. He watched the man jerk both his hands up to shield his already hurt eyes, eliminating, for the moment anyway, the threat posed by his gun.

Cort Wesley was just about to leap back over the counter, when he caught more shapes pushing their way inward against the flow of panicked park-goers fleeing the area. He dropped down again, shielding Luke with his own frame just as fresh gunfire started—four guns, his hearing told him, all nine-millimeter pistols. Then a fifth was added to the mix, evidence of the original shooter regaining enough of his senses to rejoin the attack that blistered his ears and sent splinters and shards of wood spewing into the air.

"*Dad!*" Luke wailed again.

And Cort Wesley felt the tug of helplessness that was no stranger to anyone who knows combat. But that tug had an entirely different feel when something much more was at stake than just himself or his mission. He had to protect his son. Priority One.

Which meant taking out the five gunmen with his own Glock stowed back in his truck, locked up inside in compliance with park rules.

Cort Wesley's battle-tested mind churned through everything it had recorded near the shooting gallery, searching for some weapon, some equalizer. Cooking grease, hot coffee, the oil used to make the popcorn . . . What about turning the big Clydesdale horses giving wagon rides into a stampede?

"Stay here, son!" Cort Wesley ordered, no idea what he was going to do for sure, once exposed beyond the shooting gallery.

"*Dad!*"

"Do what I say!"

Cort Wesley realized he was squeezing the boy's arm hard enough to make him wince, stripping his hand free just as he heard the loud grating sound of an engine racing in the red, a vehicle risking its transmission to surge right into the middle of the gunfight. There was a screech of tires, followed by the sickening thud of steel meeting flesh and bone. Cort Wesley peeked over the counter to see Guillermo Paz barreling toward the shooting gallery in a massive, extended-cab pickup truck.

10

San Antonio

Paz spun the truck into a whiplash turn that left its passenger side blocking the front of the shooting gallery, providing additional cover for Cort Wesley and Luke. Paz was firing out his open window with an M16 even then, still firing when he threw the truck's door open and lunged out. In the same motion, he managed to hurl a second assault rifle up and over his truck, dropping it straight into Cort Wesley's waiting hands. At near seven feet tall and all of three hundred pounds, Paz might have been the biggest man Cort Wesley had ever seen, but in moments like this he moved like a gazelle. His motions flowed in an eerie rhythm, as if thought and action had merged into one.

His huge shoulders, encased in an army green canvas shirt, vibrated as he continued to fire, M16 rotating in the neat arc the shooters had formed. His bullets trailed them in neat three-shot bursts, Cort Wesley adding his own fire to the mix in the next instant. He used the counter as a springboard to reach the bed of Paz's truck, hitting the trigger the moment his feet touched down.

Paz's fire was trained to the right at that point so Cort Wesley worked his to the left. He recorded the shape of the man Paz had plowed over bent and broken in the middle of the midway. Paz had already left a second gunman splayed atop a picnic table and Cort Wesley's fire spun a third into the abandoned popcorn cart, spilling it over to the pavement. They opened up together in the next instant, their twin streams effectively crisscrossing to hold the final two gunmen at bay behind concrete-encased trash receptacles.

"Let's go, outlaw!"

No time to reflect or reconnoiter, not even any to breathe, before Paz was behind the wheel of the big truck again, gunning the engine. The man seemed to live in an entirely different plane of existence, no wasted thought, motion, or action whatsoever.

"Luke!" Cort Wesley called.

To his credit, the boy popped up immediately, climbing atop the counter to accept his father's helping hand into the big truck's cab.

"Go!" Cort Wesley yelled to Paz, slamming a hand down on the truck's roof to signal him on.

And Paz tore out of Six Flags Fiesta just as he'd torn into it, Cort Wesley waiting until he was sure no more gunmen were about before climbing into the truck's rear seat.

"The Ranger sent me, outlaw," Paz said, his massive hands swallowing the wheel as he made straight for La Cantera Parkway and the I-10 beyond it.

And then it all clicked into place. "Dylan . . ."

"He's fine, the Ranger too. Kind of under arrest, though."

"Kind of?"

"There were casualties up in Province as well."

"Providence," Luke corrected from the passenger seat, eyeing Paz as if he were an animal in a zoo with no bars separating them. "And I recognize you. You . . . you were there the day my mom was killed."

"He saved our lives in Mexico not long afterward, Luke," Cort Wesley reminded, the rationale sounding feeble even to him.

Paz tilted his gaze toward the boy, as he gave the truck more gas. "And the man you see before you now was reborn that day. I can't change what I've done, only what I can do from that moment forward." With that, Paz extended his cell phone back to Cort Wesley. "The Ranger wants you to call her. In Providence. There were five gunmen up there too."

"Coordinated attacks, then."

Cort Wesley could see Paz's saucer-like eyes peering into the rear-view mirror. "Nothing new, outlaw."

PART TWO

A genuine Texas Ranger will endure cold, hunger and fatigue, al-most without a murmur, and will stand by a friend and comrade in the hour of danger and divide anything he has got, from a blanket to his last crumb of tobacco.

Andrew Jackson Sowell, *Rangers and Pioneers of Texas*

11

Ana Callas Guajardo led the two men, her most trusted captains, around the lee of her sprawling home toward the stables that were her pride and joy. "I'm disappointed in your failure, gravely disappointed, but I'm not angry. Anger accomplishes nothing. Bob Parsons, the great CEO who founded Go Daddy, says that when you get knocked down, the sooner you get up and get back to business, the sooner your failure can be rectified. Do you understand what I'm saying?"

"We took elaborate precautions," said Juan Aviles Uribe defensively. A former major in the Mexican *federal* police force, Uribe had lost an eye in a shoot-out; the menacing black patch he now wore made the nests of scar tissue that dotted his cheeks stand out all the more. "There's nothing linking the men we used back to us."

"That's not what I asked you, Major. I asked if you understood that now we must find a way to turn your failure into success."

"We will need more men, *jefa*," Uribe said, missing the point.

"Because your preparation and planning fell short. You underestimated the opposition in spite of my warnings. Bob Parsons also says that most mistakes stem from subjective sources, limited information, and inaccurate assumptions."

"I am just a soldier," snapped Colonel Ramon Reyes Vasquez in a voice that sounded more like a slurred growl. "I don't understand all this."

Vasquez wasn't tall but he was almost absurdly broad, with a chest that looked like a rack concealed beneath his sweat-soaked shirt. It was said that Vasquez kept a piece of every man or woman he'd ever killed. A personal collection he showcased only for himself. Some dared suggest he was not a man at all, but a *chupacabra*, a mythical Mexican vampire-like beast best known for leaving its victims, both animal and human, drained of blood. But he walked with a slight limp from shrapnel still lodged in his hip from one bomb blast and had lost a good measure of his hearing to another, which had felled a dozen men while leaving him as the lone survivor.

Guajardo's gaze bore into him. "All you need to understand at this point is that the Torres boys are still alive and that is the failure that must be rectified."

The two men looked suddenly uncomfortable in her presence, unaccustomed to taking orders from or being criticized by a woman. But Ana Callas Guajardo was no ordinary woman. Far from it. She occupied a very rare place in Mexican culture as a political power broker and kingmaker whose party had returned to power in the most recent election, in large part thanks to the millions she had plunged into her presidential candidate's campaign. His victory had increased her power many times over, making her someone to be feared and respected at the same time, but mostly feared. The respect came from her status as Mexico's wealthiest woman, having built upon her father's vast success. The fear stemmed from the ruthless manner with which she pursued her fortune. Business was a war, every deal a battle where prisoners were left dead on the battlefield. Even the cartels grudgingly accepted the reasonable peace over which she now presided because it served their business better as well.

The cartel leaders had taken Ana Guajardo lightly at first, until they quickly discerned how little her appearance suited her or the position she occupied. Her flawless skin looked perpetually and naturally tan. Her eyes were steady, calm, and reassuring, belying the true intentions and ambitions of a woman who crushed her enemies and used her supporters for the sole purpose of increasing her own hold on power. She had been pictured on the front pages of Mexican newspapers and websites at gala events and openings, equally at home there as she was in dark, dingy buildings where her less savory associates were head-quartered.

"I was clear in my warning not to attack the Torres boys in the presence of their father or this Texas Ranger," Vasquez groused.

"But that doesn't explain the failure on the fairgrounds, does it? The roots of that failure lie in yet more poor preparation on your part."

"We could not anticipate the appearance of *Angel de la Guarda, jefa*."

"And what if you had? Would you have needed a hundred men, a *thousand*?" Guajardo shook her head, her impatience showing in a flush of red through her features. "This Guardian Angel, as you call him, is just a man who bleeds like any other."

"Guillermo Paz may be a man," Uribe echoed, "but he doesn't bleed like any other. He earned his nickname from first protecting Mexican peasants from the local cartel lords and soldiers and then exacting his own revenge upon them."

"So he's a better man than you."

Uribe stammered over a response, Vasquez picking up for him. "The cartels put a price on his head that no one has dared try to collect."

"A truly dangerous man, *jefa*," Uribe said, finding his voice.

"I know," she told them both. "Guillermo Paz once worked for me."

12

QUINTANA ROO, MEXICO

"It was through Chavez," Guajardo elaborated, "when we were doing some business down there and Paz was part of his secret police. We needed a village cleared so we could exploit the mineral rights. Chavez ended up keeping them all for himself."

"I'm surprised he avoided assassination, *jefa*."

"He had Paz."

Guajardo stiffened as their stroll brought her stables and riding pen into view. Not far away, a withered shape in a wheelchair baked in the sunlight under the careful watch of a white-garbed male attendant. Her two captains made it a point to ignore Ana's wheelchair-bound father, not even acknowledging his presence as the attendant leaned over to check his pulse. Ana Guajardo's father had built this entire sprawling estate in Quintana Roo around those stables, constructing the riding pen in a way that allowed view of the horses from all sides of the hacienda but the rear. The four-story, ten-thousand-square-foot home was finished in an elegant cream stucco beneath a clay-colored roof with an overhang supported by majestic pillars modeled after renderings of ancient Aztec temples.

Concealed within this beauty, though, was the highest level of concrete and steel construction, capable of withstanding a Category Five hurricane. All the windows were made of bulletproof glass with fitted hurricane shutters for extra protection. The main rooms were outfitted with forty-five-foot-long, low-arching boveda brick ceilings, and each of the six bathrooms was finished with handmade Mexican tiles. The seven bedrooms all opened onto large balconies; the main, seven-hundred-square-foot veranda off the second floor overlooked a tennis court Ana Guajardo never used and a swimming pool she had not once swam in. Nor had she ever visited one of the beaches, among Mexico's most beautiful, located just five miles away, because there was always too much else to do.

"I knew of Paz's connection to the Ranger, not the cowboy," Uribe defended. "And I didn't know, no one knew, he was still in Texas."

Guajardo stopped within clear view of her horses at play in the field. "But we know now, don't we?" She took a quick glance toward her father, then returned her attention to Uribe and Vasquez.

"We won't fail next time, *jefa*."

"You're right, because there's not going to be a next time," Guajardo said suddenly. "The Torres boys are not your problem any longer—they are mine. That will free you to focus on the bigger picture."

"What picture is that, *jefa*?"

"Our coming attack against the *Estados Unidos*."

Guajardo's captains looked at each other, unsure they'd heard her correctly.

"*Jefa?*" Vasquez raised.

"Did you say *attack* the United States?" followed Uribe immediately.

"I need fifteen hundred pilots," she told them both, "perhaps as many as two thousand."

"*Airplane* pilots?" Uribe posed in disbelief.

Guajardo remained utterly calm, her gaze fixed on her frolicking horses as she replied.

"They are not thoroughbreds, you know," she said from the edge of the pen they'd just reached. "They are *paso fino*, horses raised for the mountainous regions of South America. The first two were gifts from my father's associate Juan Arrango in Colombia. I was a teenage girl when a stable boy, a peasant, saddled his first mare wrongly. My father made me watch as he took a hatchet and chopped the boy's hand off for punishment while two workmen held him down."

Vasquez and Uribe grinned in approval. Both had heard the story before. The legend was well-known, one of the many tales that had helped foster the Guajardo family's well-earned mystique and reputation for ruthlessness. Nothing inspired fear more than a myth like that.

"These horses remind me of what I came from," Guajardo continued. "I look out at my *paso fino*, and I remember my roots as well as those who sought to destroy my family. That is why I brought those children to die at my own hand in Willow Creek. That is why the Torres boys should be dead now too. Because only when the past is laid to rest can the future truly rise. And six days from now, *mis compadres*, that future begins with our attack. Come, there's something else you need to see."

She led them past the horse pen into the lavish, rolling fields abundant with exotic flowering trees and plantings native to the Yucatán and others, which Guajardo had paid exorbitantly to have transplanted and then maintained. There were Chak Kuyché, also known as Shaving Brush Trees, colored a deep wine-red color, and perfumed flowers in white and magenta. Mixed in among these were Royal Poinciana and orchid trees that seemed in perpetual bloom.

Guajardo's flowering fields ended at a drop-off, beyond which a stretch of land had been cleared for several acres, surrounded on three sides by native brush that grew wild and untamed. Vasquez and Uribe saw a foreman wearing a wide-brimmed hat supervising the work of flattening and leveling the land with a combination of heavy rollers and payloaders. He noticed Guajardo and tipped his hat, as she led her two most trusted officers forward.

"The pilots needed for the attack will be trained right here," she said, just loud enough to be heard.

Vasquez and Uribe exchanged a befuddled glance, having no idea how that could be possible in such a limited space, but not about to challenge Guajardo on the point. Just as they never challenged the story of her father hacking off a boy's hand for mis-saddling a horse.

"The work goes well, Cesar?" Guajardo asked when they reached the foreman.

"*Sí, señora*, very well."

He tipped his hat reverently to her again and that's when Vasquez and Uribe noticed his other arm dangling useless by his side, ending in a stump where his hand had once been.

"Six days," Ana Guajardo told them. "In six days, our war begins."

13

SAN ANTONIO

"Where's it stop, Ranger?" Captain D. W. Tepper asked Caitlin from across his desk, showing his disgust in the scowl that seemed to deepen the furrows carved into his leathery face.

Those furrows looked more like shadows nesting in his skin, courtesy of a four-bulb overhead light fixture that currently had only one screwed in. The result was to cast only the area before his desk in any decent light, Caitlin feeling it spraying down over her while Tepper himself moved in and out of the spill with each rock of his chair forward.

"There was no other choice I could see, Captain."

"You talking about killing four men in Providence or calling in Paz to kill three down here? You know, San Antonio does have a police department that, last time I checked, had a working phone number."

"And how do you think ordinary cops would have fared in Six Flags last night?"

"Guess we'll never know."

"I do," Caitlin said, half under her breath.

"They've got guns too, Ranger."

"But scoring one hit per magazine doesn't cut it against what Cort Wesley was up against."

Earlier that day, Cort Wesley and Luke had been waiting when Caitlin and Dylan emerged from the jetway at San Antonio International Airport.

"You came yourself?" Caitlin said, after they hugged tightly.

"I didn't trust the job to anyone else and I wasn't about to leave Luke alone."

Caitlin noticed him take a sidelong glance, as if to wonder what might be there. "But you didn't come alone, did you?"

"Nope."

"Paz?"

"Paz," Cort Wesley nodded.

"Where is he?"

"I have no idea. He called in some of his men too, but I haven't seen any of them either."

"And you won't. He's probably using some of those Venezuelan rebels from his native Mayan region; he's been recruiting them since our friend Jones, Smith, or whatever he's calling himself these days let the colonel off his leash."

"Homeland Security's personal hit squad."

"Now ours," Caitlin said, not bothering to disguise the irony in her voice.

Caitlin watched Tepper swallow hard, his face looking like stomach acid had splashed up into his mouth. "You have dragged the entire nineteenth century into the present with you, Hurricane. I'm starting to think the only solution to me not finishing my career as a crossing guard is finding a time machine to whisk you away to where you belong."

"It doesn't concern you that somebody sent ten Mexican hitters to kill two teenage boys?"

"It does indeed, only a little more than you calling in that one-man cavalry of yours." Tepper leaned back out of the reach of the light and shook his head.

"Look me in the eye and say you blame me, D.W. Tell me you wouldn't have done the same thing from fifteen hundred miles away."

"How's it feel to have gunned men down in a whole new time zone, Ranger?"

Caitlin shook her head, suppressed rage flushing blood through her face. "Just who murders kids, anyway?"

"Strange you should ask," Tepper said, extending a file folder across the desk. "Because we got five others killed in a ghost town by the name of Willow Creek."

14

SAN ANTONIO

Caitlin held the folder stiffly, but didn't open it. "You say Willow Creek?"

"You look like you've seen a ghost, Caitlin."

"I might as well have."

"Come again?"

"Willow Creek doesn't strike a chord in you?"

"Why should it?"

"My granddad never told you."

"Told me what?"

"About his first day as a Ranger, D.W."

"Sure, he did. He and your great-granddad William Ray were holed up in a saloon celebrating with whiskey—at least William Ray was celebrating. I seem to recall Earl telling me one glass stayed his limit from that day on. Believe the town was called Smokeville."

"Nothing about a boy wandering out of the desert with a drawing of monsters in his pocket?"

"Uh-oh," Tepper said, upper lip curling back from his teeth.

"What's wrong, Captain?"

Tepper waved a thin, knobby, nicotine-stained finger across his desk. "You got that look, Ranger, the look that says calling nine-one-one or summoning the whole goddamn Fifth Army can't save us from what's coming."

"It's just a story, D.W., and one it's time you heard."

15

WILLOW CREEK, TEXAS; 1919

William Ray and Earl Strong, with the still nameless boy latched to him for dear life, rode across the desert to Willow Creek, a town too close to the Mexican border for comfort. It was a blistering hot day for this time of year, the harsh land giving up a pleasant breeze to temper the air a bit.

The ride south to Willow Creek, six hours on horseback, meant the boy had been walking for at least four times that, likely setting out through the desert sometime yesterday morning or early afternoon. The trek had taken them past the same rolling tumbleweeds Earl had plucked from the boy's hair, along with bleached branch and tree remains having the dried texture of driftwood. More and more these days, motorcars were showing up even in small Texas towns, but Rangers to a man still patrolled on horseback, not about to entrust Henry Ford's invention for travel through the badlands and back roads they covered.

"Only thing those motor buggies got over horses," William Ray Strong was fond of saying, "is they don't shit. Then again, that oil they belch smells a hell of a lot worse."

William Ray's hope was to make the town before nightfall, no real desire to face whatever had sprayed blood all over the boy after dark.

"Tell me about Willow Creek, son," he prodded Earl.

Earl felt the boy's grasp tighten at the mere mention of the town's name. "Sir?"

"It's part of your Rangering patrol. That means you gotta know it inside and out."

"Not much of a town these days," Earl recalled. "Had a boom for a time when the plan was for the railroad to cut through it years back. But the boom died when the railroad got rerouted."

"On account of . . ."

"Mexican bandits. 'Cause of the nearby water and hills, bandits looking to make time and avoid detection are known to pass through border towns just like Willow Creek."

"Meaning we best keep an eye out, doesn't it?"

"It sure does, sir."

"You ready for your first gunfight if that eye spots something?"

"Hard to say right now. Not at all hard once my Colt clears its holster."

William Ray looked down at the Model 1911 Springfield .45 caliber pistol holstered on his own hip, its squared design distinguishing it from the .45 caliber revolver he'd given Earl as a gift on his eighteenth birthday. "You wanna trade?"

"No, sir."

William Ray grumbled something under his breath and prodded his horse for just a bit more speed. He'd first been issued the eight-shot Model 1911 for combat purposes in 1916 when he helped lead General John J. "Black Jack" Pershing and his five thousand soldiers on a retaliatory raid against none other than Pancho Villa, leader of the Mexican revolution. After attacks by Villa's rebels in Texas claimed the lives of U.S. soldiers and citizens, William Ray was called in on orders from President Woodrow Wilson himself because no one knew the terrain and the territory better than he. During his days riding with the legendary Captain George W. Arrington of the Frontier Battalion, Ranger incursions into Mexico were so frequent as to be like side trips with trails traversed so often the Rangers' horses knew them by heart.

"Don't be so quick to dismiss this Model nineteen-eleven here, son," William Ray said, their horses continuing to amble slowly through the desert. "Got itself quite a history in its own right. See, Ranger Earl, over in the Pacific, U.S. troops were armed with thirty-eight-caliber double-action revolvers that barely slowed the Filipino tribesmen down. There were tales of Moro warriors absorbing multiple bullets while they continued to hack away with their *kris* knives at the GIs. Got so the need for more firepower grew so desperate that old stocks of Model Eighteen Seventy-Three, forty-five-caliber Colt revolvers were returned to active service, many of which dated back to the Plains Indian Wars, where they took down those Moros just like they dropped the Apache and Comanche."

"Well," Earl Strong said to his father, "I wonder who we'll be taking down today."

"You smell that, son?" William Ray asked as they approached the outskirts of Willow Creek.

Earl realized the boy was digging into him tighter with his fingers, as if he'd caught the scent too. "Afraid I don't, sir, not yet."

The breeze was blowing up from the southwest, the town's direction. Earl Strong couldn't smell a thing besides the heat dust baked into the air, his own sweat, and the fear on the boy, who clung tighter to him the closer they drew to the home he'd fled.

As soon as they hit the end of the town's single main road, Earl caught the aroma on the air he knew could only come from dead bodies. The main thoroughfare was rimmed by a few nests of small homes set back on either side and dotting the surrounding flatlands. All were colored brown to match the mud that dominated the streets in the rainy season. Today, though, dust hung in the air like a cloud, whipped up by the wind into mini-tornado spouts to leave residue on everything it touched. Remnants of the railroad were still in place in the form of piles of rails and ties gathering dust and a partially dug bed that looked as if it had been abandoned almost the very day it had been started.

Both Rangers saw the buzzards circling overhead and swarms of black flies hanging above the street like storm clouds. A number of bodies grew visible once they drew to within a couple hundred feet of the center of the street, mere dark specks at first growing rapidly until the shapeless, flaccid forms of what had been human beings little more than a day before became clear. The Strongs' horses caught the scent on the breeze and fought their riders a bit, flaring their nostrils and whinnying.

"This ain't good," said Earl, feeling the boy's fingernails digging into his flesh through his shirt now. The kid was whimpering, sobbing, mumbling words Earl couldn't discern.

"About what I expected," William Ray followed.

The boy was shaking terribly by the time they stopped and dismounted well short of the bodies that had attracted the flies and buzzards.

William Ray crouched before the boy this time. "Son, we're gonna leave you in charge of our horses. Now, what you gotta know is that, like Rangers, these horses are duly sworn to protect innocent Texans from harm. Anybody tries to hurt you is gonna have to go through a couple tons of angry muscle to get it done. Nod if you understand."

The boy nodded. Once.

"Blackie," William Ray said to his horse, "you know the drill."

And the horse flipped its head, shaking its mane, as if to acknowledge the Ranger's words, before moving closer to the boy and nuzzling him with its mouth.

"Atta boy," William Ray muttered, yanking his Winchester rifle from its saddle sheath and jacking a round into the chamber.

"Guess that explains the real reason why you don't cotton to those motorcars much," Earl said, as they moved down the center of the street through the last of the day's sun.

"How's that?"

"Can't train a car to babysit."

William Ray's hand stayed close to his .45. "How many reside here, Ranger Earl?"

"Fifty these days, maybe give or take ten. The rest of civilization lies more to the north, from where we came, plenty safer from Mexican bandits. Means any other survivors probably would've lit out that way too."

"Yup, that's what I was thinking. Why don't we go see what we can see, Ranger Earl."

The first body they came upon lay in the center of the street between a saloon on one side of the street and a shuttered livery on the other. A big man wearing suspenders but missing his boots, a double-barreled shotgun still in his hands when William Ray turned him over.

"Man's been shot front and back, Dad," Earl noted.

William Ray was checking the shotgun. "Both chambers empty, meaning he got off at least two shots. You see that brighter patch up where his heart used to beat?"

"Yes, sir."

"I'm guessing there was a badge there and we're looking at the local law. Came out of the saloon after somebody, when he got opened up on from both directions."

"So they took his badge as a souvenir."

"Sound familiar?"

Earl was about to say it did indeed, from the many battles Rangers fought against Mexican bandits, when William Ray spotted something glinting in the sun atop the gravel street. "Well, look what we got here. . . ."

He knelt down and plucked a shell casing from the street. "Looks like somebody put one more into him for good measure from in close. Give me a read on the caliber, Ranger Earl," he followed, handing the shell to his son.

"Seven millimeter," Earl noted.

"Keep talking, son."

"Fired from a Mauser pistol, kind unique to Mexico. Standard army issue, as I recall."

"Carried by Pancho Villa's men too, I seem to recall."

Earl handed William Ray back the shell casing. "Kind of bullet you see displayed in those bandoliers Mexican gunmen and soldiers are known for wearing."

That was enough to push them both into silence, recalling the boy's drawing, until William Ray finally rose and tilted his gaze toward the saloon. "Let's go see what they left for us next, son."

If Earl's count was correct, most of the remaining townspeople had gathered here, the body count inside stretching into the dozens. Black flies swarmed wildly about, making the air look stained dark in patches. William Ray and Earl figured the heat had started turning the bodies sour ahead of normal timing. It was one thing to see the remains of outlaws, criminals, or would-be gunmen made brave by drink. It was another to see women and children among the fallen. It was enough to make William Ray and Earl feel their mouths go dry and stomachs quake with bile and gas.

"What you make of the spacing of the corpses, Ranger Earl?"

"I'd say a bunch were lined up against the wall and executed."

"Anything else tell you that?"

"Well," Earl said, feeling about that wall, until he came to what he was looking for and pried it out. "How about this?" he asked and handed his father the bullet he'd pried free. "Seven millimeter," he added.

William Ray nodded in agreement. "Yup, a Mauser for sure." Then he shook his head, his expression that of a man who'd just eaten an onion and washed it down with straight lemon juice. "But what could account for a massacre like this?"

Earl was crouching over the bodies now, moving from one to another. "Well, to start with, I don't believe this was Pancho Villa's work, sir."

"Son?"

"His ammo supply's dried up to just about nothing since he mixed it up with General Pershing. I heard told to save bullets he took to executing two prisoners at a time with a single bullet."

"Bet that didn't go so well."

"Point being that whoever mowed these folks down was firing about as random as it gets." Earl tilted his gaze behind him now. "As many rounds found that wall back there as did flesh. They were firing like they enjoyed it, like it was sport."

"What in hell were they doing in Willow Creek? Better question being what the hell went wrong when they got here?"

Earl rose, brushing off his pants as if to ward off the stench. "Maybe we got the timing wrong. Maybe that sheriff and his shotgun started things and the killers didn't want to leave any witnesses after they took down the bodies we saw in the street. Or maybe they were making the point that they were just not to be messed with."

"Maybe that boy can tell us," William Ray had just added when Blackie neighed loudly outside.

He held his son's stare as they moved for the door and burst out from the saloon side by side, the dusk sky giving up riders coming in fast from the south and the Mexican side of the border.

Earl and William Ray stood their ground, Earl with the Colt drawn now and his father with the Winchester grasped so tight his hands had turned bright red.

"You remember what I told you before?"

"No man in the wrong can stand up against a fellow that's in the right and keeps on a-comin'."

"True enough. Now let's kill us some men," said William Ray Strong, eyeing the badge pinned proudly to his son's shirt.

"That's if they are men," Earl replied, thinking of that drawing the boy had done of skeletons wearing bandoliers. "You can't kill something that's already dead."

"You ever try that, son?"

"No, sir."

"Then you can't be sure, can you?" William Ray hocked up some spittle and steadied the Winchester higher, as the oncoming riders kicked up a torrent of dust in their wake. "Anyway, welcome to the Texas Rangers."

16

SAN ANTONIO, THE PRESENT

"I never heard old Earl tell that one," Tepper said when Caitlin had finished. "I'm guessing it wasn't zombies with skulls for heads that came riding in."

"That's besides the point."

"What is the point, Ranger?"

"Five kids found dead in the very place where a whole town preceded them over ninety years ago? You trying to tell me that's a coincidence?"

"Here we go again. . . ."

"Where's that exactly, Captain?"

"To a place where the legendary Caitlin Strong sees the forest but not the trees."

"And your point is?"

Tepper just shook his head. "Know why I can't retire? Because Austin can't find a single man willing to become your superior. I think they might start Texas Ranger Company G with you as the sole solitary member."

Caitlin looked across the desk at him. "By the way, I never did thank you, Captain."

"For what?"

"The lights at St. Anthony's school."

Tepper pretended to be baffled. "I have no idea what you're talking about, Ranger. And you best get a move on; chopper leaves for Willow Creek in twenty minutes."

17

Caitlin covered the four hundred miles to Willow Creek in the helicopter recently allocated to Ranger Company F. The airborne route was a straight line over what to a great extent was a scrub-riddled wasteland dotted by the shells of towns along the Mexican border that had died when their water dried up and the modern world seemed to forget them. It was like an alley of emptiness and despair roasting in the sun, lifeless save for prairie dogs, mule deer, grazing pronghorn antelope, and small piglike animals called javelinas that thrived amid the brush of this semiarid desert.

She'd been told the helicopter had come from an allotment dispensed by Homeland Security, and she could see her old friend Jones's prints all over the deal, a lame attempt at making nice after he'd hung her out to dry the year before. Accompanying Caitlin was Frank Dean Whatley, who'd been the Bexar County medical examiner since the time she'd been in diapers. He'd grown a belly in recent years that hung out over his thin belt, seeming to force his spine to angle inward at the torso. Whatley's teenage son had been killed by Latino gangbangers when Caitlin was a mere kid herself. Ever since then, he'd harbored a virulent hatred for that particular race, from the bag boys at the local H-E-B to the politicians who professed to be peacemakers. With his wife first lost in life and then death to alcoholism, he'd probably stayed in the job too long. But he had nothing to go home to, no real life outside the office, and remained exceptionally good at performing the rigors of his job.

"You seen the crime scene photos local authorities forwarded to us on this yet?" Whatley asked her.

"I didn't even know there were any."

"Got transmitted this morning via e-mail. I'd show them to you," Whatley said, tapping the worn and cracked leather case in which he carried the tools of his trade, "but the ride's hard enough on the stomach as it is."

He left things there and Caitlin didn't press him for more. Instead, she let her mind wander to the times these lands would have been occupied by all manner of bandit and renegade Indian whom the Texas Rangers had battled alone for decades. Before her great-grandfather William Ray Strong had come to Willow Creek, he'd served in the famed Frontier Battalion after the battalion's glory days were done and the ranks of their enemies had been decimated. The years that followed had been especially hard on the last of the old-school Rangers, what with the appearance of motorcars and organized crime. The Frontier Battalion, she guessed, didn't know how good they had it compared to twentieth-century Rangers, who were up against as many guns to go with far more sophisticated criminal networks thanks in large part to the drug war Captain George W. Arrington never had to fight. Yet she knew that men like Arrington would have adjusted just fine, because that's what Rangers did.

Caitlin hadn't realized Frank Whatley had pulled a manila folder full of pictures and was reviewing what they were about to find in Willow Creek right now.

"Prepare yourself, Ranger," he warned.

"For what?"

He looked up at her, face ashen, folder trembling in his free hand. "The worst thing you ever saw in your life."

18

San Antonio

"Those your sons?" Miguel Asuna asked Cort Wesley, wiping the grease from his hands with an already soiled cloth.

"Dylan and Luke," Cort Wesley told him, watching a mechanic go over the finer points of a street rod's engine with the boys, all their heads hidden by the raised hood.

In all probability, of course, the street rod had been stolen. Back when Cort Wesley was working for the Branca crime family, Asuna's body shop had doubled as a chop shop where stolen cars were brought to be disassembled for parts. He'd once heard Asuna boast he could strip a Mercedes in thirty minutes flat, something confirmed by Miguel's younger brother, Pablo, who was as close to a best friend as Cort Wesley had until he was tortured and killed by having his face jammed up against a fan belt.

Miguel Asuna was twice the size of his little brother, and by all accounts was still living and working on the fringe of the law. He also maintained great contacts south of the border, since that was where the bulk of his pilfered parts, and entire cars jacked to order, ended up.

As a result, his body shop was filled to the brim, every stall and station taken, with not a single license plate to be seen. The shop smelled heavily of oil, tire rubber, and sandblasted steel. But the floor looked polished clean, shiny with a coat of sealant over the concrete that showed not a single grease stain or even a tire mark. For obvious reasons, Asuna kept the bay doors closed and, with the air-conditioning not switched on, the whole shop had the sauna-like feel of heat lamps switched on to dry paint faster.

"I don't recall my little bro ever mentioning your kids to me," Asuna said, still eyeing Dylan and Luke.

"I wasn't exactly on good terms with them back then—or *any* terms."

"So how's fatherhood treating you?"

Cort Wesley rustled a hand through his hair. "You notice how much more gray I got than the last time you saw me?"

"Welcome to my world, *amigo*." Dylan poked his head out from under the hood, drawing Asuna's stare again. "My daughter's got pictures of some TV star all over the walls looks just like your oldest there."

"I can get you his autograph, if you want."

"Your oldest's or the TV star's?"

"You're funnier than your brother, Miguel, but he wasn't very funny at all."

A workman dressed in denim overalls Cort Wesley didn't recognize from the floor when he first arrived approached Asuna and whispered something in his ear. Asuna nodded, the man taking his leave without regarding Cort Wesley.

"Javier says you're not alone. He says somebody's ghosting you."

"I know."

"You know?"

"Extra layer of protection."

"You dragging shit with you into my shop, *amigo*?"

"Just adding it to your already hefty pile, Miguel."

Asuna forced a smile. "I let you insult me because of the high regard my little bro held you in, even though helping you is what got him killed." He tossed the rag aside and folded his arms over a grease-splattered white T-shirt. "I'm having a psychic moment here, you needing this extra layer of protection's being what brought you through my door today."

"Can you tell me today's lottery number?"

"No, but I can help you pick the winning ponies running at Retama Park Racetrack," Asuna winked.

Cort Wesley noticed Asuna's eyes looked too small for the rest of his face, the result being to encase them in folds of misplaced skin. "You didn't ask me why I'd brought my sons with me."

"Is it important?"

"It's what brought me here, Miguel." Now it was Cort Wesley who focused his gaze on Dylan and Luke. "Somebody went after them last night to get back at me. Revenge, something like that."

Asuna nodded, sending tangles of hair tumbling over his forehead. "And I'm supposed to find out who's got a hard-on for you, that it?"

"So to speak. Whoever it is has plenty of muscle: they sent ten gunmen, five for each kid."

Asuna whistled. "I can ask around, but it could be a pretty long list I come up with. You've made a lot of enemies south of the border, *amigo*, and you can add a bunch more after you got sprung early from that prison the Mexican authorities thought they'd socked you away in forever."

"Just lucky, I guess."

Asuna uncrossed his arms, his eyes suddenly filled with a playful glint. "How's that Texas Ranger you been shacking up with?"

"A better shot than ever."

"Got you in her bull's-eye, eh, *amigo*?"

"She shows up here someday, you better be somewhere else."

Miguel Asuna took a step toward him, playful glint gone from his gaze. "You ever think all these problems you got now started when you met her? I mean, goddamn, didn't you used to be the most feared man in San Antonio, maybe the whole state of Texas, which is sure saying something, and nobody'd even dare look at you crossways. *Madre de Dios*, now you got death squads hunting your kids."

Cort Wesley could feel the heat radiating up from his pores. The body shop was steamy and smelled strongly of fresh auto paint and lacquer, but the heat he felt came from the inside, bubbling over to the point where he involuntarily hardened his stare.

"Somebody figured killing my boys would be worse than killing me, Miguel. I look forward to you helping me set them straight."

"Will do, *amigo*, but you'd better watch your back. Somebody who sends ten hitters to nail a couple kids is sure to do anything it takes to put you in a world of hurt."

19

WILLOW CREEK, TEXAS

The chopper landed in what had been the center of Willow Creek's main thoroughfare back when it was still a town, a safe distance from the sheriff's deputies who'd set up a perimeter in a grove of blue oak trees. Amazing how unforgiving land becomes once it's abandoned, sucking everything that had once composed a town back into the ground from where it came.

According to D. W. Tepper, sheriff's deputies from Brewster County had responded to a call from hikers exploring the nearby mesas who'd spotted what looked like bodies, but were chased away by the stench and flocks of carrion birds. Now, as she approached alongside medical examiner Frank Dean Whatley, she saw those deputies standing downwind of the bodies, still close enough to mandate them brushing aside a stray from the swarm of flies buzzing about.

The closer she drew, the more Caitlin wished she'd forced herself to at least glimpse Whatley's folder of crime scene photos to prepare herself. No matter what Captain Tepper had said, or the pictures Whatley's descriptions had left imprinted in her mind, she knew she wasn't ready for what awaited her in the afternoon shade of the small grove dwarfed by the mesas stitching a jagged line across the desert. The air this time of day was colored red by a combination of the sun's reflection off those mesas and the clay dust kicked up from the nearby hillsides. Caitlin could already feel a layer of it coating her skin and sunglasses, and recalled tales of guns jamming from too much caking up in the barrels.

"Oh God," Whatley muttered to himself, and Caitlin thought of him losing his own son to violence at a young age. He wasn't wearing sunglasses, so she couldn't tell whether the tearing in his eyes was due to the dust's assault or his own sadness over rekindled memories.

Close enough to the grove now for the stench of death to reach her, Caitlin figured Whatley was both right and wrong in the original assessment he had provided. The image of flies, maggots, and carrion birds feasting on the remains of what had been children indeed ranked among the worst things she'd ever seen, filling her with a sense of dread like none she'd ever experienced. If there was someone out there who could do this to children, then where was the hope, what was the use?

The only answer was to find the culprit.

Caitlin couldn't think, didn't want to think, of anything else. The mission, the duty, is what drove her and made visits to crime scenes like this a moral imperative; infusing her with the resolve she needed. The monsters had to be caught. Otherwise, they just kept killing, and more children would find themselves the subject of crime scene photos and fodder for the scavengers of the world.

A few years back, Caitlin caught her first glimpse of the work of the serial killer behind hundreds of murders that became known as *Las Mujeres de Juárez*, the Women of Juárez. She and fellow Ranger Charlie Weeks were looking for drug-running tunnels dug out of the desert floor east of El Paso when they came upon the body of a young woman that had been rolled down the embankment of a two-lane amid stray tires, broken bottles, and fast-food wrappers. She was naked save for a pair of lace-up sandals that must've been knotted too tight to remove. A pool of dried blood had painted the ground beneath the body, spreading outward from the woman's rectum, up which a sharp object later identified as a railroad spike had been wedged to shred her intestines.

It had surely been, Frank Dean Whatley reported, an agonizing death in keeping with the pattern already developed for *Las Mujeres de Juárez*. Evidence of torture and rape was present in virtually all the murders, Caitlin learned, in spite of which virtually no progress at all had been made on either side of the border. That is, until circumstances placed the serial killer on a collision course with her that ended with his death down in Mexico.

The difference was that the victims of that monster hadn't been children. The death of a child was bad enough on its own, the murder of a child that much worse. But the mass murder of *five children*?

Simply unthinkable, even as she and Whatley stopped with the sight plain before them. The whole scene had a surreal aura to it, the impact not quite reaching her through the haze of the dust-filled air. If not for the smell, it could have been a life-sized still shot lifted from a direct-to-DVD movie or an image conjured up by a twisted mind to be projected for all to see.

But it was real, a fact that slowly dawned on Caitlin as she edged closer to the bodies just beyond the coroner.

"They've been dead forty-eight hours, give or take," he said, crouching over his worn black case. "Cause of death on initial view seems pretty clear and identifiable as . . ." He stopped suddenly. "How much of this do you want to hear, Ranger?"

"Want—none. Need—everything."

Whatley, continuing to show more emotion than Caitlin had ever seen from him, nodded grudgingly and fit a headpiece with a micro-phone attached and rigged to a recording device over his balding scalp. "Cause of death will go down as exsanguination from severed carotid arteries. Spacing of the bodies indicates they were killed from left to right, what appears at first glance to be oldest to youngest, with the body lying slightly ahead of the others being the first to go." Whatley took a deep breath, looking up at Caitlin to give her the option to tell him to stop. "Initial survey unable to determine the order of the disem-boweling that preceded the exsanguination in the victims but, er, indi-cations point to the fact that they were still alive and in great agony when their carotid arteries were severed."

"You can be specific, Doc. Don't hold back on my account."

But it was clear that was exactly what Whatley was doing. "I can fill in the blanks later in my report, Ranger."

Caitlin couldn't help but recall another young boy's picture of mon-sters that had struck Willow Creek nearly a century before in 1919.

"What did this?" she heard herself ask.

"You mean . . ."

"I mean, as in weapon."

Whatley eased a few instruments from his black bag and moved to inspect the oldest boy's wounds. The positioning of his body indicated he had moved forward to defend himself or, perhaps, the other children. Something, some ill-defined sense of the scene, told Caitlin there'd been only one killer, even though Whatley had said nothing to that effect yet. The instruments he laid out looked to Caitlin like sophisti-cated measuring tools, even before Whatley emerged with an old met-ric ruler.

"Degree, angle, and jagged nature of wound indicates sharp force trauma consistent with tearing," Whatley said into the microphone he kept adjusting to make sure the recording would come through clearly. "Consistency of wound depth indicates a person familiar with the blade's use, but deepening depth of cut similarly indicative of a suspect not used to effects on human anatomy or live creatures in general."

"What do you mean, Doc?"

Whatley glanced up at her, looking neither perturbed nor impatient with her interruption. "There's lots of knives, Ranger, and lots of knives can kill, sure, just about all of them. There are slicing knives, paring knives, scaling knives, carving knives. This has the look of something altogether different from the product of any of those."

"Can you be more specific?"

"Best guess?"

"Best guess."

Whatley went back to studying the jagged wound that had spilled the oldest boy's insides at his feet. Caitlin tried not to picture the struggle, the screams, the other children frozen in terror. Whatley moved his gaze closer, using a simple magnifying glass now.

"If I had to say, it would be a blade more conducive to skinning or field dressing an animal. Say, either a clip point or a drop point knife, as indicated by the size and distance between serrations. You must know what I'm talking about from hunting."

"No, sir."

"You never hunted with your dad or granddad?"

"Not even once, and neither did they. Earl and Jim both believed they saw plenty of blood without spilling any more and hunted more than their share of men. Just not for sport, Doc."

Whatley turned his weary gaze back on the bodies, limbs strewn over one another in what at first glance looked like a single clump. "Too bad whoever did this didn't feel the same way, Ranger."

20

WILLOW CREEK, TEXAS

Caitlin tried to hold her eyes on the bodies but still couldn't for very long at all, sorting through the meaning of Whatley's words. "So you're telling me a first-timer did this?"

"First-timer with a knife, anyway. Otherwise, they would've chosen a blade more suited to the task."

Caitlin thought for a moment. "Can't see this as anything but pre-meditated, Doc. That means the killer used whatever knife it was for a specific reason, to make a point maybe."

"Any idea what that point might have been, Ranger?"

"Not yet, Doc, but I will. I promise you that much."

"There's something else. Judging by the wound angle, especially at the entry point here," Whatley said, indicating a spot on the wound that had dried a purplish black color, "the suspect wasn't much taller than this victim. The cut is virtually straight in, no downward angle. And I'd also say you're looking for someone of average strength at best."

"Another kid maybe?"

Whatley held her gaze for a long moment, as if trying to see beyond her eyes to the depths of her thinking. "You ever meet a kid who could do something like his?"

"I'm just trying to get a handle on things, Doc. Consider all the possibilities. What do you make of the victims' clothes?"

"School uniforms would be my guess."

"You mind checking a label for me?"

Whatley peeled back the collar of the oldest boy's shirt with a hand encased in a plastic glove. "Spanish," he said, as if that surprised him. "These kids must be Mexican."

"Somebody takes them out of school and brings them up here to kill."

"For all the sense that makes. . . ."

"It's there. We just can't see it yet."

Whatley rose from his crouch, stumbling slightly on the ground overgrown with tree roots that had begun to poke above the surface. "It's never that simple with you, Ranger."

"I don't want us ruling anything out right now, Doc. Maybe a more detailed examination of the wound will tell us something more we can use."

"If you're talking about trying to get a match on the knife that did this, forget it. Maybe a million drop and clip point knives get sold in Texas every year. Makes for a difficult database to build."

"Anything else you can tell me about the blade be appreciated all the same."

Whatley took a deep breath that stopped halfway through, all the color washed out of his face. "I was at Waco, you know."

"No, I didn't."

He seemed unsteady on his feet, his voice cracking. "Never thought I'd get those burned bodies out of my mind. But they didn't seem real, nothing left visible that was even remotely human, like something out of a horror movie. But this," Whatley continued, stealing a glance back at the bodies and swatting away some flies buzzing before his face, "this is real."

Caitlin could only look at him.

"I thought after the day I identified my own son's remains there'd be nothing that ever scared me again." This time Whatley's gaze lingered longer on the tangle of limbs and young faces twisted in agony behind him. "Looks like I was wrong."

Caitlin was spared a response when her cell phone rang, jarring both of them, and she excused herself to answer it with the number for Company F headquarters showing in the Caller ID.

"Where are you, Ranger?" Captain Tepper greeted.

"Where do you think I am, D.W.?"

"Well, get back in the chopper and get back here on the double."

"What's wrong?"

She could hear Tepper stripping off the cellophane on a fresh pack of Marlboros. "Enough shit's about to hit the fan to fill a cesspool, Caitlin, and you're standing right in front of the blow."

21

SHAVANO PARK, TEXAS

Cort Wesley was tossing a football around with Dylan in the front yard of their house, while Luke skateboarded on the vert ramp they'd built out of plywood and cinder blocks.

"Dad?"

"What?"

"You spaced out again," his oldest son told him. "What's up?"

"What happened last night's not enough for you?"

"I think it has something to do with that stop we made before, on the way back from the chop shop."

"Not at all," Cort Wesley lied.

"There's a Brindles Ice Cream just down on Heubner," Cort Wesley said, the engine still running after he parked in the lot of the Wells Fargo Bank on Vance Jackson Road. "Take your brother and get something."

Cort Wesley handed Dylan a twenty and eased open his door.

"Can I drive?" Luke asked.

"Sure you can, son: year after next."

Cort Wesley stepped down, leaving the door open so Dylan could come around from the passenger side. Only the boy had already hopped over the console into the driver's seat. He closed the door and backed up, and Cort Wesley watched him pull out of the parking lot before entering the bank. He was late for his appointment with assistant manager Royce Clavins, but, fortunately, Royce was still in his cubicle, waving him in as he spoke on the telephone. He'd hung up by the time Cort Wesley reached him, powdery dry hand extended across the desk.

"So what can I do for you, Mr. Masters?" Clavins asked, sitting back down as Cort Wesley took the chair in front of his desk.

"You can start by calling me Cort Wesley. We did go to the same high school."

"I seem to recall you kicking the shit out of me on at least one occasion."

"Puts you in good company, Royce."

Clavins waved him off. "Water under the bridge, Cort Wesley." He cleared his throat. He had gone bald young and didn't bother to hide it, having shaved his scalp for at least a decade now. Today he'd left some stubble in place and it looked like a grease smear in the cubicle's overly bright lighting. "So I reviewed your situation."

"My *situation*?"

"As in financial. We're glad you kept us on as your bank after your wife's passing."

"She wasn't my wife, she was my girlfriend. And her passing came as a result of a bullet."

Clavins cleared his throat again. "I'd like to help you, Cort Wesley."

"People who say that usually can't."

Clavins leaned forward and folded his hands before him. "You have . . . well, let's call it an unusual credit history."

"How's that?"

"No credit cards, no car loans, no mortgage, no IRA, no lines of credit. Just the one bank account and your sons' college account."

"I'm a dinosaur, Royce. I like to use cash. But unfortunately I've hit a bit of an economic dry spell and, since you've got kids of your own, I don't have to tell how expensive they are to raise. So I came here to review my options."

Clavins started opening and closing his fingers, Cort Wesley fighting not to show how annoying that was. "Your only real asset is the house your wife—excuse me, girlfriend—had insured under a separate policy to pay off the entire mortgage in the event of her . . ." The banker let his remark trail off and cleared his throat again, then raised a hand to his mouth long enough to stifle a cough. "The current assessed value is just short of four hundred thousand dollars, which would normally make you a perfect candidate for a mortgage to take advantage of the great rates we're offering."

"Normally?"

Clavins stifled another cough, fidgeting nervously now. His gaze cheated beyond the glass partitions of his cubicle as if to reassure himself there were others inside the bank. "You don't have any W-twos to prove a viable means of income and your credit, well, we discussed that problem already."

Cort Wesley was starting to feel warm, each shift of his frame seeming to crack the stiff upholstery.

"The only asset you can borrow against is that college fund set up with your girlfriend's life insurance payment and—"

"No."

"No?"

"Not interested, Royce. Those dollars are not to be touched. Let's try something else."

Clavins started to lean forward again, but stopped and settled as far back as his desk chair would let him. "That's what I'm trying to tell you, Cort Wesley. There *is* nothing else. But, look, since you say your financial issues are short-term, what's the harm?"

"That money stays where it is, Royce."

"It will. You'd only be borrowing against it and I'd be able to lend you whatever you needed at three percent. How's that sound?"

Cort Wesley rose, feeling his pants and shirt peel away from the tight faux leather fabric. "Like I've got to think of something else."

Clavins rose, almost reluctantly it seemed, and just as reluctantly extended his hand across the desk. "If you change your mind . . ."

"I won't."

"But if you do."

Clavins tried to hand Cort Wesley a business card, but he strode out of the cubicle without taking it.

"You were all sweaty when you met us in the ice cream place," Dylan said, holding the football now.

"It's hot out, in case you didn't notice."

"Also seems strange to me you left us on our own. Then I figured you knew he must have been watching."

"Who?"

"The big guy," Dylan said. "And he's watching us right now, isn't he?"

Cort Wesley didn't bother denying it, looking at his eighteen-year-old son and wondering which one of them was in charge here. "He or his men, yeah."

"That's a good thing, isn't it?"

"It sure is, under the circumstances."

Dylan stiffened a little and his next throw was short and off line. "He doing this to make up for the fact he had Mom killed?"

Cort Wesley held the ball until he could get his mind straight again. "You'd have to ask him that, though I don't want you in his company."

"He saved yours and Luke's life last night, didn't he?"

"That coach from Brown called," Cort Wesley said, eager to change the subject. "Estees."

"It's pronounced Es-*tes*."

Cort Wesley tossed the ball back to Dylan, his shoulder starting to ache a bit. "Anyway, it sounded like you impressed the hell out of him."

"I did?"

"He'd just finished watching that game film you put together before he called."

Dylan passed the ball from his right hand to his left and back again. "So what's the bad news?"

"Your weight. Coach Es-*tes* doesn't think a hundred fifty-five pounds is gonna cut it at that level. Says if you put on twenty more and keep your speed in the forty below a four-seven, there'll be a spot for you. He wants you to call him tonight. I've got his number inside."

"Damn," Dylan said, finally tossing the ball back Cort Wesley's way.

"Funny, that's exactly what I said."

Dylan's features tightened. "He ask about last night?"

"That was the main reason for his call. To make sure you were okay. He wasn't a hundred percent it was even you, until one of the news reports mentioned a Texas Ranger. The follow-up is sure to cover Caitlin in all her glory."

Dylan rolled his eyes and caught Cort Wesley's next throw on his fingertips. "I'm sure she'll just love that."

"Anybody sends a news crew here, you can be the one to stay between them."

The boy pursed his lips and blew out some breath. "You better teach Luke to shoot for real this time, Dad."

Cort Wesley was spared a response when Miguel Asuna pulled up in a pickup truck with a huge light rack atop its roof.

22

SHAVANO PARK, TEXAS

Asuna climbed out accompanied by a man with a beer keg for a torso and cheeks as red as a fire engine. Asuna approached Cort Wesley, while the other man leaned against the big truck, making it wobble slightly.

"We need to talk, *amigo*," Asuna told him, his light grin and cocky sneer missing. His normally playful eyes shifted about uneasily, as if certain there were things about he couldn't see.

"Nice to see you too, Miguel."

Asuna's gaze moved to Dylan. He seemed to relax slightly. "So you're a football player."

"Trying to be," Dylan told him.

Asuna moved closer. "I hear you're one tough *hombre*. And not just from your father either."

"Can't believe what he says, anyway," the boy quipped, smiling at Cort Wesley.

"He was my late little bro's best friend. Saved his life even. Not the only man he did that for either." Eyes back on Cort Wesley now. "Let's take a walk, *amigo*."

Cort Wesley let his gaze wander to the man with a beer keg for a torso.

"He's here for protection, that's all."

"Whose exactly?"

"Hey, you got soldiers from a death squad watching you from shit knows where, who am I to take chances?"

Cort Wesley stiffened. "I'd ask you to watch your mouth in front of my son, Miguel."

Asuna waved his hands apologetically. "Hey, *lo siento*. I'm sorry, okay? Now let's take that walk."

Cort Wesley gave Dylan a long look before joining Asuna on the sidewalk. They started down the street, passing homes with similarly well-manicured lawns, and a combination of Volvos, minivans, and portable basketball hoops occupying the driveways.

"What's got you so spooked, Miguel?"

"What's got me spooked? A few hours ago, you asked me to check some shit out. So I checked the shit out. That's what's got me spooked."

Cort Wesley felt the tightness return to his shoulder and just about everywhere else. "Keep talking."

"You asked me to look into who's coming after you, targeting your kids."

"I know what I asked you."

"Well, I did it. See, there's a kind of rule of law at play here, *amigo*. You want to do violence of that scale, you gotta inform certain parties so they can make sure they stay clear, get alibied up. They don't like your plan, they say so and you go away."

"So?" Cort Wesley prompted when Asuna stopped there.

"So nobody asked permission to do nothing. The network I'm talking about, remnants of the old Mexican Mafia La Eme combined with MS-Thirteen, didn't have a clue about who's behind what happened last night at Six Flags."

"I'm guessing things don't stop there, Miguel."

"You're right, they don't. I asked around, talked to the kind of people who know what's what south of the border. That clear enough for you?"

"Crystal. Now get to the point."

"You got your share of enemies in Mexico for sure, but none of them have much interest in messing it up with you. That stretch you did in Cereso Prison made you a kind of legend. What was it they called you?"

"*El Gringo Campeón.*"

"Nice."

Cort Wesley realized his head was hammering, his blood feeling superheated as it raced through his veins. His heart seemed to bang against his chest wall.

"Where's this leading, Miguel?"

"Last night wasn't about you."

"Bullshit. Ten gunmen went after my kids at almost the same time in two different states. What else could that be about?" And then Cort Wesley realized, his skin going cold so quickly, it felt like it'd been sandblasted on the surface. "Oh shit, it's Caitlin. They were coming after Caitlin. . . ."

But Miguel Asuna shook his head. "Not her either, *amigo*."

Cort Wesley struggled to make sense of what he was hearing. "No, no, Miguel. My oldest has been in his share of scrapes, but my youngest? Come on, don't try to tell me this was about *them*."

"It wasn't," Asuna said, almost too softly to hear.

"Miguel, if you don't start speaking a language I can understand, all the human beer kegs in the world won't be able to protect you. What went down last night had to be about *something*."

"Oh, it was, *amigo*, and some*one* too. For sure."

"You plan on telling me who?"

And Cort Wesley felt his stomach sink to his feet when Asuna answered him.

23

MEXICO CITY

Ana Callas Guajardo sat in the rear of the presidential limousine, enjoying the cool blast of the air-conditioning. She kept the window cracked open just enough to hear Mexican president Hector Villarreal address a jam-packed crowd in the Zócalo, the capital city's sprawling open-air plaza reserved for only the most special of events. The Zócalo has been a gathering place for Mexicans all the way back to the Aztecs, serving as the prime location for the major public ceremonies and military performances, anything with great pomp and circumstance. The plaza was enclosed by buildings on three sides and bracketed by towering flagpoles showcasing the Mexican flag billowing in the breeze.

Guajardo had watched many a swearing-in, issuance of a royal proc-
lamation, military parade, and Holy Week ceremony from the rooftop
Portal de Mercaderes restaurant, looking east to the entire complex
known as the Palacio Nacional. From her vantage point today, in the
secured VIP parking area next to an equally famed cathedral, Guajardo
could hear the president just fine but couldn't see him thanks to distance and the shaded stage on which he stood. She had already reviewed
his speech carefully, enough to arrange for one particular section not to
be loaded onto the teleprompter.

Villarreal reached that part of his speech, stammering briefly before
springing into ad-lib format while never covering the subject Guajardo
had removed from his prepared words. She could hear the tension in his
voice as he struggled to keep his composure and figure out what to say
now that there was no speech scrolling before him.

Ana Guajardo slid the window all the way up, the oppressive heat
and humidity having become too much to bear. She knew Villarreal's
speech was over when the Zócalo erupted into cheers and applause at
the end, followed by music as the president left the stage.

Then, moments later, a security guard yanked open the door so the
president could vanish into the air-conditioned cool of his limo.

He sneered at the sight of Ana, shaking his head. "It was you,
wasn't it?"

"Of course it was, *señor presidente*."

He snickered, pouring himself half a glass of American single-malt
scotch whiskey and adding ice cubes. "You make my title sound like a
punch line."

"Because you have turned the office you hold into one."

Guajardo let her gaze drift out the window again at the crowd dissipating in all directions. From the rooftop restaurant, it would've had
the look of ants scattering from their nest. She had first watched events
in the Zócalo with her father, the great man having chosen to mentor
her over her brother, whose behavior had proven a burden for the Guajardo family. Her father had given him innumerable chances, finally re-
nouncing the young man after his embarrassments and indiscretions
became too much for the storied family to endure.

As a young girl, Guajardo recalled the Zócalo being little more than a decaying concrete block dotted with light poles and train tracks and a single flagpole rising from the center. By the time her father began bringing her with him to watch major ceremonies from the rooftop he'd personally rented for his guests only, the train tracks and light poles had been removed and the entire Zócalo repaved with pink cobblestones.

Coincidentally, the next time the plaza fell into disrepair was right around the time her father was reduced to a vegetative state thanks to a four-story plunge off his bedroom balcony. As much a testament to him as anything, Ana had personally underwritten the effort to raise the three hundred million dollars needed for a complete repair and upgrade of both the Zócalo and the surrounding buildings. Today it stood as a monument to Mexico's potential to succeed and thrive with no help whatsoever from the United States, which, in her mind, sought to keep her beloved country impoverished to suit its own ends.

"How did you know I didn't commit the speech to memory?" Villarreal asked, after taking a hefty sip of whiskey.

For someone who didn't drink, like Guajardo, the scent was overpowering, reminding her of the antiseptic smell that hung over her father, admittedly preferable to the stench sometimes rising from his diaper. "Because that would have required you giving up time from your precious whores," she told the president of Mexico.

"My private life is none of your business," Villarreal said, stiffening. "And, by the way, at least I have one."

The remark stung her, but Guajardo did her best not to show it. "You should watch your tongue, *señor presidente*."

"Don't call me that."

"Why? It's what I made you."

"Because you have no respect for the office."

"The office I put you in, you mean. The office you seem determined to disgrace, wasting the efforts and dollars of those I organized to bring our party back to power."

Guajardo's Institutional Revolutionary Party, the PRI, had held office for seventy-one consecutive years until being defeated in 2000 by the leftists. It had been the last election championed by her father, robbing him of much of his power and influence before the fall that robbed him of everything else after another failed election six years later. The election that finally allowed Ana to redeem the family name came in 2012, the time being right and Villarreal making the ideal candidate given that his ambition was matched only by his willingness to accept whatever means led to their mutually desired ends.

"By dollars," the president of Mexico said to Guajardo, "I believe you mean the ones spent to buy votes, a scandal that has now embroiled my entire administration."

"Do you have any idea how many supermarket discount cards we had to distribute in the poor regions to bring you to power?"

"What about the other means of coercion that were employed?"

"Please don't tell me you're surprised."

"No, *señora*, just revolted. Everything you touch you leave dirty. But I have no intention of taking the fall for you. I'm going to fight this all the way and, if necessary, expose the corruption at its roots."

"Is that a threat, *señor presidente*?"

"You went too far and your penchant for excess threatens to bring all of us down." Villarreal held her gaze smugly, secure in the notion his point had been made. "I guess even your money can't buy everything."

"You're right, *señor presidente*; it can't buy strength, something you are sorely lacking. You appease the Americans at every turn. You are their lapdog at the expense of your own people, who are fed up with being at the beck and call of the Americans, who care only for their own interests. Who hide behind the lone issue of drugs to rationalize the portrayal of our country as a moral cesspit. But where do they think the guns are coming from that kill our own people because your friends the Americans would prefer all of us dead?"

Villarreal shook his head. "I don't know what's more scary: hearing you say that or the fact that you really believe it."

"Then you've chosen sides."

"I have no idea what you're talking about."

"You will soon enough. But you've made my decision easy."

"And what decision is that?"

"I'm going to violate one of the rules of business that I live by, that being to hire people you trust and let them do their jobs. That has clearly not worked out in your case."

Villarreal leaned forward. "I was elected, *señora*. You didn't hire me."

"All the same, *señor presidente*, I'm firing you. Best to admit mistakes quickly instead of pretending they'll go away on their own."

"You can quote Steve Jobs all you want, but running a country is still far different from running a company. And the side I've chosen is Mexico's."

Police sirens began to wail, a pair of officers on motorcycles drawing up even with the limousine on either side, the presidential convoy ready to ease into motion enclosed by a pair of hulking Chevy Suburbans loaded with members of the Mexican Special Police both fore and aft.

"Where did you get your vehicles, *señor presidente*?"

"A gift," Villarreal said, continuing to sip his drink.

"From the Americans, of course. I come here today because I am in need of one as well."

"From *me*?"

Guajardo removed an envelope from her handbag. "Just a routine pardon for a prisoner being held at Cereso Prison."

"Is it a name I know?"

"The last name, anyway: the pardon is for my brother, Locaro."

Villarreal took the envelope, leaving his gaze on her. "The same brother who threw your father out a fourth-floor window."

"He's the only brother I have and it was off the balcony," Guajardo corrected, "not out a window."

Villarreal signed the letter inside without regarding it and handed the envelope back to her. "Now, if you'll excuse me, *señora* . . ."

Guajardo made no move to reach for the door. "No, *señor presidente*, I will not excuse you."

The president of Mexico stiffened. "You need something else?"

"Yes," Ana said, leaving things at that for now.

"If this is about my policies—"

"This has nothing to do with policy. Politics has nothing to do with policy and neither does governing. It's all about power. The parties I represent spent a dozen years waiting for our return to power, and I don't dare risk squandering our resurgence now, especially in light of what is to come."

"And what's that?"

Guajardo smiled smugly. "Let's just say that in a very short time your American friends will no longer be in a position to do you any good at all. Too bad you chose the wrong side. Otherwise we could have done business together for a long time to come."

Villarreal almost laughed. "You're going to take on the Americans now? Declare war on the United States?"

Guajardo's smile vanished. "The war I'm about to wage doesn't require a declaration."

"Perhaps I should make some calls to Washington to alert them."

"You better make it fast. Because you are going to resign, *señor presidente*. I will make sure no charges are ever brought against you and that you remain a wealthy man for the rest of your life. You will want for nothing."

"Except my reputation, my legacy."

"I'm buying them out to better serve our cause in the wake of what is to come."

"And what is that exactly?"

Guajardo looked at him without responding.

"You know," Villarreal resumed, "I always knew you had no heart. Now I see you have no soul." He paused and sucked in a deep breath that left his face bent in a scowl. "But you've gone too far this time, first with the vote buying and now trying to brush me aside. You underestimate me, you have always underestimated me. You will pay for this and you will pay dearly. I will fight you every step of the way."

"There's not going to be any fight—it's much better to resign than have scandal force you from office."

"A scandal that you perpetuated."

"No," Guajardo told him. "I was speaking of something else entirely."

"And what's that?"

"Those pictures of you with a prostitute."

"*What?*"

"I've seen them, *señor presidente.* They're quite revealing. Not much left to the imagination."

His face started to pucker in anger, then slowly relaxed to the point where it softened into a narrow smile.

"You would blackmail the president of Mexico?"

"I would extort the man I *made* president of Mexico, because there are some things bigger than both of us."

Villarreal seemed to think of something and stretched his hand out to add fresh ice to his drink. "I'm a single man. Me sleeping with pretty young women is likely to make me more popular instead of less." He leaned forward to refill his glass.

"Who said it was a young *woman* those pictures show you with?"

Villarreal stopped his reach halfway to the ice bin. The rocks glass slipped from his fingers, its contents spilling on the thick carpet at his feet.

"You like to believe you're God, but you're really the devil, aren't you?" he asked, lips quivering in anger.

"In my experience, *señor presidente,* they're very much the same thing."

Villarreal's hateful sneer suddenly morphed into a tight grin born of a newfound confidence. "And what do you think the Americans will say when they learn the truth behind my ouster?"

Guajardo's features flared, her tight hold on her composure relinquished briefly. "Are these the same Americans who would keep us an impoverished nation to suit their own ends? The same Americans who loudly lambaste our drug-ridden culture while secretly celebrating the fact that it keeps us a second-rate people? The same Americans who proclaim their disgust with our immigrant workers while knowing their economy would collapse without the cheap labor we provide? Those Americans?" Guajardo settled herself, barely able to suppress her grin. "Trust me, *señor presidente,* when I tell you they'll have far more important things on their minds by the time you resign from office and far more pressing problems to contend with."

Something in her voice, her demeanor, prickled Villarreal's skin with goose bumps. "What have you done?"

"It's what I'm *about* to do. If you want to warn your American friends, be my guest. It's too late for them, and for you."

Villarreal wanted to laugh, but all that emerged was a chortling chuckle. "You really think you can defeat the United States of America?"

"Oh, absolutely," Ana Guajardo said, reaching for the door handle. "Absolutely."

Part Three

Boys, you have followed me as far as I can ask you to do unless you are willing to go with me. It is like going into the jaws of death with only twenty-six men in a foreign country where we have no right according to law but as I have [gone] this far I am going to finish with it. Some of us may get back or part of us or maybe none of us will get back. . . . I don't want you unless you are willing to go as a volunteer. . . . Understand there is no surrender in this. We ask no quarter nor give any. If any of you don't want to go, step aside.

Texas Ranger captain Leander McNelly (1875)

24

"That boy look familiar to you at all?" D. W. Tepper asked as Caitlin Strong studied the picture he'd handed her, a typical school photograph taken of a boy in a standard school uniform, his smile showing braces over his teeth.

Night had fallen just as her chopper had landed back in the city, and the result was to cast Tepper's office in even darker tones. He held a fresh cigarette in his hand, the smoke sifting in and out of the narrow light as it wafted upward. He hadn't turned on his desk lamp, choosing instead to leave the blinds open to let in the meager spill of the street-lights beyond to supplement the single bulb in the overhead fixture. He'd switched off the air-conditioning in favor of leaving the window open, explaining why the office smelled lightly of the hibiscus trees and flow-ering bushes down below. Tepper always said he hated the smell of fresh air, but the clacking of the blinds against the window frame indicated he was getting used to it.

"Put it out, D.W."

"I just lit it."

"Can't blame me for trying. Damn," Caitlin said, giving the photo another look. "It was the smile that threw me. This boy wasn't smiling when I saw him in Willow Creek, but he had braces for sure, wearing the same school uniform," she added, certain this was the oldest boy Frank Dean Whatley had examined at the crime scene, the one who'd been killed first likely trying to protect the others.

"Would've celebrated his fourteenth birthday next week." Tepper shook his head, his expression wrinkling to the point it looked like he was chewing on razor wire. He took a hefty drag on his Marlboro and blew out the smoke to follow the last wave in floating upward to hover over the half-lit room. "So don't tell me to put my goddamn cigarette out, Ranger."

The clacking of the blinds against the window frame seemed to get louder as Caitlin regarded the picture again, the boy framed against a stock background looking younger than fourteen. "Hell, I'm close to asking you for one myself."

"You're gonna need more than one, Caitlin," Tepper said, his steely eyes drooping a bit.

Caitlin started to flap the picture, then stopped when she felt it was disrespectful. "Where'd you get this, D.W.? And what's it got to do with what you told me over the phone?"

"The boy disappeared from his school two days back, the morning of the day he was killed. His name, according to school records, is Daniel Sanchez. But that's not his real name, Ranger. His real name is Daniel *Sandoval*."

"Jesus Christ" was all Caitlin could say.

She'd first met the murdered boy's father, Fernando Lorenzo Sandoval, while he was a patient at Thomason Hospital in El Paso, where he'd been transported after a bomb narrowly missed killing him just across the border in Juárez. The cartels gunning for Sandoval, then one of the few Mexican government officials willing to confront them, sent a hit team to finish the job but ended up taking a whole intensive care ward hostage. Caitlin had rectified the situation pretty much on her own and, as a result, began a lasting relationship with Sandoval, who understood the meaning of a debt.

Before long, he had risen to chief of the Chihuahua State Investigations Agency and declared an all-out war against the drug cartels he firmly believed were tearing apart the fabric of his country. That made him even more of a target for them than he already was, the only Mexican official Caitlin had ever met with the *cajones* to battle the cartels on their own violent terms. He'd become a virtual phantom, as a result. No one knew where he lived, and one legend said he slept in a different place every night. Another insisted that the government had built an elaborate network of tunnels beneath the country that Sandoval and other officials now used to get around without ever showing their faces. Caitlin figured the mythology suited Sandoval well, and he exploited it to the fullest in his capacity as the country's chief drug enforcer. He even once recruited Guillermo Paz to build a private army to aid his efforts, an army that somehow had ended up in the service of a shadowy division of Homeland Security.

"Has Sandoval been informed yet?" she asked Tepper.

"We only just got what I'd call a positive identification," Tepper told her.

"I'd like to be the one who gives him the news, Captain."

"Not necessary, Ranger."

"I didn't say it was. I want him to hear it from somebody he knows, somebody he knows will make sure the right thing gets done for his boy."

Tepper rolled his eyes, the motion so drawn out it looked as if they had gotten stuck halfway around his forehead. "Sure. And for you the right thing always involves folks getting shot."

Caitlin held up the school picture of Daniel Sandoval. "You didn't see what somebody did to this boy and the others."

"I saw the pictures."

"There's something else: Willow Creek, Captain."

Tepper shook his head and smacked his perpetually chapped lips. "Where you going with this, Ranger?"

"That those kids were killed in Willow Creek for a reason. The site was chosen. The crime scene had the sense of something like a ritual to it. We need to find out why, we need to find the connection to what happened in that town a century ago."

Tepper shook his head and lit a fresh cigarette. "And why's that exactly, Hurricane?"

"Because the original massacre happened on April twenty-four, nineteen-nineteen, D.W."

"Oh boy . . ."

"Yeah," Caitlin nodded. "Those Mexican kids in Willow Creek were murdered on the same day."

25

Willow Creek, Texas; 1919

The riders continued to storm toward William Ray and Earl Strong, emerging out of the dust cloud as three figures riding abreast of one another. The Strongs relaxed only slightly when the riders slowed at the outskirts of town and approached the Rangers' position in the center of the single thoroughfare, lifting their hands into the air and slowing their horses to walking speed.

"*Buenos días*," the man in the center greeted, much of his face hidden in the shadows of a huge sombrero and further obscured by the coming of night.

"*Buenos días*," William Ray returned, noting the Mexican's disdain at the sight of the *cinco pesos* badge pinned to his shirt lapel, shiny amid the patches of sweat that had soaked through. "I'm Texas Ranger William Ray Strong and this here's my son, Texas Ranger Earl Strong. You can lower your hands now, but don't let that give you any wrong ideas. I'm a pretty fast draw myself but my boy, Earl, here'll shoot you as you sit 'fore your hands clear your holsters."

The leader climbed down off his horse, brushing back his wind-blown and dirt-encrusted poncho that looked too thick for the season. "I am Captain Fernando Lava of the Mexican Federal Army."

"This be the same *federales* disbanded after Huerta was forced out of office in nineteen-fourteen?"

Lava took off his sombrero, revealing a nest of thick, sweat-dampened hair and a crease halfway down his forehead where the sombrero had left its mark, along with a scar on his right cheek shaped like a question mark. He had icy eyes that seemed colorless at first glance and an almost crystal shade of blue at second. The other *federales* remained on their horses."

"Some of us proved more stubborn than others; this scar you see on my face came from a branding iron."

"What happened to the guy wielding it?"

"He came to a violent end later," Lava said, noting the even older Ranger badge young Earl was wearing. "Something I imagine any *el Rinche* can understand."

William Ray saw no point in mincing words or making conversation. "Since you're here, I imagine you know the rest of the town is dead."

"Not exactly, *señor*. See, we are trailing the men who did it."

Night had taken firm hold of the sky by then, the lessening light making the mesas look like jagged walls rising for the sky. Having no desire to continue their discussion near so many dead bodies, they found an arroyo maybe a mile out of Willow Creek secure and defensible enough to let them build a fire. The three *federales* and two Rangers sat down on opposite sides of the fire in the cooling air. This as the now confirmed lone survivor of the massacre rocked nervously back and forth atop the barn coat Earl had spread out for him beneath a makeshift lean-to he'd built against the base of a blue oak tree as heat lightning lit up the sky to the west.

William Ray showed Lava the drawing the boy had made of skeletal demons wearing bandoliers. "So if it wasn't monsters, who was it exactly, Captain? I'm thinking maybe more of Pancho Villa's boys," he added, referring to the Mexican revolutionary leader who'd already staged several cross-border incursions.

"We are some of Pancho Villa's boys," Lava told him. "We fight for him now, because of the *monstruos* we are tracking and what they are bringing out of our country."

Lava reached into the single pocket William Ray had mistaken for a patch on trousers that billowed in the night breeze. He emerged with a small husk of what looked like dark blown glass, sealed with a tiny stopper at its one open cylindrical end.

"Christ on a crutch," William Ray muttered, rising to extend his hand over the fire to take it.

"Opium," Earl said, before his father had gotten himself settled back down.

"The young *hombre* is right," said Lava. "These men must have intended to use Willow Creek as a staging ground for their business north of the border, setting up what we believe is a distribution network."

"Distribution network? That's a mighty fancy term for the captain of a disbanded outfit."

Lava used a stick to adjust the logs on the fire, spraying glowing embers into the air that flamed out before reaching William Ray. "Forty years ago, the Chinese brought opium with them to Mexico. It has thrived, thanks to our climate and the fertile lands of the Sinaloa province, ever since then. Export into your country through California out of Mexicali and Tijuana has been thriving since nineteen-sixteen thanks to that region's governor, Esteban Cantú. Now Cantú is expanding his territory through Texas and towns like Willow Creek, and he does this with the blessing of none other than Mexico's president, Venustiano Carranza."

"Now why would Carranza do that?"

"Because he and Esteban Cantú are cousins, *señor*."

The fire framed William Ray's face in its light, making his wrinkles look more pronounced and deeper, while hiding the sudden intensity his glare had taken on as Lava continued.

"*Señores*, if Carranza isn't stopped, he will crush the revolution with more drug money and spread his poison all across your country." Lava swallowed hard, the air sticking in his throat. "I have seen what opium has done to my country, the lives it has destroyed, the families it has ruined. I have seen how men like Carranza and Cantú use it to line their pockets and control the weak and less fortunate."

William Ray leaned close enough to the fire for its reflection to seize his eyes. "How much of this opium we talking about exactly?"

Lava shrugged, looking grim. "It is grown all over Mexico now. Poor and peasant farmers have been enlisted as slave laborers, their land taken from them, their crops uprooted so opium can be grown in their place. They live in fear of *esos Demonios*."

"*Esos Demonios?*"

"*Sí*," Lava nodded. "Killers recruited from the very worst of Carranza's soldiers, now assigned to his cousin as a private army. They are called that for good reason, reasons you have now seen firsthand."

William Ray Strong slapped his knees and rose, his face suddenly out of the firelight's reach, which made him look headless. "Least we know who we're up against."

"*Sí*, but some say *esos Demonios* are invincible, that they cannot be killed."

"Guess we'll see about that," William Ray told him as the crackling flames rose enough to frame his eyes in their glow, "won't we?"

26

San Antonio

"There it was, D.W.," Caitlin finished. "The virtual beginning of the Mexican drug trade. By the nineteen-thirties, marijuana had pretty much replaced opium as the smugglers' drug of choice, but the original supply routes remained in place."

"You got me on the edge of my chair, Ranger," Tepper said.

"My granddad never told you about all this?"

"Him being there when pretty much the bane of our modern-day existence got started? Bits and pieces maybe," Tepper frowned. "Maybe I just forgot. I'm older than dirt, you know, so I am entitled." He hesitated, making the clacking of the blinds against the window frame seem louder. The single bulb in the overhead fixture flickered, then locked back on. "Except I don't see how this all squares with those murdered kids in Willow Creek, 'sides the date."

"Me either, Captain. But right now that's enough to tell us there's something else going on here. The killer was making a point two days ago." Caitlin realized she still held the picture of Daniel Sandoval and handed it back to Tepper. "How'd you come by that photo, anyway?"

"You're not Fernando Lorenzo Sandoval's only friend in the States, Ranger. He was looking for anybody who could help him find his boy." Tepper let the cigarette smolder in his hand, his expression flattening. "I can't imagine being in that situation. Don't even know what I'd do."

Caitlin thought of Dylan, how she'd felt when he was kidnapped by Mexican white slavers in league with the Hells Angels two years earlier. "I know it would likely involve guns, D.W."

"Guns aren't the answer to everything, Hurricane."

Caitlin pointed toward the picture Tepper had laid down on his desk blotter. "Compare that to the crime scene photo of what somebody did to this kid and tell me if you still feel that way."

A knock fell on the door, the two of them turning toward it at the same time to see a familiar broad-shouldered man standing in the doorway with a smirk stretched across his face.

"Hope I'm not interrupting," said the man they knew as "Jones."

27

SAN ANTONIO

He looked to be in better shape than the last time Caitlin had seen him, just before he made a quick exit from the scene, leaving the Rangers to contend with a homegrown terrorist plot all on their own. Caitlin couldn't say exactly what Jones did with Homeland Security, and doubted that anybody else could either.

She'd first met him when his name was still "Smith" and he was attached to the American embassy in Bahrain, enough of a relationship formed for the two of them to have remained in contact and to have actually worked together on three more occasions. The first two had ended exactly like the last, with Jones failing to live up to his promises and always succeeding in living down to Caitlin's expectations.

Tonight, the thin light kept Jones's face cloaked in the shadows with which he was most comfortable. Caitlin tried to remember the color of his eyes but couldn't, as if he'd been trained to never look at anyone long enough for anything to register. He was wearing a sport jacket over a button-down shirt and pressed trousers, making him seem like a high school teacher save for the tightly cropped, military-style haircut.

"You wanna shoot him, or should I?" Captain Tepper posed to Caitlin.

"Hey," Jones said back, flashing his ever-present smirk before she could respond, "maybe you never received the helicopter I sent you folks to make amends."

"You wanna make amends, Mr. Smith, you better start with a jumbo jet."

"It's *Jones*, Captain, and haven't you seen what William Faulkner said about the past?"

"Just because it may not be dead doesn't mean you don't deserve to be, *Jones*," Caitlin said, before Tepper could get his own response out.

Jones stepped into the room and closed the door behind him, looking up at the weak spray of light as if wondering what was wrong with the fixture. The open window seemed to bother him as well, and he took a slight step to the side to take himself from the vantage point it provided from outside. "Don't take things so personally, Ranger."

"Don't expect me to forget what a gutless asshole you are."

Jones feigned hurt, sucking in a dramatic breath. "Maybe I just came here to check on your well-being. That shoot-out last night in Providence was all over the wire."

"What wire is that?"

"The one circulated among people like me who take notice when incidents of that magnitude spring up."

"You're a piece of work, aren't you, Mr. Jones?" Tepper groused, shaking his head.

"Just doing my job, Captain."

"That's what worries me," said Caitlin.

Jones snapped his gaze toward her. "Maybe you should take your act on the road, Ranger. A regular fifty-state tour, see if you can leave a body behind in each of them."

"Maybe one of those bodies will be yours."

"Ouch! You hurt me," Jones said evenly.

"You don't give a shit about that any more than you give a shit about keeping your word."

"But I do give a shit about somebody messing in my business."

Caitlin moved closer to him, the two of them lost to the room's shadows as she smelled the stale residue of whatever cologne he had sprayed on before making the trip from Washington. Close enough to be just a step from getting right in his face.

"What's that supposed to mean, Jones?"

"You contacted one of my people without authorization. You involved one of my people in a public gunfight that threatened to unpush all the buttons I pushed to keep him in this country without fear of arrest."

"*Your* people?"

"I'm holding Paz's leash. He's my dog now."

"You sure you want to refer to him that way? I don't think the colonel would like it."

"I control him, Ranger."

"The only person who controls Paz is Paz, Jones. You'd be well advised to remember that."

"It's a different world now, a whole new reality. I get that, Paz gets that, now you need to get it. I've tamed him. He understands where the line is and not to cross it."

"Right, that's what those paramilitary types in Houston thought. Remember what he did to them?"

Jones glanced at Tepper, back at Caitlin, then at the two of them. "That's not what brought me here, anyway."

"No?"

"Fernando Lorenzo Sandoval did, specifically what happened to his son and the fact that you used to be running the investigation."

"Used to be?" Tepper raised.

"We'll take things from here, Captain, if it's all the same to you."

"And what if it isn't?"

Jones pretended to consider the question. "What's the lowest of the low when it comes to Ranger duties?"

"Dealing with you," said Caitlin.

28

SAN ANTONIO

Jones smirked. Again. It looked like a practiced gesture for him, as if he spent hours in front of the mirror perfecting how to make it the default setting of his expression. Caitlin wondered if the appearance was covered in some secret Washington handbook under a chapter labeled "Condescending."

"I thought you were going to say killing me instead," he said.

Caitlin shook her head. "No, people be lining up for that job, me first."

"You said *we'll* take things from here. Is this 'we' as in Homeland Security?" Tepper asked Jones.

"You coming to your senses, Captain?"

"Just asking a question, Mr. Smith."

Jones let the taunt go this time. "Then the answer is 'close enough.'"

"Don't tell me," said Caitlin. "Homeland's working with Sandoval now too."

"Also, close enough. Have I made my point?"

"Oh, you made it, all right," said Tepper. "But that doesn't mean we have to listen."

Jones fixed his gaze all the way on the captain now. "Maybe I wasn't making myself clear."

"I'll thank you not to come down here and shit where I live, sir," Tepper told him, putting out the cigarette that had burned all the way down. "People get killed in Texas, it's the Rangers' problem, not Washington's."

"This is different. And your cooperation is necessary so as not to impede our efforts on negating the effects of the Mexican drug trade."

Tepper looked at Caitlin. "Is this guy for real?"

"Uh-huh. Unfortunately."

"I see what you mean about him now." Tepper fixed his gaze back on Jones. "I should've put a warrant out on you the last time you fled the state."

"I didn't flee."

"How would you put it, then?" Caitlin asked him.

"Voluntary recall. And now I've come back to make up for my not saying good-bye last time by telling you to back off this investigation and Fernando Lorenzo Sandoval."

"Sorry," Caitlin said, shaking her head. "No can do."

Tepper leaned back in his chair and lit a fresh cigarette, the old springs creaking under the strain. "As luck would have it, Sandoval happens to be right here in Texas now. For some secret meeting up in Austin."

Jones's eyes widened, his nostrils flaring like he was about to lunge across Tepper's desk. "That's classified information, Captain. I need to ask exactly how you came by it."

Tepper took a deep drag on his Marlboro. "Come by it? We're the *Texas Rangers*. Who do you think is handling security for this thing?"

The air came out of Jones's expression.

"Oh," Tepper continued, "guess nobody told you that, did they?"

"At least he didn't have to make the trip all the way from Washington this time," Caitlin said to Tepper. "And I've got a shorter trip to meet up with Sandoval."

Jones glared at her, Caitlin feeling as if he were firing needles with his eyes. "You'll do nothing of the kind, Ranger."

"So who's going to tell him about his son?"

"That will be handled in due course."

Caitlin could only shake her head. "You really don't give a shit, do you?"

Jones reached past her to pluck the school picture of Daniel Sandoval from Tepper's desk. "How do you think your office came by this, Ranger? I'm the one who circulated it, trying to help Sandoval get his kid back."

"That's a moot point now, sir," Tepper told him.

"But I'll be sure to tell him about your good intentions," Caitlin added.

Jones sidestepped to block her path to the door.

"You know what, Jones? Stay there." In his face now, balanced on the toes of her boots to better look him in the eye. "Please."

That brought Tepper up out of his chair. "No, Mr. Jones, don't stay there. This office is too goddamn dark to find all the blood that'll have to be cleaned up if I let Hurricane here have her way with you."

Jones met Caitlin's stare again and held it. "You really want to do this?"

"You really want to find out?"

"The two of you wanna take this outside?" asked Captain Tepper.

"Just give me the okay, Captain."

"I'm much too big a bite for you, Ranger," Jones said with a wink.

"Careful, Jones. Texas has its own Stand Your Ground law now. I could shoot you right now and let things get sorted out later."

"Enough!" blared Tepper, dissolving immediately into a coughing spasm that doubled him over. "Jesus H. Christ, Hurricane, you are determined to see me dead."

"Jones is ahead of you on my list, D.W."

"You back off this and I disappear again," Jones offered.

"And I'm just supposed to forget about the fact that somebody murdered five kids in a ghost town?"

"*Mexican* kids, Ranger."

Tepper had finally stopped coughing, the attack leaving him red-faced with his eyes dripping water. "We're not backing off a multiple murder on Texas soil. No way, no how. Not unless the president himself gets me on the phone, and I'm not even sure I'd take his call on the subject. Rather see Texas secede from the Union than let whoever killed those kids get away with it, and I don't care if they were Mexican, black, white, or polka dotted."

"I can have the FBI replace you on the investigation, and I'll oversee it personally," Jones told them both.

Caitlin could only shake her head. "That was a joke, right?"

"The real joke is that you have no idea what you're messing with here, the thousands of hours of manpower and countless resources we've put into this operation and the meetings going on in Austin."

"Heard they were secret," said Tepper.

Jones moved his eyes from him to Caitlin. "Not anymore, it seems. I'm telling you we're this close to shutting down a big portion of the drug trade and I can't risk five dead Mexican kids jeopardizing all that."

"I owe a pretty big debt to the father of one of them, Jones. And in case you've forgotten, Paz used to work for Sandoval before he went to work for you."

"I'm an equal opportunity employer."

"You're an equal opportunity asshole. I'm going to tell Sandoval about his son. If he wants to call me off, I'll consider it. If he doesn't, you can go fuck yourself."

Jones shook his head, scowling. "You're not going to stop until you flush your whole career down the drain by missing the pot when you piss."

"I'm a Texas Ranger, Jones. It comes with the job." She held her gaze on him, trying to make herself remember the color of his eyes this time, as she continued. "Captain, that meeting in Austin still on tomorrow?"

"As far as I know," Tepper told her.

"Then I think I'll be paying Sandoval a visit first thing."

29

Cort Wesley was seated on the front porch swing, shotgun lying over his lap, when Caitlin headed up the walk from her SUV.

"Didn't know if you'd be coming by tonight, Ranger," he said, letting himself smile.

She sat down next to him, feeling the swing rock slightly before Cort Wesley's feet stilled it. "The way things are, where else would I want to be?"

"How are *things*?"

She sighed deeply and rested her head against his shoulder, feeling the strength and power of his muscles. "Got on that flight this morning at six a.m. with no sleep at all. I'm flat exhausted."

"I got enough caffeine in my system to make a lawn mower run."

Caitlin eased herself off him. "What's wrong, Cort Wesley?"

"Isn't the obvious enough?"

"I always feel your muscles relax when I press up against you. Not tonight."

He kept his eyes fixed forward. "I did some checking."

"Into what?"

Looking at her now. "Whatever it was I did to make someone go after my boys that way."

Caitlin felt herself stiffen. "You gonna tell me what you found out?"

"This isn't about me. It isn't about you either."

She reached out for his shoulder, her touch only making the muscles more rigid. "Then who is it about?"

"The boys' mother, Maura Torres."

30

Guillermo Paz climbed the steps of the McKinney Humanities Building on the campus of the University of Texas San Antonio checking his watch to make sure he wasn't late. There was an evening class that covered the work of Friedrich Nietzsche, the scheduled start time making him think it would be composed mostly of adults in the continuing education program.

Turned out he couldn't have been more wrong.

Paz squeezed himself into yet another tiny desk in the rear and watched the classroom quickly fill around him with kids who looked no older than the outlaw Cort Wesley Masters's oldest boy. He checked out a dry erase board that filled out the whole of the front wall and saw "Freshman Introduction to German Philosophy" written there.

Oops, Paz thought.

Still, he hoped to attain some enlightenment anyway from a middle-aged professor wearing a corduroy jacket with patches on the elbows and a shock of wild gray hair. The professor stuck an unlit pipe in his mouth, only to remove it when his gaze fell on the seven-foot freshman seated at a desk that looked miniaturized in comparison to his bulk. The professor, whose name according to the dry erase board was Litsky, seemed about to speak, then changed his mind and stuck the unlit pipe back into his mouth.

Paz aimed his gaze at the door, prepared to make a graceful exit, until Professor Litsky opened the class with, "What do we know about Friedrich Nietzsche?"

That was it. Hooked now, Paz resigned himself to staying while committed to remaining as scarce as possible this time. No more outbursts or incidents requiring calls to security like the night before across town. Litsky looked like a man who knew his shit, guaranteeing Paz a better experience than the last one. In any event, it had to be better than what he was getting from the priests who'd been hearing his confessions for five years now while offering him nothing more than the penance he wasn't seeking.

Litsky continued to look around the room in search of a raised hand. Finding none, he spoke himself.

"Allow me to start, then. Nietzsche purported to have been greatly influenced by the writings of Arthur Schopenhauer, whose outlook on life was relentlessly pessimistic."

At last, Paz thought, leaning forward.

"But to consider his own writings to be on the level of Schopenhauer's, to even consider Nietzsche a philosopher at all, is an absurdity."

Uh-oh . . .

"Nietzsche is among the most well known and least effective of the German philosophers. He hid behind diatribes that were more like slogans without holding any real meaning. He spoke to a lost generation and continues to speak to those who are similarly lost and looking to rationalize the corruption of their own souls."

Paz managed to hold his tongue.

"Even his famed concept of the *Übermensch*, the notion of a superman, makes no sense and holds no ethical, spiritual, moral, or psychological value. The celebration of his writings is nothing more than a fraud perpetrated on all of us who know better."

Paz could hold his tongue no longer. "What is great in man is that he is a bridge and not an end."

"Excuse me?" Litsky asked, pretending to spot Paz for the first time.

"That's a quote from Nietzsche. Maybe you need me to interpret it for you, Professor."

"I'm quite capable of interpreting it for myself, thank you."

"Then why don't you for the rest of the students?"

Litsky took a few steps closer to him. "Are you even registered for this class?"

"I'm auditing. The credit means nothing to me, just the experience."

"What's that mean exactly?"

Paz realized the eyes of all the freshmen students were now on him, their mouths having collectively dropped at the realization of his presence. "You should know."

"And why's that?"

"It's a paraphrase of more of Nietzsche's thinking, the concept of translating will into power and the notion of experience for its own sake without specific gain."

Litsky seemed to ponder that briefly, before realizing the class was no longer looking at him. "What was your name again?"

"The doer is merely a fiction added to the deed."

"Is that an answer?"

"Don't you recognize it, Professor? It's a quote from Nietzsche. If you're going to put the man down, you should at least have an idea of what he said."

Some of the other students chuckled. A few slapped their knees, growing more animated in support of Paz. He knew he should have left the classroom then and there, but didn't.

"For Nietzsche, you see, Professor, the deed was everything. Accomplishment, resolution, achievement. Get it?"

"I believe you're missing the point."

"And what point is that?"

"Nietzsche's very rejection of the commonplace, what normal people call life."

"See, you just made *my* point for me."

"I most certainly did not! And you, sir, do not belong in my classroom!" Litsky charged, finding courage in the certainty Paz would not assault him in front of two dozen witnesses. Probably.

"I'm disappointed," Paz said, shaking his head. "See, the man of knowledge must be able not only to love his enemies but also to hate his friends."

Litsky looked at him questioningly.

"That's another Nietzsche quote. But you don't know it because you're not a man of knowledge, are you?"

"I'm calling security," Litsky said, fumbling in his jacket pocket for his cell phone. "Class is dismissed."

But no one moved.

"I said class is—"

"They heard you, Professor," Paz interrupted. "But it looks like they're ahead of you on the assignment. See, no price is too high to pay for the privilege of owning yourself."

"Hello," Litsky was saying into his phone, having trouble getting a connection. "Hello!"

"Your students have minds of their own. They think for themselves. Hey, maybe you're not as bad a teacher as I thought."

Litsky gave up on the cell phone, glanced toward the door.

"Feel free to dismiss yourself, Professor," Paz told him. "Or stay for the lesson."

"*Lesson?*" Litsky posed in disbelief.

Paz nodded, more dawning on him as his own thoughts unspooled. "Of what Nietzsche really meant by his notion of the *Übermensch*. He's trying to show us that for society to be able to live up to its true potential it needs a whole new system of values and beliefs. So I read this and it's like the man is talking about *me*: a *superman*, whose values change as the world around him changes. This is someone who, by trusting his own intuitive sense of what is good and evil, succeeds better than any other. The key is fluidity—that's what reading Nietzsche taught me, along with the fact that the world doesn't change us as much as we change the world. You see what I'm getting at?"

"Sir, I do not!" Litsky insisted, raising his voice to imitate bravado.

But the rest of the students were nodding. "Your class does. I bet they also get the fact that this superman is someone who in discovering himself also discovers that it's in his best interests to reject any outside notions about values, trusting rather what he finds within himself as the absolute truth. He creates his own good and evil, based on that which helps him to succeed or fail. In this way good is something that helps one to realize his potential and evil is whatever hampers or stands in the way of this effort. You get at least *that* point?"

"Not in the slightest."

But the class was nodding again. "I believe your students do, and I haven't even got to the part about it's the example of the superman that allows us to see how much is actually attainable in the world. In creating his own system of values, he continually tests himself, always refining those values to be better and better still. In this way the *Übermensch* rises above the values of the masses until he reaches the top of the food chain and his particular moral superiority becomes the guidelines for the rest of society. *Madre de Dios,* don't you get it yet? Don't you see where I'm going with this?"

Litsky could only stand there, his knees beginning to shake.

Paz rose to his full height grinning with his glistening eyes focused squarely on Litsky. A urine stain began spreading down the man's trousers. Paz started toward him and the urine stain immediately thickened, even as Paz veered toward the door, meeting the captivated stares of as many of the students as he could.

"Funny how you can't see something that's been right there in front of your face all along. Me being an *Übermensch* in the true Nietzsche definition of the word explains just about everything, where I fit into the great cosmic picture. 'Courageous, untroubled, mocking, and violent—that is what wisdom wants us to be,' says Nietzsche. Well, I don't know about wisdom, but I do know that's what I need to be if I'm going to be successful this time, because 'it's the still words which bring the storm.' " Paz reached the door and held his gaze on Litsky one last time. "That storm's coming, and it's going to be the worst one I've been up against yet. I see that now."

He started through the door, stopping when Litsky's next words froze him.

"He who fights monsters should be careful lest he become one himself."

Paz winked, letting the whole class see him smile thinly. "No worries, Professor, because I'm already there."

31

Caitlin held Cort Wesley's stare until he squeezed his eyes closed and rubbed the lids.

"Who told you that?" she asked him, her words sounding lame.

"It doesn't matter who told me. All that matters is it's true."

"Whoever told you could have been wrong."

"They're not wrong, Ranger. I stayed out of my boys' lives for fourteen years because I didn't want them dragged into my shit, and now I find out there was a whole other pile of it building."

"What else?"

"What else what?"

"What else did your source tell you about Maura Torres?"

"Nothing."

"And that was enough to make you buy into this hook, line, and sinker?"

"Yup. Because it's the only thing that makes sense."

Caitlin started to speak, stopped, then started again. "Why don't you let me check this out?"

"Go ahead. You won't find a damn thing. Nothing in Maura's past at all, least not on the surface. Whatever she was involved in, whatever almost got my boys killed, is buried real deep, Ranger."

"Tell me about Maura Torres, Cort Wesley," Caitlin said, after a pause dominated by the tree branches scratching at the porch eaves over them.

"There's nothing to tell."

"Make believe I'm not a Texas Ranger."

In spite of himself, Cort Wesley smiled thinly. "That's goddamn impossible and you know it."

"Okay, say I *am* a Texas Ranger and you're coming in to make out a report, based on some suspicions you've got. Guesses, assumptions—not allegations."

"There's nothing, Ranger."

"You're telling me Maura Torres is pure as the driven snow we almost never see in Texas."

"I am."

"Make believe she's not your boys' late mother."

He rose and squeezed the porch railing with both hands, eyeing Caitlin sideways now as she rocked slightly in the swing. "What do you think I been doing out here while I was waiting for you?"

"Thinking about her."

"Didn't I just say that?"

"What about her background?"

"We never talked about that much, hers *or* mine. She was first generation American, born on a farm somewhere in Texas. Her parents came over here as migrant laborers and fought the battle to become citizens. They were sworn in together on the same day. I remember a picture of Maura as a little girl at the courthouse ceremony. She'd raised her right hand in the air too, even though she was already a citizen thanks to birth. I don't think I've ever seen prouder folks in my life."

"Any other pictures?"

Cort Wesley shook his head. "Not that I've ever seen, at least not any from those days."

Caitlin churned her tongue around the inside of her mouth, which had felt like all the moisture had been sucked out since last night in Providence. "What about that aunt in Arizona?"

"Maura's older sister," Cort Wesley recalled.

"Maybe she knows something more."

"I guess," Cort Wesley said, looking down.

"You don't exactly seem enamored by the prospects."

"To put it mildly, we've had our differences. To put it plainly, she hates my guts."

"Well, that places her in good company, anyway."

Cort Wesley mustered a smile and retook his seat on the swing next to Caitlin. "Yours included?"

"Depends on the day."

"How about the night, Ranger?"

"To know you is to love your boys, Cort Wesley."

That almost got him to laugh. "Now there's a backhanded compliment if I ever heard one."

"You wanna know what I think?"

"Why ask if you're going to tell me anyway?"

"I think you should let me talk to this aunt, Maura's sister."

"She won't talk to you."

"Why's that?"

"Because she hates you about as much as she hates me for helping me keep custody of the boys. Woman's a bitch. Even Maura couldn't stand her."

"Well, last time I checked, Cort Wesley, Arizona had a police department we can ask to talk to Maura's sister on our behalf."

"Some things I need to do myself, Ranger."

Caitlin laid her head against his shoulder. "You want to tell me what else?"

"What else what?"

"What else has got you all tied into knots?"

"All this isn't enough?"

"There you go," Caitlin said, rolling her eyes.

Cort Wesley eased himself away from her. "Huh?"

"You get nervous," Caitlin told him, "you start asking questions. But danger doesn't get you nervous, anxiety does. Danger just puts you on edge. That's different."

"Okay, I'm anxious."

Caitlin shook her head. "You want to try this again?"

Fidgeting, Cort Wesley rose and moved back to the railing, squeezing it hard enough to flush his hands with blood. "Cut me a break here," he said out toward the front lawn, "will you?"

She resisted the temptation to join him by the railing, knew she should've left things there but couldn't help herself. "You can't talk to me, who can you talk to, Cort Wesley?"

"Ranger, I'm not gonna say this—"

Her phone rang, sparing him the need to finish his statement. Caitlin wasn't going to answer it at first, then changed her mind when the Caller ID read HEADQUARTERS.

"Checking to see if I'm home safe, Captain?"

"Not exactly, Ranger," said Tepper. "I hope you're sitting down."

"Why?"

"We got tentative IDs on the other kids found in Willow Creek and you're not gonna believe it."

32

SAN ANTONIO

Cort Wesley decided to stay out on the porch, standing with his elbows perched on the wooden rail overlooking the front yard, when Caitlin went upstairs to try and sleep. The night was comfortably cool and clear enough to see just about every star in the sky if he'd been looking.

Suddenly, he smelled talcum powder layered thick and heavy to disguise a bad scent like a blanket tossed over a fire to smother it. He looked to his right to see the ghost of old Leroy Epps standing there, his thin, liver-spotted hands squeezing the railing in identical fashion to Cort Wesley's. His lips were pale pink and crinkled with dryness. The thin light from the overhead fixture's single low-wattage bug bulb cast his brown skin in a yellowish tint. He smiled when he saw Cort Wesley looking his way.

"*'Bout time you noticed me, bubba.*"

"How long you been standing there, champ?"

"*Far as you're concerned, since right now.*"

"Guess you heard."

"*From where I stand, I hear everything. See it too. You should know that by now. Looks like the merry-go-round's spinning again.*"

"When's it stop?" Cort Wesley asked his old friend's ghost.

Leroy Epps had been a lifer in the brutal Huntsville prison known as the Walls, busted for killing a white man in self-defense; it was his friendship and guidance that had gotten Cort Wesley through his years in captivity. The diabetes that would ultimately kill him had turned Leroy's eyes bloodshot and numbed his limbs years before the sores and infections set in. As a boxer, he'd fought for the middleweight crown on three different occasions, knocked out once and had the belt stolen from him on paid-off judges' scorecards two other times. He'd died three years into Cort Wesley's four-year incarceration, but ever since always seemed to show up when needed the most. Whether a ghostly specter or a figment of his imagination, Cort Wesley had given up trying to figure out. Just accepted the fact of his presence and grateful that Leroy kept coming around to help him out of one scrape after another.

"*Well,*" he said, "*that's not what brought me here tonight.*"

"No? What did, then?"

"*Wind's kicking up, fixing to blow in something big.*"

"All the things you can see, you gotta tell me something I already know?" Cort Wesley said to him.

"*It's different this time. What's brewing seems to come from my neck of the woods.*"

"The dead?"

"*The past, bubba. You gonna be running into plenty from my side of the fence along the way.*"

"Nothing new there."

Epps took his eyes off Cort Wesley and gazed into the night. "*Gotta buy a ticket there are so many whose attention you've grabbed. Yup, you and the Ranger have done spun the wheel of time backwards, that's what you've done.*" Epps looked back at him. "*So I figure I better stop by and let you know you're playing to an audience.*"

"You mind asking them what was it Maura Torres did that's put my boys in danger?"

"*They don't talk much, bubba. Not nearly as social as me and more than a little jealous that I've got a foot in both worlds.*"

Cort Wesley swallowed hard. "What about Maura?"

"*She's here. Not right now but she checks in from time to time. And she's much appreciative of the work the Ranger gal's been doing with her boys.*"

"I'm going to Phoenix to speak with Maura's sister."

"This the one that hates your guts?"

"The very same."

"Well, that oughtta go well, bubba."

"I'm hoping maybe she knows something that can help."

"The dead sure can be a pain in the ass, can't they?"

Cort Wesley just looked at him.

"Maura wishes you'd felt for her the way you feel for the Ranger."

"Different times, champ, and I was an altogether different man."

"Yup, you done proven the old at-tage wrong, bubba."

"What's that?"

"The one saying that people don't change, not really. Well, whoever wrote that book didn't know you, that's for sure. Your life's got so many different curves, even one of them race car drivers couldn't follow the course. But this stop's the one I fancy most."

"Nervous father without a clue who's trying to kill his kids?"

"Father who loves his boys more than life itself and will stop at nothing to protect them. You mind if I asks you a question?"

Cort Wesley's eyes answered for him.

"How come you don't just ask the Ranger gal for the money you need?"

Cort Wesley considered a range of responses before opting for the truth. "Pride."

"Stupid."

"I guess."

"You guess?"

"I get the point, champ."

"You mind if I asks you another question?"

"Maybe I should say no this time."

"If things were switched, wouldn't you want her to ask you for help?"

"That's not fair, champ."

"Oh no?" Leroy Epps paused long enough to nod a few times, his tired eyes looking even more watery in the night. *"I ever tell you I broke horses back in the day?"*

Cort Wesley held Epps's milky, bloodshot gaze. "As a matter of fact, no."

"Was just a boy myself at the time, working on a ranch in Alabama. They always brought me the toughest cases, not just because I was the best at breaking 'em, but also because if a nigger like me got busted up, nobody'd care much." Epps stopped, looking past Cort Wesley or maybe through him. *"Reason I mention that is it's kinda what the Ranger's done for you, except the comparison's off: Ranger didn't break you, bubba, she fixed you."*

Cort Wesley waited for old Leroy's stare to meet his again. "You say you can see things."

"Not everything all at once, bubba. More like the view through a telescope, all narrow and confined. Guess there's limits, but I really don't get all the rules 'cept there's less of them than you think."

"Reason I raise that is I've never asked you before what that view's showing. But this is different, just like you said, champ."

Epps nodded, looking sad. *"Would if I could, bubba, but there's too much blur right now."*

"But my boys, just tell me they're going to be all right."

Epps shrugged, his bony shoulders poking up through his shirt, the yellow tint to his skin making him look more sickly than dead. *"End's not written quite yet, bubba."*

"Then maybe a pen would do me more good than a gun this time, champ."

Epps's expression remained flat, the bug light staining the whites of his eyes yellow. *"You're gonna have to spill blood to win this one, not ink."* Then he looked back into the night again.

"What is it you're not saying, champ?"

"I'm not saying."

"Too late for that now."

Epps continued to stare straight ahead. *"I was here last night when you got home with your youngest after that gunfight."*

"I didn't see you."

"No, but I believe he did."

"That can't be good," Cort Wesley said, feeling something sink in his stomach.

"No," Epps agreed, his grim tone lacking its typical reassurance. *"It ain't good at all."*

33

"They normally don't let visitors in this late."

"They made an exception in my case," Ana Callas Guajardo said to the man seated across the table from her.

"It's also the wrong day."

"Is it now, Locaro?" She leaned forward, undaunted by the manacles chaining the man's wrists to the table and legs to the chair. "Maybe I should leave, eh?"

Locaro's face was a mass of scars and stray patches of beard stubble stuck between ridged layers of tissue that looked like callus. It might have been more dramatic, even fitting, to say these were the product of one battle or another. The truth, though, was that they were a genetic defect, something to do with the skin malfunctioning at the cellular level. Kept reproducing cells and storing them inside the clumps that made his face look like a mogul-laden ski slope. The clumps were like boils, occasionally leaking pus that made people seated or standing near him in public relocate in a hurry. As a teenager, Locaro had once taken a tweezers and nail file to them, succeeding only in making things worse.

The half-light of the small room cast shadows over Locaro's face that seemed to get trapped between the ridges. After only a few moments in the room with him, Guajardo found herself nearly retching from the stench of his unwashed body and oozing pus, which looked shiny when the meager spill of light found it dotting his face.

"You want me to leave?" she repeated.

"Did I say that?"

"You didn't say anything."

"What are you doing here, *mi hermanita*?"

"I've arranged for your release. You've been granted a full pardon."

Locaro showed no reaction or emotion at all. He just sat there, rocking his chair back as far as his manacles would allow. "What do you need me to do?"

"No thank-you, no show of appreciation after three years in solitary confinement?"

"I like being alone."

"And you haven't been allowed in the yard, even alone, for nearly a year after killing, what, your fifth prisoner?"

"Sixth. And two guards," Locaro added, almost proudly.

"I need you to kill two children," Guajardo told him.

Locaro scratched at the ridges dotting his face, wiping the pus off on his prison-issue trousers. "You spring me from here to take out a couple kids?"

"They're protected."

"By who?"

"Texas Ranger and her boyfriend."

"Boyfriend?"

"The Ranger's a woman."

"Caitlin Strong . . ."

"You know her?"

"I know she's a woman."

"Her boyfriend did a stretch in Cereso not too long ago." Guajardo held Locaro's gaze to see if a spark of recognition flared, continuing when it didn't. "Cort Wesley Masters."

His eyes widened slightly. "He killed almost as many men as me while he was in here. Got away with it clean 'cause it was in those death fights. I offered a guard *mucho dinero* to let me fight him. Tough *hombre*."

"Too tough?"

"Nobody's too tough."

"There's more."

Locaro leaned forward again. "You got my attention."

"Colonel Guillermo Paz."

Locaro's cheek quivered, like a nervous tic.

"And he's got backup of his own," Ana told him.

"Then I'll need some too."

"Tell me where to find it."

"You won't have to go far." Locaro looked about dramatically. "Here in Cereso. Men almost as bad as me, just not as pretty," he said.

Guajardo waited for a smile to accompany the quip, but none came. "How many?"

"A dozen, ten maybe. I'll give you the names."

"That's a lot of pardons to pull off."

"You want these kids dead, that's what it'll take given the opposition, *mi hermanita*."

Ana Guajardo stiffened. "I haven't been your sister for a very long time."

Locaro smiled, starting to cross his arms until remembering the manacles that creaked under the strain. *"Tu eres el motivo de mi existencia,"* he told her. Then, adding with a smirk, "You are *still* the fountain of my being."

She needed him and he knew it. Guajardo hated needing anyone. But there were limits to everything, even money and power, and it was left to the likes of her brother, Locaro, to deal with those limits.

"After all," Locaro added, taunting her, *"la familia lo es todo."*

"I'll need the names of the men you want released."

"Do you have a pen?"

"They wouldn't let me bring one in here. Said you killed a man with one by stabbing him through the eye."

"Almost forgot that one, *mi hermanita*."

"Prison can make a man soft. So tell me, *mi hermano*, are you still the man I remember?"

Locaro laid both hands on the table and stretched the chain binding them together. He grinned as he squeezed his fingers into fists, the veins bursting from his wrists and forearms, his hands trembling, as he began to force them further apart. Guajardo thought she heard a grating sound, followed by a crackling before the chain split at a link in the center.

Still grinning, Locaro folded his hands behind his head. She could smell his sweat now, adding further to the stench that rode him like a swarm of insects.

"Any other questions?" he asked his sister.

But her eyes were fixed on the smartphone that had just beeped with an incoming message.

"I have to be going," Guajardo said, rising after she'd read it.

"Trouble?"

"There is always trouble, *mi hermano*."

Locaro grinned. "This is different. I can tell. Ever since we were children, I've been able to tell."

"Tell what?"

"The face you make when someone crosses you. So calm, pleasant. Almost like you're grateful to have a chance to destroy them."

But Ana Guajardo's expression remained flat. "And there are several now I must destroy."

Part Four

Boots above the knee and leather leggings, a belt three inches wide with two rows of brass-bound cartridges, and a slanting sombrero make a man appear larger than he really is, but the Rangers were the largest men I saw in Texas, the State of big men. And some of them were remarkably handsome in a sunburned, broad-shouldered, easy, manly way. They were also somewhat shy with strangers, listening very intently, but speaking little, and then in a slow, gentle voice; and as they spoke so seldom, they seemed to think what they had to say was too valuable to spoil by profanity.

Richard Harding Davis,
The West from a Car Window

34

Caitlin Strong was standing in the lobby of the Four Seasons Hotel Austin the next morning, when Fernando Lorenzo Sandoval emerged from the elevator enclosed by three of his bodyguards. He spotted her a few moments after her eyes fixed upon him, enough time for her to see his appearance was dapper and polished as always. Not a single black hair out of place and bronze skin so even in tone and shade that his face looked to be sprayed on. His cream-colored linen suit fit him perfectly over tasseled loafers with no socks. Caitlin imagined in another life he might have been a movie star, bearing a strong resemblance to a famous Latin actor whose name she couldn't recall but thought might have begun with Fernando as well.

Sandoval smiled in recognition, but the gesture seemed forced. As he moved to approach her, casting an unspoken signal to his bodyguards, Caitlin could feel the confident air and swagger befitting the most hunted man in Mexico nowhere to be found, sucked out of him by worry over the fate of his missing son. His gaze held hers, seeming to grasp some meaning, some portent, in it, enough so that his eyes had begun to mist up by the time he reached her.

Caitlin had been to the elegant Four Seasons before, but remembered the lobby being brighter. This morning it seemed only half the lights had been turned on, casting the rich mauve, cream, and olive tones in a twilight-like glint, Sandoval's face looking shiny under the spill of a single fixture that found him as he reached her. He stretched his right arm outward, she thought to shake her hand, but then his grasp fastened on her elbow instead, the grip flaccid and quivery.

Caitlin held his stare as long as she could, more passing between them in those moments than any words could produce because there were no words that could capture the pain of the news she had brought with her. Looking at him in the glare of a bulb that seemed ready to burn out, she felt glad she'd insisted on being the one to do it.

Sandoval had separated himself from his family to keep them safe under new identities layered so deeply even the cartels wouldn't be able to find them. Every step he'd taken, every move he'd made in the last few years had been done to make his own children safer, looking forward to the day when he could put all this behind him and return home.

Over now. Finished. Done. All for naught.

"Let's go outside, Ranger," Sandoval said, his voice cracking and hand slipping off her elbow.

35

Scottsdale, Arizona

"Why we going to visit someone none of us even likes?" Dylan had asked that morning after Cort Wesley told him and Luke where they were going.

"Figure it out," Cort Wesley said, not in the mood to parse words.

" 'Cause you don't want to leave us alone."

"Close enough."

"What else?" Luke asked.

"I'll explain later."

"What's wrong with now?"

Cort Wesley shot his younger son a look, normally enough to silence him but not anymore, not today.

"You figure Aunt Araceli might know something that can help you figure this out," Luke surmised, "why someone's after us."

"Help?" Dylan chimed in, rolling his eyes and flipping the hair from his face. "She didn't like Mom, she could care less about us, and she hates Dad."

Luke looked to his father to say his brother was wrong about that, but Cort Wesley could only muster a shrug.

He'd called Araceli Ramirez, Torres being her maiden name, the night before.

"What do you expect me to do?" she'd interrupted, before he was even finished explaining things to her.

"Help me figure this out, that's all," Cort Wesley said, keeping his tone low and measured.

"Here's what I've figured out so far: my sister's dead because of you."

"And somebody tried to kill your nephews two nights ago."

"Wouldn't have happened if you'd let me have custody like I asked."

"You were a stranger to them."

"And what the fuck were you? How about a criminal, an ex-con, a contract killer, a mob enforcer, a drug dealer? How's that?"

"I was never a drug dealer. And none of that had anything to do with Maura getting killed."

"No? Then what did?"

"Something else. My fault, all the same—I'm not denying that. I just wish you'd keep your facts straight," Cort Wesley finished, immediately regretting the break in his tone but unable to stop himself now. "I'm going to say it again. Someone came after your nephews and it was because of Maura, something in her past."

"How the hell you know that?"

"I do, that's all. You may not think you know anything that can help, but you're the only one who might. Just let me know if we can head out your way tomorrow," Cort Wesley said, emphasizing the "we."

"Knock yourself out," Araceli Ramirez told him.

*   *   *

She'd been married twice, the first time to a Major League baseball player whose arm she'd broken in a tussle after he'd come home drunk and belligerent one night too many. Her second marriage was to a Phoenix-area businessman who owned a chain of car washes and was president of the local Chamber of Commerce. Cort Wesley thought they had two kids, but it might have been three.

They'd taken a seven a.m. Southwest flight to Phoenix, arriving in really no time at all given the time differential. Cort Wesley rented a car, insisting on printed-out directions because he hated the talking monstrosities that seemed to enjoy telling him that he'd missed his turn. Bad enough his kids were already smarter than he was; he didn't need a machine that was too.

Let On-Star, or whatever it was called, try raising two teenage boys now targeted by contract killers.

Somehow that thought made Cort Wesley smile, as almost everything did when he was alone with his boys. Circumstances aside, he'd learned to appreciate the company he knew was fleeting, even with their typical teenage back-and-forth banter. Luke had gotten to the age where he wasn't afraid to snap back at his brother and, for his part, Dylan had begun to appreciate Luke was no longer a pushover. Maybe even grudgingly accept that his younger brother now was pretty much a spitting image of him from four years ago.

When they'd witnessed their mother murdered as she stood in the front doorway.

That thought shocked Cort Wesley back to reality and he busied himself with the directions to Araceli Ramirez's home that he'd committed to memory. She lived in Pinnacle Peak Heights, one of Scottsdale's finest neighborhoods—perfectly befitting the wife of a car wash and Chamber of Commerce baron. The name suggested a gated community with fake cops patrolling in tiny fuel-efficient cars with police lights affixed to the roofs.

As it turned out, the community wasn't gated, just lush and spacious with plenty of space between homes on lots that looked to average well more than an acre. The whole community just didn't look real, more painted onto the desert, and Cort Wesley actually wanted to touch a home or some landscaping just to make sure it didn't rub off on his fingers. The palm trees and garden shrubbery looked to be of a uniform height amid lawns so well manicured he figured they might have actually been artificial turf. He'd heard fake grass was quite the rage in the desert these days and wondered what it felt like underfoot.

The street on which Araceli Ramirez lived featured a beautiful view of the mountains overlooking the scene to the east, and he imagined the lit-up city would look just as spectacular to the west after dark. Cort Wesley wasn't at all jealous, but he was surprised by the means with which his boys' aunt found herself living.

"My older sister's a bitch," Maura used to say, whenever Araceli came up in conversation. "A real bitch."

Man, he could almost hear Maura's voice in his head right now.

"Why you smiling, Dad?" Luke asked him, while Dylan remained lost between his headphones.

"I was just thinking of your mom," Cort Wesley said, instead of making something up.

"Man, check this place out," came Dylan's voice from next to him in the front seat.

He'd spotted Araceli Ramirez's address ahead of his father. A beige-colored stucco exterior enclosing four thousand square feet of living space off a large circular drive on a cul de sac. Cort Wesley pulled in slowly, figuring the car wash business must be very good indeed based on the majestically maintained landscaping amid a fenced two-acre spread within which the palatial two-story home was centered. The sun beat down on it from a cloudless sky and, as Cort Wesley wound his way toward the clay-colored cantera stone walk fronting the house, the automatic sprinklers snapped on.

Real grass, he realized, having figured Araceli more for the fake kind based on what he knew of her.

Dylan and Luke trailed him out of the rental car and up the walk, passing a tiered fountain dribbling water en route to the front door. And that's when Cort Wesley stiffened, something making his defenses snap on. He knew that sensation all too well, mostly from war, some inexplicable part of his brain and being picking up some cosmic vibrations his conscious mind had missed. He'd given up trying to figure it all out and just accepted it since it had saved him so many times.

But why now, why here?

Almost to the door, Cort Wesley froze, making sure his boys were shielded behind him.

"Dad?" he heard Dylan say, holding off on a response.

Because the front door was cracked open six inches maybe, enough for Cort Wesley to feel the cool air fleeing from inside and hear the steady hum of the central air conditioner.

"Stay here," he told his sons, and eased his way though the door.

36

Austin, Texas

The Four Seasons had been built amid a lavish garden setting on San Jacinto Boulevard in the center of Austin. It faced Lady Bird Lake, just a five-minute walk from the bustle of Congress Avenue and ten from a bridge a massive colony of vampire bats called home, having roosted on its underside for literally decades.

Caitlin hadn't even asked D. W. Tepper about the availability of the chopper provided to Company F by Jones. Instead, unable to sleep soundly, she rose before dawn and found Cort Wesley in the very same spot on the front porch where she'd left him. Driving long distances, especially along briefly empty stretches of the flat Texas four-lanes, was great for clearing her head, though not this morning. This morning she was bringing news of a child's death to a father.

Now she sat with Sandoval in matching adjacent, cushioned chairs shaded by twin umbrellas in the hotel's open parklike area en route to the pool. To Caitlin it had the feel of a golf course minus the flags, holes, and bunkers, the light green grass moist with a recent watering and trimmed close to the ground. Trees rimmed the space and Caitlin thought she might have heard the bubbling of a fountain intermixed with traffic sounds that reminded her she was in a city.

She looked at Fernando Lorenzo Sandoval, trying to find the right words before she simply eased the school photo of his son Daniel from her pocket and extended it toward him. He took the picture in a trembling hand, barely regarding it before wiping his eyes and returning his gaze to her.

"Where?" he managed.

"He was found with four other children in a Texas ghost town called Willow Creek."

Caitlin caught Sandoval's eyes raising at the mention of the town, the spark of recognition clear. But then his expression flattened again, his lips started to quiver. He eased his upper teeth over the lower one to still them.

"How?" Sandoval asked, squeezing the arms of his chair so tight his hands flushed with red.

"Why don't we leave that for another time?"

"*How?*" he repeated.

Caitlin leaned forward, canting her body to ease closer to him and stopping just short of reaching out to touch his arm. "Mr. Sandoval, sometimes you need to just trust your friends about certain things."

"And you're my friend?"

Caitlin nodded. "I believe I am, sir, yes."

Sandoval held her gaze, his eyes going glassy again. "I wonder if you hadn't saved my life in El Paso, if my son would still be alive." He swallowed hard. "This was my fault, wasn't it?"

"On the surface, that would be my first thought, but—"

Shaking his head now, as he interrupted her. "All the precautions I took . . . Everything thought out, every possible layer of protection . . . I didn't just give my family a new identity, I built them a new life entirely separate from mine." Sandoval started to swallow again, but his throat seemed to clog before he finished the effort. "I haven't even seen Daniel for almost a year now. Except once, when I showed up at one of his soccer games. In disguise so no one would recognize me, even him.

I promised myself I'd only watch a few minutes to avoid risk. Then I promised myself I'd leave at halftime, then after a little of the second half." His eyes grasped hers desperately. "I was still standing there when the team left the field. Daniel walked right past me. His team won in overtime." He stopped long enough to take a deep breath. "I moved my wife and daughter into hiding as soon as word reached me about my son. If this was the work of the cartels . . ."

"It wasn't, sir. We've now identified the other four kids who were found in Willow Creek with your son," Caitlin continued, easing her smartphone from her pocket and locating the pictures Captain Tepper had e-mailed her the previous night. "Could you check these out and tell me if you recognize any of the faces?"

"I thought you said they'd already been identified."

"They have. But I want to see if they're familiar to you."

Sandoval scrolled through the pictures in cursory fashion before handing the phone back to Caitlin. "I don't know any of them. Who are they, Ranger?"

Caitlin jogged through the pictures herself as she responded. "Three are children of two of the biggest drug cartel leaders in Mexico."

37

Scottsdale, Arizona

Cort Wesley saw the bodies first, then the blood. Araceli Ramirez and her businessman husband lying facedown on the stone tile floor. He felt chilled, immediately conscious of the central air-conditioning filling the house with supercooled air and recalled Maura saying how much her sister detested the heat.

"You want me to check upstairs?"

Cort Wesley turned toward Dylan, now standing just inside the open doorway with Luke peeking out from behind him. "No," he said, instead of reprimanding the boys for disregarding his instructions. "Not much doubt what's gonna be up there and I don't want you seeing it."

Cort Wesley moved from the foyer into the sprawling living and dining room combination, careful not to disturb the crime scene. Funny how having a Texas Ranger in his life had changed his thinking in such things.

This was bad, very bad. It wasn't about Maura Torres at all, but her whole family. Someone exacting revenge, payback, comeuppance—whatever—for something that must have happened long before that Maura had never shared with him.

"Ain't this a mess?" said Leroy Epps, suddenly standing between the two corpses, avoiding the blood pools. *"How'd this go down, bubba?"*

"Happened early this morning."

"How you figure that?"

"Kids' backpacks are still in the foyer, like they were packed for school."

Old Leroy cast his bloodshot gaze back that way. The backpacks were out of sight from here, but Cort Wesley thought maybe ghosts had no trouble seeing around corners. *"Two backpacks meaning two more bodies upstairs, boy and a girl judging by the colors. What else, bubba?"*

Cort Wesley continued forward, close enough to Leroy Epps to smell the talcum powder slathered over his skin and fresh root beer soda on his breath. "Low-caliber shots to the head. One each. Very professional."

"Dad?" Dylan prodded.

"Whoever did this," Cort Wesley continued to Leroy Epps, "didn't need to do any more than that to make their point, champ."

"Who you talking to?" Dylan persisted.

"Just thinking out loud."

"Then who's 'champ'?"

Cort Wesley swung toward his oldest son. "Maybe you should take your brother back outside."

"We're safer in here."

"Killers are long gone."

Dylan and Luke both looked past their father toward the bodies, stray clumps atop the polished tile. Both wearing light-colored clothes that beneath the dull recessed lighting looked like extensions of the floor.

"*He's right, son,*" Leroy Epps said, and for an instant, just an instant, Cort Wesley thought he caught Dylan looking the ghost's way. "*You make your way into the kitchen, bubba, check and see if there's any root beer in the fridge.*" His big, dull eyes regarded the corpses again. "*Don't suppose they'll be drinking it anytime soon.*"

"Maybe he can help protect us," Dylan was saying now.

"Who?"

"Whoever it is you're talking to."

"Myself. I told you that."

"Sure, Dad," the boy scoffed, "whatever you say."

"*Boy's got himself an attitude, don't he?*"

"Guess he takes after his father, champ."

Dylan rolled his eyes. "There you go again."

Old Leroy looked from the bodies to Dylan and Luke. "*Whoever did this likely ain't finished. And if they happened to be figuring on you coming here . . .*"

"Tell me something I don't know."

"*How 'bout help just arrived, bubba.*"

And Cort Wesley turned to find Guillermo Paz looming in the doorway.

38

AUSTIN, TEXAS

"The second-oldest boy and youngest girl were brother and sister, the children of Alejandro Luis Rojas, second in command of the Juárez cartel. That leaves one boy and one girl, each ten years old. The boy was the son of Juan Ramon Castillo, ranking member of the Sinaloa cartel cadre. The girl was the daughter of a high school teacher from Mexico City who's currently sick in the hospital."

"A teacher," Sandoval repeated.

"Which tells me this isn't about drugs, sir. It's about something else, and I want you to know I won't rest until I determine exactly what that is."

"It makes no sense," Sandoval said, sounding like someone else entirely to Caitlin. "Risking the wrath of some of the most powerful men in Mexico . . ."

"No, sir, it doesn't."

"*Ay Dios mío*," Sandoval managed, drifting backward until his shoulders sank into the rear cushion.

"What is it, Mr. Sandoval?"

His eyes found hers again. "Willow Creek, Ranger."

"I imagine you don't believe that's a coincidence any more than I do," Caitlin said, recalling the rise she'd gotten out of him when she mentioned the town's name.

"Not at all, Ranger," he told her, leaning forward. "Not at all."

39

AUSTIN, TEXAS; 1919

"I don't believe I heard you correctly," Adjutant General James Harley said, after taking a hefty swig from his bottle of milk of magnesia.

"I believe you did," said William Ray Strong, leaning as far back as the stiff, high-backed wooden chair set before Harley's desk would let him.

Harley held the bottle of antacid up for William Ray and his son, Earl, to see. "You know why I been living on this stuff? On account of the shit pulled by the likes of you."

William Ray knew full well he was referring to the most infamous episode in the Rangers' storied history, that being a massacre of fifteen Mexican civilians the year before in the tiny community of Porvenir, Texas, on the Mexican border in western Presidio County. His son, Earl, had shown him a widely circulated picture of Captain Monroe Fox and two other Rangers on horseback with their lariats around the bodies of dead Mexican bandits. That past January, numerous similar reports had led to an investigation by the Texas Legislature in the person of Representative José T. Canales of Brownsville. After hearing testimony, the legislature passed a bill that reduced the number of Rangers, pretty much bringing an end to the days of glory that had culminated with the exploits of the Frontier Battalion in which William Ray had served.

For his part, Adjutant General Harley, the de facto supervisor of all Ranger companies, had fought to preserve as much of their legacy and number as he could. Try as he may, though, he was unable to convince lawmakers that the breakdown of law and order on the border during the Mexican Revolution necessitated the appointment of hundreds of new special Rangers without sufficient training or seasoning in keeping with the organization's storied tradition. The fact that these "wildings," as Harley called them, were the true culprits fell on deaf ears and he announced his retirement effective in just a few months' time once the hearings had concluded. As a result, his modest office in the State House was already littered with boxes in various stages of packing.

"You know how many Mexicans Rangers are accused of killing in the last decade?" Harley challenged William Ray, laying his bottle of milk of magnesia back on the desktop.

"No, sir."

"As many as five thousand. That's five with three zeroes. You people still think this is the last century, with Rangers having free rein to kill as you see fit."

William Ray turned his gaze to the boxes strewn about the room. "We can talk like this 'til it's time to haul that cardboard out of here, or we can get down to business."

"Business being this plan of yours to pretty much declare war on Mexico."

"Not really, since they already declared war on us by bringing their poison over the border and heading back south with cash in its stead. It's spreading east from Baja and if we don't do something about it, this will be the last century again for sure, with waves of Mexican bandits crossing the border to move opium through Texas and beyond with no Rangers there to stop them."

Harley wrinkled his nose and stifled a belch. It was raining outside and the windows rattled under the force of the wind and hail pellets that sounded like marbles when they smacked up against the glass.

"You trust this Lava?" he asked William Ray.

"I trust he's telling the truth about these *esos Demonios*. I trust that they murdered the entire town of Willow Creek. I trust that we'll see more of the same if we don't act fast."

Harley reached for his bottle of milk of magnesia and unscrewed the cap. "What do you need exactly, Ranger?"

What William Ray needed arrived in Austin over the course of the following three days in the form of a select group of Rangers.

"No one can ever know about this," Harley told him. "Governor finds out and he'll find call to hang both of us."

"He won't find out and there'll be no call."

Harley gave William Ray a long look over his desk. "I'm trusting you with what's left of my career, Ranger. Don't let me down."

"You can count on it, sir."

The first to arrive in Austin was Captain Frank Hamer, still serving a suspension for allegedly stalking, and even threatening, Representative José T. Canales for daring to besmirch the Ranger name and reputation. Hamer had already made his name as a throwback to the old-school Rangers, who used whatever methods were necessary to get whatever was needed done.

Arriving just behind him was the same Monroe Fox who had been relieved of his Ranger command and duties following the investigation into the massacre that had followed bandit raids on a number of farms. Fox had fallen on his sword, making no excuses for his actions while knowing full well he was being made the scapegoat for a decade of brutal indiscretion on the part of the Rangers, who had decided to fight fire with fire in what had become an all-out border war. A former Austin policeman, Fox was big-boned and heavyset, but with a baby face that belied the violence that, rightly or wrongly, had come to define his Ranger career.

The next member of the team was an utter stranger, given that he had only recently applied for entry into the Rangers. Manuel Trazazas Gonzaullas was the one name added by Adjutant General Harley, who requested he be reassigned from his current position as a special agent for the U.S. Treasury Department. Gonzaullas had been born in Cádiz, Spain, of naturalized American citizens visiting that country at the time of his birth. He'd actually spent several years in the Mexican army prior to going to work for Treasury and, as such, was well acquainted with the tactics and thinking William Ray's team would be facing.

The final name on his list had drawn a raised eyebrow and smirk from James Harley. "Great choice, 'cept he's been dead for a year."

William Ray scribbled an address on a piece of Harley's official stationery and handed it to him. "Then it'll be his ghost who gets the telegram."

Two days later, in response to that telegram, famed Ranger captain Bill McDonald became the last of the group to arrive, even though his death from pneumonia had been widely reported nearly a year before.

"Hell of a thing, reading your own obituary," he told William Ray Strong and his son, Earl, when they picked McDonald up at the train station.

"Something that could have been corrected, sir," Earl noted, stopping just short of asking the Ranger legend for his autograph.

"Thought about that for two seconds maybe," McDonald relayed wryly, flashing a wink. "Then I figured I could use the privacy for a change." A laugh dissolved into a retching cough that left him red-faced and heaving for air. "Not that the damn pneumonia won't get me eventually, 'less of course something else does first."

"Not on my watch," William Ray assured him.

As a legendary Ranger captain, McDonald had taken part in a number of celebrated cases, including the Fitzsimmons-Maher prize fight, the Wichita Falls bank robbery, the Reese-Townsend feud, and the Brownsville Raid of 1906. A man, it was said, "who would charge hell with a bucket of water."

"Got a question for you, sir," Earl Strong chimed in. "Did you really come up with the phrase 'One riot, one Ranger'?"

McDonald stifled another cough and winked. "If I didn't, son, I sure as hell should have."

Adjutant General Harley put "Strong's Raiders," as they came to be known, up in the Driskill Hotel on Sixth Street in the center of downtown Austin. The showplace hotel had been built by cattle baron Jesse Driskill in 1886 and was the choice locale of any number of dignitaries, including Texas governor William Hobby, who held his first inaugural ball there. Strong's Raiders met in a side meeting room adorned with ferns left over from the celebration.

"Must be allergic or something," the famed Bill McDonald said, after a fresh coughing spasm overcame him.

"Not bad for a dead man," chided Frank Hamer.

"We're all gonna be dead sooner or later. Can't control that, son, but we can control the terms of the arrangement."

"I thought you'd be bigger," Hamer told him.

McDonald looked the hulking Hamer in the eye. "Just like I thought you'd be smaller."

"You finished, ladies?" said William Ray, the lone among them standing now. "Good. Now you all know what brought you here, leaving us to consider where we go next. What you don't know is that we're not in this fight alone. There's Mexicans my boy, Earl, and I believe are in it with us who've got damn near as much to lose as we do."

"I thought you got us together to *fight* Mexicans," raised Monroe Fox, spitting tobacco juice into a glass mug.

"Apparently we got the same enemies as these particular ones."

"Revolutionaries," interjected the young Manuel Gonzaullas, summoning his own experiences with the Mexican army. "Pancho Villa's troops who are trying to overthrow President Carranza."

"Right as rain, son. Way they tell it, Carranza's got a cousin by the name of Esteban Cantú, currently the big man in Mexicali and Baja, who's sending these killers known as *esos Demonios* north of the border to build distribution channels for his opium."

Gonzaullas stiffened. "*Esos Demonios* . . . Yes, sir, I've run into them before."

"Keep talking, son," William Ray urged.

"For starters, Carranza and the politicians he controls arranged for the Federal Army to put Cantú in charge of Mexicali, Tijuana, and Baja in 1911. As governor, his first order of business was to construct a road through the mountains to join the desert with the coastal region."

"So what?" Monroe Fox challenged.

But it was Earl Strong who replied. "So he could have himself an easy route to bring opium into California."

"And that drug money," Gonzaullas picked up, "helped get Carranza elected president."

"I believe I am starting to see the connection here," said William Ray.

"To defend his distribution network, and make sure no one rose up against him, Carranza provided Cantú with this private army of *esos Demonios* gathered from the most murderous and trigger-happy soldiers he could find. So this expansion into Texas is all on Cantú, hiding behind the shield of protection offered by his cousin south of the border. But, make no mistake about it, this is about money and the power it can buy both of them."

"Son," said Frank Hamer, lurching to his feet, "I don't give a good goddamn what's it about. All I know is I don't want that shit ruining lives north of the border the way it has to the south."

The other men nodded in unison, as Monroe Fox spit more tobacco juice into his mug.

"Now," William Ray picked up, "whether it's Carranza, Cantú, or the devil himself behind these *esos Demonios* don't matter a lick. What matters is we got a meet set up with some Mexicans who got their own reasons for wanting them dealt with: three of the resistance's top commanding officers."

Bill McDonald arched his spine forward. "I got a proposal on that note."

"What's that, Ranger?" William Ray asked him.

"Let's send *esos Demonios* back to hell."

40

"These three commanding officers," Caitlin started, something clearly on her mind after Sandoval had stopped his tale suddenly. "Do you have any idea who—"

Caitlin stopped when she saw Sandoval's gaze suddenly shift about, the color starting to drain from his face.

"What's wrong, Mr. Sandoval?"

"My coffee . . ."

"Sir?"

"I asked one of my men to bring it to me out here," Sandoval told her. "He never showed up. I just realized. Must've lost myself in that story I was telling you." He tried to muster a smile and failed. "It could be nothing, I suppose."

From their vantage point, Caitlin couldn't see all the way into the lobby, and didn't feel comfortable leaving Sandoval alone to check it herself. She yanked her cell phone from her pocket.

"Company headquarters," Caitlin said, after a receptionist's greeting, "this is Caitlin Strong up here in Austin from San Antonio. I need a patch-through to the security detail handling the Four Seasons conference. . . . Called off? When? By— Never mind, sir. Just get every Ranger you can to the hotel right now. . . . Please do it, sir. I'll explain when they get here. And please alert Austin PD we have a situation."

"Ranger?" said Sandoval, watching as Caitlin ended the call but continued to hold the phone in her hand.

"Any of your men watching you now?"

"They should be."

"Signal them. Get them over."

Sandoval raised a hand slightly overhead and curled two fingers in toward him in subtle fashion, then repeated the motion when no one responded or moved into view. His eyes found Caitlin, as much angry as scared now, the reality of his son's murder returning like a sudden kick to the gut.

"We need to get out of here, Mr. Sandoval," she told him, rising as she slid the phone back into her pocket. "We need to get out of here now."

41

SCOTTSDALE, ARIZONA

Paz's vast bulk blocked the light streaming in from outside, his face shiny with sweat from the building Arizona heat.

"I didn't see you on the plane, Colonel," Cort Wesley said, as Dylan and Luke shrank away.

"Different airline, outlaw," Paz said. "I was already on the ground when you arrived. Did you know the navigation devices on the rental cars here speak Spanish too?"

"You came alone?"

Paz cast his gaze toward Dylan and Luke, both still wide-eyed over his mere presence. "Your boys are safe. Whoever did this is gone."

"That doesn't make them safe."

"I meant for the time being."

"Wait outside, boys," Cort Wesley said with his eyes fixed on Paz.

"But Dad—"

"I don't want to hear it, Dylan. Just wait outside." Cort Wesley hesitated long enough to hold his oldest son's stare, its intensity and harshness looking misplaced amid his soft features as his long hair was moved about by thin wisps that blew from an air-conditioning baffle.

"Come on," Dylan said to Luke, leading his brother out the door past Guillermo Paz, who had turned sideways to let them pass.

Paz cast his gaze toward the two dead bodies, regarding them cursorily without expression.

"First the boys' mother and now her sister," Cort Wesley continued. "Maura and Araceli Torres. That's what this must go back to. Something in the past with the Torres family, not Maura herself."

"How much do you know about that family's past, outlaw?"

"Not a damn thing, other than both Maura and Araceli were born on farms to Mexican migrant worker parents. I haven't got a clue as to where exactly and I'm not even sure their real name is Torres."

"But you're sure they were of Mexican descent."

"Maura was first generation American, Colonel. I don't think she told me any more about her family than that, and I never cared enough to ask."

Paz gazed toward the bodies again. "And the sister?"

"She hated my guts even before she blamed me for Maura's death, and fought me briefly for custody of the boys. After that, she really hated my guts."

Paz nodded, his gaze now moving outside, eyeing Dylan and Luke leaning against the rental car while seeing everything around them as well. "We don't have much time."

"Enough to search the house," Cort Wesley told him. "Enough to find something to tell us who Maura's parents really were."

With time at a premium, Cort Wesley called Dylan and Luke back inside to aid in the process. As was the case with the vast majority of area homes, there was no basement to search, so they concentrated their efforts on the first floor. Dylan and Luke focused on the sprawling kitchen that included two storage closets. Cort Wesley concentrated on the living room area, including drawers and storage units beneath the built-in birch-wood bookshelves. For his part, Paz handled the second-floor closets and the home office in a loft-style third story that had replaced the attic.

Cort Wesley was just about to call a halt to things, the police still not having been notified, when Luke appeared from the kitchen with a shoe box clutched in both hands.

"I think I found something," the boy said.

42

"Let's go, Mr. Sandoval," Caitlin said, rising stiffly having not yet decided in which direction to head.

She didn't fancy a shoot-out in the lobby with bullets flying everywhere, almost certain to find bystanders and hotel employees.

"This makes no sense," she heard Sandoval say. He was a man used to being hunted and had built his life around precautions designed to keep him a step ahead of those he targeted and who targeted him in return. Now, in the space of seventy-two hours, those layers of precaution could prevent neither the murder of his son nor an attack on his own life. "No sense at all."

Caitlin heard his words, spoken calmly with no trace of fear, only in a corner of her mind. The rest of it was racing to determine her next move, even as her hand strayed to the butt of her SIG Sauer and unclasped the holster.

"My enemies would kidnap my son, not . . ." Sandoval's voice dissolved into nothingness, sparing him completing the thought. "This is something different, Ranger, some*one* different."

They'd expect her to head through the lobby, bait their trap where they could hide in plain sight. But they couldn't hide in plain sight along the next most available escape route.

Via the pool. Where men wearing jackets meant to disguise their holsters would stand out.

"This way," Caitlin said to Sandoval, her own words an afterthought in contrast to her actions.

She had the SIG out now and held low, concealed just behind her hip. A flagstone path led along a circuitous route to the Four Seasons outdoor pool. From a distance it looked surprisingly crowded for such an early hour, the unseasonably warm temperatures likely to blame along with businessmen who must have brought their families along for an electronics convention that had filled every downtown hotel to capacity. Lots of splashing and happy yelps told her kids had laid claim to the pool, complicating the issue even further.

The gunmetal had warmed in her grasp, Caitlin noting the presence of several men in swimsuits seated on chaise lounges around the pool. Which should have been cause to relax, but wasn't.

Because whoever was behind this and the bodies in Willow Creek would never leave so obvious an escape route unguarded, meaning . . .

Meaning she'd played right into their hands, done exactly what was expected of her. Well, not quite. They'd expect her to relax now, to figure she was home free until they chose the right moment to yank weapons stuffed beneath their chaise lounge cushions and open fire. But how to tell bad guys from bystanders, how to know which to shoot with the fourteen bullets readied in her SIG?

Caitlin kept leading Sandoval on, not about to do anything to provoke the gunmen swathed in suntan lotion and lying atop towels emblazoned with the Four Seasons logo until it was on her terms.

Why do swimming pools have fire hoses?

A question she always asked herself when she spotted one curled up behind steel and glass, posed today with a different thought in mind. Caitlin veered right toward the building facade where the firebox was placed, Sandoval on her inside with the gun between them.

"Are you armed, sir?"

"No," Sandoval told her.

"I slipped my backup pistol into my jacket pocket. I want you to slip it out. Get ready to use it."

And Caitlin felt him do so as they reached the firebox, positioned in front of him as she twisted a valve to activate the water flow and yanked the canvas fire hose free of its spool. She spun, already twisting the nozzle to the "on" position, full out for maximum force.

The hose became a powerful, thrashing snake in her grasp, filled out to its full diameter in an instant as a torrent of spray exploded outward. Caitlin's first pass coated the pool-goers with a sizzling, needle-like blast powerful enough to topple a few unoccupied chaise lounges and spill some unaware guests from others to the chalkstone pavement below. She kept the spray going until three men in pool gear that looked all wrong on them fought back to their lounges after the spray had passed them.

Tucking the hose under her left arm, Caitlin raised the SIG in her right, blasting away at the men just as their hands cleared their lounge cushions with dark steel glinting in the sunlight. She fired with no discernible lag between righting her aim and pulling the trigger, the motions indistinguishable from each other. Caitlin wasn't sure how many bullets she'd fired or how many exactly had found their mark, only that all three men were down, two of them with multiple pools of blood spreading beneath them.

She heard the screaming as soon as she twisted the nozzle to the "off" position. Some of the guests clung to the meager cover provided by their lounges or toppled tables set up poolside. Others were fleeing, while still more were climbing from the pool in terror, children in tow.

Caitlin recorded all that in a kind of choppy, surreal motion even as her eyes stayed fixed on the three downed bodies shedding blood on the concrete with their weapons left baking in the sunlight.

"I'll take my second pistol back now, Mr. Sandoval," she said, still watching in case one of them stirred.

43

Mexico City

Ana Callas Guajardo entered the conference room moments before the meeting was about to start, the members of the Guajardo Enterprises board lapsing into stunned silence that left them fidgeting in their chairs.

"Please," she said, smiling at the five, who refused to meet her gaze, "don't stop on my account."

The message she'd received while meeting with her brother, Locaro, in Cereso Prison had advised her that this emergency meeting had been scheduled for the next day, called by Ricardo Salinas Velasco, who had run the company for her father and continued in that role under her. The top-floor conference room in which it was being held offered a panoramic view of Mexico City's gleaming Interlomas district through thermal windows that automatically darkened during those hours when the sun was at its strongest.

Velasco, a tall, dapper man with perfectly coiffed salt-and-pepper hair, rose stiffly from his chair, clearly unnerved by her unexpected presence. "This is a closed meeting, *señora*."

Guajardo took her customary seat at the far end of the table, well apart from the officers of her board of directors, who had clustered at the near end. The windows had darkened in synchronicity with the afternoon sun superheating the glass, casting her in a strange mix of light and shadow, her skin certain to maintain its powdery radiance with the sun's rays too muted to disturb it.

"I'm going to have to rethink my decision to keep you on in the wake of my father's regrettable accident," she told Velasco.

Velasco combed a hand through his hair, leaving stray strands clinging to his forehead. "Accident? Is that what you call it when his animal of a son threw him off a fourth-floor balcony?"

Guajardo rocked back in her chair casually, disappearing further into the shadows as she found the gaze of the one other woman in the room, Isabella Barrera. "I'm surprised to see you here siding against me, Isabella, given that I extended the due date for the balloon payment on your loan for a third time last month."

The others at the table shifted uneasily.

"Oh," Guajardo continued to Barrera, "I guess that hasn't come up in your discussions yet."

"This meeting," started Velasco, "was called to discuss the series of questionable decisions you have refused to explain despite the board's repeated requests. The purchase of this toy factory in Guadalajara, for one thing, a software company you've invested tens of millions in without a single product to show for it for another. The development of this game preserve in Los Mochis at a cost of tens of millions more, and your absurd overvaluing of that manufacturing plant in Germany previously owned by Siemens. These inexplicable investments, totaling nearly a billion dollars, have effectively liquidated the cash position of the company, forcing us to borrow well above prime to maintain our day-to-day operations around the world, even as our bond rating is threatened."

Velasco stopped, as if to await a response from Guajardo, growing antsy when none came.

"Perhaps you weren't listening to my charges, *señora*."

"Charges? I thought they were statements made in error."

"On the con—"

"I say that in full knowledge of the fact that you signed off on those investments, Ricardo," Guajardo interrupted.

Velasco's features flared. "I did nothing of the kind!"

Guajardo removed an envelope from her handbag, slid it the length of the table, and watched it stop just before it reached Velasco. He opened it and removed the four pages from inside.

"Perhaps your memory is fuzzy," Guajardo said as he unfolded the pages. "Let me refresh it. Time was of the essence to preserve that cash position you are suddenly so protective of, so I sent my assistant over while you were entertaining."

"No," Velasco said, regarding the pages now. "This was about the acquisition of that petroleum company the board voted to support. We had to act immediately. You required my signature on the board's behalf to move the deal forward."

"I'm afraid that's not my recollection at all, Ricardo." Guajardo nodded in feigned understanding. "Of course, you had done several lines of cocaine by the time my assistant arrived. She took some pictures of you with pen in hand, signing those pages now before you and not the ones pertaining to the petroleum deal. I have the pictures on my phone, if you'd like me to share them. Perhaps you should have reviewed the documents more closely before signing them."

Velasco slumped in his chair, the others sinking too, as if afraid Guajardo might be coming to them next.

"We are prepared to call an emergency shareholders meeting," Velasco managed, sounding far less threatening than he'd intended to.

"At which," Guajardo followed immediately, "I am prepared to motion for the ouster of the entire board."

"Including yourself?"

"I am preparing a new slate of officers that includes none of you. Of course, should I prevail, Isabella, your note would come due immediately. And, Germán," she said to another board member, "the cost of your private use of the company jets would need to be itemized and repaid. Alberto, meanwhile, would have no choice but to divest his holdings in the company, thereby revealing the fact that he has claimed three times their value in the numerous loans and mortgages he has taken out to support both his family and the family of his mistress."

Guajardo looked to the final man at the table, Carlos Bailleres, but stopped just short of addressing him, since he had been the one who'd tipped her off.

"So go ahead, Ricardo, call your shareholders meeting," Guajardo said, rising from her chair. "Try to oust me. It's time to clear the air, to reveal ourselves to those whose bidding this company does. I have nothing to hide. How about you?"

PART FIVE

They were the glory of the race of rangers;
Matchless with horse, rifle, song, support, courtship,
Large, turbulent, generous, handsome, proud, and affectionate
Bearded, sunburnt, dressed in the free costume of hunters.

Walt Whitman, "Song of Myself"

44

"A fire hose, Ranger?" D. W. Tepper asked, as if still having trouble believing it himself. "*A fire hose?*"

"I thought you'd be proud of me, Captain."

"And why'd you think that?"

"Because I didn't shoot anybody."

"You mean, at first."

"I got them to show themselves. Eliminate the kind of collateral damage you always accuse me of causing."

Tepper rolled his eyes and felt about his desk for his pack of Marlboro Reds. "Ranger, collateral damage follows you around like toilet paper on a boot. I'm starting to wonder if you can even breathe without somebody getting knocked over."

"Tell that to Sandoval, D.W."

Gazing out the window made Caitlin realize how late it was. The sun streamed gently through, the spring warmth at this time of day pleasant compared to the typically oppressive summer, when the sun's rays turned harsh and unforgiving. She had lost the whole day in Austin, facing a bevy of expressionless state and local investigators who claimed they were only interested in the facts, only to dispute them at every turn. Caitlin wondered if they'd been informed of a similar shoot-out that left bodies behind just a few nights earlier in Providence, a question that was answered when an ATF agent assigned to the regional office in Austin broached the subject.

"Do you consider yourself trigger-happy, Ranger Strong?"

"Not at all, sir," she'd told him.

He seemed miffed by the stridency of her response. "So we shouldn't be concerned by two nearly identical incidents in the course of a single week?"

"You should not, sir."

"And why's that, Ranger?"

"Because I didn't use a fire hose up in Providence. Are we done here yet?"

"I'd like to tell that to Sandoval," Captain Tepper was saying now. "I'd like to ask him some questions too. Except I can't, since he's dropped out of sight and is likely back underground in Mexico by now."

"A good thing, by all accounts."

Tepper formed a circle with his lips and made a whistling noise, like wind whipping through the trees. "Hear that?"

"What?"

"Hurricane Caitlin beginning to blow, the warning charts bursting beyond the red. Your friend Jones has been lighting up my phone all day, complaints coming from every agency in the alphabet about how the Rangers messed up this conference it took them three years, three decades, aw hell, maybe three centuries to set up. And, speaking of the alphabet, have you ever heard of PR?"

"What does that have to do with anything?"

Tepper rose and moved to the office's lone window, cracking it open to let the heat in as if tired of the stale recirculated air layered with nicotine. "How about politics? That mean anything to you?"

"Do I look like I'm running for office, D.W.?"

"Not what I'm talking about, Ranger."

"Then what *are* you talking about?"

Caitlin thought Tepper was looking at her as if she had just dropped in from another planet. "Know what my grandkids' favorite cartoon is right now? That one with the moose and squirrel from years ago—you know, Rocky and Bull-something. Part they like the most is when Sherman and Mr. Peabody take trips through time in the Way Back Machine. Ranger, I do honestly wish such a device existed so you could be transported someplace where you actually belong."

"What exactly did I say or do this time?"

Tepper continued to scorn her with his eyes, the ash growing on his cigarette. "You can't take a fire hose to a poolside full of people."

"You got a better idea under the circumstances?"

"Yes, I do. How about anything else? How about anything that doesn't bring complaints to Austin and beyond?"

"A man's life was at stake here, Captain."

"But tomorrow's papers won't write about that. Tomorrow's papers'll write about an out-of-control Texas Ranger spraying innocent folks with enough water to douse a brush fire."

"That's crazy."

"No, that's *politics*, Ranger. And if you haven't figured it out yet, you've gotta start asking yourself questions your granddad and even dad never had to worry about. I don't think old Earl ever used a cell phone or a computer in his life. To Jim Strong, a twenty-four-hour news cycle would've sounded like something you'd find on an energy-saver washing machine. But that's what you're up against now and it's just as dangerous as a gunman and can ambush you twice as quick. I seriously doubt even a fire hose would have much effect on the situation."

Caitlin wanted to shake her head, but didn't. "You really believe that, D.W.?"

"I believe I had to say it." Tepper plopped back into his chair and pressed out what was left of his cigarette, kicking ash up into the air. "Maybe you should tell me what you got planned next."

"How does finding the killers of those five kids in Willow Creek sound?"

"Not good enough. Gotta be more specific."

"Whoever did it used some kind of skinning knife on the victims. You need me to be more specific than that?"

Tepper leaned forward and fished a fresh Marlboro from the pack. "Remember when you tried hiding these things from me?"

"Doesn't seem like I got my point across."

"Because I could always get more. Walk outside the building, throw a stone into the air, and you're bound to hit some place that sells Marlboros." He hesitated, his eyes widening in the room's dull light, telling Caitlin he was about to make his point. "That's the way it is for you, Ranger. You can't walk from here to there without pissing somebody off or doing something I'm gonna regret later." Tepper made a show out of lighting the cigarette. "And I'm starting to figure you can't give that up any more than I can give these up. Love for you to tell me I'm wrong if you feel otherwise."

Caitlin reached across the desk, plucked the Marlboro from Tepper's mouth, and pressed it out in his ashtray. "I imagine a fire hose sprayed into you every time you lit up might force a change in thinking, D.W."

"There a point to that somewhere?"

"Only that there's a time and a place for everything."

Tepper was about to respond when his phone rang and he answered it without taking his gaze off Caitlin.

"Your point's been made, Ranger," he said, replacing the receiver. "Your friend Jones is on his way up."

45

SAN ANTONIO

"Where's Sandoval?" Jones demanded, standing at the top of the stairs where Caitlin had intercepted him.

"Who called off the Ranger detail?"

"Answer my question first."

"Safe."

"That's not a place, Ranger."

"It beats the ground. Your turn."

"Somebody with Homeland's security code made the call."

Jones rose to the top step, even with Caitlin now. He liked sticking out his chest and straightening his spine as gestures of intimidation.

"Where is Sandoval?"

Caitlin held her ground, hands planted firmly on her hips. "Seeing the sights."

"Bullshit."

"Call it whatever you want."

"What I want is for you to come clean and start helping me pull this op out of the shredder."

"Don't think I'm following, Jones."

He shook his head, all pretenses of calm and moderation gone from his demeanor. "You have any idea how much we've got riding on Sandoval?"

"What's going on here has nothing to do with that."

"I don't give a shit. He belongs to us. That means if you want to meet with him again you go through me."

Caitlin moved so close to him she could feel the heat of his breath. "The man just found out his son's dead. Does that mean anything to you?"

Jones stiffened, fighting against the step back he clearly wanted to take with Caitlin giving no ground. "This is business."

"I'd like to show you a picture of what was done to Sandoval's boy. You ever go hunting, Jones? Because hunters got this knife they use for skinning and field dressing an animal. Killing with a weapon like that isn't quick and tends to be pretty awful. How much more of a picture do I need to draw for you before you get your priorities straight?"

Jones's expression didn't change. "Drugs have evolved into a major national security issue, and Sandoval's our best chance to do something about that."

"I'll make sure I mention that next time I see him."

Jones's features flared, his eyes widening so much Caitlin could see the thin wavy veins that looked like spiderwebs stitched toward his pupils. "So you *do* know how to reach him."

"Never said I didn't. I'm investigating the murder of his son, Jones. That requires some follow-up."

"Is it true a few of the other victims belonged to two of the biggest names in the cartels?"

"And one belonged to a high school teacher dying of cancer. This isn't about drugs."

Her response left Jones shaking his head, his neck cracking audibly. "Wake up and smell the century, Ranger. You're not the sun, you're just one of a zillion planets spinning around it. I'm sorry we can't account for your sense of morality every time we run an operation, but unless you undergo a severe change in your view of the world, you'll end up finishing out your career visiting elementary schools."

"At least that would keep me out of trouble. Bet my captain has already considered the possibility."

Jones looked down at the SIG holstered on Caitlin's hip, its clasp noticeably unsnapped. "Gunfighter hero or not, even you can't bring the Old West back. That means going through channels and accepting the chain of command is there for a reason."

"I don't answer to you, Jones."

"I want Sandoval back on the grid, Ranger. I'll give you the rest of the day."

"I don't need it. The answer's no."

"It wasn't a question."

Captain Tepper stuck his head out the door running his eyes from one to the other. "I just got a noise complaint from the building across the block asking you two to tone it down."

Caitlin's phone rang, Cort Wesley's number lighting up in the Caller ID. "I'm just taking out the trash," she said with her eyes on Jones. "Can I call you back?"

"Don't bother," Cort Wesley said. "You know the Tuscany Centre Office Building?"

"Sure."

"Then you better get over here fast, to the office of Regent Real Estate Partners, before I shoot somebody."

46

SAN ANTONIO

Cort Wesley snapped his phone closed, eyeing Dylan and Luke fidgeting in their reception room chairs, unread opened magazines fluttering on their laps with the batteries on their iPhones both drained. The long afternoon had taken its toll, even before the sun began to set outside.

"I told you I should've bought that case that's actually a backup battery," Dylan groused.

"Put a sock in it, will ya?"

"I'm just saying, that's all."

"Not today."

"Wouldn't have happened if I hadn't used up my battery finding that farm for you, Dad," Luke sighed.

"So now it's my fault. . . ."

Luke rolled his eyes.

"What?"

The boy blew the wavy hair from his face, just like his brother. When had it gotten so long? "I didn't say anything."

"When did you become such a wiseass, son?"

"While you were in that Mexican prison last year."

That got the receptionist's attention and Cort Wesley felt his skin grow even damper with sweat in spite of the air-conditioning, as he made his way back to her desk.

"Could you please tell Mr. Tawls I'm a bit rushed for time here?"

The receptionist regarded him with a scowl. "Mr. Tawls is still in a meeting. And I can't promise you he'll—"

Cort Wesley backed off, palms raised in conciliatory fashion before him until they dropped to his sides and clenched into fists. "Fine, that's fine. But you can tell him there's a Texas Ranger on the way who's not nearly as patient as I am."

She nodded dismissively, then turned her gaze on Dylan, who was only a few years younger than she. "Can I ask you a question? Haven't I seen that boy on television? Doesn't he play in a rock band or something?"

"Would getting you his autograph get me in to see Regent Tawls any faster?"

The shoe box Luke had found in their murdered aunt's kitchen drawer was full of old photographs, many with the colors washed out and edges peeling back. The pictures were mostly of sisters Maura and Araceli Torres as babies and toddlers. A few showed them as young girls and some of the shots included the girls' parents, Carmen and Mateo if Cort Wesley's memory served him right. The snapshots had been developed back in the seventies, when photo processors still used a date stamp on each shot.

The shots that interested Cort Wesley the most pictured the girls on the migrant farm where Maura may have been born. This judging by the fact that some of the shots of her at six or so months old, dated 1973, were framed against the background of what looked like corn stalks in some and dilapidated shacks typical of migrant housing in others.

Assuming Maura and Araceli's murders could be traced to the past, the original ties and roots might lie somewhere in this shoe box, starting with this farm and others on which their parents worked. But how to determine the exact locations from pictures as much as forty years old escaped him. There were no distinct clues in the form of a numbered address or convenient shot of the road running outside the property. He figured he could narrow down the list of possible farms to ten thousand maybe—not much of a help.

"I can help," Cort Wesley heard Luke say.

"Huh?"

"You said something about help."

"I did?" Cort Wesley said back, looking around to see if Leroy Epps might be somewhere in their midst.

"Uh-huh," his fourteen-year-old son nodded. "Let me see those pictures, Dad. See, I've got an app for that."

47

SAN ANTONIO

Gazing at Luke now while he waited for Caitlin to arrive, Cort Wesley remembered how the boy had used his iPhone to take pictures of the pictures he then pasted into some Google application. Then he started filling in a bunch of blanks with what Cort Wesley figured must be answers to questions.

They were in the airport waiting for their flight home, the police certain to be scouring Araceli Ramirez's house and property by now, when an e-mail arrived from Google in Luke's in-box just before his battery died. Fortunately, he'd had the search request forwarded to Dylan's phone as well.

"It's an address near Devine, Dad. Doesn't look much like a farm, though."

Luke held the phone up for Cort Wesley to see, but he needn't have bothered.

"We'll check it out ourselves when we get home."

The farm in question turned out to be located in Medina County outside of Devine, little more than a scorched cornfield just off Route 90. Amid the now-dead acreage, Cort Wesley spotted foundations and building slabs that had never been completed, taking strange comfort in the fact that he wasn't the only one experiencing financial hard times. Besides that, the sole hint the property had any life at all was a FOR SALE sign with the phone number of Regent Partners.

"Guess we're headed back to the city, boys," Cort Wesley said, flipping open his cell phone to find out where the company was located.

The afternoon sun was clinging to the sky by the time they had pulled into the parking lot near the Stone Oak Parkway just off Loop 1604, where Regent Real Estate Partners occupied half the third floor of the Tuscany Centre. The building had been finished in modern elegance with a circular extended entryway that spiraled up all three floors, having more the look of an antebellum Southern mansion than a Texas office suite. It was located within easy view of both Frost and IBC bank branches, filling Cort Wesley with fresh concern over the disaster of a meeting he'd had with Royce Clavins at Wells Fargo the day before.

He hadn't called for an appointment because he knew he wouldn't get one. Cort Wesley was used to having people see him when he wanted them to, letting them or their gatekeepers know there was really no choice to be had.

Amazing what you could accomplish with the right look, as effective a weapon as a bullet.

The difference today was that he had his boys with him and somehow he couldn't be that person, the one who breathed intimidation and could chew through people like they were gum. But he'd had enough of waiting to see Regent Tawls to forget they were there. Focused on the inner office he intended to storm straight into, he stopped as Caitlin stepped through the entry door and let it close behind her.

"I didn't miss anything, did I?"

48

Locaro hadn't killed in a very long time, unless his time spent in Cereso Prison was included in the count. It didn't seem fair to do that, given that with few exceptions he'd had little choice and had extracted no pleasure at all from the process. And if he hadn't enjoyed it, how could it count?

Part of the thrill of killing came from the possibility of the same happening to him. That's why Locaro enjoyed battle so much, charging into opponents with gun firing even as their rifles clacked off rounds that whisked so close to his head he could feel the heat. He loved to look death in the face so he could spit in its eye. Beating it back meant beating God, and beating God made him . . .

What did it make him exactly?

Locaro's thinking on the subject pretty much ended there. He thought God in particular and religion in general was a crock of shit.

Look at me, I believe in nothing, and no one can kill me. If there is a God, how could I exist?

A fair question and one he had come to ruminate over for long stretches while in solitary in Cereso. Solitary deprived the senses of natural light, the passage of time, and normal cycles. It had left Locaro with no company other than his thoughts, filling him with a vast appreciation for life led without limits and rules. He was not a great thinker, was barely literate in fact, but thoughts and words were nothing compared to deeds, and Locaro preferred to measure himself by their sum as calculated by the bodies he left behind.

He'd served his sister well in her battles to consolidate enough of Mexico's warring drug cartels to keep them, at the very least, from undermining her efforts or threatening her subtle hold on power. With the possible exception of Colonel Guillermo Paz, the mythical *Angel de la*

Guarda of the peasants, no one was more feared by the cartels than Locaro.

The thought brought a smile to his lips as he approached the cantina located in a kind of netherworld, perched as it was between the old and new cities of Juárez, known to be a hangout for the soldiers of the cartel based there. The cantina boasted no sign advertising its presence, its sole patrons drawn from those who already knew of its existence.

Locaro hitched up his safari jacket to better hide the sheathed machete hidden beneath it. The blade was old, slightly rusted, and tarnished, but honed to a razor's edge. He preferred the machete because he'd killed with it before, the first time as a mere boy. And Locaro was a firm believer in the spirit of such weapons; like a man, one that has already killed took to killing again much easier.

And this machete had killed very often indeed.

Locaro didn't believe it was imagination alone that made it feel lighter to the touch, seeming to thirst to be drawn from its sheath and whipped around through the air.

He entered the bar as if he were air, drawing no initial attention at all. Locaro liked bars because they were dark, and in dark places people did not notice the oddities of his appearance as quickly, did not notice his powerfully squat build and his face, which one Mexican cop had once mused looked like a rotten tomato field.

Locaro had hacked all four of the cop's limbs off with this very machete while he was still alive.

He stopped in the center of the bar, counting the number of patrons as the sour, rancid smell rising off him finally drew their attention. Many looked toward his face, turning away at the sight of the scaly lumps of flesh dotting his cheeks, oozing the viscous pus that was the source of the stench, not wanting to risk meeting his eyes. Locaro made no move from there until the first pair approached him smiling, their hands on the butts of their holstered revolvers. Their gait slightly drunken, their eyes full of disinterest and breath reeking of cheap tequila.

"*Buenos días, señor.*"

Locaro said nothing.

"*¿Quién es usted?*"

He just stood there.

"*¿Qué quieres?*"

Locaro shifted his shoulders to bring the machete within easy drawing range.

"*¿Cual es el problema?*"

Locaro yawned.

"What's the problem, *señor*?" the second man asked him in English this time. "Why you smell like my ass?"

Locaro was looking at both of them when the other man went for his gun.

Had anyone been outside in the street, they would've heard a single gunshot followed by a scream shrill enough to bubble eardrums.

But it was nothing compared to the ones that followed, intermixed with gunshots whose muzzle flashes lit up the windows like strobe lights, and the screams lingering well after the echoes of the rounds had ceased. In the naked light of the bar marred by cigarette smoke and thick, putrid air, glints of steel were caught through those same windows, accompanied by a strange crunching that sounded like stone being cut by a jigsaw.

When he was finished, Locaro exited still holding the machete, now covered in so much blood it looked as if someone had tossed a red blanket over him. He continued on down the street, when the cell phone his sister had given him rang. He lifted it from his pocket in a blood-soaked hand and flipped it open.

"How are you, *mi hermano*?" Ana Callas Guajardo asked him.

"Readjusting to life on the outside, *mi hermanita*," Locaro replied, his breathing and pulse rate having already returned to normal.

"Can your adjustment be completed by tomorrow night?"

Locaro wiped the blood from his forehead with the already speckled sleeve of his safari jacket and gazed back at the cantina, the door flapping against its frame now.

"I believe so."

"Then have your men ready, *mi hermano*. It is time for the Torres children to die."

49

SAN ANTONIO

"Miss anything?" Cort Wesley asked, as Luke rushed to hug Caitlin, followed in more leisurely form by Dylan. "Do you ever?"

"From time to time." Caitlin could feel the receptionist's eyes glued to her. "I see you still haven't been granted an audience."

"And I'm about to start tearing down the walls."

She separated herself from Dylan and started toward the receptionist's desk. "I got this, Cort Wesley."

But he fell in behind her anyway, the young woman following her approach every step of the way.

"Ma'am," Caitlin said, "I believe you know who I am."

"Are you allowed to give autographs?"

"I guess so, though I don't know why'd you want one from a simple law enforcement agent like myself. Right now, I'd like you to buzz Mr. Tawls and tell him there's a Texas Ranger here to see him."

The receptionist had the phone at her ear. "There's someone here to see you, Mr. Tawls. . . . No, someone else. A Texas Ranger." Eyes glued to Caitlin now. "Caitlin Strong." She hung up the phone. "You can go right in."

And Cort Wesley followed her through the door without asking if it was okay.

* * *

Caitlin smelled the cologne before she even glimpsed the big man swathed in it. Regent Tawls had played on the defensive line in college back in the sixties and had gone soft in all the wrong places. His big-boned frame now sagged in the middle, his considerable stomach pushing the boundaries of his suit coat and shirt. A crackling sounded as he pushed himself from the chair, the seat of his pants peeling up off the upholstery, to which perspiration had glued it. His face was plump and round, looking like an overgrown baby's. Drawing closer, Caitlin saw it was shiny with sweat that similarly blotched his shirt in discolored patches.

Tawls wiped his hand with a handkerchief and extended it across his desk, eyeing Cort Wesley with no small degree of trepidation. "A pleasure, Ranger, a pleasure to meet a true hero of the state of Texas."

Caitlin took his hand, finding it still damp and wondering what it had felt like before Tawls had dried it. "Ranger Caitlin Strong, sir, and this is Cort Wesley Masters. Mr. Masters has uncovered some information pertaining to a current investigation I'd like to ask you about."

"I'm all ears, Ranger," Tawls said, forcing an overly bright smile born of some extra-strength teeth whitener.

"Sir, your family once owned a farm just outside of Devine off Route Ninety, a property you are currently attempting to sell through your real estate interest. I believe you took over its management sometime in the early to mid seventies. Is that correct?"

The moment froze between them, the smile slipping off Tawls's face and leaving Cort Wesley to wonder exactly how Caitlin had come by that information.

"Yes or no, Mr. Tawls?"

"Yes, Ranger, yes." He forced another smile. "Some of the best feed corn you ever saw."

"But that's not all you grew, sir, was it?"

"Ma'am?"

"I believe you had occasion to meet my father, who was also a Ranger, sometime around nineteen-eighty. Jim Strong."

Tawls stood there, his breathing so loud it sounded like a vacuum cleaner powering down. His eyes suddenly looked small, twin holes drilled in his flabby face. The smell of sickeningly sweet aftershave was overpowering this close to him and Caitlin caught just a whiff of the sour odor he'd doused himself to hide.

"I was asking you about your past encounters with my father, Mr. Tawls. I believe they involved you reserving a substantial stretch of your acreage in Medina County for marijuana growing."

Cort Wesley felt the floor go wobbly beneath his feet.

"I've heard it told you were one of the most prominent marijuana growers of your time. My father wasn't able to do much about it, since the local law and political types earned plenty off your profits. But he did investigate that suspicious fire that burned almost all your bud crops to the ground. Don't believe his hard work ever did yield the perpetrator, though, did it?"

Tawls's only response was even louder breathing that had turned wet and wheezy.

"Mr. Tawls?"

"No, Ranger, it didn't."

"A damn shame." Caitlin aimed her gaze back at Cort Wesley. "Now, Mr. Masters here has some photographs that may help us finally nail the man who cost you all those millions in lost profits."

It took a few moments for Tawls to realize Caitlin was waiting for a response.

"I sold my farm a decade later and went into real estate. Since then, the property's gone through a bunch of owners who never did much besides flip it, the most recent of which gave me the listing a few months back. He didn't even know I was the original owner," Tawls added, shaking his head.

"Cort Wesley," Caitlin prompted.

He laid a series of photographs down on Regent Tawls's desk blotter picturing what could only be Maura Torres as a baby, toddler, and young girl in the company of her own parents and sister in photographs dated between 1973 and 1980.

"Do you recognize these people, Mr. Tawls?" Caitlin asked him, hesitating just long enough before continuing. "Please, take your time before you answer."

"Yes," Tawls said, after putting on a pair of reading glasses and studying the pictures closer.

"Do you know who they are?"

Tawls eased a few of the pictures back toward her, leaving damp fingerprint stains atop the likenesses. "I believe the man's name was Mateo Torres. His wife was named Carmen. I don't recall either of the children's names."

"Could the baby have been named Maura?"

Tawls shrugged. "Could have been anything. I don't believe we were ever introduced."

Caitlin ignored the snippiness of his remark. "But your memory is strong otherwise. I think that's because you have a reason to remember Mateo Torres, don't you?"

Tawls drummed the desk with his fingers before answering. "Is this off the record?"

"We're not investigating you here, sir. At least, not yet."

He swallowed hard, having trouble meeting Caitlin's gaze now. "Mateo Torres and his business partner stole from me, Ranger."

"You report that to my father?"

"I couldn't, on account of what it was he stole."

"Marijuana," Caitlin figured. "How much marijuana, Mr. Tawls?"

"A whole truck full. They stole the truck too."

"And this would have been . . ."

"Nineteen-eighty, just like you said. Torres's daughter you're so interested in must have been about seven at the time."

Caitlin stole a quick glance at Cort Wesley. "What about this business partner of his?"

Tawls searched out another picture with his eyes and pointed at it. "That's him there standing with Torres, his little girl about the exact same age as . . . Maura, was it?"

"You recall the other man's name, sir?"

"Cantú," Tawls told her, "Enrique Cantú."

PART SIX

Night and day will the ranger trail his prey, through rain and shine, until the criminal is located and put behind bars where he will not molest or disturb peaceful citizens. For bravery, endurance and steadfast adherence to duty at all times, the ranger is in a class by himself. Such was the old ranger, and such is the ranger of today.

Ranger James Gillet,
Western Horseman Magazine (1881)

50

"I know what you're thinking, Ranger," D. W. Tepper said from the other side of the Denny's booth where he'd met Caitlin for breakfast the next morning. The restaurant was situated just short of the River Walk and still offered the best breakfast in town.

"What am I thinking, Captain?"

"That this Enrique Cantú was somehow related to Esteban Cantú, the provincial governor who started the whole damn Mexican drug smuggling business by bringing opium into California through Baja."

"Man gets celebrated as a hero for all these public works projects he undertook to build the roads that made life a snap for his smugglers. But I don't think that at all, sir . . ."

"That's a relief."

". . . I know it. I did some research to confirm my suspicions, D.W. Turns out Enrique Cantú, business partner of Mateo Torres, was Esteban Cantú's grandson. That means we now have something directly linking Maura Torres's father to the drug trade."

Tepper settled back in the booth and stretched his arms out to either side, forgetting about his eggs. "What else?"

"D.W.?"

"You got that look that says you got something you're not ready to tell me. You mind if I take a guess?"

"I'd love to hear it."

"We got five dead kids in what's left of Willow Creek at the same time Mexican hitters go after Dylan and Luke Torres."

Caitlin took a bite of her bagel, saying nothing.

"I knew it," Tepper followed.

"Seems about as obvious as it gets, Captain," she said between chews.

"The connection lying somewhere on Regent Tawls's marijuana farm back around nineteen-eighty." Tepper thought for a moment. "You said Tawls told you Enrique Cantú and Mateo Torres stole a truckload of marijuana from him?"

"They stole the truck too," Caitlin nodded. "It was my dad's case, though it seems Tawls wasn't very cooperative."

"You figure maybe he's more involved in all this than you think?"

"He's no killer," Caitlin said, shaking her head. "Tawls's receptionist asked for my autograph."

"You give her one?"

Caitlin nodded. "On the way out."

Tepper rubbed his forehead, leaving a red welt that began to fade as quickly as it came. "Only time I ever did that was in an elementary school they sent me to speak at with your granddad. He had a line of kids out into the playground waiting for him to sign while I got ten maybe and then went to take a piss. I came out of the bathroom, went to lunch, and Earl was still signing when I got back."

"He never liked to disappoint people."

Tepper hesitated, holding his next forkful of eggs suspended between the plate and his mouth. "What else is on your mind, Ranger?"

"Just this Torres and Cantú stuff."

"You wanna be more specific?"

"I'm still trying to figure things out, but I believe it all goes back to nineteen-nineteen again. . . ."

51

Strong's Raiders met their Mexican counterparts for the first time in mid-May, crossing the Rio Grande in a trio of Ford trucks over the Laredo International Foot Bridge into Nuevo Laredo. The bridge had been destroyed by a flood in 1905 and had taken six months to repair. Lava, the Mexican soldier William Ray and Earl Strong had first met in Willow Creek, had set up the meeting, the subject being how to take down *esos Demonios*, Esteban Cantú's soldiers currently carving a bloody distribution network across the border into Texas.

Lava had chosen a cantina featuring electricity for the meeting, the officers and soldiers inside surprised when a twelve-year-old boy known for giving free shoe shines entered instead.

"I have a message for you," the boy said to Lava.

The message directed Lava to bring the three generals, and only the three generals, to a spot on the shores of the Rio Grande protected by the Chihuahuan Desert to the west and the Sierra Madre Oriental mountains to the east.

"I don't like surprises," William Ray said in English and then repeated it in Spanish for Lava and the generals once they arrived at the rendezvous. "And the number of horses I saw tied up around town told me a lot more than just the four of you might be attending our meeting."

His face was lit by the crackling flames of a fire that sent embers twisting away into the breeze lifting off the river. His skin shone thanks to the desert heat even at night this time of year.

"It's mutual interests that have brought us here," William Ray continued, "and it's mutual interests that we're gonna keep in mind ahead of everything else. You need to be rid of *esos Demonios* for your side to bring down Carranza, and we need to be rid of them to keep the shit they carry from poisoning the state of Texas. Question being how best to go about that."

"*Señor*," started Lava, serving as spokesman for the generals, "it is our feeling we cannot defeat *esos Demonios* here in Mexico. They have too much power and inspire too much fear in the people. We are worried our soldiers would run from them at the first sign of battle."

"Well, I thank you for your honesty," said William Ray, "and truth be told, I was thinking the same thing, though for a different reason entirely. We don't want to fight these demon soldiers on their own turf. Question being how do we lure them into a trap we can spring?"

"I believe we're going about this in the wrong way," said Frank Hamer, no longer able to restrain himself. "All tactful and shit."

"What would you recommend, Frank?" William Ray asked him.

"For starters, I'd take the fight directly to Cantú. Pay him a visit up close and personal like."

"Lava, what you have to say on that front?"

"*Señores*, Cantú has many enemies. He is very cautious in his movements and very well protected when he goes anywhere. No one has been able to get to him."

"Texas Rangers ain't tried yet," Frank Hamer reminded, suppressing a laugh.

"I don't believe that's a bad idea, just not on its own," noted Manuel Gonzaullas.

"What's that mean exactly, son?" William Ray asked him.

"Cantú is not a man likely to respond simply to threats."

"Knowing Ranger Hamer here, simple isn't in his vocabulary, and I imagine he's got something bigger than what you'd think of as a threat in mind."

"I do indeed, starting with the barrel of my old Colt."

Gonzaullas avoided Hamer's gaze in responding. "Cantú must have known this battle was coming when he expanded his business east into Texas. That means he's prepared for whatever we throw at him."

"That is true," Lava echoed, as Pancho Villa's three top generals who'd accompanied him nodded in virtual unison. "We would be better served focusing our attention elsewhere."

"I believe there's a way to make our point to Cantú so he gets the message we want sent," Bill McDonald suggested, swallowing air to stifle a fresh coughing fit. "That being we keep our focus trained on these *esos Demonios* of his. We've all had our share of scrapes with Mexicans of this kind, and these might be worse or better depending on your thinking, but they're Mexicans all the same. We know how they think and how they'll respond."

"Captain McDonald," began Earl Strong, "with all due respect, sir, you didn't see what they did in Willow Creek. I'd argue that this is a new kind of enemy we're up against, chosen specifically for their ruthlessness and desire to kill pretty much everything in their way. Just the way it's gotta be for Cantú to make the inroads he needs in Texas for his smuggling operation. Makes it all the more important we stop him here and now. Be a lot harder to do that once he's got things built up on our border with Mexico the way he did it in Baja."

"Now you're talking, son," said Frank Hamer.

"*Señores*," began Lava, as the Mexican generals shook their heads vociferously, "taking *esos Demonios* on in Mexico would be suicide, even for the likes of you."

"Who said anything about taking them on in Mexico?" raised William Ray Strong.

52

San Antonio

"The Battle of Juárez," Tepper realized.

"Happened just the next month, in June of nineteen-nineteen," Caitlin told him.

"What you're saying doesn't exactly match how history ended up weighing in on the subject, Ranger."

"Truth be told, my grandfather never said much about things beyond that. It was one of the last tales he ever told me, like he was saving it for the end. Turned out to be the one he never got to finish," Caitlin said, suddenly sad over the memories stirred of her legendary grandfather, making her miss the man who'd practically raised her even more.

Tepper ran a finger in and out of the furrows lining his face before responding. "You ever figure Earl never finished the story 'cause he had reason not to?"

"I suppose that's why I never looked for all the answers before."

"But here you are doing that now."

"Something connects the attempts on Dylan and Luke Torres's lives with the other murdered children in Willow Creek. And that something is somehow related to Mateo Torres and Enrique Cantú stealing marijuana from Regent Tawls's farm back in my father's day. I find out how all that fits together and I can get to the bottom of who's behind the killings."

"Same party is likely to try for Cort Wesley's boys again, Ranger."

"I've thought about that too."

"Not even your friend Paz can keep them safe forever," Tepper said, a degree of both caution and harshness framing his words.

"Who said anything about Paz?"

"You didn't have to. Man walks on water now, thanks to your friend Jones . . ."

"*My* friend?"

". . . like he's been given a damn free pass for every bad thing he's done. In my mind, a man saying he's sorry for shooting you in the gut don't make it hurt any less."

Tepper shook his head and looked for a fresh cigarette to light, as Caitlin's cell phone rang and she excused herself to answer it.

"Regent Tawls calling, Ranger," said the familiar gravelly voice. "I believe there's something I left out of our conversation yesterday."

53

Ana Callas Guajardo always took a security detail with her when she traveled to visit her business interests in Guadalajara. Two cars, one leading and one trailing the bulletproof Lincoln Town Car in which she rode. Kidnapping was big business in this part of the country and Guajardo knew the power she held didn't render her immune to that.

For any number of years Guadalajara had escaped the drug violence that plagued the rest of Mexico. That was, until relatively recently, when the Zetas, a cartel composed primarily of former soldiers from Mexico's Special Forces, saw an opportunity to take over the city's methamphetamine trade lurking beneath the surface of what many called the Silicon Valley of Mexico.

With good reason. Sitting on a mile-high plateau in western Mexico, Guadalajara had sprouted into the country's main producer of software and electronic and digital components. Guajardo knew that telecom and computer equipment manufactured in the city accounted for over a quarter of Mexico's exports in electronics and that companies like General Electric, IBM, Intel, Hitachi, Hewlett-Packard, Flextronics, and Oracle had set up shop there. All welcomed by Guajardo in no small part because they enabled her to better keep her own modest software company under the radar.

She'd named the company Zuñiga after Tlajomulco de Zuñiga, the sprawling slum-riddled county where both her parents had been born. Zuñiga was nestled amid other companies and buildings just like it in a software park located on the western edge of the city. Guajardo's convoy passed through security en route to an underground garage where more armed security personnel would be waiting.

A captain in the *federal* police saluted her stiffly as she emerged from the rear of the Town Car and escorted her into an elevator with two more of his men and three of hers. They rode not up, but down, to a secret, secured floor of the Zuñiga building where two-dozen software engineers toiled without distraction or danger, including the two Americans who'd been supervising the final stages of this part of her operation for over a year now.

The elevator doors opened and Guajardo felt immediately chilled by a blast of reprocessed air. Strange how, as she grew older, she found herself colder more times than she could ever remember. A priest whose church she'd leveled because it sat on land too valuable to leave to God had once told her the depths of her soul were a frozen wasteland. In moments like these, when she felt so chilled, Guajardo couldn't help but take him literally.

The lighting down here was dimmer than above, more ambient and less harsh, as she let the entourage lead her along the hallway to an open door at the end.

"No way, dude," she heard emanating loudly from within, "Chamberlain's got Russell beat six ways to Sunday."

"Chamberlain?" a second voice came back.

"Wilt the Stilt, man, Wilt the Stilt. Scored a freaking hundred points in a single game."

"Oh yeah. But how many championships did he win? No, dude, Bill Russell is the man!" A brief pause followed as Guajardo neared the door, then, "He shoots and . . . *scores*! Game over, man, game over!"

The two young men high-fived each other and then quickly stiffened, spotting Guajardo standing in the doorway, her guards stationed just out of sight beyond.

"And what about the game I hired you to play?" she asked them.

54

One of the young men switched off the 3-D video game as Ana entered the room and closed the door behind her. In the brief glimpse Guajardo had caught, the basketball players had seemed amazingly lifelike, right down to the sweat dripping off their bodies to disappear into some virtual ether. She actually found herself looking at the top of the conference table to see if the basketball was still resting there.

"You developed this," she said to the two young men. They'd turned the room's lights down to better enjoy the video game, an ashtray on the table lined with the refuse of marijuana cigarettes rolled in cigar paper. A sweet grape smell hung in the air, mixing with stale cannabis yet to be washed out by the air-conditioning that hummed softly in the background.

"Sure did," said the taller, bushy-haired one, whose eyes were glassy over the grin that looked painted onto his face. John. Last name not important.

"In our spare time," added the squatter one, whose khaki pants fit him too snugly. David. Last name not important.

"Spare time," Guajardo noted, not bothering to hide her displeasure. "I'm surprised you had any, given the responsibility with which you've been entrusted."

"That's because we're the best," John said, rising to pull a chair back for Guajardo. "Let us demonstrate, my lady."

She took her seat, holding his gaze sternly the whole time. The other one, David, took a fancy remote control device in hand and began working the buttons. Suddenly, a three-dimensional map of the United States appeared before her, the state of Texas even with Guajardo's face until the map began to rotate.

"First subject of the day," John said. "Population distribution."

Working in tandem with him, David pressed some keys on the remote and various shades of red, ranging from pink to rose to scarlet, appeared in varying swatches across the map. The largest centers of population were the darkest.

"Here's a simple fact, my lady," John continued. "Eighty-two percent of the population of the United States is concentrated in roughly ten percent of the country's landmass. You can see why that's important to our plan."

"I believe I do."

"Second subject of the day: what this means exactly. Let's look at things in terms of sports. Baseballs, basketballs, and footballs."

"Because we'd already created the icons," David chimed in, looking up from the remote. "For those games we've been working on."

"In your spare time," Guajardo echoed.

"Right. Sure."

"Basketballs first, fifty-eight hundred of them."

With that, tiny basketballs appeared all over the moving map. Tightly clustered and even layered over one another in the more populated areas, but with space to spare in the light-colored pink places.

"Next," Jon picked up, "footballs. There are about ten thousand of those."

The footballs flashed on the map as green oblong shapes with almost identical distribution density as the basketballs.

"And now baseballs, numbering just over a hundred thousand."

The baseballs appeared as mere pinpricks across the map.

"For our purposes, let's eliminate the baseballs," John told Guajardo. "That leaves us with only the footballs and the basketballs. Focus on that ten percent area accounting for eighty-two percent of the total population, and this is what you're left with."

"How many basketballs?" Guajardo said, rising to better acquaint herself with the three-dimensional map.

"Roughly two thousand."

"And footballs?"

"Thirty-five hundred would be a fair estimation."

"And if you reduced the number of basketballs to fifteen hundred or so?"

David worked the keys on the remote, doing just that. Guajardo watched basketballs drop off the projected map into nothingness.

"Seventy-five percent of the population would still be affected," John told her.

"But the remaining twenty-five wouldn't be far behind," David added. "Thanks to the ripple effect. We've done a lot of research into the ripple effect."

"Show me," Guajardo ordered. "Show me this ripple effect."

John took a hefty swallow before nodding to David, who returned the map to its original scope with the total number of all three balls displayed at once. The result was a congestion of colors and shapes that made for a vast rainbow-like blotch.

"Zero hour," John said.

And a few keystrokes from David later, a large percentage of the footballs, baseballs, and basketballs concentrated in the most populated areas of the United States vanished.

"Zero hour plus one day."

Another hefty portion of balls dropped off the map, spreading beyond the brightest population grids.

"Zero hour plus three days."

And with that the rest of the balls in those areas were gone, leaving only those concentrated in rural and less populated areas in place.

"Zero hour plus four days."

The balls were all but gone.

"Can't be a hundred percent sure of the time frame," John reported, "but this is well within the margin of error, my lady."

Ana Callas Guajardo found herself staring at the map spinning slowly over the table before her, all but a very, very few of the balls that had formed all that clutter missing.

"Game over," from John, grinning now.

"Yeah," David echoed, summoning the best Spanish he could muster with a slight giggle. "*Se acabó el juego.*"

55

"You're kidding, right?" Cort Wesley said to Dylan.

"It's the district championship, Dad. I'm captain of the goddamn team."

"I believe I already know that, and I'd appreciate you not taking that tone with me."

The last of the afternoon sun was fading from the sky, the first signs of dusk appearing to appear in the form of shadows stretching over the lawn and beginning a steady climb up the porch steps. Cort Wesley hadn't switched the porch light on yet, making Dylan's face look darker and older. Too much like his mother, especially today. Last thing Cort Wesley needed.

He realized he was blocking what little light there was and stepped aside to little effect.

"What tone?" his oldest son asked him.

"There you go again."

"What?" Dylan snapped, exasperated.

"Rolling your eyes."

"I didn't roll my eyes."

"Yes, you did."

Dylan blew the long hair from his face. The fading light seemed to steal the whites from his deep-set eyes, narrowed harshly now on Cort Wesley.

"You see me do that too?" he asked, before storming into the house, stopping on the lip of the doorjamb. "I just wanna play in the championship game. I just want a normal life. Is that too much to ask?"

"Right now it is, yeah."

He slammed the door behind him, and Cort Wesley turned around to find Caitlin Strong standing there on the grass just short of the porch.

"Thought I heard you," he managed.

"I tried to be quiet."

"I'm surprised you didn't chirp up to take Dylan's side. Good thing he didn't notice you, or I'd have someone else to be pissed at."

Caitlin started up the stairs, drawing even with the edge of the shadows. "Cort Wesley—"

"I don't want to hear it, Ranger."

"You don't even know what I was going to say."

"Dylan wants to play in the lacrosse game at St. Anthony's tomorrow night."

"I know."

"You *knew*?"

"That there was a championship game at the school tomorrow night." She reached him on the porch and laid her hand on a shoulder that felt like banded steel, hot to the touch, as if it had been baking in the sun. "But that's not what I'm here about."

"Like you need a reason to come by?" he asked shaking his head, his emotions twisted like cheesecloth.

"I had another talk with Regent Tawls, Cort Wesley."

56

SAN ANTONIO

"What can I do for you, Mr. Tawls?" Caitlin had asked earlier in a day spent mostly following up on leads buried long in the past. She'd put her phone on speaker and laid it between her and D. W. Tepper atop the Denny's booth.

"Well, something occurred to me after you left. You were asking about those two little girls in the pictures you showed me, one of which was Maura Torres."

"What about them, sir?"

"I believe I may have left you with the impression that they were born on my farm."

"Not really," Caitlin told him, realizing her oversight. "I never asked the question directly."

"Well, the answer would've been that the Torreses and Cantús showed up for the season with those infants in tow back in the late spring or early summer of nineteen seventy-three."

"I showed you a number of pictures, Mr. Tawls."

"Both girls practically grew up on my farm. It's how I knew time was passing, when they'd show up like clockwork every year for the planting and then again for the harvest. They must've been seven or eight when their daddies stole my plants."

"Meaning marijuana."

"Don't make me confirm that over the phone, Ranger."

"You're not being investigated, Mr. Tawls."

Caitlin could hear Tawls breathing loudly on the other end of the line. "Different times, Ranger."

"You don't owe me any explanations, sir. Your record's clean as a whistle since then, not another spot on it."

"That was my last experience with that kind of crop. After those two spics stole from me, burned my fields, and stole my truck I decided I'd had myself enough of that world."

"Don't call them that, sir."

"What?"

"Spics. It's beneath a man of your standing."

Tawls took a big breath and let it out hard enough to make Caitlin think static had overtaken the line. "I suppose you're right, then as well as now. I bulldozed that part of my fields and turned the whole stretch into a playground for the local kids. Might still be there today if the drought of nineteen-ninety hadn't put me out of business for good."

"Can you tell me where those girls were born, Mr. Tawls?" Caitlin asked him.

"Not for sure. But I do know the other farm they both frequented was located in the lower Rio Grande Valley. Believe the spread belonged to the McClellan family."

"Mr. Tawls?"

"Ma'am?"

"I'm glad you stopped growing marijuana."

Tawls sighed, the sound garbled by the speaker. "You ever need to check out some property, just give me a call."

"Will do, Mr. Tawls," Caitlin said, hitting "End."

Tepper had already paid the check and they walked out of Denny's together.

"The Rio Grande Valley," he said, lighting his morning Marlboro. "Rangers got their own history down there during the farmworkers strike. My first assignment was greeted by a shovel swipe that almost splattered my skull like the melons they were growing. I remember counting myself fortunate to be alive."

Caitlin plucked the cigarette from his mouth and stamped it out under her boot. "Too bad it didn't stick, D.W."

57

SAN ANTONIO

"Why's all this important?" Cort Wesley asked when she was finished, dusk already fading to night by then.

"I'm not sure yet. Something in those pictures . . ."

"Like?"

"You tell me."

"You're the Texas Ranger."

"But this is all connected to someone trying to kill your kids, Cort Wesley," Caitlin said, wishing she could snatch the words back out of the air.

Cort Wesley's nostrils flared as his gaze narrowed. Big bugs called crane flies that had staked a claim in San Antonio buzzed the air around both of them. Cort Wesley started to raise a hand to swat one, then changed his mind.

"*My* kids, Ranger? You got as much say on their upbringing as me, and don't try to tell me otherwise."

"Then why didn't you tell me?"

"Tell you *what*, Ranger?"

"About your visit to the bank."

Cort Wesley turned away, swatting at the crane flies now. "I'm making believe this is Dylan. Spares me from doing it to him instead."

"It wasn't Dylan who told me."

He stopped swatting and swung back toward her. "Luke? When did that boy grow a mind of his own?"

"While you weren't looking."

"Couldn't help yourself, could you?"

"You tend to lose me in moments like this, Cort Wesley."

"You didn't come here intending to even raise the subject. But once the opening presented itself . . ."

"Banks aren't normally very hospitable to people like you."

"You mean because I've been in jail on both sides of the border and register an incomplete on my credit score?"

"You need money."

"You know any other reason to go to a bank? The bodyguard business has slowed down a bit, since I'm not exactly welcome anymore south of the border."

Caitlin shook her head. "And you expected to find a sympathetic ear in Royce Clavins?"

Mention of the banker left Cort Wesley raising his brow. "Luke didn't know the name of the man I met with."

"No, I figured that out all by myself. Clavins is an asshole, Cort Wesley. Always was, always will be. Next time he goes out of his way to help somebody will be the first. All the more reason you should have come to me first."

"You think it's easy?"

"You damn near bit my head off when I didn't acknowledge my stake in the boys. So you bet I think it should have been easy."

She watched his shoulders stiffen, the veins in his neck pulsing with tension, the crane flies suddenly steering clear of him. "I'm not touching Maura's insurance money, Ranger. Not borrowing against it either."

"I wouldn't want you to. I did fine when I sold my condo and bought the house where I grew up for a song in one of those short sales. Anyway, I got Clavins to agree to let me be co-signer on a loan that doesn't have to go anywhere near the insurance money."

"What'd you have to threaten him with, Ranger?"

"Nothing. I just reminded him about what he smelled like after you stuffed him in the trash can on a regular basis in high school. Believe he'd do just about anything to avoid that experience again."

"Get back to those pictures you were talking about," Cort Wesley said, eager to change the subject.

"Not until you get back to Dylan wanting to play in the championship game tomorrow night."

"You first, Ranger."

Caitlin went back to her most recent conversation with Regent Tawls and the two girls in the pictures being born at a farm in the Rio Grande Valley in 1973. "I think whatever's got the boys targeted begins down there, where their mother was born. Something maybe we can use."

"Against who?"

"I haven't figured that part out yet. But there's something all wrong about this I haven't got my mind around yet. Two farms, two little girls the same age, the stolen marijuana . . ."

"I don't think Maura ever said a word to me about her father."

"Maybe that's the reason. Because he was a drug dealer in league with a relative of the man who started it all by bringing Chinese opium through Baja."

"So how does a guy with that kind of heritage, like Cantú, end up working migrant farms through Texas?"

"Well, his grandfather Esteban Cantú didn't hold on to all his power very long. He was forced out as provincial governor of Mexicali in nineteen-twenty and not a peep was heard from him after that. Like he flat-out disappeared."

"Not surprising, given that I seem to recall you mentioning your granddad and his father went up against him right around then."

"Except my grandfather never finished telling me the story."

"Doesn't mean the Strongs didn't have a part in ending his political career. Your family does have a pretty decent record when it comes to taking down the worst bad guys unlucky enough to cross its path."

"Right now," Caitlin told him, "the only bad guys I care about are the ones we're after today. How'd you like to take a drive down to the Rio Grande Valley and the McClellan farm tomorrow?"

"With you?"

Caitlin shook her head. "I've got other plans," she said evasively. "You ready to talk about Dylan?"

"Sure, if I knew what to say." Cort Wesley plopped himself down on the porch swing, forcing it to rock backward. Caitlin watched him shaking his head, the toughest man in Texas brought to his figurative knees by his headstrong son. "Normally when I'm backed into a corner, I come out fighting. But this kid's got me boxed in against the ropes."

"You sound like your friend Leroy Epps."

"Damn ghost wasn't around when I needed him this afternoon." Cort Wesley's gaze sought Caitlin out, looking more vulnerable than she'd ever seen him before. "Dylan didn't tell me he wants to play, Ranger, he didn't ask me if he could play. He told me he *was* playing. Plain and simple. No room for argument. Then he asks if he can take my truck to get new tape for his damn stick. What the hell did I do wrong here?"

"You shoot him?"

"Nope." Cort Wesley slapped his knees loud and suddenly enough to send the crane flies scurrying in the porch light. "Way things are going I figure I'm gonna need all my bullets, starting tomorrow in the Rio Grande Valley."

58

With the moon directly overhead, Guillermo Paz stood outside the San Fernando Cathedral on Main Plaza in San Antonio, studying the plaque that proclaimed it to be the oldest cathedral sanctuary in the United States. Jim Bowie was married here before dying at the Alamo at the hands of Santa Ana, who used the building as an observation post. The cathedral claimed that Bowie, along with Colonel William Travis and Davy Crockett himself, had been ceremonially buried in the church's graveyard as their official resting places. But Paz knew of other locations that made the same claim. Since the heroes' bodies had all been burned after the famous battle, he supposed anybody could claim anything they wanted to.

Paz mounted the stone steps and entered the chapel to the smell of age, dust, and the lingering scent of cheap perfume left over from visits by tourists in the late afternoon. The last time he'd been here, the floors had just been refinished with a fresh coat of lacquer, the wooden pews restored to their original condition as well. That was a source of great pride to Paz, given that the money he'd left behind on a previous visit had funded the improvements. He'd even done some of the work on the roof himself, enjoying the hot sun burning his naked back and shoulders along with the view of the world provided from up on the hot slate.

Paz smelled candles and light incense, wondering why exactly he'd stopped his search for meaning here in favor of trying night classes at local colleges. Those classrooms lacked the scents of warm lavender and sandalwood, which partially explained his discomfort within them, even before the pompous professors started talking. It was the same smell he recalled from his youth growing up in the slums of Venezuela, where the local church provided the only refuge from the gang-riddled streets, making him feel truly at home as he made his way to the confessional perched in the church's rear.

Paz squeezed himself into the confessional and eased the door closed behind him. An armrest lay just below the confessional window, on which he had once carved the letters P-A-Z with a twelve-inch commando blade to leave some trace of his presence behind. The renovation his donation had financed had allowed that armrest to be refinished or replaced, and tonight Paz set about replacing his original mark. He was working the tip of his knife carefully to form the base of the "P" when the confessional window slid open, leaving only the screen between him and the priest.

"Have you missed me, padre?"

Paz could hear the slight gasp and shuffle, as the old priest shifted his legs to be able to leave his side of the confessional quickly if need be.

"I wanna apologize in advance for defacing church property," he continued. "But I realized that maybe it was a mistake giving up some of the things I used to do. Like maybe I was after more change than I really needed."

"My son?"

"You're probably wondering why you haven't seen me in so long."

"Well, I . . ."

"No worries, Father. Coming back here feels like coming home."

"Have you been . . . somewhere else?" the old priest asked, still groping for words.

"That's a good question, the answer being yes, in a figurative sense, anyway. My mind and spirit have been other places because I wasn't sure I could find what I was looking for in places like this anymore."

"Finding what you seek from God takes time, my son," the priest said sternly, finding his voice.

"And that's the point, padre. I was looking for easy answers, the kind that reinforced what I was already thinking. Believe I'd forgotten what places like this are all about."

"That it's not about the finding," the priest picked up, "it's about the seeking. The process bears its own rewards."

"You know me too well," Paz told him, "and I guess that was a lesson I needed to learn on my own." He finished the loop on the "P" and moved his knife to begin carving the "A." "That's why I decided to go back to the things that got me this far to begin with. Don't worry, I'm gonna leave another sizable donation to let you repair whatever needs to be fixed. Too bad it's not that easy with the soul, eh, padre?"

"Amen, my son."

"You know why I'm here?"

"I know why you've come in the past."

"And here we go again. My Texas Ranger and her outlaw need me in a big way. It's nice to be needed."

"Exactly as God feels," the priest tried to joke.

"Well, He's got me beat there for sure. But the thing is, it's different this time."

"Different how?"

Paz started carving the center bar of the "A" in his name on the armrest, brushing the stray shavings aside. In the confessional's dim light, he watched the wood specks sprinkling the air like faerie dust and hoped they left their own kind of magic.

"You remember me telling you about my mother?"

"You believed her to be some kind of witch, I seem to recall."

"What we call a *bruja* in our language, Father. She saw things, *felt* things. Her crazy warnings kept me alive as a boy, helped me steer clear of trouble. I already told you about that priest from the slum where I grew up in Venezuela, right?"

"The one who was killed by the gangs?"

"The very same. I was supposed to be with him that afternoon, but my mother wouldn't let me leave our shack when I was supposed to because she saw what was going to happen, saw me being killed too. I got to the church just as the gang was attacking him. I've never forgiven myself for not being there, convinced to this day I could have done *something*."

"Not according to your mother, my son. And how old were you?"

"Eleven."

"But years later . . ."

"I hunted down the men who killed the priest, the ones who were still alive, and killed them. It didn't make me feel any better. But help-ing my Ranger, *that* makes me feel better."

"You said this time was different."

"I'm getting to that. As I get older, I get more like my mother, the visions and shit. They used to come and go, now they just come, in my dreams mostly."

Paz could feel the priest stiffen on the other side of the confessional as he started in on the "Z." "My son, the church does not think kindly of such things. Some might even call it sacrilege."

"But you believe in miracles, don't you?"

"The church does, yes. Of course."

"Then why not consider this a miracle?"

The priest cleared his throat. "I recall you saying before how things had come to you in your dreams, mostly about the Texas Ranger you always refer to."

"This is different, padre. In my dream, there were men in a bar, bad men. Then a man entered who was even worse. I don't think he was human."

"What makes you say that?"

"The way he killed the men around him, each and every one of them. The last two begged for their lives and he cut their heads off."

"Not human, you say," the priest said, after a pause.

"I've learned there are plenty of things in this world we can't explain."

"But this man was no miracle, my son."

"No, he's a mistake of nature, a violent aberration. I only dream about things that are destined to cross my path or the path of my Ranger. That means he's coming this way. That means he's coming soon."

"You don't sound like that bothers you much."

Paz completed the "Z" and brushed the freshly carved letters clean of any shavings. "I'm protected now, padre."

"God protects us all."

"This is even better: the United States government. It's like every bad thing I've ever done in my life has been erased, the tablet wiped clean."

"But not the memory, my son. You'd be wise to remember that, lest you find yourself straying down old paths."

Paz shifted his vast bulk to ease closer to the screen. "That's the problem, Father. I don't do as well serving others as I do serving myself."

"What about serving God?"

"Same thing in my mind. I mean, where else could these visions be coming from? And that's the thing."

"What's the thing?"

"Serving the government types who wiped my slate clean has left me empty. I lost my sense of purpose and even stopped dreaming. Started going to college classrooms to find answers that weren't there because I was asking the wrong questions. Then my Texas Ranger called and the dreams started again."

Paz could see the priest nodding on the other side of the confessional. "Bringing you back to your one true self, your one true nature. This Texas Ranger has lent purpose to your life, but beware of that on the chance it's a false purpose."

"How could that be?"

"It justifies a part of your nature and being that frightens even God Himself."

"You just said we're here to serve Him and, pardon me if this comes out the wrong way, I doubt anything really scares the big guy very much."

"No," the priest said, "only when man tries to be as He is."

"You think that's what I'm doing?"

"I think that's what whoever's coming this way is doing. I think you are indeed doing God's work when you stop him."

"So what's the problem, padre?"

"Only God has no better, my son."

Paz reflected on that briefly. "Maybe not, but He's got the devil and I think that may be who I saw in my dream. I think that's who's headed here now."

59

"I don't know about this, Ranger," Fernando Lorenzo Sandoval said in response to Caitlin's proposal.

"I'd suggest, sir, that what you have in common with these two other men vastly outweighs your differences right now."

"In common with criminals?"

"Grieving fathers, Mr. Sandoval. Last time I checked, even cartel heads grieve."

Caitlin made the call from her cell in Cort Wesley's living room just before midnight, not feeling much like going home. She'd convinced Cort Wesley to try and get some sleep and volunteered to take the first watch.

"Mr. Sandoval?" Caitlin prodded, after he remained silent. She could feel him stiffening over the phone, heard a soft, guttural whimper.

"You're asking me to meet with two men committed to killing me," he said finally.

"Two men who lost their children just like you did, sir. I think that trumps everything else, and for now I'm asking you to help me do my job."

"*Your* job?"

"Your boy and those other kids were killed in Texas. That makes it my job, and I will see that job done by bringing whoever's behind this to justice. But I need your help to do that, I need all of your help. I need to figure out what links two major cartel heads with the leader of Mexico's antidrug resistance."

"What about the father of the final victim?" Sandoval asked her.

"Jesus Aguilar, a schoolteacher from Mexico City, remains hospitalized with terminal cancer."

"No involvement in drugs?"

"Not besides chemotherapy. The daughter he lost in Willow Creek was ten years old, Mr. Sandoval. I can interview him separately if necessary."

Caitlin left it there, not bothering to mention the teenage sons of Maura Torres. Caitlin wondered what Maura thought about the role she'd taken in her sons' lives, wished she could speak with her the way Cort Wesley seemed to with Leroy Epps. She'd spotted the spectral images of her father and grandfather often enough to know there was plenty about this world nobody really understood, and was probably better left that way.

"Mr. Sandoval?" Caitlin prodded, listening to him breathing rapidly over the otherwise quiet line.

"When would you like to set the meeting, Ranger?"

"I'm thinking late morning tomorrow."

"*¿Eso es imposible!*"

"That explains my thinking perfectly, sir. I'll send word on the location and will rely on you to contact the two cartel leaders. No extra guns, no entourages. The three of you let it rest for a few hours to help me catch a killer."

This time the silence lasted so long, Caitlin figured Sandoval had hung up or was about to. Then his voice finally returned.

"I'll be waiting for your call, Ranger."

60

SAN ANTONIO

Cort Wesley couldn't sleep. If Caitlin Strong hadn't been downstairs watching the house, he'd have been able to pass it off to his own sense of hypervigilance when it came to protecting his sons. But that wasn't it at all; the future was more his concern right now.

Spending your life as a soldier, an enforcer, and then a resident of the Walls correctional facility in Huntsville tends to make mundane day-to-day worries the stuff of other people's lives. But trying to play father to a pair of teenage boys had confronted him with a host of things he'd never had to consider before.

Like how much money it costs to raise them and keep them happy. That's what Cort Wesley wanted more than anything, and up to now he'd done a pretty good job. But selling the house and moving to an apartment or rental trailer like the kind his own father had spent his last drunken days in wasn't a good bet to continue that trend. And on top of everything else killers were undoubtedly still gunning for Dylan and Luke, and he had no clue how to find those killers first.

"*Bubba?*" came the voice of Leroy Epps.

"Where you been, champ?" Cort Wesley asked, sitting upright in bed.

In the darkness of the bedroom broken only by the moonlight slipping through the window, Leroy was just a dark shape set against the wall, standing there as if he'd been painted onto it.

"*Here and there. Heard you calling for me.*"

"I didn't say a word."

"*Your thoughts did the talking for you,*" Leroy said, stepping away from the wall so the moonlight both framed and passed straight through him. "*You're nothing like your own daddy, bubba.*"

"No, he was a drunk who liked it when I snuck a peek at him beating my mom when I was a boy. Said it made me hate him and hating him made me tougher. Maybe he was right."

"*That the sum total of your thinking?*"

"Need more time than we've got to cover all of it."

"*Don't know about that—I got all the time in the world, bubba. It don't actually pass where I be.*"

Cort Wesley rose from the bed and moved to the window, blocking the shaft of moonlight that had been illuminating Leroy Epps. "I used to think he stopped mixing it up with me because he was afraid of getting beat himself, given my size and strength by the time I was fifteen. Then I realized it was something else he was afraid of, champ."

"*What's that?*"

"Being alone. After my mom died, if I ran off he'd have nobody and even a degenerate violent drunk like Boone Masters doesn't want to live out his life that way."

Leroy smiled tightly, still reluctant to show the teeth that had gone brown with rot in the last months of his life, even though Cort Wesley was pretty certain death had restored their luster. *"I knew we'd get around to that."*

"Get around to what, champ?"

"Your boys and the Ranger gal downstairs. Hardly makes you alone like your daddy. Last thing you got to worry about in the world."

"There's people out there who want to take all that away. And that scares me more than anything."

"Nope," Leroy Epps said, shaking his head.

"Nope, *what?*"

"Nope, what scares you the most is your oldest likely going off to college next year with his younger brother not far behind. Being alone didn't scare you before 'cause you didn't know no damn difference. Now you got something to compare to the alternative and you don't like them prospects one damn bit."

"Any words of wisdom beyond that, champ?"

"Maybe you can learn something from your daddy."

Cort Wesley tried to make him out clearer through the darkness. "Come again?"

"No need to on account of you hearing me fine the first time. Boone Masters done one thing right, even if it wasn't the right thing to do."

"Do all ghosts talk in riddles?"

"Wouldn't know, bubba. I don't talk to many. Doesn't work that way where I be now. Anyway, that one right thing your daddy did was teaching you how not to be a father. I'd venture to say that avoiding his example has changed you as much as a man can change for the better." Leroy started to fade out, Cort Wesley able to see right through him to the moonlit wall when his form suddenly thickened again. *"Oh, almost forgot to tell ya. Ranger gal fell asleep downstairs. You may want to check on her."*

PART SEVEN

The Texas Ranger Frontier Battalion developed a reputation for individual daring and success in restoring order to lawless areas—a reputation which helped enshrine the legend of the Texas Rangers in popular imagination.

Randolph B. Campbell,
Gone to Texas: A History of the Lone Star State

61

Caitlin saw the spire of San Agustin Church rising over the plaza rich with tourists strolling past sidewalk kiosks and open storefronts, snapping pictures with their cell phones and fishing cash from their wallets. She had switched off the air-conditioning and opened her SUV's windows after being waved through the Customs stop. The air here just across the border, mere miles away from where Strong's Raiders had met with Pancho Villa's three generals to plan their response against *esos Demonios*, was dry, dusty, and laced with the scents of grilled food sifting out from restaurants featuring open fronts.

She finally found a parking space down the street from a Mexican restaurant called Los Jocales. Caitlin entered to find it all but deserted as the staff prepared for the busy late-morning and lunchtime rush. She'd set the meeting in the same back alcove where Cort Wesley Masters had been brought after being sprung from prison by Jones the year before. Approaching the bead curtain separating the alcove from the rest of the restaurant, Caitlin saw three figures sitting in silence inside. The lights in this part of the restaurant had yet to be switched on, and the result was to place the figures in shadows broken only by the spill of light coming in through the spacious windows that formed the entire side wall beyond the alcove. She thought she smelled cigarette smoke and saw wisps of it rising as she drew closer, parting the beads to find the eyes of all three men fastened upon her.

Sandoval rose respectfully first, waiting for Alejandro Luis Rojas and Juan Ramon Castillo to join him before bowing his head slightly. Rojas and Castillo nodded her way, Caitlin doing a mental review of both as they retook their seats, even as she felt the thick tension that had settled between Sandoval and his mortal enemies.

Alejandro Luis Rojas, second in command and chief enforcer of the Juárez cartel, was a ruddy-looking man with a dark pockmarked complexion and stubby, callused hands that looked like a farmer's. His forehead was stitched by permanent lines that ran across it in slight waves. He brushed his thick black hair straight back and Caitlin noticed dried flecks of hair dye dotting the shoulders of his white button-down shirt, the sleeves of which were rolled up just past the elbows.

Juan Ramon Castillo, fourth in the chain of command for the Sinaloa cartel, but currently number one given that the three ahead of him were all in prison, was rail thin and bookish-looking thanks to a pair of spectacles he wore on the tip of his nose. Caitlin noticed that one of the lenses was cracked and his belt was struggling to hold his trousers over his narrow hips. Nonetheless, the intensity of his gaze and general flatness of his expression mirrored Rojas's in both respects, the two of them looking as if the emotion, the very life, had been washed from their features. There was no fierceness, no hatred, no unnerving sense of awareness of the power each held, not even any grief. Caitlin guessed the unusual nature of this meeting was to blame, both these men and Sandoval at a loss to find the proper face to wear for a tragic occasion that, however temporarily, had joined them in a common purpose.

"I want to thank all you gentlemen for coming," she said when she reached the table. At that point, Caitlin cautiously eased the SIG Sauer from its holster, ejected the shell from the chamber and popped out the magazine, laying all three down before her. "Seems like the right thing to do given what's brought us here, and I appreciate the three of you all coming alone."

"Anything that helps us find the killer of our children," said Rojas, the last of his words spoken softer through a lump that Caitin saw was actually visible in his throat.

"Perhaps the guilty party sits at this table now," Castillo followed, holding his gaze on Sandoval. "I would not put it past some to have orchestrated this entire ruse to cloak their own part in weakening our operation."

"You think I'd sacrifice my own son to such a cause?" Sandoval asked him.

"The only body I've seen is *my* son's. I have no way of confirming the other deaths, do I?"

Rojas nodded slowly in assent, echoing Castillo's words.

"I saw the bodies," Caitlin told all three of them. "It was the Rangers working with Mexican authorities who made the IDs. If this were a trap, it'd already be sprung. And I got my own reasons for wanting this to go smoothly."

"Perhaps you should share them with our new friends," Sandoval suggested, eyeing both of them.

"Two boys have been targeted north of the border as well, two boys who mean a lot to me."

"Spoken in the present tense," Castillo noted, "while we speak in the past."

"You have other children, don't you, *Señor* Castillo?"

Castillo bristled at Caitlin's remark.

"Two to be exact," Caitlin continued, "both born to your mistresses. How long you think it'll be before the killers catch on to that fact and come after them too?"

"I can protect my own without help from *los diablos tejanos*."

Caitlin held his stare. "Well, right now this Texas devil needs to remind you that wasn't the case four days ago, sir."

Rojas leaned forward, his hands coiled into fists so tight that the veins looked like branches growing out of his skin. "So what do you want from us?"

"To find out what the three of you, and *Señor* Aguilar, have in common, because that's why five children are dead and others are in danger."

"You think we haven't searched for that answer ourselves?" challenged

Castillo, shaking his head. "You think we wouldn't have found it if such a thing truly existed?"

"Reason for that being," Caitlin told him, "is that you've been looking in the wrong place."

62

SAN ANTONIO

"I've gotta be back in time for the game tonight," Dylan told Cort Wesley, pulling his boots on. His hair was still damp from the shower and he smelled like the liquid soap Caitlin used because he said it made his skin feel better.

"So you don't want to come along."

"No, Dad, I do. We just have to make sure I'm back. It's the district championship."

"Still?"

"Huh?"

"I thought maybe something had changed from the first fifty times you told me."

"Ha-ha. Very funny, Dad. Remind me to laugh later." He pushed his foot the rest of the way into his boot and stood up. "Where we going again?"

It wasn't anything like boosting refrigerators with Boone Masters, but this was still the first time Cort Wesley had ever taken Dylan with him on a trip like this, specifically to the Rio Grande Valley and the farm where the daughters of both Mateo Torres and Enrique Cantú had been born in 1973. He hadn't asked Luke to join them and his younger son would've likely rejected the proposition anyway since he hated missing any school, a freshman now already thinking of grades, college, and test scores.

Man oh man, is this really my kid?

The night before he'd gone downstairs as soon as Leroy Epps was gone to find Caitlin sleeping by the window in front of which she'd moved an old upholstered armchair. Instead of rousing her, Cort Wesley had covered Caitlin with a blanket and smoothed her hair.

"I'm taking Dylan with me tomorrow," he said softly. "Figured it's time the boy sees how the world works." Or maybe he'd said "how I work," his actual words blunted by memory.

Cort Wesley was glad Caitlin was asleep so she couldn't argue the point with him any more than his mother had when Boone Masters took Cort Wesley on his first job, where he'd watched his father pick the lock on a storage depot overhead door and boost a bunch of major appliances.

"Reason we pick instead of cut, son," his father had explained, "is on account of the fact the owners won't know they been robbed right away. And by the time they do, these fridges, ranges, washers, and dryers'll be in people's homes at a serious discount. Hell, we might be back another couple times before they notice anything's missing at all."

Cort Wesley had to ride atop the big boxes piled into the truck bed on the way to the dusty warehouse where Boone Masters stored his merchandise. Maybe today he'd tell Dylan all about that. Something to pass the time on the hundred-thirty-mile drive that couldn't pass slowly enough.

Except Dylan lost himself in iTunes playing through earbuds that tuned him out to the rest of the world, including Cort Wesley. His eyes were closed five minutes after they hit the 101 going south, and Cort Wesley couldn't tell whether he was asleep or awake, since the earbuds shut out pretty much all ambient sound that included anything even remotely passing for a conversation.

Once, after stealing another glance toward his oldest son, Cort Wesley caught a glimpse of Leroy Epps in the backseat.

"Bright idea I had, champ," he said, shaking his head, "real bright."

Epps shrugged, just about to respond when Dylan opened his eyes and plucked the buds from his ears. "You say something, Dad?"

Cort Wesley checked the rearview mirror to find Leroy gone. "Just thinking out loud, son."

Dylan nodded and glanced into the backseat. "Hey," he said, holding up his iPhone, "you want me to play this over the Bluetooth?"

63

Nuevo Laredo, Mexico

"*. . . you've been looking in the wrong place.*"

The eyes of all three men remained fixed on Caitlin after she said that.

"Which assumes you've been looking in the right one, Ranger," said Castillo, his hooded eyes still trying to size her and her intentions up.

"I believe I've got a notion, sir, yes. I believe this is about revenge for something you gentlemen had nothing to do with yourselves."

Rojas and Castillo started to look at each other and then stopped, the bond between them broken momentarily by a sudden awareness of their violent rivalry.

"*¡Eso no tiene sentido!*"

"No, *Señor* Rojas, it doesn't make any sense, at least no more than murdering innocent children."

"You really think you need to keep reminding us of that?"

"Yes, yes, I do, given that priorities could change in a hurry otherwise."

"So if it was not something we did . . ."

Caitlin looked toward Sandoval. "You remember telling me what you knew about the formation of Strong's Raiders back at the Four Seasons in Austin?"

"Of course."

"Most important being the part about those three generals from Pancho Villa's army William Ray Strong, my granddad, and the others met over the border not far from this very spot. They gathered around a campfire to figure out how they were going to defeat *esos Demonios*," Caitlin said. "Hatched a plan to flush them across the border and take them down in El Paso. But I'm guessing things didn't go as planned, did they?"

"No, Ranger," Sandoval said, while the cartel leaders exchanged a wary glance, curious as to where this was going. "Not at all."

Caitlin finally took the chair set at the head of the table. "Why don't you tell us why, sir? Why don't you tell us what went wrong?"

64

EL PASO, TEXAS; 1919

"What the hell is this?" William Ray Strong wondered, as soon as Strong's Raiders pulled into El Paso just after dark on the evening of June 14, the day before the plan to take the fight to *esos Demonios* was to happen.

Pancho Villa's three generals, who had spoken only through Major Lava, would marshal all their forces in mounting a daring attack on the *esos Demonios* stronghold in Juárez. The object of the raid was to force the enemy to retreat in the only direction available: north, over the International Bridge into El Paso, where Strong's Raiders would be waiting. At that point Villa's troops would hold their position on the Mexican side of the bridge to prevent *esos Demonios* from staging a return or retreat, boxing them in and leaving the rest of the battle in the hands of the Rangers.

"Six against a hundred, maybe twice that number if we're lucky," William Ray mused to Earl Strong, as they rode into El Paso in a boxy Ford with two rows of seats inside and one on the out. "Lousy odds . . . for them."

Earl had smiled back at him. The trailing car, being driven by Monroe Fox with Manuel Gonzaullas riding shotgun, had its backseat occupied by four Thompson machine guns and three Browning automatic rifles. The plan was for Fox and Frank Hamer to set up two of the BARs on rooftops at the south end of El Paso's main drag, a stone's throw from the International Bridge, while Gonzaullas and old Bill McDonald aimed Thompsons out fifth-story windows on both sides of the street nearer the center. The Strongs, for their part, would be on the ground, ready with both their twelve-gauge pumps and Thompsons slung from their shoulders by thick leather straps.

The idea, as William Ray explained it, was to catch *esos Demonios* in a classic crossfire. By the time they recovered their wits, he and Earl would move in from the head of the street and treat the enemy with the same consideration with which they had treated the residents of Willow Creek.

"You okay with this?" William Ray asked the newest Texas Ranger before they'd set out, struggling not to mix too much worry with his words.

"Why wouldn't I be?"

" 'Cause it means killing lots of men."

Earl fished William Ray's chewing tobacco pouch from his lapel pocket and packed a wad into his mouth. "These stopped being men when they gunned down women and children. Shooting them ought to be no different from shooting a rabid dog."

William Ray slapped his son in the back, sending the wad of tobacco jetting from his mouth and leaving Earl spitting out the leftover juice.

"That's what I needed to hear, boy. Just like ducks on a pond."

Earl was still trying to rid his mouth of the awful taste, hocking up more and more spittle to little effect. "Except in the daylight we'll be ducks too."

William Ray winked at him. "Didn't tell you what else I got planned, did I?"

The "what else" turned out to be "smoke candles" of the sort invented by Robert Yale in 1848 and based on the principles of seventeenth-century Chinese fireworks. The smoke candles he and Bill McDonald had mixed up the night before were simple enough contraptions con-

sisting of cylindrical cardboard topped with an inch-long fuse. A Comanche Indian chief with whom William Ray had made peace had
taught him how to make a slightly different version, calling them "magic
balls" because they were round in shape. William Ray improvised on
that, but not the relatively simple ingredients that included sugar, sodium bicarbonate, and a chemical called potassium chlorate.

When the time came, he explained to Earl, the four Rangers with
the high ground would light and hurl them into the cluster of *esos Demonios* already reeling from the heavy onslaught of fire. William Ray
and Earl would then use the camouflage provided by the smoke to take
the fight to the Mexicans, while the other Rangers mowed down any
who escaped the death circle.

But all that had gone to shit as soon as they reached the outskirts of
El Paso and glimpsed what awaited them there.

"What the hell you mean?" William Ray said to the first army officer
brave enough to approach the leader of Strong's Raiders when he
reached the head of Central Square in El Paso.

Before them the entire area—streets, rooftops, plazas—had been
taken over by elements of the United States Army. And not just the
relatively token force assigned to guard the city from any possible in-
trusion or attack from across the nearby border. From the look of
things, this was a major detachment of troops and ordnance that included artillery out of Fort Bliss, seeming to William Ray like preparations for a full-scale war.

"We've got our orders—that's what I mean, sir."

"Well, son, so do we. From the governor of Texas himself."

"Well, ours come from the president of the United States. I believe
he outranks your governor."

"Who's in charge here, son? I need to give him a piece of mind and
find out what the hell is going on."

* * *

The officer in charge was Brigadier General James B. Erwin, who'd set up his field headquarters in a makeshift command post to the rear of the Eighty-Second Field Artillery regiment in El Paso's Union Stockyards.

"I was told to expect you, Ranger," Erwin said, extending a hand instead of bothering with the gesture of a salute.

William Ray didn't take the hand at first, then finally did out of respect for the man's service. They must've been about the same age with the battle scars and weary eyes to prove it. "Told by who exactly, General?"

Erwin smiled like a man used to being in charge, just as William Ray was. "Let's just say the people responsible for your orders."

"Which have plainly changed by the look of things."

"You've done your part," Erwin said, leading William Ray aside and then moving to steer him away. "Now let us do the rest."

He reached for the Ranger's elbow to better do the leading, but William Ray snapped it away and Erwin looked down to see his own elbow grasped instead. "My *part*, sir, is to have at it with a few hundred monsters pretending to be men. Since you're here I'm gonna assume you've heard of them. *Esos Demonios.*"

"Let go of my elbow, please, Ranger."

"I'd like an answer to my question."

"You mean, assumption. And I'll thank you to release my arm first."

William Ray finally did.

"Yes, I've heard of *esos Demonios.*"

"That it?"

"It's more than you're entitled to know. This mission is being undertaken on the orders of the president himself, who, by the way, has authorized me to thank you for your service on his behalf."

"What the hell's that supposed to mean?"

"We owe all this to you, Ranger."

"Owe all *what* to me, General?"

Erwin stiffened slightly and didn't answer William Ray's question.

"How 'bout I take a crack at things, then? Way I see it, if you're stopping our plan to wipe out these monsters, it's because you're fighting on the same side; with Carranza and Cantú against Pancho Villa and his fighters."

"I don't know anyone by the name of Cantú," Erwin said smugly, not bothering to deny the rest.

"Then let me shed some light for you. Esteban Cantú is the cousin of President Carranza and the provincial governor of Mexicali, a position he's used to build his own personal opium smuggling route into California. Now he's moved his opium business east to Ranger country, forging a second major entry into the country with *esos Demonios* killing anyone in their path to build a distribution network. That killing includes the entire population of a town called Willow Creek."

Erwin just stood there, maybe listening but maybe not.

"There a problem with your hearing, General?"

Erwin realized William Ray had raised his voice just enough to attract the attention of some junior officers standing close to them. "I'll thank you to address me in a more respectful tone, Ranger."

"And I'll thank you to *kiss my ass*!"

Erwin started to move closer to William Ray, but stopped when he felt the heat radiating from within the Ranger's flannel shirt.

"You used me and my men, General."

"I did no such thing."

"The people you represent, then."

"I represent the same people you do."

"No, sir, that is not the case at all. See, me and my men represent the dead folk of Willow Creek. We speak for them on account of nobody else seems to give a shit. So the way I figure it, you used the opportunity of Pancho Villa risking an attack in Juárez to flush *esos Demonios* toward us here in El Paso to finish Villa and the threat he poses to your friend Carranza off once and for all."

Erwin neither confirmed nor denied his assertion, his gaze remaining flat and noncommittal in the light of lanterns strung from poles.

"You wanna tell me what I'm missing here, General?" William Ray asked, sensing there was something else going on.

"That isn't your concern. And this isn't your fight anymore. Take your men and leave the fighting to mine."

"What am I missing?" William Ray repeated, holding his ground as a gesture from Erwin drew a host of infantrymen to both sides of him, hands too close to the triggers of their carbines for comfort. "Who exactly was it let you know what we were up to?"

The night's heat was already oppressive before factoring in the fires that pumped more of it through the air, making the stockyards feel to William Ray Strong like he'd entered hell itself. All manner of insects and mosquitoes buzzed the air, thirsty for blood and, maybe, sensing its spill coming. The stench of a different spill from fresh slaughter in these very yards hung like a cloud, impervious to the wind as if it formed more of a wall.

"You know why they call a certain species of beetle June bugs, General?"

"Because I assume they come in June."

"That's the thing of it—they don't; they come in July. Next month, not this."

"What's your point, Ranger?"

William Ray got right up in Erwin's face before responding, the infantrymen enclosing the general tensing but still frozen in place. "That whoever called them June bugs to begin with was full of shit. Just like you."

65

NUEVO LAREDO, MEXICO

"Pancho Villa reached the outskirts of Juárez about the same time your great-grandfather reached El Paso, Ranger," Sandoval continued.

"In keeping with his part of the plan," Caitlin followed, "having no idea he'd already been betrayed, sold out."

"I always assumed the Americans were behind that. A change in priorities. They saw the plan Strong's Raiders had put into place as the means to help President Carranza crush the Villistas once and for all."

"That wasn't the case at all, sir—at least, I don't believe it was." Caitlin held her gaze on Alejandro Luis Rojas and Juan Ramon Castillo, the cartel leaders. "And I believe that betrayal is the reason we're all here today . . . and why your children were murdered."

Rojas swallowed hard while Castillo's stare grew more rigid and hateful, aimed at no one in particular.

"What you're suggesting," Sandoval started, seeming to lose his train of thought in mid-sentence. "It doesn't make any sense."

"Finish your story, Mr. Sandoval," Caitlin prompted. "Then I'll explain what I'm getting at."

Sandoval needed to collect his thoughts before resuming. "Villa launched his initial attack on Juárez not long after midnight on June fifteenth. His troops cut through barbed-wire barricades with wire cutters provided by Strong's Raiders and entered the city, the advance done in a way to keep their bullets from flying across the border into America."

"But Villa didn't lead the battle himself, did he?"

"No, it was led by his godson, General Martin Lopez, because Villa was sick."

"He was sick all right, sir, sick after he was tipped off about the betrayal. Just because he'd come too far to retreat doesn't mean he was ready to sacrifice himself in the battle."

"I never thought of that. . . ."

"But you've thought about what happened next."

"The Villistas made progress initially, until General Erwin ordered his troops into action," Sandoval expounded. "He'd cobbled together forces from the Twelfth Infantry and Eighty-Second Field Artillery, along with regiments from the Fifth and Seventh Cavalries. His attack began with the shelling of Juárez Racetrack, where Villa's forces were concentrated."

"And by that time," Caitlin recalled, "the Mexican troops had returned to their fort, leaving it strictly to the American forces to put down the Villistas. Suggests a lot of coordination, doesn't it? Suggests that the battle was over before it even began. *Esos Demonios* weren't even in Juárez at the time. Villa's men had walked straight into a trap."

"All very interesting," said Castillo, each word measured and pronounced in perfect English. "But what does all this have to do with the child I lost in your country?"

"I'm getting to that, sir," Caitlin told him.

Rojas leaned so far forward in his chair, it seemed he was about to stand up and Caitlin was pretty certain his gaze had darted out beyond the bead curtain to make sure no one was laying in wait beyond. "And how do we know you haven't lured us here on a similar pretext? How can we be sure this isn't a trap as well?"

"Because if I'd set that trap, *señores*, it would've sprung already." She hesitated long enough to let them weigh her words. "We need to listen to the rest of what Mr. Sandoval has to say to fully understand why what happened in that battle in nineteen-nineteen ended up getting your children killed almost a century later."

Castillo and Rojas looked at each other, then back at Caitlin, nodding simultaneously.

"Mr. Sandoval," she prompted.

"There's not a lot more to tell," Sandoval sighed. "After the artillery shelling, Erwin sent his thirty-six hundred men across the Rio Grande to engage the drastically weakened Villistas. But that too was a trap meant to get Villa's forces to stage a retreat that subjected them to relentless shelling by Erwin's artillery. Salvo after salvo lobbed across the border, the shrapnel rounds wiping out entire sections of the Villistas at a time. When the Americans reconnoitered at daybreak, they found a host of adobe structures leveled where the resistance fighters had fled. There were bodies everywhere; weapons, ammunition, horses and mules left behind when the survivors fled to melt back into their everyday lives. For all intents and purposes the revolution ended that night. Villa managed to flee and muster what was left of his forces together again, but in their weakened state they were crushed in Durango."

"Leading ultimately to Villa's surrender in nineteen-twenty," Caitlin interjected.

"He managed to stay alive for three more years until he was finally murdered in July of nineteen twenty-three by assassins likely dispatched by Alvaro Obregon, President Carranza's successor, who had no interest in honoring the terms of Villa's truce with his predecessor."

"Now we wish to hear from you, *el diablo Tejano*," Castillo said to Caitlin, no longer bothering to hide the disdain in his voice. "We wish to hear what all this has to do with the murder of our children."

"I did some research before I came down here, sir," Caitlin told them all, "research into some men who strolled through history anonymously with blood coating their hands. I believe the blood they caused to be spilled in nineteen-nineteen is what caused the deaths of your children today. All the times this story's been told and their names never even get mentioned."

Rojas finally came all the way out of his chair and pressed his fingertips into the tabletop. "Who were these men?"

"What were their names?" Castillo added, rising too.

"You both need to be sitting down to hear this."

But neither moved an inch. "We're fine as we are," said Castillo.

"Suit yourself," Caitlin told them. "Turns out those three generals Strong's Raiders joined forces with were the ones who betrayed Pancho Villa. They had their own reasons for doing so, reasons that ultimately brought down Esteban Cantú, at the hands of William Ray and Earl Strong, I figure."

"But who were these generals?" asked Sandoval.

Caitlin hesitated, meeting the drug cartel leaders' stares before resuming. "Their names were Rojas, Castillo, and Aguilar."

66

TEXAS-MEXICO BORDER

Caitlin's SUV edged forward amid the line of cars waiting to make it through the border checkpoint. It was taking no more time than usual, but her impatience to get back to the case at hand made it seem interminably longer.

Back in Nuevo Laredo, all three men had been speechless when she revealed what she believed they held in common, dating all the way back to 1919 and Strong's Raiders.

"What about me, Ranger?" Fernando Lorenzo Sandoval had asked. "Since my grandfather was not one of Pancho Villa's generals."

"I'm still working on that, sir. There's got to be something else connecting you to the group, just like there's something connecting Maura Torres."

"You're saying this is about revenge," said Rojas, his tone more measured and less confrontational. "You're saying someone's getting back at us for something from a past we had nothing to do with."

"I suppose that's not how whoever's behind all this sees it, sir."

"What else is it you're not telling us?" Castillo asked her.

"I'm not telling you anything more until I'm sure."

Caitlin needed to get back to San Antonio to pick up her investigation, so distracted that she barely noticed she'd finally reached the checkpoint.

"Identification, please," the border agent asked, after she eased the SUV into park.

Caitlin routinely handed over her Texas Ranger ID and badge, thinking nothing more of it until the border agent stepped back and was almost immediately joined by two more, one of whom was considerably older.

"I'm going to have to ask you to step out of the car, ma'am."

Caitlin didn't budge. "What's this about?"

"Step out of the car, please."

With that, another pair of agents came up on the passenger side of her SUV, studying her through the windows.

"Ma'am?" the older man prodded.

"It's *Ranger*, sir," Caitlin said, easing the door open and stepping out.

"I'm going to need you to surrender your firearm too," he said next.

Caitlin did so slowly, making sure her intentions could not be confused. "What's this about, sir?"

"National security," he told Caitlin, as the four younger agents moved up to enclose her.

67

"Cort Wesley Masters? No shit!"

"And this is my son Dylan. Seems like you've heard of me."

"I have indeed," said Jan McClellan-Townsend, the older woman who now ran the McClellan family farm. She'd married an Easterner and moved to Massachusetts, of all places, until her husband died. Around the same time no one else in the family was interested in continuing to run the farm's day-to-day operations, so Jan had returned home to take over the business in the heart of the Rio Grande Valley, followed in rapid succession by three of her four kids, who'd all sworn off ever even looking at the fields near which they'd been born again. That kind of stuff, she explained, was in the blood like it or not. "I believe my father and your grandfather did some business together."

Cort Wesley looked toward Dylan, who'd removed the earbuds he'd worn through the duration of the drive from San Antonio and now looked genuinely interested. "True enough. My grandfather broke plenty of bones on behalf of men like your father back during the farmworkers strike of sixty-six, maybe sixty-seven. Mixed it up with more than his share of Texas Rangers at the time."

"Maybe so, but that's not how my dad knew him. My dad knew him for the same reason I know you: the drug business."

"You worked for the Branca crime family out of New Orleans," Jan McClellan-Townsend continued, making Cort Wesley briefly regret that he'd dragged Dylan along for the ride.

She was a rangy, tall woman, wearing baggy blue jeans and cowboy boots that looked as old as she did. Her radiant blue eyes made Cort Wesley figure she'd been quite a catch in her time and remained attractive considering the wear of running a farm and her sixty-plus years. Her skin was sun-darkened bronze and boasted nary a wrinkle. She had ash-gray hair she'd never colored and didn't bother much with based on the way it fell limply past her shoulders.

"Am I talking to you or your father, Mrs. Townsend?"

"Call me Jan, please." Her eyes fell on Dylan. "Shouldn't you be in school?"

"My dad figured this trip might be educational in itself."

She studied the boy closer. "Believe I've heard of you too, at least read about you in the paper."

"I've been in my share of scrapes, ma'am, but I'm going to college next year."

"Where?"

"Brown I hope. To play football."

Jan McClellan-Townsend's eyes glistened. "Brown *University*? I've got a grandson there. He's gonna be a sophomore. I'll give you his e-mail address." She looked back toward Cort Wesley. "Used to be phone numbers." On Dylan again now. "When I grew up, phones had cords and rotary dials and the word 'texting' didn't exist yet. Now when my grandkids come to visit, I can't get them to look up from their damn phones. Threw my grandson's in a horse trough a few years back. Then I felt bad about it so I bought him one of those I-whatevers."

"Like this," Dylan said, flashing his iPhone 5.

"Don't put it too close to me, son, or it may go a-flying."

"We were talking about how your dad knew my grandfather," Cort Wesley said, returning to the matter at hand.

"*We* weren't—you were. I was talking about other stuff with your boy here," she said with a wink cast Dylan's way.

"Then let me put it this way, Jan: how was your father mixed up in the drug business?"

"You still with that Texas Ranger, Cort Wesley?"

"Our relationship make the society columns again?"

"When the most famous gunfighter in Texas takes up with the most famous outlaw in Texas, it tends to cause a stir."

"You're only half right on that, Mrs. Townsend."

"Jan. Remember?"

"That depends on where this conversation goes next."

She nodded, seeming to agree with him as she looked back at Dylan. "You remember playing show-and-tell in school, son?"

"Sure."

" 'Cause that's what we're gonna do now," she said to both of them. "Play a little show-and-tell."

68

LAREDO, TEXAS

"I gotta hand it to you, Jones," Caitlin said, when he finally showed up at the border crossing nearly two hours after she'd been detained by border agents. "Every time I forget all the reasons I've got to shoot you, you come up with another."

"Just trying to make you as miserable as you make me, Ranger," he said, taking off a cowboy hat that was too small for his head and holding it before him. "Like it?"

"It makes you look like Roy Rogers. A genuine fake cowboy."

"I thought old Roy was a real one."

"Not by my standards."

"Meaning he didn't gun down enough people in the name of justice."

"We finished here? Because I've got a pressing engagement back in San Antonio," Caitlin said, thinking of Dylan's lacrosse game.

"We're just getting started, Ranger." Jones spun a chair around and sat down straddling it. "I want to make sure I'm clear on everything here. You actually met with Sandoval and two of the top cartel leaders in Mexico. In the same room. At the same time."

"I believe I informed you of that intention."

"I didn't think you were serious."

"You ever known me to be anything but?"

Jones could only shake his head. "You managed to get two men we've been hunting out of hiding together with the proxy we've got hunting them." He shook his head again.

"Proxy," Caitlin repeated. "That what you call all the men you almost get killed these days?"

"What happened in Austin isn't on me, Ranger."

"Oh no? And I seem to remember warning you there was more going on here than you were willing to accept."

"That's because we've already got enough going on. And in the past seventy-two hours you compromised two of my assets, Ranger."

"I thought they were proxies."

"You have any idea how much we've got invested in Sandoval and Paz? No? I didn't think so. Enough for me to give you this little demonstration of what life is like on the other side."

"Tell me something, Jones: do you ever actually listen to yourself talk?"

"Enough to hear me tell·you the shit you've been pulling has to stop."

"So all this, having me detained, is about showing your power."

Jones stepped aside so Caitlin could see the door. "You're free to go, Ranger. But next time I might not arrive in such a timely manner."

Caitlin looked down dramatically, seeming to gaze at the floor.

"Am I missing something here?" Jones asked.

"No, sir, I was just checking to see if I was quaking in my boots."

"See this?" Jones held his palm even with Caitlin and then brought it upward over his head. "That's called the upper hand. You'd be wise to remember that."

"Yeah? Well, the only thing that upper hand is good for is pulling on your pud."

"Am I not getting through to you here?"

Caitlin looked toward the door again. "I think I'll head off, since I'm free to go and all."

Jones stiffened as she neared him. "Your act's wearing thin, Ranger. You had me for a while, but it's all getting a bit tired now. Political realities don't mean any more to you than rules, and I find it truly amazing that higher powers than me haven't forced you into early retirement."

"With a gold watch or a bullet, Jones?"

"You know what I mean."

"Actually, I don't. Not at all. Not even close."

"You jeopardized two years of work when you decided to contact Sandoval on your own."

Caitlin let him see her weighing his words. "I don't do exactly that, and he's dead now. Or maybe that didn't occur to you."

"And maybe the leak that gave up his identity originated in your Ranger Company office. Not that I'm accusing you; after all, your captain talks like he's suffering from Alzheimer's. Maybe he called to order a pizza and just happened to tell the delivery boy about the secret anti-drug strategy meeting going on in Austin."

"Strategy meeting?"

Jones nodded, his expression deadpan. "What they call it when you have a meeting to discuss strategy."

"I'll be sure to let Captain Tepper know of the high esteem in which you hold him," Caitlin said, fitting her Stetson back on.

"You're to have no further contact with either Sandoval or Paz."

"You tell that to Paz?"

"Look around you, Ranger," Jones said, making a show of running his eyes around the cramped office that smelled vaguely of body odor and stale onions from fast-food meals. "There's a million places like this I can put you in to make you disappear, for good if I want."

With that, he pulled her SIG Sauer from inside his jacket and handed it to her butt first, then followed up with the magazine. "I'll ask you not to load your weapon until you're back across the border. Just following procedure."

"Is that what you call it?" Caitlin asked, holstering her pistol and pocketing the magazine.

"What would you call it?"

"Waiting until you're out of my range, Jones."

"You really that good a shot, Ranger?" he smirked.

"You really want to find out?"

69

"What is it exactly you want to show us, Jan?" Cort Wesley asked, as Jan McClellan-Townsend wound amid her orange and grapefruit groves in what felt like a turbo-charged golf cart. The air smelled of sweet citrus, somehow making it feel less hot.

"My family built this farm up from nothing," she said reflectively, ignoring his question. "Started with ten acres and built it to what you see now. For quite a time, people thought that old movie *Giant* was based on this spread. Maybe it was," she added, jerking the cart to a sudden halt that jostled Dylan in the back. "Of course, I don't believe Rock Hudson's character ever grew marijuana on his land."

"You talking about your father?"

But Jan was looking at Dylan again. "Why'd you bring him with you, Mr. Masters?"

"That's Cort Wesley, ma'am."

"You mean Jan."

"Jan."

"Stop avoiding my question, Cort Wesley."

"You ever plant or pick crops with your father, Jan?"

"Of course."

"Then you just answered your own question."

"Have I?"

"A few nights back," Dylan started, "a bunch of Mexican gunmen came after me."

"I take the fact that you're still here to mean they weren't successful."

Dylan's gaze moved to Cort Wesley. "I think my dad wants to let me play a part in finding out why before they come back."

"Sure," Jan McClellan-Townsend said to Cort Wesley, "that's just like picking oranges."

"Or marijuana," Cort Wesley nodded.

The woman turned her gaze on the fields of citrus that seemed to stretch on forever. "This was the patch of ground my father cleared to do it. Times were tough and he was overextended at the bank, three mortgages or at least two, thanks to devastating droughts that covered three straight seasons. It was either that or lose the property." She looked back at Cort Wesley. "From my viewpoint, he made the right choice."

"I didn't come here after that."

"Then why did you come here?"

"To ask you about a couple migrant workers and their families from that same era: Mateo Torres and Enrique Cantú."

Jan McClellan-Townsend's eyes narrowed in surprise and then she smiled. "You pulling my leg here, Cort Wesley?"

"Not at all, Jan."

"You mention those names, but really don't know?"

"Know what, ma'am?"

"When my father decided to branch out into marijuana farming, Torres and Cantú were the ones who grew it for him."

"It was their specialty, as I recall," she continued. "Rather specialized field at the time, but there were a host of specialists south of the border, and my father was lucky enough to have some contacts in that field from a business perspective."

"My grandfather," Cort Wesley realized, "Boone Masters senior."

"Among others, but as I've heard it told it was indeed Boone senior who connected my dad up to Torres and Cantú. They were just starting up, dirt poor at the time with nothing to show for their expertise. That's what drove them into Texas in the first place. In Mexico their skill growing cannabis was a dime a dozen. But Texas, good ole Texas, was a real emerging market. All this money being made from a true cash crop just a few miles away, what'd everybody think was going to happen? Texas was perfect for it. Local elected law was easy enough to buy off and there weren't hardly enough Rangers to walk every field in the state."

Cort Wesley fished the old photos Luke had found in Araceli Ramirez's kitchen from out of his pocket and flipped through them. He located the one picturing both families, children and all, from 1973 and handed it to Jan McClellan-Townsend.

"Yup," she said, "that's them for sure. The Cantús on the left and the Torres family on the right."

Cort Wesley took the picture back, seeing a trace of Dylan and Luke in both Mateo Torres and his wife. Not much, but enough to notice how Maura had come by her strong features and, by connection, how her sons had done the same.

"Babies look close to the same age."

"They should," Jan McClellan-Townsend said, the sun having shifted enough to catch her in its rays while leaving Cort Wesley in the shadows. "They were born the same day in seventy-three."

"Some coincidence."

"If that's what you want to call it."

"What would you call it?"

"The Torres woman gave birth to twin girls at a time the family couldn't afford to provide for the one they had. The Cantús had a son and desperately wanted a daughter. Call it an arrangement of convenience, Cort Wesley."

Cort Wesley cocked his gaze back toward Dylan as he fit things together in his mind. "The Cantús adopted one of the infants?"

"Well, I think the fathers shook hands on the deal. Back in those days, when it came to migrant workers, that was enough." McClellan-Townsend stepped out of the golf cart to stretch, her back and knees cracking like silenced gunshots. "Got so Cantú and Torres built themselves quite a franchise as growers, moving from farm to farm and training the other workers on how to tend the crop after they'd nursed it from seedlings. They had a true green thumb, Cort Wesley, and that pun is intended given how much cash they made for the landowners. But this farm held the first crop they tended and they always kept that in mind."

"Even after they stole the crop of a man named Regent Tawls and burned up his farm?"

Jan McClellan-Townsend shook her head slowly, smiling as she regarded Dylan again. "Your daddy sure can put two and two together, can't he? Let's just say, Cort Wesley, that the two families became victims of their own ambition, coming to a bad end as a result. Happened about seven, maybe eight years after that picture you showed me was taken. But you need to get the rest of the story straight."

Cort Wesley thought of another old-fashioned snapshot he'd just flipped past, one picturing Maura right around the age of seven, the latest of any found in Araceli Ramirez's shoe box. "How's that exactly?"

"To start with, Cantú wasn't that family's real name."

"No?"

Jan McClellan-Townsend shook her head. "Enrique was born to the daughter of Esteban Cantú, who I'm guessing you're familiar with. But he decided to take her name back instead of going by his father's, figuring the familiarity some people had with it might help in his business dealings."

"What was his real name?"

Jan frowned, struggling to remember it until her spine straightened and she tapped the soft roof of the golf cart. "Guajardo, I think," she said. "Yup, it was Guajardo."

70

QUINTANA ROO, MEXICO

"When you said pilots," Juan Aviles Uribe started, as he walked alongside Ana Callas Guajardo in the clearing carved into her vast stretch of acreage, which extended all the way to the edge of the jungles of the Yucatán, "I had no idea you meant . . ." He let the remark trail off, still amazed by the sights around him.

"Toys," grunted Ramon Reyes Vasquez, her other most trusted captain, shaking his head. "How do you expect to do any damage to the Americans flying toys?"

The "toys" he was referring to were among the largest radio-controlled model airplanes in the world. A variety of models produced in monster scale compared to their far smaller, and more truly toylike counterparts. The bodies of the bomber, fighter, fixed-wing, airline, and biplane models had been custom fashioned out of lightweight plastic, fiberglass, and polymers with one additional major ingredient molded into every inch of the design.

The key ingredient for Guajardo's purposes.

Some were powered by mini turbine jet engines, others by turbo props. They averaged fifteen to twenty feet in length, with wingspans stretching equal to that in some cases, and heights of up to six feet when the tail fins were included. It took only limited imagination to picture miniature crews manning the cockpits and, when viewed alone with nothing to betray their true scale, the radio-controlled planes looked every bit the same as the full-sized versions on which they'd been modeled.

Guajardo ignored Vasquez's caustic comment and turned back to Uribe. "But you found me the men I needed. You did the job expected of you."

Vasquez grunted again, insulted by her slight.

Right now, the latest hundred of the men supplied by Uribe were learning how to master the elaborate remote control device, held in both hands at once to better allow for supple and rapid maneuverability with the thumbs. Even at this size and scope, the model planes were easy to control given that there was little to learn beyond takeoff, in-flight maneuverability, and landing. The onboard sensors accounted for variations in wind speed and current and made the adjustments automatically, while each plane's course could be followed on a miniature screen built into the remote control.

"What's the range?" Uribe wondered.

"One mile," Guajardo told him. The roar of so many engines forced her to raise her voice to be heard. Around her the sweet smells of her flowering trees and plants were overcome by the lingering heavy scent of gasoline vapors, more fuel than she had anticipated being required to drive the remote-controlled planes' hundred-horsepower engines. Guajardo had gotten the idea for this stage of the plan after learning that the manufacture, distribution, and even flight plans of any and all model aircraft were not regulated in the least. And by manufacturing them down here, no one even knew they existed. "More than enough," she finished.

Vasquez uttered a low guttural sound, something like a growl, still not able to grasp the machines' purpose and potential. Guajardo was not surprised, given that she had not selected him for command responsibility based on his skills as a thinker. He'd been chosen instead for his ability to instill fear in the minds of those who served under him, the greatest deterrent to betrayal and double-cross in a business and culture driven by both.

"These were built a retooled toy manufacturing plant I purchased in Guadalajara," she continued. "The reason the models are so varied is that the purchase orders had to be made to look legitimate, especially since each is supposedly manufactured to order. A fleet of identical model craft could have raised eyebrows."

But Vasquez remained unimpressed. "This is your grand plan, what you have staked so much of our resources on?"

"It's part of my grand plan," Guajardo told him patiently, "but far from all. Just the only part of direct concern to the two of you."

"Toys will not bring the United States to her knees," Vasquez persisted, "no matter how many of them you manufacture."

Uribe smiled smugly, believing he had now figured everything out. "Unless they were carrying germs, *micros,* or whatever."

"*Microbes,*" Guajardo corrected. "But our fleet will not be carrying any microbes or any weapon at all."

"Then how do you intend to attack the Americans?" Vasquez huffed, making no effort to hide his disdain or cloak his displeasure.

"There are many forms of attack, and the one we are about to launch will not harm a single American physically, not even one."

Vasquez had turned red in the face, his massive shoulders seeming to grow wider still in the confines of his sweat-dampened olive drab shirt. "You said we'd be bringing the United States to her knees."

"I know, and it is no less true today than when I said it, *comandante.*

But did you honestly think we were going to wage a traditional war against America?" Guajardo shook her head to further emphasize her point. "I have worked for five years building a plan of attack that would hurt our enemy in ways she cannot possibly imagine. What happens when you drop an atomic bomb?"

"People die," Vasquez replied smugly, back in his element.

"And afterward?"

"More die. From the radiation."

"The results of our attack will be similar in that its effects too will linger. That was always the prime component for me. Buildings can be replaced or rebuilt. Lives can be mourned and avenged. But I sought a means to hurt America in a way in which the pain would linger and linger and linger, perhaps beyond our lifetimes, potentially forever."

Vasquez and Uribe ducked instinctively to avoid one of the giant radio-controlled planes coming in for a landing. Others buzzed the sky far overhead, birdlike specks on the horizon. The ones flying nearer to the ground struggled for space to maneuver, too close to their counterparts for comfort.

"But not from these toys alone, of course, *jefa*," Uribe said respectfully.

"As I told you, they are just one element of my plan."

"Then your plan cannot come too soon; the Texas Ranger investigating the killings in Willow Creek was spotted across the border earlier today."

"Caitlin Strong," said Ana Guajardo, struck again by the irony that another Strong was investigating a second mass killing in the same town divided by a century. Or maybe it wasn't irony at all, maybe it was something else. "I'm taking measures with her involvement in mind."

As if on cue her cell phone rang.

"I'm in San Antonio, *mi hermanita*," Locaro's strangely soft voice greeted. "Your information was correct."

"Kill as many as you have to, *mi hermano*, but there's been a slight change in plans. . . ."

71

"Sorry I'm late, Cort Wesley," Caitlin said, after squeezing through the crowd to take a seat between him and Luke in the bleachers overlooking the St. Anthony's playing field.

"Where you been?"

"What'd I miss?" she said, settling down.

"Just the warm-ups. Game's about to start. Now answer my question."

Caitlin smiled at Luke and wrapped an arm around his shoulder. "There was a misunderstanding at the border."

"This misunderstanding have a name?"

"Jones. He's not too pleased I've been messing with his people."

"*His* people?"

"That's the way Jones sees it."

Cort Wesley gnashed his teeth, the muscles in his shoulders rippling under his shirt, recalling his own interactions with the man. "Maybe I should've plucked out his eyes when I had the chance."

"Dad," said Luke, frowning.

"You never met the man, son. You need to give me a pass on this one."

"On one condition," the boy said, as the crowd rose for the national anthem.

"Name it."

"We just enjoy the game."

"We'll enjoy it a lot more if St. Anthony's wins," Caitlin said, easing her arm from Luke and focusing all her attention on the field as the school band faced the home side of the field.

72

For a moment, Locaro didn't recognize the song the band was playing. It had been so long since he'd heard the American national anthem, and when he did it stirred nothing but hate in him. That's what made this night so enriching, so rewarding.

He looked at his release from Cereso Prison as rendering him immortal in the sense that he'd already accepted death upon his life sentence there. Being released had made him feel freer than he could ever remember. No one could hurt him, no one could stop him. He was playing with the house's money here, God's money, even though he neither believed in nor prayed to Him. Locaro worshipped violence in its purest form, a means to an end. The men he'd killed in that Juárez bar had no idea of the meaning taking their lives had for him. The act had renewed his spirit and purpose, filled him with a vast surety of his potential to achieve whatever ends he sought by similar means. Tonight Locaro would kill again, but tonight it would be toward a specific purpose instead of just sport and practice.

Until wielding his machete about through muscle and flesh, he'd remained unsure of what his years in Cereso had done to his speed, reflexes, and embrace of the very act itself. But as soon as he'd cut his first man in that Juárez bar, he knew. The tightness in his spine, the pleasant flutter in the pit of his stomach, the pleasure he took in the sound of their screams and the terror in their eyes. When the light was right, he could follow the machete arcing through the air in their reflection, seeing his victims' deaths coming just as they did.

And tonight there would be more, lots more.

Somewhere in this crowd lurked the man he'd never gotten the chance to fight when they'd been in Cereso at the same time. From his windowless cell in the solitary wing he could hear the crowd roar through the many bare-knuckled brawls that kept the vast prison population from killing Cort Wesley Masters. He'd stay alive only so long as he remained *el Gringo Campeón*, certain to be killed the day he lost.

Locaro realized his men, fellow prisoners sprung from Cereso as well, had all clamped their hands over their hearts. So he did too as "The Star-Spangled Banner" played on, shifting in his wheelchair to better ready the machete to draw.

73

San Antonio

"We got plenty to talk about, Cort Wesley," Caitlin said, as they retook their seats, both of them joining the crowd in applause as St. Anthony's took the field, their face-off man moving to the center circle.

"We sure do, Ranger."

"You found what you were looking for?"

"I believe so, and it looks as if you did too."

"And then some. I know the motive behind the murder of those children in what's left of Willow Creek. I had it figured pretty close, but to look at those men at the table, those fathers . . ."

She let her voice trail off, the crowd erupting as St. Anthony's won the face-off and went on the attack, back passing to set up their offense with their front line jostling and twisting for position in front of the goal.

"Goes back to the past, Cort Wesley," Caitlin resumed.

"Doesn't it always?"

"Tell me about your field trip to the Rio Grande Valley with Dylan."

Before he could start, Dylan cut in front of the goal, took a perfect pass at stick level, and shot in the same motion. The ball zipped past the goalie, hit the back of the net, and dropped.

The crowd on the St. Anthony's side lurched to its feet en masse, hooting and cheering the goal. Caitlin turned toward the scoreboard now flashing a one for the home team.

"To begin with," Cort Wesley started, when they sat back down, "Enrique Cantú and Mateo Torres weren't your average itinerant migrant workers, Ranger. They specialized in cultivating a certain kind of crop already known to flourish south of the border before it came north to Texas."

"Marijuana," she said softly, so Luke wouldn't hear. But his attention was rooted squarely on the game, watching his brother's every move even on the sideline when Dylan came out for a breather with the rest of his line.

"And that's not all. Cantú wasn't that family's real name. Enrique chose to use his mother's maiden name instead of his father's: Guajardo."

"You've got my attention, Cort Wesley."

"I've saved the best for last, Ranger."

But the crowd erupted again before he could continue, when the St. Anthony's goalie made a spectacular scoop save on a rocketed, bouncing shot, cradling the ball in the box while looking for someone to clear. Everyone on the home side sprung to their feet again, except for a grouping of military veterans watching the game in wheelchairs from field level just off a back sideline.

Locaro didn't understand the game at all and didn't care. He cared only about the player wearing the number forty-one burgundy jersey for the St. Anthony's side, the player who'd scored the first goal.

Dylan Torres.

All that stopped Locaro from giving the order to his snipers to open fire was being still unsure of where the younger Torres boy was located in the crowd on the home side of the field. One of his men was already seated there, constantly shifting position in search of him.

"*Lo encontré, jefe*," Locaro heard through the tiny wireless bud in his ear that looked like a hearing aid. "I found *el muchacho americano*."

Locaro raised the hand holding a similarly small transmitter. "*Prepárense para disparar*," he told his snipers camouflaged on the school roof. "Prepare to fire."

* * *

"The two little girls in those pictures were sisters, Ranger," Cort Wesley continued.

Caitlin looked at him, forgetting the game and the noise.

"Twins," he elaborated, "both born to Carmen and Mateo Torres. But they couldn't afford to raise both of them, so the Cantú family offered to take one in."

"A third sister," Caitlin realized, "along with Maura and Araceli. That means her life's likely in danger too, and her family's. What was her name, Cort Wesley? Did Jan McClellan-Townsend tell you that?"

Cort Wesley nodded. "Ana."

"Ana Cantú."

"Not Cantú, remember? Ana *Guajardo*," Cort Wesley said, the row just behind them jostling as a small Latino man wearing a baseball cap squeezed into a seat behind Luke.

74

SAN ANTONIO

With his man in the crowd now in place, Locaro saw no reason to wait any longer. His snipers' instructions were to take out as many players as they could measure in their sights in rapid succession. Two of them, placed strategically apart from each other on the rooftop. In the chaos that followed, Locaro and his remaining men would storm the field blazing an indiscriminate path through the resulting panic while Locaro himself took care of Dylan Torres. By then, he fully expected the protective forces of Guillermo Paz to have joined the fray as well, and it unnerved Locaro no end that neither Paz nor his men seemed to be anywhere about. He could only hope that the guise formed by the wheelchairs and fake military uniforms complete with various medals awarded for distinguished service would hold long enough.

Locaro shifted positions again, stretching his arms high over the wheelchair to better ready the draw of his machete, his chosen instrument of death since he'd killed his first man while working citrus fields as a boy in Texas.

In that moment, Ana Guajardo was thinking about that very same day. Remembered because it was just after her seventh birthday, in 1980. Ana had watched as the man, a newly hired American work foreman, had pushed her mother. Then slapped her. Then shoved her to the ground. Then dragged her off into the nearby fields.

Her father had been taken away a few weeks before by *la policía*. Ana didn't know what her father had done, and refused to cry when her father had been arrested and handcuffed to prove she was brave, eyeing the uniformed figures with contempt. Locaro had come to her then, wrapping an arm knobby with muscle for a boy around her shoulder and leaving it there to reassure her she was safe, that he would protect both her and her mother.

The day the man had dragged her mother off into the citrus fields was hazy, more like a dream than a memory. Ana remembered following them into the groves of thick stalks that smelled like skunk, clinging to the hope that Locaro would somehow follow to keep his promise. She remembered looking about for Locaro, thought of crying out his name but didn't.

Her mother and the new foreman whose clothes smelled like piss were mostly lost to the shadows cast by the thickly congested plantings that shifted slightly in the breeze. He was lying prone over her, Ana following his strangely gyrating motions. As he moved up and down over her mother, an old shriveled orange appeared amid the plantings, sent rolling toward her until it came to a halt against the sandaled foot of her brother, Locaro.

He held a finger to his lips to signal her to be quiet. Then Ana watched through the strange haze as Locaro moved soundlessly into the thick foul-smelling grove. Watched as he stooped to retrieve a machete another worker had left behind. Watched him bring the machete, which looked absurdly large in his grasp, overhead and lash it downward.

It stuck in the neck of the new foreman who stank of piss and Locaro pulled it out, the man jerking a hand up to the bloody gash. Ana remembered that Locaro's next strike partially severed the hand, and his third strike found the original gash and dug deeper.

The blood became a spurt, a fountain, the new foreman falling over sideways when he tried to rise. Ana watched Locaro leap over their mother onto him, slicing down with the machete again and again until he was covered with the blood and what was left of the man no longer moved. In the haze of memory today, Ana remembered wiping blood from her own face and clothes, wondering how it had sprayed so far. She had no recollection of her mother from that point, only of Locaro leading her back to their small shack that seemed so empty since their father had been taken away. Her mother had taken her out back and hosed off the blood, Ana figuring she must have done the same to herself first. So brave and strong, the way Ana would be someday too. Locaro had hovered nearby the whole time, her protector then and forever.

Ana often dreamed of that day but never recalled all the details upon waking. As if her brain sought to hide it from her to spare her further pain. What happened that day remained cloaked by a sheer curtain that revealed only shapes. Ana supposed she should be grateful for that much, and yet sometimes she woke at night screaming with some terrible truth revealed by the dream lost before she caught her next breath.

Locaro was only just beginning to realize how different he was from other children when he'd killed the new work foreman, how much bigger and stronger he was than they. But there was something more, something Locaro found in the mirror in the wake of killing for the first time with the machete he'd washed in the clothes trough and hidden under his bunk. His head looked funny even to him; block-shaped with a ridged, almost simian forehead that seemed to hang out over his brow. His neck was too small for his squat, barrel-like frame, making it seem as if his head was an extension of his shoulders. His fingers were short, stubby, and strangely gnarled. One of his eyes hung noticeably lower than the other and always drooped.

Only the older boys dared make fun of him and, after killing the work foreman, he began responding to their insults with unbridled attacks, launching himself on them in unrelenting fashion until others pulled him off. Locaro learned then the lesson that size was not nearly as important as will, translating desire to action without hesitation. It was a lesson that stayed with him all the way into an adulthood that saw his appearance neither change nor worsen, but merely stay the same. A blown-up version of the very same frame and features that made him reviled as a boy, save for the unfortunate addition of a skin condition that left his face marred with oozing boils and the pockmark scars left behind when Locaro picked at them with a knife.

His sister was the only one who viewed him without revulsion. From the day that he'd killed his first man, they became inseparable. But even Ana couldn't grasp how much he had enjoyed the feel and smell of blood upon him. He began to thirst for it, never happier than when it spilled or sprayed from his victims.

Blood *was* life, after all.

"*Fuego*," he ordered his snipers, hand at his mouth, finally ready. "Fire."

Just as the Torres boy whipped another blistering shot with his webbed stick into the goal.

75

San Antonio

Caitlin and Cort Wesley joined the rest of the crowd on its feet, cheering for the goal that put St. Anthony's up two to nothing.

"You need to explain this game to me again, Cort Wesley."

But Cort Wesley's eyes had darted back toward the school building to their right, gaze canting upward.

"Something's going on up there," he said without looking back at her. "Someone's on the roof. Something's wrong."

Then he was in motion, shoving his way through the crowded row still celebrating Dylan's second goal. Caitlin reached over to Luke to take him in tow with her to follow, when a shape from the row above lunged over her for the boy.

Something *was* wrong, Locaro realized.

The sniper fire hadn't started, even as a commotion broke out in the stands right around the location of the other Torres boy.

Locaro looked to his men gathered in wheelchairs, dressed as American Army veterans, which had provided them field access to view the game. They had been saluted instead of searched, the players on the home team making a show out of shaking all their hands in a kind of reception line before pregame warm-ups.

The unexpected gesture had unnerved Locaro, especially when he shook the hand of Dylan Torres, though not as much as the current state of affairs here and now did.

Something had happened to his snipers. His plan had gone to shit.

Which meant it was time for a new plan. His snipers were gone, taken out. But he had his men. He had his machete.

And Guillermo Paz was somewhere about.

It could only be Paz, Locaro thought as he lurched out of his wheelchair, yanking the machete from beneath his fatigue jacket and charging toward the playing field.

His men fell into a surge behind him, whipping out their guns.

Jesus Christ, Cort Wesley thought, recognizing what was coming in the last moment before the men disguised as disabled veterans launched their attack.

He'd reached the aisle by then, thundering down it with Glock drawn, the crowd just starting to realize that something was about to go terribly wrong, rising to its collective feet, prepared to flee en masse when the staccato din of automatic fire sounded from high in the bleachers. The entire crowd forced downward, the attackers steadying their weapons as they charged over the edge of the field.

Cort Wesley's thoughts came in fragments, snippets. He felt his feet stop churning amid the jostle of bodies around him, saw his own pistol coming up, thought having yielded to instinct, trying to find Dylan amid the burgeoning chaos.

Ready to fire when he thought of Caitlin and Luke now trapped somewhere behind him.

Ready to fire as a pickup truck with double rear tires crashed through the fence surrounding the complex from the near side and tore onto the field.

Caitlin intercepted the figure in midair, the blade he held glinting in the bright stadium lighting just inches from Luke. She grabbed him by the hair and shoulder at the same time and flung him backward, where he crashed into seated patrons not yet aware of the maelstrom about to consume the field.

She lost her grasp on him, but never lost sight of the knife, lunging up and over her row of seats as gunfire erupted somewhere below.

Cort Wesley was living the nightmare. Again. It came to him often in the uneasiest nights of his sleep when worry over the future of his sons consumed his thinking. He'd finally slip off to find himself in a firefight with the Iraqi Republican Guard back in the Gulf War. In the dream, they kept coming no matter how many he shot or how many fresh mags he jammed into his M16. It was like being trapped in a video game, only the ground was sinking beneath his feet and Cort Wesley found himself fearing the eternal promised darkness more than the Iraqis' Russian-made bullets or shrapnel.

Tonight the stands remained firm beneath him as he fired, emptying the Glock's magazine toward the dark-clad men disguised as disabled veterans. He thought he counted seven in total, including one who looked like the base of an oak tree in motion, reddening blotches on his face shimmering in the stadium lights.

From this distance he managed to drop only two of the seven, taking them in the face or skull above their body armor. Their fall had no effect on the remaining five, neither slowing nor stopping them from opening fire into the sudden rush of panic that had overtaken the field with St. Anthony's home burgundy jerseys and the white uniforms of the visiting team.

Where was Dylan?

That thought formed as breath bottlenecked in his throat and misty froth burst from several visitors' uniform tops as they were hit with bullets that spun the still-helmeted players around or felled them where they stood. Now the stands had erupted in full-fledged panic, Cort Wesley struggling to hold his ground, not even remembering slapping a fresh magazine into the Glock.

No way he could reach the field to stop the madness before it converged on Dylan, he thought as Guillermo Paz burst up through the pickup truck's sunroof, opening fire on the gunmen disguised as veterans with twin submachine guns as its double rear tires thumped across the field.

Caitlin lost track of Luke in the crowd surge that seemed to be moving in all directions at once. It was like getting sucked into the funnel of a tornado, but the knife-wielding man had got sucked into it too.

She shoved a woman aside and then yanked on someone's ponytail to reach the attacker again after he'd briefly broken free. His knife must have been knocked from his grasp on impact and he was just retrieving it from the floor of the steel bleacher when Caitlin pounced on him. She got his knife wrist pinned with her left hand and began whaling at him with her right. Hand laced into a tight fist with fingers pressed high into the pads. She led with her knuckles, pounding him again and again and again, long strands of his blood coughed into the air until his nose mashed under her fist and the strands gave way to a geyser. She was vaguely aware her hand looked painted red and could feel the stray flecks spraying up into her face.

"Caitlin!"

Luke's voice. Luke hugging her, trying to pull her off, the man's features unrecognizable below, his face a mass of pits, hollowed and broken flesh. Caitlin felt the boy tugging at her, her gaze shifting in search of Dylan to the field now awash in panic, muzzle flashes, and the echoing din of gunshots.

76

San Antonio

Cort Wesley hurdled the interior fence enclosing the field and outdoor track. He had no recollection of pushing his way through the panicked crowd to get this far, only dimly aware of the chorus of screams and staccato bursts of fire from Guillermo Paz's twin submachine guns. Paz's huge, dark shape looked to be part of the big, black pickup from which he had burst. There were bodies everywhere, many still writhing, and the endless swell of panicked kids and adults stole any chance of him finding Dylan in his sights.

Cort Wesley entered that swell, the feeling like being swept under by an ocean wave. The panicked crowd even seemed to suck the oxygen out of the air, making it hard to breathe, the world turned oven-hot, those he pushed his way past literally steaming to the touch.

"Dylan!" he yelled out. "Dylan!"

He could barely hear himself, but he screamed the boy's name again, his left arm carving the way forward while his right hand clung to the pistol. The body of a boy in a burgundy uniform nearly tripped him up, and Cort Wesley dropped to a crouch with his heart lurching against his chest wall, breath held until he saw it wasn't Dylan; then both sadness and rage consumed him when he saw there was nothing left to be done for the boy.

Beneath the heavy spill of the stadium vapor lights, he could now see more bodies dotting the field. He'd just steered toward another shape wearing a burgundy uniform top crumpled on the field turf when a teammate pushed fleeing bystanders aside so he could drop down to help. The boy shed his stick, knelt by his fallen teammate's side, and tore off his helmet to let a nest of long black hair swim freely.

Dylan! It was Dylan!

Cort Wesley surged forward, noticing crazed shadows of the panicked projected against nearby buildings by the sodium lights, cast as massive sentinels looming over the chaos. He was halfway across the field when the crowd buckled and pushed back against him, the massive pickup from which Paz was firing scattering them as a pair of the killers dressed as disabled veterans closed on Dylan.

Locaro pushed his way through the crowd that had engulfed him on the field, flinging anyone aside when they loomed too close. His eyes swept the blood-strewn scene he'd created, his ears awash in the sounds of screams and the gunshots of his remaining men.

He'd focused his attention initially on the uniformed police assigned to the event, four of them woefully inadequate to respond with mere pistols. Locaro killed them with his machete, moving from one to another to clear the way for his men to storm the field.

But events continued to conspire against him. First his snipers had been taken out, then two of his men were dropped where they stood by someone firing from the crowd.

The woman Texas Ranger maybe, or the outlaw father of his target. Uniform number forty-one currently lost from sight.

But the Venezuelan, the muck-dwelling Mayan, Guillermo Paz made for his biggest problem. The Ranger's and these boys' protector roaring across the field in a truck from hell, holding the remainder of his men at bay, shooting two more down. That left only two still with him on the field to join the search for the older target, while all the panic the attack had created stole sight of him from the younger one in the stands.

Locaro couldn't help but smile, loving the world being made before him. He didn't want to let go of the sights, sounds, and smells, wanted them to go on forever.

But Locaro saw that wasn't going to happen, as his final two men closed on a boy wearing a burgundy uniform numbered forty-one.

Caitlin felt Luke clinging fast to her as they pushed down the bleacher steps for the field, gunshots continuing to echo through the night.

Not once had she experienced anything like this, guessed even the prison and labor riots her father and grandfather had been called in to stop couldn't compare. She remembered going to football games herself, a cannon ignited whenever the home team scored, leaving the smell of sulfur and cordite to waft across the stands. The smell was similar tonight, the gunshots coming in pops not unlike Fourth of July firecrackers.

She finally reached the waist-high chain-link fencing but held her ground, suspended between staying here to protect Luke and joining Cort Wesley on the field in search of Dylan.

What if Dylan came this way instead? What if Cort Wesley somehow missed him?

That made her decision easier, dragging Luke in tighter against her with the SIG palmed in her free hand. Caitlin was running her gaze over the panic still dominating the field when a sliver in the crowd opened up, allowing her to catch enough of a glimpse of a St. Anthony's player kneeling by a fallen teammate to know it was Dylan. Knew it before she even saw his number or hair swimming past his shoulders.

Knew it even as a pair of gunmen finally cleared the crowd enough to find him in their sights.

Cort Wesley saw them too, desperately trying to find enough of a window through the crowd to fire and too far away to bother mounting an effective charge.

If he opened fire now, he was certain to hit bystanders, accomplishing nothing. If he didn't, the killers had a clear path to Dylan, accomplishing less. The situation was further muddled by so many parents and team supporters wearing replica burgundy team jerseys, adding another element to the madness. They seemed everywhere now, mirror reflections of Dylan and his teammates, like the downed one over whom the boy was now kneeling.

But the crowd blocked Cort Wesley's sight and path again, leaving the two gunmen a much clearer path to Dylan, as Guillermo Paz's pickup surged the rest of the way through the crowd. Its huge tires ground wildly, kicking up the black pellets that helped provide traction on the turf. Scattering bystanders from its path and grazing those who didn't lurch aside fast enough.

77

SAN ANTONIO

Caitlin was a good shot, but this was going to need a better one, along the lines of Earl and William Ray Strong. Frontier shooters who lived as long as their skills permitted and not a day more. She could only wish either of them, or even her father, Jim Strong, was with her now to take the shot she couldn't risk through the crowd still fleeing in all directions across the field.

In that moment Paz's pickup truck crossed her line of vision. In that moment she grasped his intentions and flinched involuntarily, tensing with the certainty of what was to come.

The pickup roared past Dylan, putting itself between him and the two gunmen in the last instant before they opened fire. Their bullets pinged into the truck's heavy steel frame, a burst of wet mist from the grill indicating at least one had pierced the radiator. But the truck surged on, still picking up speed.

Caitlin actually covered Luke's eyes in the moment before impact, the big truck's extended after-market grill slamming into both men at once, hurtling them like bowling pins in separate directions. A combination of the impact and bullet spray sent the pickup whirling into an uncontained spin, the G-forces at that speed sufficient to topple it over. Caitlin saw the huge form of Paz either leaping out of it or being ejected to safety.

Then her eyes were drawn to the origin of fresh screams to see the stout man who looked overgrown with muscle hacking his way through anyone in his path with a machete that showered blood into the air like rain.

"Stay here!" she ordered Luke, pressing him against the corner of a concession stand. "I'm going to get your brother."

Incensed after the collision killed his last two men, Locaro decided to finish the boy his way, on his own. This is where guns had gotten the team he'd brought with him; dead, all of them. The best he could find, desperate to breathe the air outside of Cereso Prison again, men as tough as they came killed by their reliance on weapons they falsely believed rendered them invincible.

Locaro would never make that mistake. Locaro avoided guns at all costs, preferred the old ways for the terror they inspired in his enemies. He could find no trace of Paz anywhere around the toppled truck, leaving him an easy path to the uniformed boy still crouched over his teammate, hand pressed to stanch the blood oozing from a chest wound.

Locaro continued to use his machete to clear that path, showered again in the blood of his victims and finally meeting the boy's gaze when he drew to within twenty feet, *thwacks* of bullets against his flak jacket stealing his air.

Caitlin was ready to fire when she saw Cort Wesley shove more bystanders aside and take up a shooter's stance. He was still fifty feet away from the shape only vaguely resembling a human being that was about to kill Dylan, his initial shots somehow squeezed between more of those fleeing.

Those bullets barely slowed the man down, as if he were made of steel instead of flesh and bone. But Caitlin steadied her SIG once more, ready to try for an impossible shot.

Cort Wesley didn't have time to aim his initial shots, hoping only to slow the machete-wielding madman long enough to allow him to sight in for a kill shot to the head. While in Cereso he'd heard rumors of such a man languishing in the stench-riddled bowels of the prison from which no one ever emerged. A man whose final act as a free man had been to hack off the arms of two of the Mexican policemen who'd come to arrest him for throwing his own father off a fourth-story balcony. Then he'd dropped his machete and sank to his knees laughing.

Cort Wesley knew in that moment this was the same man, wished he'd gotten his chance at him in the dusty ring forged out of the prison yard when fights to the death were all that had kept him alive. Then he wouldn't have needed to deal with him here. He fired two more shots for the man's head, the first aimed high to stretch over the heads of on-rushing bystanders and the second jerked errantly aside when a flood of them crossed his line of vision at the last moment.

Just one bullet left now.

Cort Wesley didn't hesitate, couldn't hesitate. Fired with a reasonably clear shot. Saw the man-monster reel sideways, hand to the side of his head where the bullet had impacted. Coming away with an ear in his hand and turning toward Cort Wesley.

With a smile.

Cort Wesley in motion now, sprinting, knowing there was no way to reach the man-monster before the man-monster reached Dylan.

Still dazed from the heavy fall, Guillermo Paz finally made it back to his knees, as tall even then as many of those rushing past him. He had his knife in hand, ready to hurl it toward Locaro at the first opening of space. Locaro still holding his severed ear as he swung back toward the oldest son of Cort Wesley Masters, who had taken something else in his grasp.

* * *

Dylan had known the boy at his feet was dead, had known it for some time, but still couldn't bring himself to move his hand from the wound, as if applying pressure might miraculously bring him back to life. Who knew?

Only when the stump-shaped man who looked pumped full of air discarded the ear his father had shot off did Dylan release his hand from his friend's chest and grasp the lacrosse stick by his side. He brought it up from his knees, the ball he'd scooped up before the killing started still trapped in the webbing, and fired a shot as if the man bleeding down the side of his face was the opponent's goal.

High for the corner.

Aiming for his third goal of the night.

The ball struck the man square in the forehead, halting him as if someone had just slammed on his internal brakes. His eyes remained open the whole time he dropped to his knees and then keeled over, freeing Dylan to return his hand to the hole in his dead friend's chest.

He felt that hand being pried off by his father, no idea how much time had passed or where his dad had come from.

"Let it go, son, let it go."

Dylan let his father move his hand away, saying nothing, not even feeling himself breathe as he spotted Caitlin rushing toward him too. Then his gaze shifted sideways toward where he'd dropped the killer, who looked somehow like the Michelin Man, with a lacrosse shot.

But he was gone.

"Where's Luke?" Cort Wesley asked when Caitlin reached them.

She turned back toward the field-level concession stand that they'd taken cover alongside of, Luke certain to be in her view from this angle.

"Oh, shit" was all Caitlin could say.

Because he was gone too.

PART EIGHT

Free as the unchained winds that sweep the boundless prairie, he was a terror to the incarnate Mexican Devils, a sworn foe to the Indians, who with torch, tomahawk and blood-freezing warwhoop terrified helpless women and children; the ranger, characteristic exponent of the Anglo-Saxon race, drove every enemy away from him and established peace and contentment.

Katie Daffan, *Texas Hero Stories* (1908)

78

Captain D. W. Tepper's face was ash white, his expresion utterly flat with an unlit Marlboro hanging out the left side of his mouth. He reached Caitlin, who'd just separated herself from Cort Wesley and Dylan, and flung the cigarette aside.

"Witness statements aren't worth shit," Tepper told her. "Near as we can figure, the same Mexican who shot up the crowd made off with Luke on foot. No one saw them enter a vehicle and we can't find a single person who saw the man you and Masters figure was the leader flee the area. Hell, maybe he just goddamn disappeared." He swung his gaze back about the chaos that continued to dominate the field under the harsh glow of the stadium lights that now sliced through a slight mist. "Have you ever considered another line of work, Ranger?"

"Not until tonight, Captain."

"Good thing maybe," he said, expression looking as if it were caught halfway through a belch.

"You blaming me for this now?"

Tepper's expression didn't change, his bony shoulders stiffening as if to keep from turning back toward the utter carnage littering almost the entire field that was dark with drying patches and pools of blood. "No, Caitlin, I'm not. I'm just asking because that's the way I feel right now." He started to turn to regard what he'd just walked away from, but stopped. "I was at the scene after a nutcase named George Hennard crashed his pickup truck into Luby's Cafeteria in Killeen and then shot up a whole bunch of folks eating their lunch. I was one of the first inside of the Branch Davidian complex in Waco, and haven't been able to get the smell of burned hair and flesh out of my mind since. You wanna tell me what chance I ever have of sleeping again after this?"

Caitlin returned her gaze to the carnage that looked day-glow bright under the sodium vapor lights, the litter of bodies being properly cataloged and zipped into bags while blood-soaked EMTs and volunteers rushed wheeled dollies across the turf, over a field where a district championship lacrosse game should have been played out instead, now turned into a triage unit.

"Who was he?" Tepper asked her. "That freak show of a man who got away somehow."

"I have no idea, Captain."

"I think I do," Cort Wesley said, standing back a ways with his arm stretched around Dylan's shoulder, spine held so straight he looked a half foot taller.

"For all the good that does us," Tepper said, after Cort Wesley had finished describing what he'd heard while in Cereso.

"Somebody got him out of there, Captain," Cort Wesley told him. "And now he's got Luke."

Tepper held his expression steady. "We got roadblocks in place in a five-mile radius. We got choppers, and dogs, the Highway Patrol, and the ghosts of every dead Ranger out there looking."

Cort Wesley shook his head and ran his tongue around the inside of his parched mouth. "None of it matters. They'd have the escape route planned out. They could have killed Luke, but they wanted him alive."

"Because whoever's behind this knows we're getting close," said Caitlin grimly, her determination growing with each word. "They needed leverage, something to hold us back. Means they've gotta keep him alive, Cort Wesley, and that means we're going to find where he's stashed no matter what it takes."

If the assurance meant anything to him, he didn't show it. "You shouldn't have left him, Ranger," Cort Wesley said almost too soft to hear, as if the words belonged to somebody else.

"Dad," Dylan started.

"Quiet, son," Cort Wesley snapped, never taking his eyes off Caitlin. "We just can't help ourselves, can we? No matter when and where the bell goes off, we're off racing to the fire and everything else be damned."

"This one's on me, Cort Wesley. I don't know what I was thinking."

"I do," said Captain Tepper. "I know exactly what you were thinking because it's what you're always thinking, and this time it caught up to you." He shook his head. "What is it about you that attracts this shit? I swear, Ranger, you are like some kind of super magnet dragging every monster the good Lord ever made straight to you." Tepper raised another cigarette to his mouth and started a lighter toward it. The lighter trembled in his hand but he managed to touch it to the Marlboro's tip, eyes retrained on Caitlin. "You know how I always tell you to ease back on those hurricane force winds that blow with you?"

"Category Ten you've called them."

"Well, this time I'm gonna find shelter in my basement and let you go at it."

"D.W.?"

Tepper turned away, continuing to puff on his Marlboro as he responded. "No reports, no actuarials, no travel logs, no time sheets, no gas vouchers, no powdering your nose, and no missing what you shoot at. As of now you are on special assignment and nobody needs know where or how, and that includes me. In fact, all I ever want to know is that it's done once and for all. You find out the why, you find out the who, Ranger, and you leave them the way they left our people here tonight. That clear enough for you?"

Caitlin could only nod.

"Your granddad used to put men on the chain when he cleaned up

Sweetwater during the oil boom. I expect you to wrap that chain around as many deserving necks as you can find. Just get that boy back."

Then, shaking his head, he walked off, leaving Caitlin with Cort Wesley and Dylan.

"What now, Ranger?"

"We go old school, Cort Wesley, just like Captain Tepper said."

79

San Antonio

"You go on ahead," Caitlin told him. "I'll meet you at home. Got somebody else I need to talk to first."

Cort Wesley held his gaze on her the whole way back to the parking lot, while Caitlin looked about until she spotted a figure standing by the glass of the press box, the one spot in the stadium lost to darkness. She located the back stairs leading up to it behind the home section of stands and found the single long table set with folding chairs still littered with notebooks and laptops, the attending press having fled in such a hurry that they'd left them behind.

"His name is Locaro," said Guillermo Paz, stepping into a thin sliver of light so she could see him. "He used to keep reasonable order between the cartels. For a time they needed to seek his permission before killing a major public official or rival. Our paths have crossed before."

Caitlin looked at Paz through the darkness between them. "I'm trying to understand something here, Colonel."

"What's that?"

"Some problems I'm having with how things got handled tonight."

"Are you talking about you or me?"

"Guess we've both had better nights, haven't we?"

"My men took out the snipers," Paz said defensively, unnerved by

Caitlin's criticism. "We thought we had them trapped. The wheelchair guises took even me by surprise."

"Is that it or did you force Locaro's hand so you could let it play out just the way it did?"

"You rushed the field instead of staying with the boy. I guess that makes us both prisoners, Ranger."

"Of what?"

"Our natures."

"That's a goddamn cop-out and you know it."

"You're raising your voice because you're mad at yourself."

"But I'm talking to you." Caitlin again turned her voice toward the window. "This didn't have to happen."

"And it didn't have to end the way it did."

"You know what, Colonel? I'm starting to think you're no different from the man who had the mother of Cort Wesley's boys killed. Maybe I had you wrong. I think maybe you knew it was Locaro all along tonight. I think maybe you wanted this to happen," she added, casting another gaze outside a window now dappled with flashes of red from revolving lights both leaving and entering the scene.

"Keep going."

"Excuse me?"

"It helps to turn your anger on me, so you won't turn too much of it on yourself. You're capable of hurting yourself more than any of your enemies, Ranger, but that makes you weaker and thus vulnerable to them."

"So you're saying what? I should just forget the fact that I got a boy kidnapped tonight while you let a war break out?"

"We did what was right for one moment, not the next. And it's in that moment we must judge ourselves."

"Is that how you've lived with all this shit for so long, Colonel?"

"I used to have a different approach than you, Ranger."

"How's that?"

"I used to remain above it all without feeling, until our paths crossed for the first time. Now I live within it, the same way you do."

"Means you get to experience pain, Colonel. How's that feel?"

Now it was Paz who turned his gaze toward the window. "I'm not finished with Locaro yet."

"And I won't rest until I bring Luke back safe and sound."

They looked at each other again.

"That's how we live with all this, Ranger."

80

MEDINA COUNTY, TEXAS

"Thanks for coming on such short notice, Mr. Tawls," Caitlin greeted, not shaking the man's hand since it would've hurt too much with the bruised knuckles of her right hand wrapped in gauze.

The first thing Regent Tawls glimpsed after he closed the door was a man digging a hole on the outer rim of the wasteland that had once been his farm. The man's bare chest showcased banded muscles across his arms and shoulders and pectorals that looked like baseballs tucked into his chest. At this time of the morning, when the sun was right, he could distinguish the burned patch of earth that had ruined the dreams bred from his life when he was still a young man. But it was the bare-chested man with thick shovel in hand that continued to claim his attention, as he approached Caitlin Strong.

She'd called Regent Tawls and asked him to meet her on the site of his former farm in Medina County just outside of Devine after the indescribable violence at St. Anthony's school had culminated in Luke's kidnapping the night before. She managed to steal some sleep in fits and starts broken by nightmares featuring the monster of a man named Locaro hovering over her bedside.

"The boy's mine now," he told her with a grin and, for some reason, the thing she recalled most clearly was a stomach-turning stench that rose off him.

The sun-scorched ground on what had been Regent Tawls's farm was brown, impossible to distinguish where the refuse of crops grown ended and dirt began, although both smelled musky and sour beneath an unforgiving sky. Looking at the surroundings now, it was hard to picture life ever having sprouted from it, like regarding a massive above-the-earth grave where the dead were still awaiting last rites.

Moments before she watched Regent Tawls pull onto the property in his white Cadillac, which shimmered in the sunlight. The heat rose from its hood in visible ripples that continued to churn as he exited and approached her, forcing a smile even as the buttons of his shirt showed the strain of keeping his stomach contained. His walk was more of a lumbering gait, his cheeks shiny with perspiration that also dappled his forehead in actual drops, his eyes squinting to better make out the solitary figure digging away at the hard ground that fought his efforts every step of the way.

"I appreciate you meeting me out here," Caitlin continued.

"Well, Ranger, truth be told, I thought you might have an eye on the property," he said with a smile, a bad attempt at humor that produced no response from Caitlin.

"I believe there are some things you've been leaving out of your story about what happened here in nineteen-eighty."

The smile slipped from his face, his eyes darting back toward the hole digger in the hope he might be gone. But instead, he had seemed to redouble his efforts upon Tawls's arrival. "And what things would those be?"

"Well, sir, I did some back checking to the original investigation and reports," Caitlin told him. "My dad was one of those investigating the theft and the fire in the fall of that year. You were very cooperative at first, full of information, clues, and even indications where you thought the likely culprits could be found."

"So what's the problem?"

"Maybe you didn't hear me say 'at first.' When Jim Strong came back for follow-up, you clammed up. Suddenly had nothing to say, and you even retracted some of your earlier claims and insisted some of the information you'd furnished had been given in error. Have I got that right?"

"Not to my recollection, Ranger. But you know how many years ago this was now?"

"Yes, I do, sir, down to the day, and there are some things I can't expect a man to forget, lying to the Texas Ranger investigating a theft from his farm and subsequent arson being one of them. Something like that tends to stick."

Tawls shrugged his already slumped shoulders. "Like I said—"

"I know what you said, just like I know what you said all those years ago. Problem is, it doesn't add up; or what it does add up to creates a significantly different picture from the one you've been sketching."

"Ranger, I—"

"You see the news last night about what happened at St. Anthony's High School?"

"The lacrosse game shooting? It's been on the air nonstop. It's . . . horrible," Tawls managed, immediately looking as if he wished he'd chosen a different word.

"Sir, I believe whoever's behind that incident, which included the kidnapping of a teenage boy, is very much connected to what happened on this farm of yours here in nineteen-eighty. I believe there's plenty more you haven't told me that you're going to tell me now."

Tawls looked about the wasteland around him, hoping to see someone else about besides the hole digger. A hitchhiker, squatter, vagrant, potential buyer—anything. But there was no one. Just him, a hole digger, and a Texas Ranger known for planting more bodies in the ground than any gunfighter in Texas history.

"You know what he's digging?" Caitlin asked him, joining Tawls's gaze toward the outer reaches of his former farm where the sour ground had taken on the texture of concrete.

"I'd rather not speculate, Ranger."

"Let me put it this way, then, sir: do you have any idea how many bodies of Mexican bandits and Comanche are buried in this area, maybe right here on this very land?"

"Quite a few I've heard told," Tawls said, swallowing hard.

"Many of them planted by the Texas Rangers and dumped in makeshift graves where they've yet to be found to this day." Caitlin took a step closer to him, angling herself to block his view of the hole digger. "You know the Comanche could fire arrow after arrow without hardly a pause and those Mexican bandits often outnumbered the Rangers ten to one, but those Rangers prevailed. We're still prevailing, Mr. Tawls, but it's been a long time since we've been in the grave-digging business." She turned sideways so he could see the hole digger again. "That changed last night. All bets are off now. On top of that kidnapping, we've got fifteen dead so far and five times that hospitalized, and it's a miracle there weren't more of both. I can't tell you much more, but one thing I can tell you for sure is anyone who stops me from doing the job I'm sworn as a Ranger to do might as well be six feet under for all I care. And I won't give it any more thought than the Rangers who preceded me with bullets as well as shovels. Are we clear so far?"

Tawls shielded his eyes to better see into the sun, to where the bare-chested hole digger had stopped his toils and was now leaning against the shovel, seeming to look right back at him.

"I asked if we were clear," Caitlin repeated.

Tawls barely managed a nod. "I promised never to breathe a word of this. Not then, not now, not ever."

"Promised who?"

"This young Mexican cop who paid me a visit a few weeks after the fire."

"You tell him your story?"

"I didn't have to. He already knew it. Said the fact I'd been burned out gave it away."

"Wait a minute, this cop came up from *Mexico*?"

Tawls nodded. "Said he was part of some new task force or something. Said there wasn't much he could do for me, other than help me gain the justice I deserved. Said they'd likely already dumped my crop by then and were likely hiding out down in Mexico. He wanted to know everything I could tell him about Enrique Cantú and Mateo Torres. He promised me justice in return for me clamming up to anyone else in on the investigation. That included your father."

"And you went along with him?"

"He made it plain I didn't have a choice, threatened me with extradition to face charges in Mexico if I didn't do everything he asked."

"It didn't occur to you to share this during our last conversation?"

"I don't recall you asking me about it. I answered your questions then, just like I'm answering them now. Don't pin this on me. I'm sorry about the people who were killed or hurt last night, and I'm sorry about that kidnapped boy, okay?"

"So long as you can assure me you're telling me everything this time."

Tawls sighed deeply, his squinting into the sun having folded the excess flesh around his eyes into layers. "Nineteen-eighty marked the official end of my tenure as a grower. Guess I just wasn't cut out for that sort of thing."

"I imagine you made plenty before that day came."

"I was underinsured. Believe me when I tell you I came out on the short end of things."

"What about the Mexican cop?"

"Never saw him again. You want to know what happened from that point, you'll have to ask him."

"What's his name?"

And Caitlin felt her mouth drop as Tawls provided it.

81

Medina County, Texas

Cort Wesley waited until Regent Tawls had driven off before pulling his arms back into his shirt and traipsing toward Caitlin. His hands were raw and he could feel the dull sting of blisters already forming from driving the shovel head into dead ground that felt like highway hardpan. But the discomfort felt better than the gnawing that had plagued him since Luke's kidnapping the night before. For some reason he'd always thought his younger son was somehow immune to the shit he dragged behind him. It was always Dylan who suffered for his transgressions and his very being.

Now all that had changed and Cort Wesley had a stale and bitter taste in his dry mouth ever since he'd realized Luke was gone the night before. No call had come yet, but it didn't have to; the kidnapping was a message in itself, a message Cort Wesley wasn't about to comply with.

"Wish I could saddle up with you on this one, bubba," said Leroy Epps, suddenly by his side. *"Get that boy of yours back."*

"Oh, we'll get him back, champ. You can bet your life on that."

"It's not worth much at this point, but I'll see if I can check on him all the same."

Cort Wesley reached Caitlin without recalling the rest of the distance covered, certain the grim, determined look painted on her worn features matched his own.

"We're headed to Mexico, Cort Wesley, to follow up a lead you're not going to believe."

He tossed the shovel into the overgrown weeds and brush, wanting everything it represented out of his life and Luke back in it. "Got another stop I've gotta make, Ranger. In the Rio Grande Valley."

"Jan McClellan-Townsend?"

He nodded. "Regent Tawls isn't the only one who's not telling us everything he knows."

82

SAN ANTONIO

Guillermo Paz impatiently waited for the confessional window to open, drumming his fingers on the P-A-Z he'd carved on the armrest. Outside, thunder had been rumbling all morning in a sky divided between sun and clouds. No rain had fallen while its promise remained, the humidity continuing to climb with the temperature seeming to put the entire city in a foul mood that rode Paz like a layer of grease he couldn't sponge off.

Finally, he heard a creak and the familiar priest's face appeared behind the screen. The whites of his eyes grew big with recognition as he settled himself in as comfortably as he could manage.

"Bless me, Father, for I have sinned and I mean really messed up this time. Forget our talk from the other day, this is the real deal."

"I'm listening, my son."

Paz regarded his carved name. "I wish I could fill these letters in. I'd like to break the wood up with my bare hands and build you a whole new confessional, since I'm not worthy to have my name displayed in a church."

"What changed?"

"Not me, padre. I thought I had, but I guess I was fooling myself. Last night, my Texas Ranger caught me with my pants down."

"My son?" the priest raised, clearly uncomfortable with the direction the confession seemed to be taking.

"No, nothing like that, just a figure of speech. I think I fooled myself into thinking I had everything figured out."

"Go on."

"Auditing college classes in search of some kind of enlightenment? Who I was fooling?" Paz hesitated, hands grasping the armrest and testing the strength of the brackets that attached it to the confessional wall. "You see what I'm getting at?"

"You felt God no longer had the answers you sought."

"No, padre, that's where I had it wrong. It was more like I figured I was beyond asking the questions, like I had all the answers. What a crock of shit, if you'll excuse my English."

"You're excused, my son."

Paz put more pressure on the armrest bearing his name, hearing a creak as it began to give. "Is fooling yourself a sin, padre?"

"It can be, depending on what it leads to."

"Because I fooled myself into thinking I'd changed, but last night my Texas Ranger showed me how wrong I was."

"What happened last night?"

"I'd rather not get into that," Paz said, scratching at the wood now, as if to cover the carving of his name.

"You must."

"You already know."

"How can that be?"

"It's front-page news."

"Lord in heaven," the priest said, crossing himself as he realized.

"Yup, I was there and so was my Texas Ranger. Guess that comes as no surprise to you."

"What did you do wrong, my son?" the priest asked haltingly, the words slow coming out of his mouth as if he dreaded the answer.

"It's not what I did wrong, so much as where I *went* wrong. That make any sense, padre?"

"Not really, no."

"It's like this. After it was over, my Texas Ranger made me realize that I wanted it to happen. I wanted it to happen, maybe so I could prove myself to her again."

The priest shifted uncomfortably on the other side of the window. "Haven't you proved yourself enough?"

"I said 'maybe' because I don't think it's about that at all anymore. I think it's about me moving from one challenge to another to suit my own needs. My Texas Ranger made me realize I'm a selfish *bastard*, a real *cabrón* if you get my drift."

"I speak Spanish, my son."

Paz found himself feeling better, his breaths coming easier, yet still detached from the man he thought he'd become. "I've shared a lot with you, and I still don't know your name."

"Father."

Paz almost laughed, suddenly thinking of his boyhood in the slums. Of fending for himself and his family while growing up, stealing the food they ate until his mother found out and threw everything out, insisting she'd rather they go hungry.

"Wanna hear something, *Father*? Last night, the way my Texas Ranger looked at me reminded me of how disappointed my mother was when she caught me stealing bread," he continued, shaking his head even as his eyes misted up. "I don't think I've ever felt worse in my life. Until last night when my Texas Ranger looked at me the same way."

"Your point, my son?"

"What if a man can't change no matter how much he tries, padre?"

"His actions can be changed, but not the circumstances that brought him to be. You search for answers to find the path you're already on."

Paz had trouble forming his next question for the old priest, as if dreading the answer. "Was last night a misstep on that path?"

"That remains to be seen."

"I think I need to start the process over, from scratch."

"It's something different now," the priest told him. "After last night."

"What's that?"

"What every man who comes to question his actions seeks: redemption."

"To win my Texas Ranger over again? To win over *God*?"

"Neither: to win over yourself."

Paz leaned back against the wall, his breaths coming easier, the mist gone from his eyes as if the past had never happened at all. "Know something, padre? You remind me of that old priest back home when I was a boy. Carrying a bag full of food, gunned down in the street by the gangs he wouldn't give in to. I watched it happen, I watched it happen and there was nothing I could do. But you know what, padre?"

"What, my son?"

"I can do something now."

83

CIUDAD MIER, MEXICO

Caitlin Strong waited by the old train tracks in a town that no longer existed. The roots of Ciudad Mier dated back to the Spanish colonial era, but those roots were dead now, along with everything else associated with the town.

The once thriving ranches that formed the backbone of the town had been abandoned, empty save for overgrown weeds and bramble and the rotting bones of livestock picked clean by carrion birds and rodents. The rural roads where children once walked from the center of town lugging groceries back home were empty save for shell casings left behind by the armed drug cartel soldiers who began kidnapping those children for sport as much as money. They'd use them to practice with their latest weapons, leaving their unburied bodies behind to be picked at just like the livestock.

The residents had fled the violent onslaught, owed as much as anything to the town's location on the U.S.-Mexico border just south of Laredo. Strategic in the sense that it offered convenient access to any number of lucrative drug smuggling routes north into the United States. The once thriving town had fallen as collateral damage to an endless war, in this case between the Gulf cartel and the Zetas for control of those new *rutas*. First, firefights led to the shutdown of schools and public services. Then public officials were murdered by one side for siding with the other, creating an endless circle of death that turned the town utterly lawless and sent its residents fleeing in the night with only what they could pack in their vehicles.

For their part, the train tracks looked like the town's spine: half-buried, bent and broken. But this was where Caitlin had been directed to wait, on a bench beneath a crumbling wooden overhang that creaked behind each blow of a hot breeze that left dust mixing with perspiration on her face.

Suddenly she felt a vibration under her feet, followed by a rumbling that shook the decaying wood of the unused station that otherwise featured only a burned-out building with a sign still intact reading TA-QUILLA, or ticket office. Then, from out of the wasteland to the south, a dust cloud appeared accompanied by the repetitive mechanical wheeze of what could only be an old, steam-powered locomotive.

Rising to her feet, Caitlin actually felt chilled by what seemed like the very real possibility that this was one of the fabled ghost trains of lore, thundering toward the station only to speed right past it with the souls of the damned peering out the windows in search of their lives. But this train slowed as it approached, its brakes grinding into a lingering squeal as it huffed and snorted to a stop directly before her.

Seconds later the door before her opened and Fernando Lorenzo Sandoval stepped out onto the stoop. "Come inside, Ranger."

84

"Your hand," Sandoval said, noticing the bandage. "That happened last night?"

"I'm afraid it didn't do us much good, sir."

Inside was cool, the interior plush, the old steam-driven train having been retrofitted and rebuilt with equal measures of security and luxury. Sandoval's personal security forces were omnipresent, and it looked as if he could have fought a war with the ordnance that had been packed on board.

They sat opposite each other in a sitting area inside a train car that served as his office and the operations center for the Mexican government's all-out war against the cartels. All the furniture, including their chairs, was bolted to the floor. The tinted, bulletproof windows made it impossible for anyone to see in from the outside, and there was an armed guard posted outside either end of the car.

"I was sorry to hear about the Torres boy's kidnapping," Sandoval said, his expression honestly pained and looking much like it had back in Austin after Caitlin had broken the news to him about his own son.

"Something I didn't tell you back in Austin, sir," Caitlin told him. "Near as we can tell, your son tried to protect the others. Says a lot about the kind of father you are and the kind of boy you raised, in spite of the obstacles you've faced. You need to keep that with you."

Sandoval's eyes began to tear up and he made no effort to wipe them. "You saved my life once, Ranger. No matter how hard I try, I can never truly make up for that."

"You can if you tell me what happened on Regent Tawls's farm in the fall of nineteen-eighty, Mr. Sandoval."

"I was little more than a boy myself back then," Sandoval reflected, his mind working to remember. "Just starting off with the Mexican *federal* police."

"But you remember the case, don't you, sir?"

"Of course I do. It was my first major arrest and prosecution. Enrique Cantú and Mateo Torres had apparently tired of serving only as growers moving from one farm to another, choosing to become distributors themselves. Their mistake was to sell their stolen product through the same man with whom the Tawls family did business. Through him, I tracked them back to Mexico and arrested both, promising I'd release the one who gave up the other first."

"It was Torres who gave up Cantú."

Sandoval looked a bit surprised. "How did you know?"

"Cantú wasn't the man's real name, though, was it?"

"I knew he was related to Esteban Cantú, the first to bring opium into the United States through Mexicali, but that's all. He stood trial in the United States and was sentenced to ten years at the prison now known as the Walls in Huntsville."

Caitlin could see the man's eyes widening, dark saucers wedged into his face.

"This has something to do with the murder of my son, doesn't it, Ranger?"

"Enrique Cantú's real name was Guajardo," Caitlin said instead of answering. "Does that mean anything to you?"

Caitlin watched Sandoval pitch back in his chair, spine stiffening and throat bulging as he swallowed hard. "Yes, it does. It means plenty."

85

RIO GRANDE VALLEY, TEXAS

"I see you brought your boy with you again, Mr. Masters," greeted Jan McClellan-Townsend, approaching as Cort Wesley and Dylan climbed out of the truck.

She smiled, about to say more when she caught Cort Wesley's dour, purposeful expression.

"No time for pleasantries today, ma'am. My younger son was kidnapped last night."

The older woman's spine arched in realization. "Oh my Lord, the terrorists at that lacrosse game . . ."

"They weren't terrorists. They were Mexican killers led by a man who's living proof we evolved from apes. This whole thing is about revenge and I think you know more about the why than you've said already."

"Just tell me what you need to know, Mr. Masters," she said, taking a deep breath.

"That's Cort Wesley, ma'am. And we need to talk about Enrique Guajardo, Jan."

The woman pretended to be surprised. "Excuse me?"

"You knew him as Enrique Cantú."

He watched Jan McClellan-Townsend stiffen. "I thought we'd been over that part."

"We had. But you left something out."

"What's that?"

"Enrique Cantú served three years of a ten-year stretch in the Walls prison," Cort Wesley told her, stiffening at the mere mention of the place he'd spent four miserable years himself. "During that stretch, prison phone logs say he called phone numbers registered to you on this farm over five hundred times, some of the calls pretty long in duration."

The woman stood board straight directly before him, saying nothing.

"Take all the time you need, Jan."

"I believe you've pretty much figured it out, Cort Wesley."

"You had an affair. I think it was ongoing over several years. I think you were the one who paid for a lawyer he couldn't possibly have afforded and paid off the right people to secure his early parole. I think you took care of his family here in the years he was in the Walls."

"Couldn't have laid it out better myself," McClellan-Townsend said with a frown, looking as grim as Cort Wesley now.

"Still a few things missing, though, aren't there?"

The woman stiffened, suddenly looking all of her years and more, her gaze seeming to be directed between Cort Wesley and Dylan. "I believe I've said everything I'm going to say on the matter. Anything else you want to know about Enrique Cantú you'll have to find up in the Walls penitentiary."

Cort Wesley took a step closer to her, sliding sideways back into her line of vision. "There's something else you need to tell me first, ma'am—"

"Jan."

"*Ma'am*, and it's for your own good."

"*My* own good, Mr. Masters?"

"I believe there's a body buried somewhere on your land belonging to a work foreman killed by Cantú's son as a young boy not long after Cantú was arrested. I heard told the case has drawn the interest of the Texas Rangers, including one I believe you're aware I'm quite close to. Now, unless you want your property torn up while you face an accessory to murder charge, you need to tell me everything you know about that."

"You're talking about Locaro Cantú," Jan McClellan-Townsend said softly, almost fearfully, her gaze suddenly empty and distant.

"I believe we are," Cort Wesley said, after exchanging a glance with Dylan.

"I should have known when you made that comment about being evolved from apes. . . . A more fitting description of a person, man or boy, has never been spoken, and I mean that entirely."

"He got away last night," Dylan said, before Cort Wesley had a chance to. "He's got my brother. I know what it's like to be kidnapped, Jan. I know how scared my brother must be and how helpless he feels right now."

The woman managed a smile, one sad enough to match her tone, unable to disguise how much Dylan impressed her. "If only my youngest daughter was still a teenager . . . So why now?" she asked Dylan instead of Cort Wesley. "Why is all this happening after so many years?"

"It has to do with my mother, Maura Torres, the twin my grandfather Mateo kept. I never met the man, but if he hadn't died before I was born, I'd have told him that was the wrong thing to do. A man doesn't give up his kids. A man does whatever it takes."

Jan McClellan-Townsend's eyes narrowed, then widened again, as she sighed deeply. "Locaro was a monster for sure, but . . ." The rest of her words dissolved into another sigh.

"Go on, Jan," prodded Cort Wesley.

"His sister, she was worse. Totally different from the other twin. There was something about that girl—Ana I think her name was—that just wasn't right. Things would happen, bad things, and she'd always be in the area, the look on her face saying plenty but not enough. I remember it getting worse right around the time Locaro took a machete to that rapist in the summer of nineteen-eighty. You're right about the man's body being buried somewhere on the farm, Cort Wesley. What you don't know is we'd had to scoop up what was left of him with a shovel. I believe Locaro was ten at the time. Ana would've been seven." She shook her head, the memories obviously painful for her. "The family left not long after that and I never saw them again."

"But you saw Enrique Cantú again, didn't you, Jan?" Dylan asked when Cort Wesley remained silent.

Jan McClellan-Townsend's eyes started misting up. She dabbed them with her sleeve and sniffled. "Some years ago, Enrique got in an argument with his son and Locaro pushed him off a fourth-story balcony. It happened in front of witnesses and he ended getting sentenced to life in Cereso Prison." She looked befuddled. "But now you're telling me he got out. How in the Lord's name did he get out?"

"We were talking about your time with his father," said Cort Wesley. "You started seeing Enrique again after you arranged for his release from prison, didn't you?"

Jan McClellan-Townsend nodded slowly, looking almost embarrassed. "I don't know the circumstances, but his wife died not long after he was paroled. I didn't see him for a stretch after that and by the time he got back in touch with me, his name was known throughout Mexico. We used to meet in as beautiful a piece of land as you've ever seen, me and Enrique, in this little stretch of paradise called Los Mochis. I believe it's been turned into a game preserve now. He'd gone back to using the name Guajardo by then."

"A game preserve?" Dylan raised.

"Where hunters pay to kill just about anything for a price, son." Her still moist eyes fixed themselves on Cort Wesley. "Guess we haven't evolved as a species nearly as much as we thought we had."

"But you seem to feel awfully bad for young Ana witnessing that work foreman raping her mother before Locaro killed him. That's a credit to the kind of person you are, Jan."

But Jan McClellan-Townsend seemed to have no interest in taking that credit, something else plainly on her mind as she took a step closer to Cort Wesley. "I believe you have your facts wrong."

"Ma'am?"

"It's Jan, and I'm talking about the truth of what really happened that day."

86

Ciudad Mier, Mexico

Sandoval rose from his chair and moved to the nearest tinted train window. "How could I not have realized?" he said, words aimed at the wasteland beyond that had been a town until just a few years before.

"Realized what, sir?"

Caitlin studied his reflection in the window, the anguish on his features slowly giving way to the arrogant resolve that had made him Mexico's foremost soldier in its perpetual war on the drug trade. "Enrique Guajardo's daughter, Ana, is the most powerful woman in my country, perhaps the most powerful person period. Her known dealings include energy and telecom holdings, stakes in major real estate developments, and full or partial ownership in a myriad of companies and conglomerates, both known and unknown. She's also one of the largest landowners in all of Mexico."

"What about the unknown ones?"

"She has supplemented her fortune by unifying the business interests of the cartels. Moving their money into vast hedge and investment funds to launder it while consolidating her hold on power. While the drug soldiers and mules kill each other in the streets, the product of their labor is invested both in holdings in North America and beyond. It all becomes a self-fulfilling prophecy. Ana Callas Guajardo grows more powerful while the drug lords become richer and more entrenched in what passes for Mexican society."

"That's why you can't touch them, isn't it, sir? That's why all your efforts have produced little more than a stalemate?"

He turned from the window slowly, as if in pain. "I take my orders from those who take their orders from Guajardo. First the father, then the daughter."

"She's not his daughter, sir."

"*¿Qué quieres decir?*"

"I mean that Mateo Torres's wife, Carmen, gave birth to twins at that other farm they worked in the Rio Grande Valley in nineteen seventy-three. Since the Torres family couldn't afford to raise three kids, they gave one of the newborn infant girls to the Guajardos, because they only had a single child: a boy named Locaro. He led the attack at the lacrosse game last night. He's the one who's got Luke Torres, sir."

"Could you give me a moment, please?" Sandoval said, moving in behind his computer.

"Locaro was released from prison three days ago, pardoned by President Villarreal himself."

"Don't tell me, at the request of his sister, Ana."

Sandoval didn't bother nodding. "What can I do to help, Ranger? What can I do to help you stop the Torres boy from joining my son?"

The sun suddenly caught Caitlin in its spill through the tinted train windows, adding to the surge flushing through her as if her blood had been superheated. "Tell me what you can about Ana Callas Guajardo and her holdings, Mr. Sandoval. Tell me everything."

PART NINE

In 1914, during the early days of World War I, the Rangers had the daunting task of identifying and rounding up numerous spies, conspirators, saboteurs, and draft dodgers. In 1916, Pancho Villa's raid on Columbus, New Mexico, intensified already harsh feelings between the United States and Mexico. As a result, the regular Rangers, along with hundreds of special Rangers appointed by Texas governors, killed approximately 5,000 Hispanics between 1914 and 1919, which soon became a source of scandal and embarrassment.

LEGENDS OF AMERICA:
"Texas Legends: The Texas Rangers—Order Out of Chaos"

87

"The time is almost upon us, *Papá*," Ana Guajardo said to her father as she pushed his wheelchair along the perimeter of the various enclosures that formed the game preserve honored with his name. "Do you know my happiest memories? The times you took Locaro and I hunting. The respect you taught us for the animals, our prey, has stayed with me ever since. The way you taught us to field dress them then and there, also with respect for what only minutes before had been a living creature. I understand now the lesson that held, I understand now you were teaching me both the value of life and its natural order. We may respect our prey but it exists to serve our ends and purpose."

Ana Callas Guajardo had turned her father's most expansive stretch of land, located on the outskirts of the Sinaloan coastal city of Los Mochis, into a wild-game preserve for hunters, both would-be and otherwise. Her thought was to provide an opportunity for her allies and those she wanted to make her allies to hunt big-game animals even Africa did not provide. Indeed, here in Los Mochis there were no government monitors, no pesky environmentalists or conservationists, to enforce rules and quotas or complain about endangered species. Those invited to Rancho Enrique had their choice among lions, tigers, wild boar, big buck dear, bison, antelope, and various types of game birds. In other words, the perfect selection to choose from for those who wanted to take a trophy of their own killing home with them. Not all the animals roamed the site at any one given time, but any could be procured with sufficient notice.

She had long thought those hunting trips with her father were about bonding, him trying to bring her closer to him after giving up attempting to do the same with her brother, Locaro. Only many years later did she understand why and how hunting had figured into it. Her brother had enjoyed killing too much, so much so that it blurred the real reason behind the trips. Her father wanted her to understand what it felt like to take a life, to feel the last of an animal's heart beating away and then field dress it while it was still warm before maggots could have their way. It was a crucial lesson to learn, testing her own limits and making her appreciate exercises of the mind all the more. Though she reviled the process, it taught Ana what Locaro was never capable of learning: the meaning of true power. Her father never put it in those words, never put it in any words really. And it wasn't the kill that mattered, it was the hunt. For the hunt made for a better life metaphor, summarized by the one point her father had made that Ana hadn't understood until many years later.

"There are only two kinds of creatures, Ana: those who hunt and those who are hunted. Animals do not choose their lot, but people do."

It was the simplest but most important lesson she had ever learned, one that stayed with her each and every day. Life was indeed a hunt, rife with prey to be stalked and commanded, if not destroyed.

And, sometimes, even killed. Her father had realized that was all Locaro was good for, so he'd given up on his son and turned to his daughter, who embraced his wisdom along with the realization that power was everything because without power there was nothing.

Ana Guajardo recalled the time her father had made her stand against a wild boar, on the verge of trampling and goring her when her final bullets at last brought it down, snorting and belching hot breath from its nose until it finally died.

"That boar I now realize, *Papá*, represented the United States, and from that day on I've learned to stand against the enemy who dwarfs us the same way the boar dwarfed me. I still have the knife I used to field dress that animal, and I'll never forget its blood and entrails spilling all over me, just like the blood of the children in Willow Creek did last week. Because now the roles have switched. We are the boar and the United States is the frightened child about to be trampled in our path. All your dreams are to be fulfilled, vengeance gained on the enemies of our people and our family. Those who would cast us off as refuse, those who would betray all that we worked to attain going back almost a century now." The smell of feces from his diaper seemed to dissipate briefly, before returning even thicker. Guajardo adjusted her father's hat to keep the sun from hurting his eyes. "Whoever said revenge is sweet was wrong, *Papá*, because it isn't, but that makes it no less necessary. We can feign strength to others but must find it in our hearts as well. And only the weak allow sins against them to go unpunished."

Ana had built this five-thousand-acre preserve as a testament to her father's vision and teachings, which had made her everything she was. The preserve was divided into eight separate quadrants enclosed by heavy steel fencing to discourage interspecies mingling that would surely turn deadly. Guajardo did not charge a fee of any of those who came to Rancho Enrique; they came by invitation only, culled from those who could advance, or had advanced, her business and political interests. The preserve allowed for the ultimate payback, rendering Ana's guests all the more beholden to her.

Rancho Enrique boasted the perfect climate and terrain to maintain the kind of exotic animals that would die most other places. There were ample grazing areas as well as open spaces atop hardened clay and cracked tundra that gave way to thick forestlands perfect for both smaller species and the hunters who enjoyed the notion of evening the odds a bit more. She felt as if this were some less futuristic version of Jurassic Park, offering a comparable experience with far more predictable species. She cared nothing for the animals—rare, endangered, or otherwise—sacrificed toward her greater ends. They were no different to Ana than ballot box manipulations, compromising photographs, discreet bribes, not so discreet extortion, or political payoffs. All merely tools and nothing more.

Her father had made his initial fortune building an elaborate marijuana distribution network through the United States following his release from prison just after her tenth birthday. She had made herself far richer, on the order of billions, by using the vast stores of laundered drug money she controlled to buy herself the entire country of Mexico. And soon, very soon, she would sit back and watch while the country she had despised for as long as she could remember became the very same backward and desperate land Mexico had so long been perceived to be.

"Why do you hate the United States so much?"

It was a question posed to her on numerous occasions, one to which Ana Guajardo had no precise answer. Every time she contemplated one, she felt a tugging on her brain, a curtain of haze trying to lift on something she could not clearly see. It couldn't be just the rape of her mother at the hands of the new work foreman Locaro had sliced to pieces with his machete as a ten-year-old boy in the Rio Grande Valley. She remembered the hose stinging her skin as her mother washed away the blood that had sprayed her. But the haze always returned before she could recall something else from that day, some lost truth that forever eluded her and perhaps held at least part of the answer others sought that she couldn't provide.

Upon learning of the moves she had made to divest their interests from American holdings five years ago, her father had summoned her to his fourth-floor office in their hacienda.

"This is business, Ana," he had scolded. "You must never let your personal prejudices interfere with business."

He had turned away, a clear sign he considered the matter finished.

"When did kissing the Americans' feet become part of our business?" Ana had challenged instead of leaving.

"You would have us sacrifice profits?"

"I would have us do business in a way that serves Mexico's interests instead of those of our American investors."

Her father had shaken his head, his look of disappointment profound. "You've made my decision easy, at last," he sighed.

"What decision?" she asked him, starting forward.

"You are not fit to succeed me. I've tried so hard to teach you, and yet you are no different from your brother. You are even worse for having squandered the chance I gave you to do great things. Now, like him, you will be nothing because you can't set aside your hate even for one moment. No matter how many times I warn you, you persist. Tell me why, Ana. Tell me why so I can help you."

But Ana couldn't, because she didn't know.

"We are done here," she remembered her father saying. "Leave me."

But Ana held her ground, risking more of her father's wrath and temper.

"*Tu estás muy débil*," he charged. "You are weak and no longer fit to work with me. You are no better than your mother, just not a *puta* like she was, sleeping with every man she could find while I was in prison."

Ana felt herself begin to shake.

"You bring me no grandchildren because you are empty inside."

That's when Ana felt something snap. She recalled picking up her pace but nothing beyond that. The haze that had enveloped her after the rape of her mother returned, clearing to find her father lying broken on the concrete drive four stories down while gardeners and security men alike looked up at her.

"I'm sorry, *Papá*," she said now to the figure hunched in the wheelchair that barely resembled the strong, vibrant man she remembered. "I'm sorry you did not share my vision for the future."

Guajardo felt a buzzing on her hip. She stopped her father's wheelchair and jerked the walkie-talkie from her belt, raising it to her ear.

"I told you I was not to be disturbed," she snapped at whoever was on the other end. Rancho Enrique offered no cell phone service and she never walked the property without a reliable alternative.

"*Señora*," said the voice she now recognized as belonging to a guard at the front gate, "there is someone here who insists on seeing you. A Texas Ranger."

"A Texas Ranger?" she said, wondering if she'd heard the man right. What could they possibly want with her? How could they have known she'd be here? "Tell him to make an appointment with my office. Give him the number."

"But *señora*, she is already on her way."

"She?"

"*Sí*, a woman."

"And you let her *in*?"

"*Ella no me dio ninguna opción*. She did not give me much choice, *jefa*. *Ella me dijo que me iba a patear los huevos*."

"I should kick you there myself for letting her in."

"There's something else, *jefa*. The Ranger told me she came here because your life may be in danger."

88

LOS MOCHIS, MEXICO

"You can see my reason for concern, ma'am," Caitlin Strong explained to Ana Callas Guajardo minutes later, after finding her in the enclosure set before an area where two African white rhinos were grazing comfortably in a field. Their tiny tails waved side to side in rhythm with the wind that blew the scents of animal musk and stale feces straight into the two women. Caitlin noticed a shriveled figure in a wheelchair huddled in the shade of a large oak tree. "I felt it was my duty to come down here and warn you personally."

"And this is because . . ."

"The same killers who may be after you came after a pair of teenage boys up in Texas. They're your twin sister's boys, ma'am, your nephews," Caitlin said, comparing Ana Guajardo to pictures she'd seen of Maura Torres. Clearly, they weren't identical twins, but the resemblance between them remained striking.

"Well, Ranger, your coming all this way is a much appreciated yet altogether unnecessary gesture," Guajardo told her, having to ungrit her teeth to manage the effort and fighting not to show her shock at the

Ranger's knowledge of her background. Caitlin Strong had wielded that knowledge like a blow, waiting for Ana's reaction to see if it had landed. "I'm very well protected."

"I imagine that's what the parents of those children we found in Willow Creek last week thought. Got them packed off safely to school, just like they did every day, only this time they never came home."

"And you believe I'm in danger because of *that*?"

"Ma'am, I believe you're in danger because of what I've managed to learn about your past. You had a twin sister who was raised by your real parents. Whoever was behind the murders of those kids in Willow Creek hired professional gunmen to kill your twin sister's sons too. Mexicans. That mean anything to you?"

"Why should Mexican gunmen, hired killers, mean anything to me?"

"Because you're so well protected. I just figured you've come to make the acquaintance of plenty of men who fit that description down here."

"Down here," Guajardo repeated, trying to capture the obvious disparagement in the woman Ranger's voice. "As in Mexico, you mean."

"Or hell, ma'am. Take your pick."

Guajardo noted an expression that might have been confused for smugness rode the female Ranger's countenance, as if she practiced it in front of a mirror. The Stetson looked too big for her tight, angular features and hint of Mexican descent in the thick portions of her hair that pushed out from the hat's confinement. She'd removed it politely as soon as she reached Ana, holstered pistol riding her hip like a steel appendage.

"Get back to why you think I may be in danger," Guajardo told Caitlin Strong.

"I wish I could tell you for sure, *Señora* Guajardo, but I believe it's about revenge for something that happened a long time ago involving my own grandfather and great-grandfather."

"A student of history are you, Ranger?" Guajardo asked with her head tilted slightly to the side, tight expression indicating that she knew Caitlin was holding something, maybe plenty, back. She wet her lips with her tongue, reveling in the challenge the way someone not accustomed to losing does. Hanging on Caitlin Strong's every word, as if ready to snap the cord connecting them at any moment, letting the Ranger think she was in control when in fact nothing could be further from the truth.

"I believe in the past, ma'am, just as much as I believe we don't understand it any better than we understand the present."

"Then I'm sure you're aware that vengeance is the purest, strongest emotion, the most powerful motivator of all."

"Especially when its roots lie somewhere back in history," Caitlin told her. "In this case to that stretch your father did in Huntsville on those drug and arson charges."

"What does that have to do with anything?" Ana Guajardo snapped, fighting the rage building inside her, summoning all her reserves to keep herself calm.

"I was hoping you could tell me, ma'am, since your brother and his men shot up a lacrosse game in San Antonio last night and kidnapped one of your nephews."

Guajardo let Caitlin Strong see her stiffen. "My brother is dead to me."

"Because he pushed your father off a balcony."

"*Threw* him, you mean."

"Your brother was released from Cereso Prison, you know."

"Maybe he had served his time."

"This was a pardon signed by President Villarreal himself. Interesting that the president of Mexico would bother intervening, don't you think?"

"I don't think anything," Guajardo told her. "It's not my concern."

"Your own brother?"

"I told you he's—"

"Dead to you, I know." Caitlin took a step closer to Ana Guajardo, out of the sun now so both of them were trapped in the shadows cast by the thick tree line. "But there's this problem I was hoping you could help me with. See, ma'am, your brother was under surveillance by undercover Mexican drug operatives at the time of your father's unfortunate fall. Those operatives can place him several hundred miles away at the time he supposedly pushed—pardon me, *threw*—your father off that fourth-story balcony. I was hoping you could help me reconcile the discrepancy."

"There is no discrepancy."

"My sources indicate otherwise."

"Then your sources are wrong. And they're wrong about me being in danger too. Please accept my assurances of that."

Caitlin hesitated, making a show of seeming to study the woman before her without responding until, "Where were you on the day your father was nearly killed?"

"You already know the answer to that: I was home. I was the one who found him broken on the pavement four stories down on the circular drive he'd only just installed."

"You also said you saw your brother on the balcony afterward. You said that to the police."

"If you say so, Ranger."

"I do, ma'am, and I also say that was either a lie or a misstatement."

"What's the difference?"

"None at all," Caitlin said, her stare holding all of its harsh intensity intact. "And if you misstated the facts about that, I wonder if you might also misstate the facts as they pertain to the murder of five Mexican children just across the Texas border who all happened to be offspring of those connected to your family's past."

Ana Guajardo refused to break Caitlin's stare. "So you really didn't come down here to warn me my life was in danger, did you?"

Caitlin ignored her question. "I've got no jurisdiction in Mexico, ma'am; you and I both know that. So whatever happened that day your father ended up in a wheelchair is of no concern to me."

"But the murder of these five Mexican children is."

"That's right, ma'am."

"Strange hearing that from a Texas Ranger."

"They were killed in Texas, but, truth be told, I'd go after anyone anywhere who targets children."

"You still haven't told me what really brought you down here, Ranger."

Caitlin started to put her Stetson back on, but stopped. "You're a very powerful woman, *Señora* Guajardo. The most powerful woman in Mexico, and maybe the most powerful person period. I know you've earned most of that on your own, but the foundation your father laid was based on the drug distribution network he built north of the border, and that *is* within my jurisdiction. So you might say we got more business between us than either of us thought, and maybe more of a connection through a shared history too."

"Are you accusing me of something?"

"Not at the present time, no."

Perhaps the intensity between them was what made the big male African rhino look up from his grazing and snort, his lazy-looking eyes suddenly tilted in their direction. Perhaps it was just coincidence.

"So you didn't come down here to accuse me and you didn't come down here to warn me," said Guajardo. "Is there another option I've left out?"

"Maybe I just wanted to get the history between our families straight in my head, how my great-granddad and granddad ran your great-granddad out of Mexicali."

Ana Guajardo's features tightened so much, it looked as if her mouth had sealed up tight.

"They have television down here, ma'am?" Caitlin continued, taunting her now. "That lacrosse game last night was televised and the cameras went right on rolling when the bullets started flying. Means you can go to YouTube and watch a lot of innocent people being killed by your brother and the men he brought with him. Back in Texas we call that a massacre and we also call it cause to leave the badges and laws behind."

"Massacres have happened on both sides of the border, Ranger," Guajardo managed, growing composed again with each word as she sought to regain the upper hand. "Have you actually heard the story of how the Strongs brought down my great-grandfather?"

"Not the specifics, ma'am, no."

"Then maybe it's time you did."

89

There was no point in leaving the city until the battle being waged by the American forces against Pancho Villa's troops was over. Knowing as much as he knew about General Erwin, William Ray Strong didn't think it would take very long either. And, in point of fact, it didn't. He and Strong's Raiders were saddling up for what all figured would be their last ride as a group when a Mexican spy taken prisoner right there in El Paso broke free long enough to push a note into William Ray's hand.

"*¡Apúrese, señor, apúrese!*"

William Ray wondered what it was he was supposed to be hurrying about, but didn't check out the note until the prisoner was dragged back into custody. Then he unfolded it and called Earl Strong over.

"Your Spanish is better than mine, son. Tell me what this says exactly?"

Earl read the note out loud in Spanish first. "*A nosotros también nos traicionaron. Nos encontramos en la cantina de la plaza central en la Ciudad Juárez, al otro lado de la frontera.*" Then he translated, "*We were betrayed too. Meet us at the cantina in the central square of Juárez across the border.*" At that he looked up at his father. "It's signed '*Los Generales.*' The Generals."

"Now, that's interesting."

"You figure it's a trap, Dad?"

Frank Hamer held up his Thompson, still oiled and ready. "I say we head down there and kill us some Mexes if it is."

"Hell," said old Bill McDonald, trying his best to stifle a cough, "I came this far to kill somebody."

"There are many cantinas in Juárez, Ranger Strong," said Manuel Gonzaullas. "How could the generals be sure you'd know the one they meant?"

"'Cause of something in the past, son. Details don't matter a mite. What matters is this tells me the note came from them, all right."

"Can't trust their kind one bit's what I say, Ranger," noted Monroe Fox.

"Nobody's asking you to come along, sir. You want to ride on home into infamy for your past indiscretions, be my guest. But I don't expect this is a chance you'll see again in your lifetime to hang up your guns the way they're supposed to be hung up."

"Aw, hell," whined Fox. "Count me in. But I'm killing the first one stares at me crossways or even looks at his pistol."

"Son, if it comes down to that, all the shooting be over 'fore you even get your pistol drawn," McDonald chided him.

"We'll see about that, Captain Legend."

The others laughed, then resumed mounting up.

"Guess we got a change in destination," said William Ray Strong, as they started off.

Strong's Raiders took to horseback for the short distance across the bridge into Juárez, still armed to the teeth and probably mistaken for a supplemental contingent of the American forces. The city remained a study in chaos with the aftereffects of the battle lingering in the form of ruptured walls, shattered glass, and stubborn smoke from the artillery shell explosions still rising. Most of the fires that had caught burned out of control with no one about to fight the flames.

But the three generals who'd requested this meeting—Rojas, Castillo, and Aguilar—must have known the cantina in question had been left whole and remained somehow opened. Actually, when the Rangers arrived they found the lights off, the door locked, and as many of the windows boarded up as the supply of lumber would allow.

"How is it those generals chose this cantina again?" William Ray heard his son Earl ask him, as he approached the door.

"Because a few years back I killed three men here in a gunfight after they refused to go peacefully across the border."

William Ray rapped hard on the heavy wooden door and was about to do so again when the door opened to reveal Pancho Villa's top generals disguised as peasants standing in darkness broken sporadically by lantern light. They had clearly opted not to join Villa when he fled south, pursued by the American forces.

"Come in," Castillo said in English, "all of you."

Inside, Strong's Raiders shoved four round bar tables together and sat with their arms crossed upon the wobbly tops while the generals explained why they had summoned the Rangers here.

"It is not too late, *señores*," Castillo started. "There is still a way to rid the world of Esteban Cantú's *esos Demonios*."

"Two days from now," Rojas picked up, "he has scheduled a military parade to honor the Mexican troops who bravely fought and defeated the forces of Pancho Villa in the battle of Juárez. Out of respect for his cousin, President Carranza," he added with a smirk, not bothering to disguise the irony in his voice.

"It will take place in the central square of Mexicali," the general named Aguilar explained, taking a tattered, hand-scrawled map from his pocket. "Cantú will surely lead the procession and all residents are required to attend. He will be accompanied by his soldiers—you know them as *esos Demonios*—and among them will be the very same men who were responsible for Willow Creek."

With that Aguilar unfolded the map and handed it to William Ray Strong, who passed it on to Manuel Gonzaullas.

"I know this place," Gonzaullas said.

"So can we do it, M.T.? Can we take out this many men at once?"

"The participants won't be expecting anything but more tequila and sangria when the procession ends. It will be hot in the sun and by the end of the route, the effects of their first round of drink will have worn off and left them sluggish. So, yes, Ranger, we can do it."

"The next question being," William Ray said, moving his eyes from one general to the next, "what's in it for the three of you exactly?"

"The war is lost, *señor*," said Rojas. "The revolution is over."

"Leaving all enterprising men like us," added Castillo, "with a need to stake out the next stage of our lives."

"You want to take over Cantú's drug business," Earl Strong realized.

"Only the business in Mexico, *señores*," Aguilar told all of them. "That is more than enough to suit our needs once Cantú is out of the way, and the three of us intend to divide our interests through the country, separate groups responsible for different regions."

"You've thought this thing out, haven't you?"

"We wouldn't have wasted your time if we hadn't, *señor*," Rojas said to William Ray.

"And we're supposed to take you at your word that you won't spread your poison across the border into Texas just like Cantú did?" raised a skeptical William Ray Strong.

"*Sí*," said Aguilar.

"You see, we'd rather keep you as *amigos*, rather than risk having you as enemies," Castillo explained.

"Even though you're not coming entirely clean?"

The three generals looked at one another.

"You're the ones who betrayed Pancho Villa," William Ray continued. "You had all this thought out and you used us to do your dirty work right from the start."

None of the generals bothered denying the assertion, Rojas speaking for all of them. "We get what we want and you get what you want."

William Ray Strong thought back to the scene in Willow Creek, feeling a grimace stretch across his lips. "You boys got yourself a deal," he said, taking the map back from Manuel Gonzaullas.

"Those Mexican bastards done fucked us again," said Frank Hamer once Strong's Raiders reached Mexicali two days later.

They'd arrived to find the city overrun with soldiers and members of the *federal* police force. Armed men were everywhere, not just *esos Demonios* preparing for the procession at the head of the street.

"This ain't good," Monroe Fox added, dressed like the others in capes and sombreros to give the impression they were no more than visitors here to enjoy the festivities.

The three generals had failed to mention the Gatling guns poised in a church steeple at one end of the Mexicali central square and jerry-rigged upon a rooftop at the other. Those guns, combined with the abundance of additional armed troops, made the formidable supply of BARs, Thompsons, 12-gauges, and .45 caliber pistols scattered through the three cars the Rangers boarded to drive here pale by comparison.

All morning the square's cantinas were packed with soldiers, locals, and tourists mixing easy among one another. William Ray dispatched Manuel Gonzaullas and Bill McDonald to hide a pair of Thompsons and scout out the remainder of the square for other potential surprises. But foremost in his mind remained the opportunity to slay those who had perpetrated the massacre at Willow Creek. *Esos Demonios* would fall hard and quick once the bullets started flying, that was for sure.

Or maybe not.

Because a few minutes later, Gonzaullas rushed up to William Ray, nearly out of breath.

"They're moving on Captain Bill!" he managed, heaving for air in between breaths.

"Christ on a crutch! Where?"

"Another cantina. Somebody recognized him and wanted to make sure he wasn't a ghost."

William Ray looked to Monroe Fox and Frank Hamer. "We need those BARs set up in the high ground. That means—"

"I know what it means," Hamer interrupted. "Taking out those Gatling guns."

"Just give me a few minutes to get Captain Bill back," William Ray Strong told him. "Then let's show these bastards what happens when you cross the Texas Rangers."

William Ray, Earl, and Manuel Gonzaullas reached the cantina just as Bill McDonald was being led out by *federal* police officers and the first beats of a drum began to pound, signaling the procession was about to start. At its very head was Mexico's first engine-driven fire truck, purportedly a gift from the governor of California. The three Rangers moved to block the path of the *federales*, Manuel Gonzaullas stepping forward to do the talking.

"There must be some mistake. Why are you arresting our friend?"

The *federal* captain, who walked with a limp, grinned, his bravado reinforced by the half dozen officers he commanded and the bevy of well-armed soldiers filling the streets and bars. "If you are his friend, then you must be an *el Rinche* too, eh?"

He grinned again, wet eyes big in the sunlight, an instant before he and the other men went for their guns. But Earl and William Ray drew theirs first, Earl opening up with his Colt and William Ray with his .45 in a blistering crescendo that accompanied the now heavier rhythmic drumbeats of the procession. More band instruments joined in, stealing the sound of the gunfight from the street, but not the sight of the *federal* and his men straining to return the Rangers' gunfire.

William Ray heard a gasp and saw Bill McDonald stagger, wincing and clasping his hand against a side leaking blood. Still firing, he moved to the Ranger legend and shielded him with his own body, supporting his weight.

"I'm okay, goddamnit!" McDonald said. "Just get me a goddamn gun!"

Earl and Manuel Gonzaullas dropped the last two policemen with their Colts, as the patrons closest to the disruption rushed to flee. The crowd just slightly beyond was clustered too tight and, to a man, too drunk to realize anything was awry until Monroe Fox and Frank Hamer started firing their Brownings from top-floor hotel windows centered in the square. Their first targets were the Gatling gun perches, way too open and the soldiers behind them much too bored to offer any resistance at all. The BARs' bullets chewed them, and the wood composite around them, to shreds.

"Let's do this, son!" William Ray, with Bill McDonald still in his grasp, yelled to Earl.

Earl finished reloading his Colt and positioned himself to provide cover for his father and Bill McDonald, while Gonzaullas rushed into a nearby building to fulfill his part of the plan. William Ray eased a gasping Bill McDonald against a nearby adobe facade, holding him steady there with his freshly reloaded .45 in hand.

"Get to it, Ranger!" he yelled to his son, who was already stripping light canvas coverings from the pair of Thompson machine guns squeezed in a gap left to drain rainwater from the flat rooftops above two matching structures.

Earl handed one of the Thompsons to his father, who, in turn, pressed his .45 into Bill McDonald's grasp. "If you get yourself killed, make sure I get this back first, Captain."

"Do my best, Ranger," McDonald said, wincing.

The loud riffs of the marching band continued to drown out the sounds of battle long enough for Fox and Hamer to train their Brownings downward on the rearmost flank of the *esos Demonios* following the band and fire truck in the procession. In their absurdly garish dress uniforms, they looked like cartoon characters falling in waves to the relentless BAR fire. The Brownings came equipped with detachable ammo boxes that held twenty 30.06 Springfield rounds that would put a man down wherever it hit him. Instinct drove *esos Demonios* to surge forward away from the heavy fire, starting to recover their senses when Gonzaullas rained a half dozen smoke grenades down from a building rooftop overlooking the central square. A few of the grenades never actually went off, but the four that did quickly sent a thick blanket of gray over the street that hung like a curtain long enough for William Ray and Earl to enter the battle with Thompsons in hand, sifting through the fleeing members of the marching band.

They scattered in all directions while holding fast to their instruments the way a gunman would his weapon. The driver of Mexico's first ever fire engine, meanwhile, lost control of the vehicle, its front end crashing into cantina tables set up on the curb and sidewalk for patrons to better view the parade. That cleared the way for the Strongs to fire straight into *esos Demonios*, who were rushing straight for them to escape the BAR fire.

Neither would talk of the ensuing moments or that day at all ever again. Even in the sometimes storied, other times muddied history of the Texas Rangers, this battle was never mentioned, not even as the fodder of legend and myth. For the Strongs there was only the sense of the Thompsons rumbling in their hands, growing so hot the feeling of a fever would linger for hours afterward. The volume of the rounds tearing out the barrels bubbled their ears before deafening them to the clatter of the ejected shells clamoring to the pavement.

Earl actually smelled nothing at all until his Thompson finally clicked empty, feeling featherlight in contrast to when he'd first hit the trigger. Then he was accosted by the smells of smoke, blood, sweat, and fear all hitting him at once in a wave so powerful it nearly buckled his knees, as he slammed a fresh drum home and laid waste to more *esos Demonios*. His heart was going so fast, it stole his breath and only William Ray's hand tugging on his shoulder got him moving from the maelstrom.

Both caught a glimpse of Esteban Cantú himself, dressed in a colorful uniform affixed with epaulets, stumbling in and out of the smoke clouds to escape the carnage. But the Strongs had other priorities ahead of chasing him down, first and foremost being Captain Bill McDonald, who'd taken another hit, this time in the shoulder. His breath sounded wheezy, as William Ray hovered over him. The surviving *esos Demonios* struggled to regroup in tandem with the *federales* and regular Mexican army conscripts who'd come to enjoy the procession. But Manuel Gonzaullas tossed more smoke bombs down toward the street, giving the Strongs enough cover to get McDonald onto his feet.

"They got us boxed in!" Earl realized.

But William Ray's eyes had fixed on Mexico's first motorized fire engine. "Not for long, they don't."

William Ray took the wheel, Bill McDonald squeezed next to him with Earl on the legendary captain's other side.

"I'm not worth the extra weight to carry, Ranger," McDonald told Earl.

"Don't you even think of dying today, Captain."

"Hey, didn't you hear?" McDonald managed between gasping breaths. "I already died, a year ago." His grin quickly dissolved into a hacking cough that brought blood into his hand.

William Ray got the truck righted and headed down the plaza amid a sudden relentless torrent of fire unleashed by the surviving *esos Demonios*. He opened up with his .45 toward them while he drove with one hand, Earl laying the Thompson's barrel on the doorframe through the open window and unleashing a rainbow of muzzle fire on the gunmen firing from that side. Bill McDonald had slumped between them unconscious, and William Ray shoved him down further to keep him safe from a stray or ricocheting bullet.

The Strongs had just run out of ammo when Frank Hamer and Monroe Fox hit the streets blasting away with their BARs, leaping up to take the handholds of the fire engine as if they were firemen wielding promised death instead of hoses. They emptied the remainder of their ammo boxes, the 30.06 cartridges chewing through flesh and bone, leaving nothing whole in their path.

"Where's M.T.?" Earl realized suddenly.

"Don't you worry about that boy, son," William Ray said from behind the wheel. "He knows how to keep his wits about him for sure, a damn lone wolf if ever there was one."

"Dad," Earl started and William Ray knew something must be serious for his son to call him that. "It's Captain McDonald. I believe we've lost him."

"Shit." William Ray tried to rouse the legend with no success as they left the plaza for the city's outskirts, Hamer and Fox still returning the fire chasing them. "I'm of a mind to turn this rig around and go for round two."

But he knew they were too low on ammunition to mount another effective attack, and the sight of the multitude of bodies fallen to the combined onslaught of the BARs and the Thompsons was plenty enough to tell him they'd won the day. Accomplished just what they came here to do, though at a terrible price given the loss of Bill McDonald.

"We had no choice here, son," William Ray said in a voice strained by the battle that had left his throat hot and dry. "No matter how many years you live from this day, you need to never forget that. Otherwise, it'll steal your sleep first and then your sanity. Just remember Willow Creek and you'll keep note of our purpose. . . . You hear me, boy?"

"I do, Ranger."

William Ray nodded, feeling the fire engine's gears buck as they left Mexicali behind them. "We didn't start this, but we damn well finished it."

90

Los Mochis, Mexico

"They did at that," Ana Guajardo finished. "And I imagine that if You-Tube had been around then, there would be a record of plenty of women and children bleeding in the street from those Thompsons and Brownings. In Mexico, we call *that* a massacre." She took a breath to steady herself. "My great-grandfather survived that day at the hands of yours, but not the fallout that followed. He left office in disgrace—the entire Cantú family was disgraced—a few months later. His political career was over and he was never heard from again."

Caitlin remained silent, at once understanding why this was one of the few, perhaps the only story her legendary grandfather had never shared with her.

"Nothing to say, Ranger? *Te comió la lengua el gato?* Cat got your tongue? I believe you've come all this way for nothing more than a history lesson. No one's been able to control my brother since my own family gave up trying. So if his trail is what brought you down here, I'm afraid you've wasted your time."

"Four of the murdered children in Willow Creek were descendants of those three generals who betrayed Pancho Villa so they could take over the Mexican drug trade, ma'am. They used my ancestors to take down yours and became the original founders of what we now call the cartels," Caitlin said finally. "The fifth victim in Willow Creek was the son of Fernando Lorenzo Sandoval, the man who put your father, Enrique Cantú, in the Walls prison. And those nephews you've never met are the grand-children of Mateo Torres, the man who gave up your father to Sandoval."

"But Enrique Cantú wasn't really my father, was he, Ranger? This Mateo Torres was my real father."

"I'd tell you to ask Enrique himself," Caitlin said, stealing a look at the man hunched in a wheelchair in the lee of an oak tree, "but I don't expect he's been in much condition to answer since suffering that four-story fall."

"If you're right, Ranger, you could very well be in danger yourself."

"Ma'am?"

"Well, you are a descendant of the man who ultimately destroyed Esteban Cantú, aren't you?" Guajardo said, fixing her harsh stare on Caitlin and letting it hang there. "I'd watch my back if I were you."

Caitlin seemed all too happy to meet her gaze. "I know my enemies when I see them."

"You don't have much family, do you, Ranger? No one, in fact."

"While you have your brother, Locaro. I thought you might like to let whoever got him sprung from prison know I'll be coming after them too, once I hunt down the killer of those children. I'm guessing you've done some hunting yourself, *señora*."

"What's that have to do with anything?"

"The children were killed with some kind of field dressing knife, for starters." Caitlin gazed about their surroundings. "And this being a game preserve, I figure you'd know your way around such a thing. Thought maybe you could give me some pointers in its use, so I'll know better the kind of killer I'm looking for. According to our medical examiner, that killer would be just about your height too."

"I believe we're finished here, Ranger."

"I'll let you know when we're done, *señora*."

"Perhaps you're forgetting your jurisdiction and that you came down here to warn me, not accuse me."

"I only accused you of being a hunter. But now that you mention it, doesn't seem as if a man like your brother would launch a random attack north of the border. Who do you suppose landed him that pardon? We find that out, we'll know who's pulling his strings, that's for sure."

"We look the other way when it comes to our families, Ranger,"

Guajardo said, stiffening only slightly. "But that doesn't stop them from being the one thing in our lives we can't replace."

"I guess if you could've replaced your father, it might've spared him that fall, ma'am."

Whatever fear or trepidation Ana Guajardo might have felt in Caitlin's presence vanished with that statement. Instead of showing anger, her expression grew almost frighteningly flat. Instead of her breathing picking up, it slowed. Instead of sneering or scowling, she simply smiled.

"Just like whoever killed those children because of the actions of men dead long before they were born must have had his reasons, or hers, and they must have believed those reasons to be true. They must have thought that the wrongs done to their family justified something so extreme. There are no consolation prizes in life, any more than there are in business. It's a zero-sum game, Ranger."

Caitlin remained just as calm. "Well, I've never heard the murder of children called a game of any kind, ma'am. And I'd say anyone who feels that way must figure they've got a reason not to be frightened of the consequences."

"Why, what makes you say that, Ranger?"

"Because they've got something bigger planned. It all comes down to timing, ma'am. Why now? Why would whoever's behind your whack job of a brother take such a chance if they didn't have good reason to figure everybody'll forget soon enough?"

Guajardo took a step closer, Caitlin planting her hands on her hips, the right one noticeably closer to her holstered pistol now. "Maybe they let their hatred stew for as long as they could. Maybe they've grown powerful enough not to fear the consequences." She hesitated, seeming to enjoy herself now. "Do you ever hunt yourself, Ranger?"

Caitlin lowered her hands again, left them dangling by her hips. "I never found much point in killing anything that wasn't trying to do the same to me."

"It's just a sport, Ranger."

"Only for those with a taste for spilling blood, ma'am. And the drug trade your great-grandfather started, the same trade Pancho Villa's generals expanded, has spilled far more than its share. Throw a stone on either side of the border and you're bound to hit someone whose family was decimated by the legacy left by Esteban Cantú. What was it you said about revenge, that it's the most powerful, the purest emotion of all?"

"Close enough," Guajardo smirked. "But I only want what's best for Mexico."

"Really? Maybe I should have a discussion with President Villarreal about that."

"Better make it fast, Ranger. Word is he's going to be stepping down soon, is probably crafting his letter of resignation as we speak."

"So you can appoint someone else from your party in his place?"

"That's the idea. Someone better able to help those of us who love our country realize the vision that's best for it."

"I love my country too, ma'am."

"There's no accounting for taste, I suppose."

"And how did President Villarreal take his demotion?"

"There was no one for him to express his displeasure to. Besides me, of course."

"Bet it was a good thing he didn't have a skinning knife available at the time."

"Not much of a weapon when it comes to killing."

"Tell that to those kids in Willow Creek, ma'am, who suffered a terrible death," Caitlin said, her eyes boring into Ana Guajardo in search of a reaction that never came.

"I'd like to help you, Ranger, I really would." Guajardo took another step closer, stopping when she banged up against something that felt like a force field enclosing Caitlin. "That's why you need to know you can't stop the storm that's coming. The best you can hope for is to find cover before it's too late."

"I'll keep that in mind."

"Then are we done here?"

"For today, ma'am, for today." Caitlin returned the Stetson to her head and started to turn, only to stop and look back at Guajardo. "But tomorrow's another story entirely."

91

Entering the Walls prison through the visitors' entrance had almost a surreal effect to it. Cort Wesley hadn't been back on these grounds, or anywhere even close to Huntsville, since his own release four years earlier, much less with his oldest son accompanying him.

Dylan had remained silent through most of the drive from Jan McClellan-Townsend's spread in the Rio Grande Valley, removing his earbuds when they reached the outskirts of the town that housed eleven of the most notorious prisons in the entire state. Cort Wesley had made an appointment with Warden Warren Jardine, who actually looked happy to see him when he was ushered into Jardine's spacious office, decorated with all forms of Texas memorabilia that belied the kind of business that went on within those walls.

"I've heard good things, Mr. Masters, good things," he greeted, shaking Cort Wesley's hand enthusiastically before his eyes fixed on Dylan with some surprise. "This your oldest?"

"Yes, sir."

"Well, son, I've heard good things about you too." Eyes back on Cort Wesley now. "You certainly seem to have turned the corner and I hope you don't mind me saying I'm proud to have played a part in that."

Cort Wesley didn't bother to tell Jardine he'd played no part at all, that being released after a DNA test determined his innocence didn't qualify as a successful rehabilitation. "I've got a younger son too," he said instead. "He was kidnapped last night."

Jardine looked caught by surprise, clearly with no idea how to respond. "I, er, I," he stammered, and then just left things there.

"I didn't tell your secretary the true subject of my visit, because you don't need any record of it in the books. But I'm here because I think you might be able to help me get my son back. You had a prisoner here in the early nineteen-eighties. Man by the name of Enrique Cantú, aka En-rique Guajardo. Believe he spent three years in your fine institution."

Jardine's entire expression seemed to sag, the life going out of his eyes. His gaze fell on Dylan again. "You wish to have this conversation in front of your son?"

"It's his brother who got kidnapped, remember? And, if you don't mind me saying, that's a pretty strange reaction about a small-time marijuana grower who not long before his arrest had bumped up to dealing. Of course, a few years after his release Cantú, Guajardo again by then, was among the richest, most powerful men in Mexico. So un-less he hit the lottery while living within your walls, I gotta figure it was something else he hit and I'd like to know what exactly."

"I could say I don't remember him," Jardine offered lamely.

"But that would be a lie, wouldn't it?"

"It was a long time ago, Mr. Masters. Lots of prisoners have come and gone."

"You owe me more than a weak memory, Warden, you owe yourself more too. Because if I don't get my son back, I'll have to go after all those who got in my way. Not a good place to be standing anytime soon."

Jardine shook his head, looking suddenly miffed. "You haven't changed at all, have you, Mr. Masters?"

"Why bother if I wasn't guilty of anything in the first place?"

"Oh, you were plenty guilty all right, just not of what made you my guest for four years."

Jardine's face took on the smug expression Cort Wesley recalled all too well from his time here. He'd aged noticeably in the past four years; his skin was paler, almost sallow, and his hair had thinned over droop-ing eyes that looked tired, sick maybe.

"You know I'm retiring next month."

"I didn't know, Warden, no."

"Forty years in Corrections is enough for any man, Mr. Masters, and I'd like to think I did some good." His eyes lowered, his shoulders seeming to sag as well. "Enrique Cantú wasn't one of those things."

"How's that, sir?"

"I was just a gun bull at the time and didn't have much to say about how things were run. What I can tell you is that Cantú spent a lot of his time inside with soldiers and heavyweights from La Eme, the Mexican Mafia, that was starting to make its presence felt in the drug world back then. He had a true gift for business, Mr. Masters, and whatever I might have been able to do to the contrary became forbidden, the word past down from on high, as they say. Cantú was off limits. He never ran a gang or spoke for his fellow prisoners; no, what he was doing organizationally was all about the world when he got out."

"You believe he was building a distribution network while inside, Warden, don't you?"

Jardine's eyes grew glassy, distant. He suddenly looked unsteady on his feet and leaned back against the edge of his desk. "Let me put it this way, Mr. Masters, for you and your boy here. I followed Cantú after his release, watched him become a major player in Mexican business and politics and listened to all the stories about how he made his stake when I knew they were all lies. Because, you're right, his initial fortune came from that drug distribution network he built on the inside in league with La Eme. Gives a whole new meaning to the word 'rehabilitation,' doesn't it?" Jardine asked, with a hint of irony in his voice.

"You know Cantú's grandfather started the whole process by smuggling opium into California. Guess you could say he was the actual founder of the Mexican drug trade."

Jardine nodded. "I've heard that, yes. And I'll tell you something else about Cantú. He spent three years here building alliances with street thugs as much as major dealers and suppliers. He taught men how to read English and lent them money he never asked to be repaid. He left here with hundreds of men in his debt and all their names and the names of their associates in his personal Rolodex. I'd venture to say he called all those debts in."

"You'd be right there, Warden," Cort Wesley told him, "you'd be damn right."

92

After leaving Ana Guajardo's game preserve, Caitlin climbed back into her SUV and switched the air-conditioning on full blast to relieve the heat flushing through her system as if she'd spiked a fever. She began the ten-hour drive back home slowly, shaking too much from knots of tension to grip the wheel tightly or give the vehicle the gas it needed to make time.

She needed those minutes to sort out her thoughts, distinguish knowledge based on surety from assumptions based on very little at all.

"That's why you need to know you can't stop the storm that's coming. The best you can hope for is to find cover before it's too late."

Recalling Guajardo's final words chilled her more than the cold blast of the air-conditioning. She'd known countless psychopaths, sociopaths, megalomaniacs, and residents of a lunatic fringe that the vast reaches of humanity went to bed every night never suspecting even existed. They shared, above all else, a uniquely self-destructive impulse that inevitably caught up with them as they betrayed themselves and their own intentions instead of letting someone else do it for them. It was a world where someone as extreme as Colonel Guillermo Paz could remake himself into a veritable moral center.

But Caitlin found Ana Callas Guajardo worse and more terrifying than any of those who dwelled on the fringe of humanity, because she lacked the self-destructive nature that doomed the others. She had said, hinted at, just enough to tell Caitlin what was coming without telling her anything. And she had practically confessed to murdering five children in Willow Creek without actually saying anything at all.

Ana Guajardo was settling all her family's old scores. The descendants of the three generals who had betrayed her great-grandfather, the current head of Mexico's antidrug efforts, who had arrested her father, and, finally, the grandchildren of the man who had betrayed her father to a young Fernando Lorenzo Sandoval years before Ana herself had likely pushed him off a fourth-story balcony. It would have all been madness had she not gone about things so systematically with utterly unrestrained violence emblematic of someone who felt either she had nothing to lose or, soon, there'd be no one to go up against her.

Caitlin believed the latter to be the case, because Guajardo's final act of vengeance would be this storm she intended to somehow rain down on the whole of the United States. The only thing she couldn't figure was why. Everything else made sense in supremely monstrous, and chilling, fashion, Guajardo's targets selected for clear reason. But taking on the entire United States, dedicating her considerable resources to what sounded like a thinly veiled major attack? That made no sense and wouldn't make any until Caitlin figured out what exactly the country had done to Guajardo to so earn her wrath. She had hinted at plenty back on the game preserve named after her father, but not that.

Caitlin had finally cooled off and her trembling subsided enough to make a call on her Bluetooth.

"You're kidding me, right?" Jones answered. "What operation of mine have you fucked up this time?"

"Can it, Jones. You still in Texas?"

"Yup, picking up the pieces of the mess you made for me, Ranger."

"Get to San Antonio. We're having a meeting as soon as I get back."

"Where are you and who'd you leave dead behind?"

"Mexico, and I didn't leave her dead at all."

"Her?"

"Ana Callas Guajardo."

"You sure know how to pick them, don't you, Ranger?" Jones asked after a slight pause. "What's this about?"

"Remember that color-coded warning chart Homeland used to use?"

"Intimately."

"What comes after red, Jones?"

* * *

Her next call was to D. W. Tepper.

"I need you to call Young Roger and get him to turn up everything he can on Ana Callas Guajardo. Tell him there's no need to go gentle with this because we've got a direct liaison with Homeland."

"Jones?"

"He has his uses, Captain."

"You were never a good judge of character, Hurricane."

"This particular storm's got nothing to do with me, D.W."

"Before I go upsetting every applecart between here and Austin, it might help if I knew what we're facing."

"Some kind of attack, Captain. An attack on the whole damn country." Caitlin heard her phone beep with another call coming in and checked the number. "Jesus Christ, I think it's her."

"Who?"

"Ana Guajardo."

93

MEXICO

"You have a change of heart, *Señora* Guajardo?" Caitlin asked, feeling colder than she could ever recall in her life.

"We left a few things unfinished, Ranger. You didn't come here to warn me, did you?"

"Not at all, ma'am. I came because I believe you're behind the killings of those children in Willow Creek and the attack on that lacrosse game in San Antonio. And you knew exactly who I was when I showed up. Almost looked like you were expecting me."

"Point taken."

"And you must be calling to make your own."

"Getting this kidnapped boy back is very important to you."

"Yes, it is," Caitlin said, starting to shake now.

"I am not without power or contacts inside Mexico, Ranger. Perhaps I can prove to you how wrong you are about me."

"And how wrong is that, ma'am?" Caitlin asked, her words like marbles rolling around her mouth.

"I believe I may be able to secure the boy's release in three days, subject to certain conditions."

"What do you need me to do exactly?"

"Nothing, Ranger, I need you to do nothing. You've clearly disturbed the interests of someone powerful and they took the boy to hold you back. So if you do nothing for, say, three days I believe, no, I'm confident, I'll be able to secure the boy's release. But you need to give me something to bargain with."

"I imagine that includes keeping what I suspect to myself."

"I believe we're on the same page here, Ranger."

A pause.

"Look at the two us, driven by our own ambitions and the legacy to succeed above all else."

Heat started to flush through Caitlin, pushing back the cold that had invaded her core. "Where you going with this?"

"We're both predators, Ranger. It's what we live for. You with your gun, me with my iPad. We live to destroy."

"You're only half right, ma'am."

"How's that?"

"I live to destroy people like you."

"And you're paying the same price I am for doing it. That's my point."

"Not really," Caitlin told her. "You got anybody you'd kill to protect?"

Silence on the other end of the line.

"I didn't think so. You got a brother who's crazy and a father you likely pushed off a balcony. You're a hunter, all right, and right now I know you've got a whole country set in your sights. Too bad I got you centered in mine. You made me an offer and now I'm gonna make you one: give it up or you'll end up a casualty of your own storm."

"A boy's life is at stake here. Do I need to remind you about that?"

"You just did, because you're scared as hell what'll happen if I don't get him back. How much you think you'll be able to enjoy your victory with Guillermo Paz and Cort Wesley Masters on your ass?"

"You forgot to mention yourself, Ranger."

"No, I didn't, 'cause I'm already there. See, *señora*, a strong rain's gonna be falling all right, but it's gonna be falling on you."

Silence followed and Caitlin thought Guajardo was about to hang up, until she heard her sigh deeply. "You're forgetting one thing about this puzzle you think you've put together."

"Am I?"

"There's still one last surviving relative of William Ray and Earl Strong, the Texas Rangers who actually destroyed my great-grandfather Esteban Cantú that day in Mexicali. Maybe these victims are being taken chronologically, starting with the children of the three generals, son of the Mexican cop who arrested my father, grandchildren of his deceitful business partner, and saving you for last. You ever think about that?"

"I'm thinking about it right now. And maybe they left me off the list because they know I'm not a little boy or girl. Killing kids, no matter in what cause or name, is coward's work, ma'am, an act of weakness no matter how the perpetrator wants to spin it. We still hang people in Texas, you know, and I'll see that person swinging by a rope if I have to string her up on a tree myself."

"Her," Guajardo repeated.

"Figure of speech, ma'am."

"That all, Ranger?"

"That's up to you."

94

Luke was scared. Luke was terrified.

They'd stuffed him in the trunk of a car with a bottle of water to drink and an empty one to use if he needed to pee. The men didn't seem to speak English and got angry every time the boy failed to understand what they were saying.

They brought him to what must have been Mexico, some stench-riddled slum, and stuffed him in a thinly walled room with plywood nailed over what passed for windows. The room, hot and stifling even at night, stank worst of all, the smell seeming to rise through the rickety floorboards, assaulting his nostrils with virtually every breath he took in. He'd heard how somebody could get used to practically anything, but Luke couldn't imagine ever getting used to this.

He'd been in his share of scrapes, but nothing like Dylan. So maybe this was his chance to prove he was just as brave and strong as his older brother. Truth was he'd always wanted to prove to Caitlin and his dad that he could handle tough things just as well, and Dylan had been the very same age he was today the day they'd both witnessed their mother shot to death.

Now Luke regretted ever wanting to prove anything to anybody. All he could do was huddle on the dirty, smelly floor with his hands tucked between his knees to still their trembling.

Why don't you just suck your goddamn thumb, you baby.

He'd barely formed that thought when the boy had the sense there was someone with him in the room. He might have dismissed the feeling out of hand had he not smelled sweet talcum powder suddenly blocking out the stench of ass and shit. The smell made Luke feel better and he actually felt himself nodding off to the sight of a smiling black man sipping root beer and telling him everything was going to be all right.

PART TEN

They may be the most fantastic organization in the world. When you've got a situation like this, they move in and they move in to stay. . . . They are there until the problem is solved.

Fort Worth Star Telegram, June 16, 1985

95

It was well after dark by the time Caitlin made it back to the city, impatience starting to get the better of her as it mixed with anxiety over her last call just after she crossed the border moments before dusk.

"All right, Ranger" said Captain Tepper, "no sign of your friend Jones yet, but Masters is here with his boy Dylan, and so is Young Roger, who's chomping at the bit to get started. He hasn't briefed me yet, but judging by the look on his face and number of machines he's got strung round the conference room he's gonna have a lot to say. And he looks a bit scared to me. You scared, Young Roger?"

"In a big way, Captain," Caitlin heard him reply. "The whole country should be scared."

"You figured all this shit out, didn't you, son?" Tepper's voice returned.

"I believe I have, but I hope I'm wrong."

The man known as Young Roger was a Ranger himself, but the title was mostly honorary, given after his technological expertise as a computer whiz helped the Rangers solve a number of Internet-based crimes ranging from identity theft to credit card fraud to the busting of a major pedophile and kiddie porn ring. He worked out of all six Ranger Company offices on a rotating basis as needed and as the investigative caseload demanded. Young Roger wore his hair too long and played guitar for a rock band called The Rats. Caitlin had never seen them play but she'd listened to the CD. Not the kind of music she preferred, but Dylan told her it was pretty good.

"Okay," Young Roger started, Caitlin hearing him clicking on a keyboard as well, "I wish you could be here to see the visuals on this, Ranger, but I'll do my best to lay it out verbally. My instructions were to give the holdings of Ana Callas Guajardo the once-over to see if I could find anything that suggested a threat, some attack about to be launched against the United States, and, boy, did I ever."

Caitlin felt her stomach quiver inside as Young Roger continued.

"Normally in such assignments I'm looking for something suggesting weaponry and ordnance. Ingredients for explosives, shipping orders with the wrong weights attached to them to suggest dummy invoices and falsified documents, manifests with plenty of lines to read between, evidence of lots of men being moved from one place to another—that sort of stuff. First thing you gotta realize is I found none of those things here, but what I found could be even worse."

The sound of fingers clicking a keyboard stopped and Caitlin wondered what everyone in the conference room was now able to see that she couldn't.

"This is a woman with diversified holdings the world over. But I decided to stick, initially anyway, with Guajardo's holdings in Mexico, specifically a number of companies spread throughout the country with the most interesting ones being based in Guadalajara."

"Why interesting?" Caitlin asked, hearing her own voice echo in tinny fashion over the Bluetooth.

"Because they were start-ups opened in the last three to five years, two especially: a software company and a toy factory refitted into a manufacturing plant. The software company because since it's been open, I can't find a single product it's produced either on its own or on a subcontract basis."

"A front, in other words."

"That was my first thought, Ranger."

"What was your second?" Caitlin asked him.

"What the hell would she need with carbon filament at a remodeled toy factory?"

"Carbon filament?"

"Its strength, especially when comprised of graphite fibers, makes it a relatively low-cost favorite of both the auto and aerospace industries. Pretty much any machine that moves and involves complex internal combustion is going to make heavy use of carbon filament. The problem in this case was the amount Guajardo, or her subordinates, ordered. Tons of it over a three-year period that was roughly a hundred times what NASA ordered. Added up, the order came to about the same amount as all three American auto companies during the same period."

Caitlin thought briefly, listening to the muted sounds wafting in over her speakers through the Bluetooth. "How come this didn't raise any flags with Homeland, NSA, or somebody else?"

"Routing orders were manipulated to disguise the amounts being sent to a single location. There were over a hundred different shipping destinations scattered all over the world that ultimately were rerouted and ended up at that old toy factory in Guadalajara."

"What's all this add up to, Young Roger?" Caitlin heard Captain Tepper ask.

"I can't tell you for sure, sir, other than to say carbon filament has plenty of military uses as well, though this amount doesn't jibe with anything I can figure. Other than to tell you my researching got the notice of some watchful eye down Washington way and forced me to get on another computer to continue my search. Only other thing I came up with of note was a number of anomalous shipments from a manufacturing plant in Germany that Guajardo purchased from Siemens, notable for the fact they followed much the same routing history as those carbon filament shipments."

"What did these shipments contain?"

"Can't tell you that, Ranger Strong. But I can tell you the weight of each shipment was just about exactly the same, leading me to believe Guajardo was putting the same thing in those boxes, no matter what the invoice might have said."

"She must've had a real good reason to go through all that trouble."

"Wish I could tell you what that reason was, Ranger."

"Can you tell me what this Siemens plant in Germany that Gua-jardo purchased manufactured?"

"They were primarily an assembly plant, and one thing sure did catch my eye."

"What's that?" Tepper asked before Caitlin could.

"Transformers, sir. Electrical transformers."

96

San Antonio

Jones climbed out of his car outside Ranger Company F headquarters just after Caitlin, jogging to catch her before she reached the door.

"This better be good, Ranger."

"Or what? You won't come to my next birthday party, so we can't play pin the tail on the asshole?"

"You're a piece of work, Ranger, the genuine article."

"How's Sandoval, Jones?"

Jones's cheeks puckered, making it look as if pen tip–sized holes had been punched in them. "I wouldn't know. I got a message he's no longer interested in working with us, that he's come to doubt we're actually pursuing the same goals."

"Smartened up, in other words."

"Or more likely got scared off by a certain Texas Ranger who's a walking tampon for all the blood that flows through Texas."

He'd intended the remark to get a rise out of her, but it produced only a smile. "Nice metaphor, Jones. You mind if I use it myself someday?"

Jones shook his head repeatedly, seemingly with nothing else to say until he resumed suddenly. "Where's the fire this time, Ranger? You know, life's gonna be pretty boring when you run out of targets to fix in your sights."

"There were plenty of them the other night at that high school lacrosse game, or maybe word of the fifteen dead and seventy-five wounded never reached your desk."

"There are some at Homeland who want to cancel all sporting events for the foreseeable future."

"I don't think Ana Callas Guajardo will have call to attack another anytime soon, Jones."

Jones's eyes widened, then narrowed in suspicion. He started to shake his head again, but stopped. "So what did the most powerful person in Mexico do to find your crosshairs, Ranger?"

"Killed five children with her own hands, but that's just for starters. I think she's planning an attack on the whole country, *our* country."

Jones rolled his eyes. "You couldn't find a bigger windmill to tilt at this time?"

"You know Guajardo, Jones?"

"Only by reputation. And why attack something you can just buy the same way she bought Mexico?"

"Oh, I don't know. Maybe it has something to do with the carbon filament she's been stockpiling."

Jones stopped just short of the door, grasping Caitlin by the elbow. The grip came accompanied by a look on his face somewhere between shock and realization, his eyes flashing like an LED readout. Caitlin thought she could feel pulses of electricity transferring out of him and into her.

"Say that again?"

"Carbon filament, Jones, tons of it. That must mean something to you."

"It means you just may have done it again. It's truly amazing, Ranger, that no matter where somebody leaves a pile of shit, you find a way to step in it."

97

The conference table was littered with fast-food wrappers when Jones trailed Caitlin into the room.

"Look who's here," D. W. Tepper greeted, quickly brushing the refuse into a nearby wastebasket. "I guess the meeting of Shitheads Anonymous can now commence."

"Stow it, Captain," snapped Jones, training his gaze on Dylan. "And somebody tip the delivery boy so he can be on his way."

"He doesn't leave my sight, Jones," Cort Wesley told him.

"No? I seriously doubt he has the security clearance to hear what I'm about to say, cowboy."

"That may be true, but the other night he knocked out a stone killer with a lacrosse ball to the skull. I believe he can handle whatever it is you have to say, and for your sake it better be something that helps me get my other boy back."

Jones chuckled and shook his head. "What is with you people? Is there something different about the water in this damn state?"

"Why don't you just stick to the subject, Jones?" Caitlin prodded.

"Fine by me, Ranger, since the quicker we get this dealt with, the quicker I can get out of this swamp. The subject is a soft bomb."

"Come again?"

"Better known as the BLU-114/B. Highly classified and probably never mentioned outside of very select circles until this very moment. We've been using soft bombs through a bunch of wars now, most prominently Bosnia. A soft bomb consists of chemically treated carbon graphite filaments that rain down on their targets in a kind of cloud, a really dense one."

"Carbon filaments?" Cort Wesley raised, the soldier in him speaking. "Doesn't sound much like a weapon of mass destruction to me."

"It isn't, not in the traditional sense, anyway. But soft bombs can be just as effective when it comes to the targets they were designed to hit."

"And what targets are those?"

"Power plants, cowboy."

Jones continued, filling in the blanks in the mental picture the others in the room were already drawing. "We used an early variation in Desert Storm, the war where you cut your teeth, Masters. Back then they were variations on the Tomahawk missile, only packed with bomblets filled with small spools of carbon-fiber wire. We rained enough of those babies down to rob Iraq of eighty-five percent of its electrical power while doing only minimal damage to infrastructure.

"Now, the BLU-114/B was an updated version of that principle and worked even better in strikes against Serbia. We put three quarters of the country into darkness and as a result were able to do things I'm not gonna mention in front of the delivery boy there. See, the updated smart bombs utilized filaments that were only a few hundredths of an inch thick. When the carbon fibers hit transformers, signal switching stations, and especially the power plants themselves, *poof!*, you've got yourself a made-to-order short circuiting which, in turn, vaporizes the carbon in its electrical arc flow, leaving no trace, and thus no evidence, behind."

Jones stopped to resteady his thoughts.

"Of course," he continued, "to manage that, the Ranger's friend Ana Guajardo would need a delivery system akin to the one we used. So unless Mexican bombers are gonna sneak through NORAD and our other air-defense networks, I'd say we've got nothing to worry about."

"Not necessarily," said Young Roger, working his keyboard again.

98

Young Roger brought up a schematic on the big-screen television to which his laptop was linked. "This is what they were building inside Guajardo's converted toy factory."

Tepper squinted to better make out what he was seeing. "Looks like a model airplane to me. Remote controlled. Used to fly them when I was a boy."

Jones moved closer to the screen, frowning. "And that's supposed to scare me? No, sir, unless we're missing something here, Ana Guajardo might as well attack the U.S. with a fleet of toy stock cars." He shook his head, his frown growing into a scowl. "You don't need Homeland Security here, you need Hasbro."

"We *are* missing something," Dylan said suddenly, drawing the rest of the eyes in the room to him. "That's not a model airplane, least not the kind you used to play with, Captain."

"Then what the hell is it, son?"

"It's known as a monster-scale radio-controlled plane. I saw one at a fair last year. Built to scale and plenty big too, maybe twenty feet long with a wingspan almost that big. Much bigger flying range than what Hasbro might make," the boy said, with his gaze moving to Jones, "but still controlled with a remote no bigger than a smartphone, maybe even a smartphone these days."

"Okay, okay," Jones broke in, not wanting to be outdone. "So what are we saying now, that Guajardo's used all this carbon filament, *tons* of it, to make miniature bombs to match her miniature fleet?"

"No," Caitlin said, breaking the silence that fell in the wake of Jones's question. "What if, what if . . ."

"What if *what*, Ranger?" Tepper prodded.

"What if these planes *themselves* were the bombs? What if Guajardo layered this carbon into the frames and blew a couple thousand of them up directly over their targets? What then, Jones?"

He was speechless for a moment, his mouth hanging open and lower lips quivering in a motion more akin to a spasm. "You'd have a hell of a mess, Ranger."

"But it wouldn't be irreparable and would leave no lasting damage," Jones continued immediately. "So if you think Guajardo's master plan is to plunge us into eternal darkness this way, you must be drinking more of that Texas water."

"Transformers," Caitlin said almost too softly to hear.

"Say that again?"

"Transformers. Tell him, Young Roger."

"Another of Guajardo's companies. She bought a manufacturing plant in Germany from Siemens that makes them."

Jones's mouth started to lower again. "Siemens makes ninety percent of the transformers in this country."

"You mean Guajardo does, Jones," Caitlin said, "and has been for as much as five years now."

"Oh, shit . . ."

"What is it?"

Jones looked like a young boy who'd been caught pinching quarters from his own piggy bank. "Looks like maybe that Texas water isn't so bad, after all."

"In the past five years, nearly three quarters of the transformers in the country have been replaced," Jones continued.

"First I've heard of that," noted Captain Tepper.

"That's because it was all done under the radar to avoid attracting attention to the fact that Homeland had identified a major flaw in the system, specifically how vulnerable the older design was to overloads and its incompatibility with newer software. So we authorized a new design built to incorporate security measures that allowed for faster and more secure switching and transfer."

"Don't tell me," said Young Roger. "You nationalized the grid so Homeland could take control, if it ever came to that."

"Gold star, smart-ass."

Young Roger flapped a frayed and tattered paperback at him called *Cyber War* by Richard Clarke. "If I'm a smart-ass, what's that make counterterrorism expert Mr. Clarke here? I've read his book a dozen times and it scares me more each time. Wanna know what I learned from it?" No one at the table said yes, but Young Roger continued anyway. "Screw with these transformers and you end up with too much power being sent down high-tension lines that deliver electricity to homes. That destroys the line, maybe even resulting in a fire. Meanwhile, the resulting power surge overwhelms household surge protectors and fries every electrical device in the house."

"You finished?" Jones asked him.

"Not even close," said Young Roger, still holding Clarke's book as if it were the Bible. "In two thousand three, a falling tree hit a power line somewhere in Ohio, creating a power surge. The backup systems that were supposed to reroute and compensate didn't do their job and fifty million people all the way to the East Coast ended up losing power— all from a single tree limb. But that just scratches at the depths of the problem we're facing here. See, the real crux of Guajardo's plot to take us back to the Stone Age is to create uneven flow through the electric generators. Alter the spin rates on the subgrid from the standard sixty megahertz, change the rotation speeds to something other than what the programming calls for, and the turbines will literally tear themselves apart. The problem being that nobody's storing these monster machines in a warehouse. They're strictly built to order, custom made, and even under the best of circumstances it takes months. Now we're talking about having to replace tens of thousands of them all at once. Years?" Young Roger asked, shaking his head as he let the Clarke book flop back to the tabletop. "Try decades. And that's years and decades with factories shut down; distribution networks of food, produce, and other essentials destroyed; and financial markets back to the era of ledger books and abacuses."

"While at the same time," Tepper picked up, "her . . . what'd you call them again?" he asked Dylan.

"Monster-scale RC planes."

"Her monster-scale RC planes loaded with this . . ." He looked to Caitlin this time.

"Carbon filament."

"Carbon filament ignite over the nation's top distribution stations and power plants serving the most populated areas of the country."

"Not too hard," added Young Roger, "considering that eighty-five percent of the population is concentrated in barely fifteen percent of the nation's area."

"We're still missing something here," said Caitlin, looking back toward Young Roger. "You said Guajardo bought a software company too, a software company that apparently wasn't making any software."

Young Roger spun the *Cyber War* paperback around. "Looks like I was wrong there."

99

SAN ANTONIO

"Her transformers would give Guajardo access to the software systems controlling them through a back door," Young Roger continued. "Just what the mad doctor ordered when it comes to launching some virus her software engineers have been developing into the power companies' SCADA—that's Supervisory Control and Data Acquisition—systems that balance the flow between each company's substations, transformers, and generators. This virus is the final piece of the puzzle that's going to shut the power grid down and keep it shut down by sending faulty signals to the devices that regulate the electric load across the country. Power surges flood the grid with no failsafe or shutdown, since the virus has effectively disabled the backup systems, blowing every generator and every circuit breaker panel from coast to coast."

"India," Jones muttered, his gaze drifting out the window.

"I'm old, sir," Tepper told him. "You mind speaking up a bit."

"One year ago in India. Biggest blackout in goddamn history."

Caitlin laid her hands on the table. "Don't tell me, Jones, it was you."

"Test run, Ranger, just to see what we could pull off by infecting their system with a virus and just a virus. Half a billion people lost power."

"But they got it back within, like, a day," Dylan pointed out.

"Right you are, delivery boy, because it was a simple worm and they were still in control of their transformers and didn't have to worry about a hard rain of carbon taking out their physical capacity to boot. And our worm didn't disrupt their system to the point of destroying their electric generators."

"But you could have, right?" Caitlin challenged.

"That's classified."

"I'll take that as a yes."

"Take it however you want," Jones snapped. "The bottom line here is we're the *United States government*, not a pissed-off bitch with a grudge. Right now all we've got is assumptions with virtually no proof whatsoever to back them up. I don't care how angry this woman is, she's not capable of pulling this off; no one is."

"You never met Ana Callas Guajardo," Caitlin told him. "My interview with her was like having an audience with the devil. These aren't assumptions, Jones, they're *intentions*. She wanted me to know she was up to something and gave me just enough hints to figure out what. Know why? Because she doesn't think we can stop her."

"Can we?" Young Roger wondered. "You know how long it took us to build the power grid that's up and running now? Over a hundred years. More than a century of work Guajardo plans to erase in a matter of hours, days at most. And I do mean erase, since a three-pronged attack like this would render every part, every segment of the grid, from power lines to substations to the circuit breakers in your house, nothing but a mess of useless junk. Could we salvage some? Sure. Is a lifetime an accurate estimate of how long it would take to bring us out of the second Stone Age? Nobody knows for sure.

"What we do know, pretty much anyway," he continued, "is what all this is going to lead to. You can forget about using your local bank or ATM, because there won't be any way to access your accounts. That means the only cash you'll have for who knows how long is what you've got in your pocket when the attack hits. Not that it matters much, because there won't be a lot of places where you'll be able to use it before too long. Any food that isn't swept up in the initial panic will spoil. Stores won't be able to sell you batteries for your flashlights, because their cash registers and inventory control systems will be gone. And whatever's on the shelves is all that's going to be there for a long time because, here's the kicker, we can also look forward to the collapse of the entire transportation system. No air traffic control means nothing flying. No switching stations means no trains running. No traffic signals means utter chaos in the streets that's certain to spread to the freeways, which are going to become one big, fat parking lot since there won't be enough early responders to respond to all the accidents or any effective way for the responders to talk to each other. In short, no way to move anything, any goods at all, anywhere. Remember, we're talking no cell service, no landlines, no television, no Internet. Maybe a few radio stations operating on backup power for a while, but that's it." Young Roger took a deep breath, his voice sounding strained and hoarse when he resumed. "Sure, the power, at least some of it, will be restored eventually, but what exactly will the country look like when the lights come back on? We're talking about civil disobedience taken to a whole new level. We're talking about an epic societal breakdown on *every* level. You want to know what Armageddon really looks like? Stay tuned."

No one at the table spoke once he was finished. No one posed any questions. They all just looked at one another amid the grim silence, until everyone's eyes fastened on Jones.

"You think Homeland Security might actually be able to help the cause this time, Jones?" Caitlin asked him.

Jones's expression looked as flat as a granite statue. "We'd need to come clean to President Villarreal of Mexico and enlist his help. But that means asking him to go up against the political power broker who runs his party and pulls all his strings. Take our side against Ana Guajardo."

Caitlin almost smiled. "I don't think he'll have a problem with that," was all she said.

100

SAN ANTONIO

"Ranger," Jones said an hour later, after emerging from behind the closed door of Captain Tepper's office, which he'd appropriated for his own use, "I don't know how you know what you know, but consider President Villarreal on board in a big way."

"He's got his reasons, believe me."

"Okay, here's the plan. Mexican troops are going to storm Guajardo's software company and manufacturing plant simultaneously. Villarreal is also in the process of obtaining what they call an *orden de apprehension*, their version of an arrest warrant, for Guajardo so she can be taken into custody."

"How long, Jones?"

"The troops are gonna hit the two locations at start of business tomorrow." He checked his watch. "A mere ten hours from now. You don't mind, I need to bring Washington up to date," he said, starting back for the door. "Nice being on speaking terms with you again, Ranger."

"Oh, you'll find a way to disappoint me," Caitlin told him. "You always do."

They all remained at Ranger Company headquarters overnight, stealing what little sleep they could on cots in a ready room that had been a workout facility until it became clear no one was using it. At nine a.m.

sharp everyone had gathered again in the conference room over dough-
nuts, bagels, and coffee, awaiting word from Jones on the results of the
morning raids on Guajardo's high-tech facilities in Guadalajara.

"Both facilities were abandoned," he reported flatly, "cleaned out
recently and fast by the look of things. We're talking nothing left behind. I'm surprised they even left the floors and ceilings."

"You think Guajardo's wise to us?" Tepper wondered.

"Even if she was," Caitlin replied before Jones could try, "it sounds
like this must have happened before I paid her a visit yesterday. Which
means the timing's just coincidence and everything's proceeding according to her plan."

"So where's that leave us exactly?" Cort Wesley posed to no one in
particular.

"Up shit's creek with a paddle we can't use," Jones told him. "The
Mexican president is moving in troops to surround that game preserve of
hers in Los Mochis, but there's no sign of Guajardo or anybody else on
the premises. Looks like it's been abandoned too, except for the animals."

"You have any recon satellite available?" Caitlin asked him.

"You got that look, Ranger."

"That doesn't answer my question."

"Depends on what they'd be reconning."

"Guajardo's game preserve."

Two more hours passed before Jones got the report from a satellite reconnaissance sweep that had used thermal imaging and density scans to
survey Guajardo's land in Los Mochis.

"Ever hear of Rio Secreto, Ranger?"

"Nope."

"It's a network of underground caves located near Mexico's Playa del
Carmen. Truly an amazing sight to behold, featuring a two-thousand-
foot river that winds its way underground, with literally thousands of
stalactites and stalagmites."

"I appreciate the information, Jones, but what does that have to do
with Los Mochis?"

"Well, it turns out Los Nachos," he said, grinning at his purposeful mispronunciation of the name, "features a similar cave system, more limestone based in this case but also surrounding what is clearly an underground river even longer than Rio Secreto."

"I'll be sure to remember that next time I plan a vacation," said Captain Tepper, the furrows and lines on his face exaggerated further by lack of sleep. His eyes drooped tiredly and the ashtray before him at the head of the table featured any number of Marlboros extinguished quickly so as not to set a bad example for Cort Wesley Masters's oldest son. "But right now I'm more worried about all of us boarding an express train back to the dark ages."

"There's definitely a structure beneath the game preserve, people," Jones elaborated. "But our initial satellite recon can't determine whether it's an extension of the underground cave system or a separate structure built to take advantage of the camouflage provided."

"Nice things, your satellites," snapped Cort Wesley, grumpy from worry and lack of sleep as well, his short coarse hair sticking up at one side thanks to a few hours spent twisting on a cot to no restful end. "They can tell what kind of vodka somebody's drinking from five miles up, but not whether a megalomaniac Mexican has built herself a lair from which to launch an attack on America, or where she's got my son stashed."

"Well, the satellites did pick up some hot spots in the grid, temperature variations usually indicative of man-made structures carved out of the ground."

"You mean like stairways, emergency escape routes, something like that?" Caitlin raised.

"That's exactly what I mean. There are four of them pretty much equidistant from one another on the game preserve."

"That's good, right?" asked Tepper.

Jones nodded. "It sure is. But what isn't good is the fact that our reconnaissance picked up no signature normally associated with a power source or any power in general. Now, boys and girls, it could be Guajardo reinforced her bunker with lead shielding to throw our birds off or is using propane to throw us off. But it could also be that there's nothing down there at all but stalactites."

Caitlin found herself staring at the remarkably detailed array of overhead shots of the game preserve taken from satellites miles up in the sky. "She's there all right."

"Why don't I put you on the phone with President Villarreal and let you convince him to attack what might be no more than a fancy zoo?"

"Because his top cadre could be beholden to Ana Guajardo, maybe even on her payroll. Leave this in the hands of the Mexican army, Jones, and you might as well start stockpiling batteries and flashlights."

Tepper shook his head and pressed out another cigarette without even puffing on it. "Oh boy, here we go. . . ."

Jones moved from the table to better face her. "Not gonna happen this time, Ranger. Mexico's an ally last time I checked and you going gunfighter down there is the last thing we need."

"Who said anything about going gunfighter? I'm going down there to serve an arrest warrant on the suspected killer of five children in Texas."

"With a signature or a bullet?"

"Whatever it takes, Jones."

"You better make it fast once you're inside, Ranger," Jones told her. "Because if you're right, I don't know how long I'll be able to hold off the Mexican army."

"You leave that to me," Caitlin said, pulling her phone from her pocket.

"Who you calling now?"

Caitlin aimed her answer at Cort Wesley. "Couple new friends of mine named Rojas and Castillo, descendants of the generals who helped my great-grandfather bring down Esteban Cantú."

Jones shook his head in disbelief, then shook it again. "You're talking about the cartel leaders, public enemies one and two."

"Not today," Caitlin said to him, then immediately looked back at Cort Wesley. "Today they're the only men who may be able to find out where Guajardo's got Luke stashed."

* * *

"I couldn't reach Castillo," Caitlin told Cort Wesley, after ending the call. "But Alejandro Rojas is calling me back as soon as he learns something. Turns out Guajardo's brother killed a bunch of his druggers in a Juárez bar before crossing the border."

Her cell beeped with an incoming text message, Caitlin lifting it back out of her pocket.

"It's him," she said.

"I need one thing from you, Ranger," the head of the Juárez cartel said, so softly that Caitlin had to press the phone tighter against her ear. "A promise that the killer of my children dies tonight."

Cort Wesley had slid over to her and Caitlin put the phone on speaker so he could hear. "You've got it, sir."

"In that case, I believe I've found where this boy is being held. . . ."

"You gonna do this alone, Cort Wesley?" Caitlin asked him, sticking the phone back in her pocket.

"You bet," Cort Wesley told her, his expression a mix of determination and renewed hope. "Just like you're gonna handle Guajardo alone."

"Not quite alone."

"You reached Paz?"

"He was waiting for my call."

"Then there's something else you need to know about Ana Guajardo, Ranger," Cort Wesley said, "something Jan McClellan-Townsend told me that I can't believe myself. . . ."

101

Just past midnight, the Blackhawk brought Paz and Caitlin right up to the edge of the game preserve, landing in a field mixed between saw grass and red clay that had hardened into a gravel-like texture. Not far away, Caitlin thought she caught a glimpse of wild grapefruit trees mixed with hibiscus and flowering pink camellias. The ground beyond the field was thick and rich, indicating an underwater source rare indeed for a country that was primarily composed of desert and brush.

Caitlin looked toward Paz, found him smiling tightly, prepared to do what he did best.

"We don't get this done our way, Colonel, the Mexican army will move in and get it done theirs."

"We'll get it done, Ranger," Paz said, even for him remarkably calm and self-assured. "We always do."

While awaiting the logistics to be finalized, Young Roger had managed to extrapolate the satellite reconnaissance provided of the area to find an aboveground entrance to the cave system and river that ran beneath Ana Guajardo's game preserve.

"Okay, Ranger," Jones said, shaking his head, "if you're right, Guajardo will have dozens of men with her. They will be well armed and likely drawn from the Mexican Special Forces, who tend to be pretty tough *hombres* themselves. And you intend to walk in there waving your gun and ask them to please not throw the switch that turns the lights out in the U.S., as you arrest their boss for murder. How am I doing so far?"

"Spot on."

"So what am I missing here?" he asked her, face taut with exasperation.

"Something you need to do for me, Jones," Caitlin told him. "Something you've done before."

102

Juárez, Mexico

Cort Wesley moved with the night. He was no stranger to the cartel-dominated streets of Juárez, but had never actually been to the *colonias*, slums that were home to thousands of peasants impoverished by a combination of the drug trade and the nearby factories that had basically enslaved them. The *colonias* lay literally in the shadow of the sprawling complexes boasting names like Delphi, RCA, and Hyundai. As he hid between two collapsed structures waiting for night to come, Cort Wesley had spotted any number of buses dropping off workers for the day shift and picking up those who would take their place in the factories overnight.

According to Juárez cartel head Alejandro Rojas, Luke was being held on a hillside of ramshackle structures in the Anapra slum by former prisoners from Cereso Prison both loyal to and terrified of Locaro. Rojas had no idea of their number, only their location on stench-riddled land built over an abandoned landfill. As night fell around him, Cort Wesley had continued to survey the squalor dominated by abandoned or burned-out cars and endless piles of trash rife with dogs and small pigs that were the only things moving by the time he slid out into the darkness. He passed a row of black crosses memorializing schoolchildren who'd been gunned down just a few months before while waiting for their bus, and angled for the hillside.

Minutes later Cort Wesley was skulking up the slight slope of the cluttered slum, squeezing through the narrow gaps between huts made of sheet metal and wood scraps with interior walls formed of corrugated cardboard duct-taped to salvaged plywood and rotted lumber. There was no power, no running water or utilities whatsoever. The ground layered over the old Anapra landfill was parched and dead, more scrub than soil. Clotheslines bent under the weight of clothes strung over them. Junk that looked like it had sprouted from the ground, seeded by the trash collected below, lay everywhere in the form of goods first salvaged and then rejected for being in too poor a condition to use even here.

Cort Wesley had an approximate location for where Luke was being held and nothing more. He'd geared up in the same fashion as he had for night raids back in the Gulf War, the biggest difference being the utterly flat land outside of Baghdad and the lack of any smell at all. He carried the Special Forces M1A4 version of the M16 with a cut-down stock, a sound suppressor, and a pair of magazines rigged together to allow for sixty shots instead of thirty with one simple flip. He wore a killing knife on one side of his belt and a holstered Glock on the other, the ammo vest worn over his flak jacket holding both smoke and fragmentary grenades. The air was thick, stale, and reminded him of the smell coming from the cesspools he'd pumped one summer as a teenager.

Cort Wesley stopped and rested his shoulders against an abandoned shanty to settle his breath. He'd avoided the rut-strewn roads formed of flattened mud to stay clear of any vehicles or gunmen. Slums like this were peaceful enough during the day, but dominated by armed roving gangs who ruled the streets at night. Last thing he needed was to find himself up close and personal with one of those before he found Luke.

"*Here we are again, bubba,*" said Leroy Epps, leaning right alongside him. "*Business as usual.*"

"You bring a gun?"

"*Nope, just a good word.*"

"Rather have an extra hand."

"*This one's on you, and that's just the way you want it. In your mind, you can't provide for your boys with your wallet, try a currency you're better with.*"

"Bullets?"

"If they was dollars, bubba, you'd be a rich man for sure. Meantime, you let me work on the cash issues. I got things covered there and that's a promise."

"Thanks, champ."

"Forget the thanks. Just kill some of those hombres for me tonight."

Then he was gone and Cort Wesley started on again.

103

LOS MOCHIS, MEXICO

Ana Guajardo grasped the handles of her father's wheelchair and eased him along one of the hallways inside her underground bunker leading toward the control room. She'd wanted him here so any part of him that clung to conscious thought might witness these final hours leading up to the fateful moment when things would turn for once and for good. How wonderful it would be to see Mexico and the United States flip-flop in terms of technological superiority—the ultimate irony, in fact. All at the hand of a woman born to a migrant farmworker who'd grown up picking fruit.

The very definition of the American Dream.

Guajardo knew her father had disapproved of her hatred for the United States. So bringing him here was not about celebration so much as victory. From the day of his plunge off that fourth-story balcony, she only hoped that he'd live long enough to see her bring down the country to which he was so beholden. Ultimate vindication that her beliefs had triumphed over his, vindication of the vision she had enacted. Ana wanted him to see it, wanted him to know, so he could die with that implanted in his mind.

Retribution indeed.

The bunker's main control room looked more like something out of NASA, with electronic, interactive maps filling wall-mounted massive flat-screen televisions. Those maps were connected to computers that would automatically update the power supply status across the United

States. The monitors shared the walls with other smaller flat screens tuned to various American cable channels. As long as those stations had sufficient power to continue broadcasting, she'd be able to follow the fall of America in real time, even as the maps would show her a moment-by-moment depiction of the actual progression of the country going dark.

"I don't believe you've met my father," Guajardo said to John and David, her code writers, who were in the midst of their final preparations to push the worm into power grids covering the entire country. "Father, these are the young men I was telling you about."

John and David both nodded toward Enrique Cantú politely, no idea how to respond to the old man who sat in his wheelchair with drool piling up on his chin and dripping slowly to his shirt. Happy to turn back to their consoles.

"And look who's here to see you, Father," Ana said, turning the chair so her father could see Locaro.

The old man passed some gas, the one person in the room not revolted by the sight of the scab-riddled depression in the side of Locaro's head where his ear had been shot off.

"I am not his son," Locaro said from his post in the room where Ana had placed him to make sure nothing went awry. "He is not my father. He is a shell, a vessel, that you keep alive with feeding tubes and false hope. You should have let me smother him."

Ana almost told him why she hadn't.

Locaro could have gone on, could have mentioned the years he had spent in Cereso, confessing to the crime to spare his sister the same fate. But he left things at that because all else, that which had come before, was gone now. There was no looking back, only ahead to an entirely new world, one where America's influence and manipulation would be lost. A world of chaos in which he would thrive.

"How long?" Ana Guajardo asked the young men back working feverishly at the head of the room, as bulbs representing America flashed on the display monitors.

"Thirty minutes until showtime," said John. "That's when we send the signal to the remote pilots to push their birds into the air. Once that's done, we activate the worm and watch the transformers blow as the system begins to overload. Then it's curtains—literally."

"The dark ages reborn," added David.

"You're both very good at what you do," Ana told them.

"With what you're paying us," said John, "we better be."

104

Los Mochis, Mexico

Caitlin and Paz moved through the darkness toward the game preserve. The special model Blackhawk would remain behind, waiting. The pilot would lift off only if Guajardo's forces appeared before they returned. Meanwhile, the Mexican army would be lying in wait, certain to make an utter mess of things if Caitlin didn't stop Guajardo before they stormed the area.

Caitlin followed an actual map to a brush-covered entrance of the underground cave connected to the bunker where she felt certain Ana Callas Guajardo was now preparing to trigger her attack. She looked at Paz, the nod they shared saying more than any words before he disappeared into the night, leaving Caitlin to ease the brush aside to lower herself into the entrance to the cave.

Moving about without detection, especially in the dark, was a skill Paz had mastered as a boy when he needed to steal food for his brothers and sisters and escape the gangs who wished to enlist him in their ranks. To this day, he wondered if the *bruja* vision and foresight he'd inherited from his mother also enabled him to move like a ghost, a *fantasma*, immune to detection.

But for Paz tonight was not just about the guards he needed to kill and power supply he needed to mark. Tonight was about finishing

Locaro, as he should have back in San Antonio. Only then would he have atoned for his failure and misjudgment back at the high school. He had gone there that night for himself. But he was here tonight for something else entirely, something that suited him far better:

His Texas Ranger.

Caitlin followed the river, more certain than ever that the other end of the underground cave would finish where Ana Guajardo's bunker began.

The sights her flashlight revealed on this path, winding its way along the river, were nothing short of spectacular. The stalactites looked like daggers of varying sizes sticking out of the cave ceiling. The feel was that of traversing a crystal palace inlaid amid still water that had a greenish tint and was rimmed by white deposits that looked something like snow.

She was well more than a hundred feet into the cave when she realized there was illumination springing from something other than her flashlight. Closer inspection revealed a series of battery-operated lanterns hanging from the walls, making it clear this was indeed to be used as an escape route from Guajardo's underground bunker in the event of an emergency.

Though the lanterns themselves gave off a single curtain of ambient light, they blended with the shading of rock formations and irregularly spaced hanging stalactites to create a dull blue hue over the water to go with the greenish tint. Caitlin continued to weave her way along the narrow path that followed the twists and bends of the underground river, radiant hues of blue and green bouncing off the water's surface. The underground cave was laced with a musky odor due to the thick moist air trapped within it, something like damp towels soaking up a basement spill, musty and spoiled.

Before long she'd come to the end of the path. Before long she'd find the underground bunker.

Caitlin shuddered, thinking of the terrible truth Cort Wesley had learned from Jan McClellan-Townsend about Ana Callas Guajardo, something the woman had likely blocked from her own memory. It made perfect sense, the final piece in a puzzle that explained her obsession with attacking the United States.

Up ahead, Caitlin's flashlight illuminated something shiny amid the rough darkness of the cavern. A door, she realized, leading into the bunker from where Guajardo was about to launch her attack.

105

Juárez, Mexico

Finding the shanty where Luke was being held, on the sloped rise riddled with raw sewage running downhill, proved more challenging than Cort Wesley had been expecting. For security, and privacy, shanty dwellers had done their best to wall off their dilapidated homes with makeshift fencing formed of a combination of salvaged Sheetrock, cinder blocks, corrugated tin left over from what passed as roofs, and rusted barrels. That turned the slum into a maze to be negotiated in zigs and zags, sometimes running up against buildings so tightly congested that there was no way to negotiate a route between them.

At this late hour, Cort Wesley had encountered no resistance or human obstacle at all. Besides sound and flickering lantern light coming from inside the shacks, the only residents he'd glimpsed were moving to or from their outhouses, which were little more than a hole dug in the ground surrounded by a curtain strung between two trees. That is, until he detected a light emanating from behind the tallest assemblage of fencing he'd come upon yet.

Reaching a barrier composed of warped sheets of tin that looked affixed together, Cort Wesley's portable GPS unit told him he was somewhere very close to the location provided by Alejandro Rojas. He calmed himself enough to see if he could actually sense his younger son beyond, if some paternal bond might provide the absolute confirmation he needed.

Short of that, he thought maybe the ghost of Leroy Epps might show up to point the way, since walls and fences far thicker than these had no effect on his vision. But Leroy was nowhere to be seen and Cort Wesley had given up looking after hearing the rustling hum of an electric generator. It was the only one he'd come upon so far in his winding trek up the slope of the covered landfill, confirmation enough that he'd found his son.

Cort Wesley eased a pair of night-vision goggles from a slot in his vest and looped them around his head, tightening the strap the way he would the more mundane sport variety. This version was still in the developmental stage, meaning no one other than men like Jones knew of their existence or had access to them. The goggles provided both enhanced peripheral vision and substantially increased comfort as well as functionality, compared to older models with which he was more familiar.

Next, he found a seam in the tin fencing that had been weakly soldered and effortlessly cut through it with the same Special Forces knife he'd used back in the Gulf War. Squeezing through the gap, Cort Wesley found himself in a sloped yard sectioned off from others by barricades of debris in the form of rusted bicycles, old pushcarts, and wheelbarrows missing their wheels and handles. The stench-riddled air told him a curtained-off cubicle contained the outhouse and, not far from that, his night-vision goggles allowed him to discern a small gasoline generator attached to a long orange extension cord that was partially buried in the ground.

Cort Wesley slinked forward, hunched low now with silenced assault rifle trained before him. There were no guards outside, but shadowy movement was clear within the shanty itself. His now clear view revealed it to be an amalgamation of three or four separate structures, distinguished by varied shades of roofing, somehow linked together to form easily the largest structure he'd come upon yet in the hillside slum.

Certain now he'd found Luke's location, Cort Wesley trained his eyes on the thinly covered slat-holes that passed for windows. As he angled his assault rifle higher, his boot snared on something; looking down, he saw a trip wire even with his foot just about to snap.

* * *

Grasping the handles of her father's wheelchair, Ana Guajardo swept her gaze about the various maps depicting the United States. She pictured all the lights on the biggest projected map going dark. It would not happen at once, but over the course of hours, even a day, for the entire effect to take hold. Once begun, the process would spread geometrically, as the failsafe measures built into the system, designed to pull power from where it was needed the least to where it was needed the most, failed miserably. Meanwhile, the rain of carbon filaments from her radio-controlled monster-scale planes detonated directly over their targets would ravage the infrastructure of the most vital power-generating plants and distribution-switching facilities.

Her greatest victory at hand, Ana turned to her brother but found him stiff and distracted, hardly in a celebratory mood.

"What's wrong?" she asked him. "Locaro?"

He snapped alert, cold dark eyes finding her gaze, his ridged face looking waxy in the ambient underground lighting. "Not all the guard posts are checking in."

"Interference, maybe."

Locaro picked at the scabbing where his ear had been, his fingers coming away wet with fresh blood. "That's what I'm afraid of, *mi hermanita.*"

Guillermo Paz barely registered the kills, the number as meaningless as the lives of the men he'd ended. They were nothing to him, soulless creatures no different from ants to be crushed underfoot. With each snap of a neck or twist of a blade through bone and cartilage, though, he felt the Ranger was that much safer, her path to victory that much easier thanks to him.

His vast size and bulk through space lacking sufficient cover should have rendered a stealthy approach an exercise in futility. Yet Paz stalked his prey with ease; even when they seemed to be looking straight at him there was no acknowledgment whatsoever of his presence or existence.

Paz began to wonder in earnest if perhaps the tales told him by his mother had more credence than he let himself believe. Beyond the visions he was convinced were true, maybe there was something to be said for some to have been blessed with phantom-like abilities, to be both man and *fantasma* at the same time.

Paz approached the next guard from the rear, his massive hands swallowing the man's head in the last moment before a crack that sounded like a thunderclap resonated through the air. Then he moved on, sensing a presence on the vast grounds around him, as cold and unfeeling as any he'd ever encountered.

"Locaro," Paz said, under his breath.

106

LOS MOCHIS, MEXICO

Caitlin reached the door, SIG in one hand and flashlight in the other. Careful to steady her feet, she located the latch and pulled. Not surprised it was locked, Caitlin eased the explosive charge from her small shoulder pack, recalling Cort Wesley's instructions on exactly how to use it.

Inside the super-sized shanty, the two gunmen poised by the window slats heard the rattle of tin cans jarred suddenly into motion, the trip wire to which they were tied jerked by a foot.

The gunmen jammed the barrels of their assault rifles through the slats, fabric brushed aside behind a torrent of wild and indiscriminate fire more unleashed than truly aimed. Three more gunmen joined them and then a fourth, their barrages lighting up the hillside with muzzle flashes and filling the air with gun smoke that wafted upward in thin clouds.

The darkness beyond gave up nothing, the men relying on the fury and spread of their bullets to cut down the man or men who had tripped their primitive defense system. Each emptied his entire magazine, the spent ones thumping to the floor an instant ahead of the clacking sounds of fresh ones being jammed home. The gunmen ready to unleash fresh barrages when Cort Wesley rose behind them.

Paz found the self-generating electrical substation well camouflaged inside the rhino enclosure, sliding past a magnificent male that regarded him with tired-looking eyes. The animal lifted its head slightly and snorted, but made no move to do anything, letting Paz pass unmolested. He met its eyes briefly, wanting to know its strength, its thinking, finding only acknowledgment of his presence.

The power station hummed softly, likely fueled by propane tanks buried underground and shielded by a metallic coating that no doubt hid its heat signature from the satellites orbiting overhead. It was bigger than Paz had expected, the size of a large car, but with different modules climbing to differing heights all camouflaged by brush planted toward that end.

Paz marked the generator with a laser and touched a button on a satellite relay clipped to his belt to send the proper signal to the fighter jets circling overhead. Moments later, a series of *poofs* sounded and the black rain of carbon filaments wafted down from the sky. The moon cast just enough of the night in a soft hue to distinguish the black mist he had glimpsed in his dreams descending in clouds that looked like thick swarms of insects.

What had the priest called it?

Redemption.

Paz heard a rustling in the enclosure's grass and swung to find Locaro standing twenty feet behind him, machete clutched by his side.

"On my signal," Ana Guajardo told David and John, ready to give the order to activate the plan that would plunge America into darkness.

Her trained "pilots" were in place across America, just waiting for her signal to take off en masse and rain carbon filament down on nearly two thousand power plants. The transformers she controlled would soon overload and short circuit, irrevocably destroyed. But her worm would first enter the grid systems through the back doors they provided, everything timed out to the last second.

Guajardo moved closer to her software experts, wanting to see the fateful strokes on their keyboards.

And that's when all the power in the complex died.

Caitlin double-checked that she had planted the explosive pack even with the door latch, just as Cort Wesley had instructed, and then eased the compression fuse into place.

"Just depress the trigger, cover your ears, and be somewhere else," he'd said.

Which was exactly what she did, the charge igniting with a loud *poof!* that rocketed the heavy door inward, exactly as Cort Wesley had promised.

Then the walls began to shake, the roof over her quaking, Caitlin quickly realizing something much bigger than the charge she'd just triggered was to blame.

Cort Wesley took the gunmen in three-shot bursts, spraying his fire left to right, then back again. The world turning an eerie shade of orange before his night-vision goggles as frothy blood bursts erupted from the holes his 7.62mm fire punched in the men holding his son hostage.

Outside, he'd extricated his boot from the wire just short of tripping it and stripped down a clothesline suspended between two trees. Still-rank, damp clothes toppled off as he strung the clothesline to the trip-wire and held it in his grasp while working his way around to the shanty's opposite side.

Once at the door there, he yanked on the clothesline to trip the tin cans strung to the wire and burst through as soon as the gunmen opened fire. He'd reached them in the front room, just as they ejected their spent magazines, a few not even managing to get the fresh ones jammed home before he opened fire.

They were nothing to Cort Wesley, the stench and ugliness of the slum itself transposed onto them. He felt no more in killing them than he had gunning down targets in the amusement park shooting gallery with Luke just six nights before.

Luke was being held somewhere else in the shanty, and Cort Wesley was now free to find him as the final body fell, scattering spent shells across the clapboard floor.

"What's happening?" Guajardo managed in the dull haze of emergency lighting.

"We've lost power!" from John.

"Everything's shutting down!" from David. "Communications up-links are gone!"

Frozen behind their keyboards and lifeless screens, the world having seized up solid before them.

"Do something!" ordered Ana Guajardo in the last moment before explosions rocked the bunker.

107

LOS MOCHIS, MEXICO

Caitlin didn't know if the shelling was the product of another of Jones's betrayals or, more likely, President Villarreal's forces launching an all-out attack on the compound ahead of schedule. She felt debris from the cavern roof rain down upon her, realizing the integrity of the entire structure could be compromised by the blasts.

Retracing her path backward now was a fool's errand at best, suicide at worst. So, wasting no more time, she ducked through the heavy door she'd blown and entered Ana Callas Guajardo's bunker.

* * *

The walls were crumbling; the walls were coming down.

Ana Guajardo's world was collapsing around her, a shrill alarm blaring through the darkness broken only by the spill of emergency vapor lights cutting through the haze. Panic had erupted, the explosions sending her people fleeing, loyalty and purpose lost along with hope.

It was the Texas Ranger, Caitlin Strong, it had to be!

Ana couldn't resist baiting her, feeling herself so superior and powerful as to be immune to any potential response. She had as much as told the Ranger what was to come, reinforcing her own words with a phone call after she realized how foolishly she'd acted. Now, to see all her work squandered, years of planning to vanquish her hatred and avenge her world lost, because of belief in the infallibility of her own convictions.

With the power gone and the bunker collapsing, Guajardo had no choice but to join the flow of her people in escape and regroup, salvage what she could from all this. She was almost to the door leading into the underground cave when she remembered her father.

"We must go back!" she said, stopping in her tracks. "My father!"

Uribe and Vasquez stopped too, but made no move to follow as Guajardo started to back up.

"Fools!" she spat at them. "You'll die for this! Do you hear me, you'll die!"

In that moment more of the ceiling gave way. When the dust cloud cleared, the two men had already moved on and Guajardo retraced her steps to find her father poised in the middle of the hallway. And in the dull haze shed by the emergency lighting through the debris cloud, she saw Caitlin Strong standing behind his wheelchair.

"I have a warrant for your arrest, ma'am, and I'm taking you back to Texas."

The black chalky dust continued to rain down from the sky even as explosions nearby rocked the ground and lit up the night. Locaro had drawn within ten feet, close enough for Paz to see blood running down the side of his face where his ear had been shot off and just the distance he could cover with his machete before Paz could draw and fire his pistol.

Locaro's eyes glistened in the moonlight as more black chalk dust fluttered to the ground between them and more sparks flew out of the generator before flames replaced them in the air. Those eyes wanted Paz to go for his gun, those eyes begged for him to do it.

But Paz went for his knife instead, all twelve deadly inches of it. It was the very knife taken off the first man he killed for murdering the priest. Paz had waited years for that opportunity and had kept the knife as both souvenir and reminder of how resolve and hate could quickly turn a boy into a man.

Locaro wheeled in, looping his machete around and downward. It sizzled through the air in a blinding arc, Paz just managing to sidestep the blow but missing with a slash of his knife. Locaro spun, continuing around in one fluid motion before Paz could respond. Paz arched his spine, midsection tucked inward so the machete tip sliced through his shirt and grazed his flesh. He felt the thin soak of blood and stinging pain, a flash erupting before him, beyond which Paz thought he caught a glimpse of his dead mother smiling.

Cort Wesley dipped and darted down narrow halls lined with small, tightly congested rooms inside the cobbled-together shacks.

A figure lurched out on his left.

Pfffffffffft!

Another on his right.

Pfffffffffft!

Two directly before him.

Pfffffffffft! Pfffffffffft!

"*Nice shooting, bubba,*" he thought he heard Leroy Epps say as one final door appeared at the end of the plywood floor, Cort Wesley's heart hammering as he moved toward it.

* * *

Ana Guajardo stood her ground, eyes locked on the pistol Caitlin Strong aimed her way.

"You're wasting your time," she managed, as more explosions rocked the bunker, sending chunks of the dirt and shale above showering downward through holes punched in the ceiling. "I'll never stand trial—in either country."

"You killed five children with your own hand," Caitlin told her from behind the wheelchair. "That means you're going to jail. Where you stand trial, that's not up to me."

Guajardo gazed about her.

"It's just us now, ma'am," Caitlin said and raised her SIG Sauer higher. "Looking at you is like looking at the pictures of the mother of the nephews you tried to kill, your twin sister. But the truth is you look nothing like her because all you know is hate and it's turned you ugly."

Ana Guajardo shook her head in disbelief, as if opening her eyes and seeing Caitlin standing there for the first time. "You really expect me to just walk out of here with you, in *handcuffs*?"

Caitlin tightened her grip on the SIG. "The alternative's worse, ma'am. But if it means anything, I understand."

"Understand what?"

"All that hatred you got bottled up inside you."

"Save it, Ranger. You haven't got a chance going up against me."

But Caitlin ignored her taunt. "Goes back to the day your brother, Locaro, killed that rapist on the McClellan farm in the Rio Grande Valley when you were seven."

"It was a long time ago. I'm way past that."

"No, ma'am, you only think you are. See, your memory got it all wrong, like some kind of defense mechanism. It wasn't your mother Locaro saved that day." Caitlin held Guajardo's stare before continuing. "It was you."

* * *

Paz recovered his senses as quickly as he lost them, the initial shock from the wound dissipating. Locaro moved in sync with him, denying him the distance he needed to draw his gun while seeming to relish the thought he might try anyway. That made Paz realize Locaro had trained too much of his attention on his holstered pistol, so he led with his knife away from where Locaro was focused.

The boldness of the move, the mere thought that Paz would tempt the reach of his machete, surprised Locaro enough to open his side for the thrust. Though he tried to twist at the last moment, Paz's blade still jabbed home between the ribs at mid-torso.

Locaro hunched and tucked that whole side in close instinctively, robbing him of dexterity as well as swiftness. Enraged, he bit down the pain and launched himself on Paz with a relentless series of sweeping strikes with his machete, all of which whisked close enough for Paz to feel the cut of air behind them. The last miss caused Locaro's rib muscles to lock up, his balance stripped as he whirled past Paz, who seized the opportunity to finally draw his pistol.

He opened fire, a trio of bullets finding Locaro's side and back before Locaro wheeled, machete coming around with him. It clanged against the steel of Paz's pistol and sent it flying, one last shot flying errant.

Bellowing, Locaro launched himself at Paz, machete looking like a loosed propeller blade spinning through the air. Then, at the last, when Paz was ready to duck beneath it, Locaro lashed out with one booted foot and then the other. Paz lost his footing, thrown backward with the ground coming up fast and Locaro rushing straight for him.

Cort Wesley kicked in the door at the end of the hall, sending it rocketing backward in a cloud of dust and splinters to reveal a man holding Luke on either side, fear bleeding from their eyes.

"*Deja caer tu arma! Deja caer tu arma!*" one wailed, ordering him to drop his gun.

Cort Wesley met Luke's gaze, saw not just hope there but also relief and certainty, certainty that his father was going to save him. Then surprise when Cort Wesley dropped his assault rifle to the floor.

"You boys ever ride a roller coaster?" he asked Luke's two captors in English. "Know what happens when you gotta puke?"

He looked at Luke as he said that. The boy's eyes widened with realization and then tightened with resolve an instant before he jerked his head downward, bending over at the waist. Cort Wesley drew his Glock in the same instant, firing twice, a bullet lodged in the foreheads of both men, who stood there for an instant with pistols frozen where Luke's head had just been before crumpling to the floor.

"You were the one who was raped that day," Caitlin continued.

Ana Guajardo had frozen, locked up solid, everything inside—from her breath, to her heartbeat, to her blood—seeming to stop. Suddenly she saw the same picture that had haunted her dreams for as long as she could remember, only now the terrified seven-year-old was looking *up* at the new work foreman who smelled like piss gyrating over her. Shoving himself inside her until the terrible pain made her bite down on her tongue. She remembered gagging, her breath stolen when the blood splattered her, feeling like rainwater against her skin. More of it showered down, spraying her face, arms, and raggedy shirt pulled up almost to her neck, Locaro's machete a blur in the air over her. Watching him kill the man who'd hurt her so badly, spilled off her now and being hacked to pieces by her ten-year-old brother. Locaro finally turning toward her, barely breathing hard, covered in blood himself. Smiling.

"You know it's the truth, *señora*, I can see it in your eyes," Caitlin told her. "Almost makes me feel bad for you, because it explains what killed you inside and left you with nothing even remotely approaching a feeling. No child should have to suffer like that, but that must've slipped your mind last week in Willow Creek. That's why you were able to kill those children the way you did, because you can't feel. But I wonder if you'll feel the needle going into your arm or the noose snapping your neck."

Ana Guajardo hadn't moved or reacted, still didn't seem to be breathing, the dull emergency lighting losing her to the shadows. "It takes one to know one, because we're the same, you and I," she managed finally, summoning the hate she knew so well. "Tell me you don't look in the mirror and see my face looking back at you, Ranger."

"All I know is I'm looking at a monster right now. And I'm gonna make you pay for what you've done."

With that Guajardo stooped to retrieve an assault rifle that must have been shed by one of her men in his rush to flee.

"Not today," she said calmly.

Paz hurled his knife from the ground, propped up on his back. It lodged in Locaro's shoulder, stopping him in his tracks five feet away, machete locked into position overhead.

Locaro jerked the blade out and tossed it aside. "You can't kill me, *India chusma*," he grunted, almost grinning.

A dark blur of motion caught Paz's eye behind Locaro, accompanied by a heavy pounding that left the ground quaking and rumbling beneath both of them.

"I don't have to."

Paz watched the charging male rhino gore Locaro from behind with its horn and then jerk him upward, spearing him deeper until the horn emerged through the thrashing Locaro's chest, dragging blood and gore with it. The massive animal continued to twist him from side to side before tossing his still writhing body to the ground and prancing proudly off.

Caitlin held her gaze on Ana Guajardo, focusing on the woman's finger as it stopped just short of the assault rifle's trigger.

"Your rapist is already dead, ma'am. You can't kill him again, no matter what you do to me or anyone else."

Guajardo's eyes widened, then narrowed hatefully, the assault rifle stiff in her grasp.

"I'm not a child, and this isn't Willow Creek," Caitlin told her.

Guajardo's expression grew strangely placid and sure. "All the same to me."

She jerked the assault rifle upward, finger finding the trigger just as Caitlin dropped down behind the cover of her father's wheelchair. Guajardo hesitated before firing.

Not long, but enough.

Caitlin fired four times from her crouch, two hits to Guajardo's chest and one to her head to go with the single miss before Guajardo ever pulled the trigger.

"I'm nothing like you," she said, more falling chunks of the ceiling entombing Ana Callas Guajardo in rubble as Caitlin rushed for the exit.

Paz was waiting when she emerged, the Mexican army already scouring the grounds to round up Guajardo's fleeing troops. The shelling had ended, the remnants of the bunker likely entombed by now with all evidence of Ana Guajardo's plot lost forever.

Which, Caitlin figured, had been the whole point.

"You've looked better, Colonel."

Paz grimaced, still in pain. "You too, Ranger."

They looked up when troop-carrying helicopters soared over the scene, lowering to dispense more Mexican soldiers.

"Government down here can't afford to let this get out," Caitlin said, as much to herself as Paz. "That means we better make ourselves scarce in a hurry. Kind of makes you wonder why we keep bothering, doesn't it?"

"The world is a fine place and worth fighting for, Ranger."

"That's Hemingway, right?"

Paz nodded. "The rest of the quote reads, 'And I hate very much to leave it.'"

"Well," Caitlin told him, "I don't suppose the two of us are going anywhere."

EPILOGUE

The New Texas needs the Rangers every bit as much as the old.

Dallas Morning News; January 30, 1994

SAN ANTONIO

Three days later, a lawyer in Phoenix contacted Cort Wesley to inform him that Dylan and Luke were the sole beneficiaries of the proceeds from the estate of Maura Torres's murdered sister, Araceli. The amount was somewhere in the high six figures and the lawyer wanted to schedule a convenient time for Cort Wesley to sign the necessary paperwork.

"*See, bubba,*" he heard Leroy Epps say, "*I told you so!*"

"You say something?" Caitlin asked him, as he pocketed his phone.

"Just thinking out loud," Cort Wesley smiled.

They sat side by side on the porch swing, watching Dylan and Luke taking turns on the half-pipe. Cort Wesley had oiled the sprockets that morning to eliminate the squeaking, and the swing rocked smoothly back and forth now.

"What about what's left of Guajardo's plan, Ranger?" he asked Caitlin.

"I couldn't tell you, Cort Wesley, other than to say Jones and his counterparts in Mexico are handling the cleanup. All those giant remote-controlled aircraft that never got airborne are being rounded up and the transformers manufactured by Guajardo's company are being retrofitted. Meanwhile, those two software geeks turned themselves in and are talking up a storm about how to prevent anyone from actually succeeding where they almost did."

Over on the half-pipe, Luke took another spill on his skateboard under Dylan's tutelage.

"Doesn't come easy for him, does it?" Caitlin said.

"That'll make it all the more worthwhile once the boy gets it right, Ranger."

"Voice of experience, Cort Wesley?"

"I was just about to ask you the same thing."

Caitlin watched Cort Wesley flinch as Luke went flying again, leaving Dylan to just shake his head with hands planted on hips. "Be plenty of folks who couldn't handle watching their kids take falls like that."

"Guess we're immune to such things."

"All being relative, of course."

Cort Wesley let out an easy breath. "Dylan just got an e-mail from Brown telling him he'd been officially accepted. An hour later comes a message from Coach Estes with the off-season football program included. I'd say he's truly excited about something other than the shit we've dragged him into."

Caitlin turned toward the half-pipe, where Dylan was shredding up a storm while Luke looked on, his board balanced against his leg. "Should give him a chance to be a regular kid."

"Somehow," Cort Wesley said, with his eyes straying to her. "No thanks to us."

Earlier that day, holding Caitlin's detailed report about what had transpired inside Ana Guajardo's underground bunker, D. W. Tepper settled back in his chair and faced her. "You really used a *wheelchair* for cover?"

Caitlin shrugged. "Accomplished what it was supposed to. And, the thing is, he was already dead when I found him. Managed to live just long enough to see the daughter who'd put him in that chair fall miserably."

"Speaking of which, Ranger, it seems strange that somebody just *happened* to leave an assault rifle behind in the middle of that floor."

Tepper took a Marlboro from a freshly opened pack but stopped short of lighting it. "Sounds to me like whoever it was put the gun there for a reason."

"I can't imagine why," Caitlin said, her gaze giving up nothing.

Tepper shook his head and lit his cigarette. "I am truly glad we're on the same side, Hurricane."

With that, he touched the tip of his cigarette to Caitlin's report and dropped it in a nearby wastebasket as the flames caught. Tepper had started to raise the cigarette to his mouth, when Caitlin leaned over his desk and plucked it from his hand.

"Me too, Captain, me too."

Caitlin continued to hold Cort Wesley's stare. "Down in that bunker, facing off against Ana Guajardo, finally brought it home to me."

"Brought what home?"

"She told me she and I were the same. The scariest thing being she was almost right, because I realized the only thing that made us different is you and those boys."

"Well, I wouldn't say it was the only thing."

"Most important, then."

"I'll give you that."

"You've given me plenty already."

"Likewise."

Caitlin eased up against him, and Cort Wesley drew her in closer still with an arm wrapped over her shoulder. "So where do we go from here, Ranger?"

"Same place as always."

"Where's that?"

The afternoon sun broke through the clouds, casting shimmering rays across the front yard that splayed shadowy patterns through the trees on Dylan and Luke on the half-pipe.

"I'll let you know when we get there, Cort Wesley."

AUTHOR'S NOTE

This is the West, sir.
When the legend becomes fact, print the legend.

Carlton Young as Maxwell Scott,
The Man Who Shot Liberty Valance

History, my good friend Steve Berry counsels, matters. It does indeed and I normally take great pride in the attention I pay to history in my Caitlin Strong books, specifically the history of the Texas Rangers. Normally.

See, I took a few liberties with this one—hence, my first stab at a proverbial Author's Note to explain myself. I refer specifically to the composition of "Strong's Raiders," who've you just met. William Ray and Earl Strong, of course, are products of my imagination, but the other Rangers are all real and all presented as they really were, more or less. More in the kind of men they were and the kind of deeds they'd done. Less in the fact that I played loose with some key facts and dates here.

The famed Bill McDonald, for example, really did die in 1918, a year before the events depicted in *Strong Rain Falling*. I needed a Texas Ranger legend and I figured I could cheat at least this once. I didn't cheat at all with Frank Hamer, as tough a Ranger as there ever was, who was famously lured out of retirement to bring down Bonnie and Clyde.

For his part, Monroe Fox never returned to the Rangers following his alleged role in a very real massacre, although that role remains in dispute to this day. As for Manuel Gonzaullas, well, I couldn't resist including a future legend in Strong's Raiders as well. And, other than the fact that "Lone Wolf" didn't actually become a Ranger until a year later (1920), his background is otherwise presented exactly as it was.

Meanwhile, the Battle of Juárez really did happen in June of 1919, but there's no evidence whatsoever that battle was in any way connected to an early fiendish force of Mexican drug dealers. But while *esos Demonios* never existed, Esteban Cantú most certainly did. And all evidence points to the fact that he did indeed run the first major drug smuggling ring out of Mexico, bringing opium into California out of Mexicali and Tijuana through Baja and beginning the scourge that ultimately begat the notorious cartels themselves.

Hope you don't think less of me or the book for these embellishments. Hey, I'm in good company; remember, the motto of the Texas Rangers—*One Riot, One Ranger*—was never actually spoken by anyone. That's why we print the legends. That's what makes us storytellers.